** DID I READ THIS ALREADY? **

Place your initials or unique symbol in a
square as a reminder to you that you have
read this title.

R · M				
ST				
IN				

WITH WINTER'S FIRST FROST

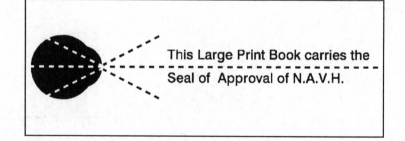

This Large Print Book carries the Seal of Approval of N.A.V.H.

AN EVERY AMISH SEASON NOVEL

WITH WINTER'S FIRST FROST

KELLY IRVIN

THORNDIKE PRESS

A part of Gale, a Cengage Company

Farmington Hills, Mich • San Francisco • New York • Waterville, Maine
Meriden, Conn • Mason, Ohio • Chicago

PJ6 31

Copyright © 2019 by Kelly Irvin.
All Scripture quotations, unless otherwise indicated, are taken from The Holy Bible, *New International Version*®, NIV®. Copyright © 1973, 1978, 1984, 2011 by Biblica, Inc.™ Used by permission. All rights reserved worldwide. www.zondervan.com
The King James Version (KJV) of the Bible is in the public domain.
Thorndike Press, a part of Gale, a Cengage Company.

Thorndike Press® Large Print Christian Romance.
The text of this Large Print edition is unabridged.
Other aspects of the book may vary from the original edition.
Set in 16 pt. Plantin.

LIBRARY OF CONGRESS CIP DATA ON FILE.
CATALOGUING IN PUBLICATION FOR THIS BOOK
IS AVAILABLE FROM THE LIBRARY OF CONGRESS

ISBN-13: 978-1-4328-6302-9 (hardcover)

Published in 2019 by arrangement with The Zondervan Corporation, LLC, a subsidiary of HarperCollins Christian Publishing, Inc.

Printed in Mexico
1 2 3 4 5 6 7 23 22 21 20 19

To Tim, I love growing old with you.
Here's to many more years!

Even to your old age and gray hairs I am he, I am he who will sustain you. I have made you and I will carry you; I will sustain you and I will rescue you.

ISAIAH 46:4

He brought me up also out of an horrible pit, out of the miry clay, and set my feet upon a rock, and established my goings.

PSALM 40:2 KJV

GLOSSARY*

Abrot: ministers' council held at the beginning of each church service outside the main worship area

aenti: aunt

Ausband: Amish hymnal

bann: a temporary period of excommunication intended to cause a change of heart and end errant behavior in a church member

bopli(n): baby

botching: clapping game

bruder: brother

daed: father

*The German dialect spoken by the Amish is not a written language and varies depending on the location and origin of the settlement. These spellings are approximations. Most Amish children learn English after they start school. They also learn high German, which is used in their Sunday services.

9

danki: thank you

dawdy haus: grandparents' house

dochder: daughter

eck: married couple's corner table at wedding reception

Englischer: English or non-Amish

Fehla: failure (in this context, sin)

freind: friend

fraa: wife

Gelassenheit: a yielding to God's will

Gmay: church district

Gott: God

groossdaadi: grandpa

groossmammi: grandma

gut: good

haus: house

hund: dog

jah: yes

kaffi: coffee

kapp: prayer cap or head covering worn by Amish women

kind, kinner: child, children

lieb: love (noun)

mann: husband

Meidung: avoidance, shunning

Mennischt: Mennonite

mudder: mother

nee: no

Ordnung: written and unwritten rules in an Amish district

Rat: official vote of the Gmay church membership
rumspringa: period of running around
schweschder: sister
suh: son
wunderbarr: wonderful

JAMESPORT, MISSOURI, FEATURED FAMILIES

The Kauffmans

Laura (widow, husband: Eli)

Children: Luke (deceased), Raymond, Kyle, Abraham, Aaron (wife: Deborah), Victoria, Marilyn, Lena, Ruby (husband: Martin)

Fifty-two grands, twenty-eight great-grands

Tamara Eicher (granddaughter, daughter of Ruby and Martin Eicher)

Hannah Kauffman (great-granddaughter, granddaughter of Aaron and Deborah Kauffman, daughter of Seth and Carrie Kauffman)

The Stutzmans

Zechariah (widower, wife: Marian)

Children: Robert (deceased), David (wife: LeeAnn), Ivan (wife: Nadia), Elijah (wife: June), Esther (husband: Joshua), Michelle, Martha (special child, deceased)

Forty-eight grands, twenty great-grands

Michael (grandson, son of Elijah and June)
Robert (grandson, son of Elijah and June)
Micah (grandson, son of Ivan and Nadia)
Dillon (grandson, son of Ivan and Nadia)
Anna (granddaughter, daughter of David and LeeAnn) (husband: Henry)
Donnie (special child, great-grandson, son of Anna and Henry)
Ben (grandson, son of Ivan and Nadia) (wife: Rosalie)
Children: Delia, Samuel, Christopher, Mia, and Mary

The Troyers/Grabers
Jennie (Troyer) and Leo Graber
Children: Matthew, Celia, Micah, Mark, Cynthia, Elizabeth, and Frances

The Ropps/Millers
Mary Katherine (Ropp) and Ezekiel Miller
Mary Katherine's children: Thomas Dylan, Dinah, Mary, Elijah, Ellen, Josiah, Angus, Beulah, Barbara
Twenty-nine grands
Ezekiel's children: Leah, Carlene, John, and Andrew
Nine grands

The Weavers/Grabers

Bess (Weaver) and Aidan Graber

Children: Joshua (father: Caleb Weaver) and Leyla

Abel and Jessica Danner (five children, grown)

Declan and Susie Yoder

Children: Wayne, Thaddeus, Mattie, Lucy, Kevin, Violet

Fred and Celeste Schwartz

Children (all adults): John, Jacob, Amanda, Sandra, Phillip

ONE

Friends warm a room better than any fireplace. Laura Kauffman laid the pinking shears on the oak table cluttered with a pile of construction paper in a rainbow of colors, Elmer's glue, scissors, crayons, pens, pencils, and markers. The sweet aroma of pumpkin-spice cookies fresh from the oven mingled with the scent of burning oak in the fireplace. The chatter of the women around her as they quilted lilted like sweet music.

She couldn't sew anymore because of her arthritis, but she could make Christmas cards. A white candle with a yellow flame glued to green paper still needed the Christmas poem inside. Her friend Mary Katherine Miller — the writer among them — would handle that part. Laura's perfect penmanship had also faded as the disease strengthened its grip on her.

Even so, at seventy-three she had no

17

complaints. Only the certainty that she was closer to the end than the beginning. Her best friends, once widows like herself, had remarried. She served as the only remaining member of an unofficial club. She had no need to marry, of course. What a silly thought. She chuckled and reached for a piece of paper. Red this time. Bright and happy like this time of year.

"I cut out my donkey." Elizabeth Troyer dropped her baby scissors and held up her contribution to the card making. The eight-year-old's burro seemed to have an extra leg. Never one to sit still too long, she wiggled onto her knees and grabbed the glue stick. "It's for Mary. So she can go to Bethlehem with Joseph and have baby Jesus."

"He has too many legs." Elizabeth's sister, Cynthia, scoffed at the ragged animal. "And he's red. Donkeys aren't red."

"I think he's quite nice." Laura smiled over their heads at their mother, Jennie Graber. She shrugged and smiled back, surely used to her daughters' bickering. "Why don't you make a big yellow star for the wise men to follow after the baby Jesus is born?"

They were so like Laura's four daughters when they were that age. Now they were married and had children — and grandchildren — of their own.

"What wool are you spinning?" Mary Katherine nudged Laura's arm. "You're a million miles away and moving fast."

"Like a tortoise on an icy highway." Chuckling, Laura removed her silver-rimmed glasses and cleaned them with her apron. "I was just thinking about how much I love the Christmas season. Everyone is so cheerful and it smells and tastes so good. I think I'll make some caramel popcorn balls and gingerbread men for the grands."

"All of them?" Mary Katherine snorted. "What are there now? Twenty-eight great-grands? That's a lot of popcorn. You'll never get the smell out of the *dawdy haus!*"

"I like that smell." The dawdy haus would smell like Christmas. Giving presents to all of them was beyond her means, but she could make a little something and hand it out when she visited on Christmas Day and Second Christmas Day. And it would keep her busy, which would keep her mind off the anniversary. "And it's not like I don't have the time."

Eli loved Christmas. He loved gingerbread men. He often stole one — or two — before she had a chance to decorate them. She could smell it on his breath when he kissed her with an airy "sorry." He wasn't sorry at all. Worse than the children. His death during the night on Christmas Eve eight years ago made the season a strange mixture of bittersweet memories. More sweet than bitter as the years passed and the anguish faded into a well-worn, treasured memory box hidden away in the far corner of her mind. If God willed it, she would see her sweets-loving husband again one day soon.

Maybe they would make gingerbread cookies in heaven and he'd steal two or three. The kisses would be all the sweeter with son Luke and grandson baby Matthew sharing them too. Her parents and grandparents and aunts and uncles and sisters and brothers and all the other family members who'd gone on before would be present for the great, unending celebration of the New World. If it were God's will, she could look forward to seeing them all for supper every night and singing every morning.

At her age she'd find a train station full of folks waiting to meet her at the pearly gates.

How prideful of her to think she'd be standing at those pearly gates. *If and when,* Gott, *on Your time, not mine.*

Mary Katherine elbowed Laura again. "Was there more to that thought or did you doze off?"

"I'm old. I have to rest between sentences."

"Like I was saying, I love the time between Thanksgiving and Christmas too. I've discovered — or maybe rediscovered — how romantic this time of year can be." Batting her pale eyelashes in pretend coquetry, Mary Katherine stabbed her needle into the burgundy material. Her round cheeks dimpled. "Ezekiel has been sneaking around the back bedroom for a week now doing something he refuses to talk about. There's strange noises floating down the hallway."

"That's because you're still practically newlyweds." Bess Graber stood and picked up her coffee mug. It appeared she might be in a family way again — a thought that tickled Laura pink. Her blue eyes made bluer than sky by her royal-purple dress sparkled with happiness. "Aidan and I spend more time thinking about what to get the *kinner* than each other now. Anyone need more *kaffi* or hot chocolate?"

"Let me get it." Rosalie Stutzman hoisted herself from the other side of the quilting frame. Like Bess, she was in a family way, only on a much larger scale. Almost eight months along and, rumor had it, expecting twins. They'd chosen her house for the frolic so she wouldn't have to drive. "My back is

21

killing me and I need to check on Delia and Samuel. They've been napping for over an hour. For Samuel, that's a miracle. When he starts school next year, no more naps."

"I'll take a cup of chamomile tea." Laura smiled up at her friend. Being retired as a midwife meant someone else would bring these new babies into the world. She stifled a sigh. No sense in regretting what couldn't be changed. "My hands and my knees ache today. It must be the cold."

"Oh, look, it's snowing." A mug in each hand, Rosalie paused at the window. "The first snow of the year. Finally."

"You never know in this part of Missouri. Snow one minute, sunshine and fifty the next." Finicky weather served as part of the charm in living in Jamesport. God liked to mix it up and keep everyone on their toes. "Snow makes it feel more like the Christmas season, though."

"That's not snow. It's freezing rain mixed with sleet." Jennie kept sewing. She was determined to get this quilt done in time to sell it at her Combination Store before the holidays when demand was particularly high. "It'll be gone by midafternoon. Which is fine by me. I'm not a fan of driving the buggy in the snow. We'll have plenty of that this winter."

Being part of the holiday hustle and bustle at the store this year sat at number two on Laura's list of chores she missed. Her knees and ankles simply couldn't handle standing for hours at a time. "I love the seasons. Every one of them. All that winter snow will make us appreciate spring flowers all the more."

"*Jah,* Miss Sunshine." Mary Katherine stuck her tongue out at Laura. "You're not the one driving into town every day to the bookstore."

"You like it, you know you do."

"Ach, there goes Zechariah shuffling out there in that slick sleet with his cane. He'll fall for sure and Ben will have a fit." Shaking her head, Rosalie trudged toward the door that led to the kitchen. "The man seems to have lost what sense the *gut* Lord gave him along with his health."

"Ben loves his *groossdaadi.* I'm sure he feels responsible, too, since his *daed* gave him a turn at watching over Zechariah." Laura made her tone soothing. Plain families took care of their old folks. They were gifts. Not burdens. Rosalie knew that. "I read that confusion can be a symptom of Parkinson's in the book I checked out from the library."

"You were reading up on Parkinson's."

Jennie giggled. "Sudden interest in another aspect of the medical field?"

"Just curious." And sympathetic. Getting old, although a gift, could be a tough row to hoe. A disease like Parkinson's was no walk across the pasture. "I like to be helpful if I can."

"Uh-huh."

"What's he doing out there?" One hand holding back the folds of the green curtain, Bess pressed the flat of her fisted hand on the window and wiped away condensation in a widening circle. "It looks like he's filling the bird feeder. In this weather?"

"Tons of birds are looking for food in the winter. They don't all migrate like the purple martins." Laura rose and went to stand next to Bess. Cold air seeped in around the window's caulking. She shivered. Lately, she didn't have as much body fat to keep her warm as she once had. If her dress hems were any indication, she'd somehow lost a few inches in height as well. Old age had mysterious ways. "Looks like he's hooking up one of those buddy propane heaters. The birds will love a heated birdbath. You just turn on the pilot for heat."

"Since when did you become a bird lover?" Mary Katherine's voice held suppressed laughter. "Or, have you been brushing up so you can carry on a conversation *with* the bird lover? Everyone knows Zechariah is crazy about them."

"Don't be silly." All her knowledge of birds had been acquired since her retirement from midwifery. She sat on the dawdy haus porch and watched the purple martins, cardinals, blue jays, and sparrows wrangle as the spring evenings lengthened into summer. The fresh breeze turned into a languid rustle of leaves weighted down by summer humidity. Hummingbirds zipped around the orange and yellows of the Pride of Barbados and the esperanza, keeping her company.

A Janette Oke book, a mason jar of homemade tea, and some decent bug spray helped pass the time. Visits from her kiddos too. Lots of visits over cookies. Lots of storytelling. Boo-boo kissing. They and the birds were her companions when her now-remarried friends filled up their lives with husbands and couple-y things. "They like the black oiled sunflower seeds. I like sunflower seeds now and then too."

The other women joined in a chorus of laughter. "Maybe you should run out there and chat with Zechariah about where to buy them," Jennie suggested.

"Or where he bought the heater," Bess added.

"You girls are too silly. Besides, I think Rosalie is having a word with him." Laura tapped her gnarled finger on the cold windowpane. Rosalie had donned her coat and rubber boots in order to follow Zechariah outside. From her gesticulations and Zechariah's overt turning-of-the-back, the exchange pleased neither one of them. "He's not so thrilled with her either."

A few seconds passed. Rosalie threw her hands up, whirled, and marched back to the house. She tromped in the front door and stopped on the braided rug to tug off her muddy boots. Balancing her unwieldy body proved a challenge. She propped her hand on the wall and grunted as she shed the boots, followed by her coat. "I thought Ben was stubborn. Now I know where he gets it. Zechariah is the most stubborn man who walks the earth." Her cheeks were red and her *kapp* damp with melting sleet. "He's had that stomach flu that's going around. Fever, vomiting, diarrhea, the whole kit and caboodle. Yet he insists on parading around half-dressed —"

"Rosalie! Half-dressed?" Iris Kurtz chortled as she placed her baby Thomas on her shoulder and patted. Thomas obliged with an enormous belch. She laid the four-month-old in Delia's old playpen and scurried to the window. "Looks to me like he's wearing pants and a shirt. Thank the gut Lord."

"You know what I mean. No coat." A pained look on her face, Rosalie rubbed her belly. "Ach, indigestion. I hope I'm not getting that flu. I can't afford to get sick. Who'll watch the *boplin*? Not Zechariah. He doesn't get around well. He can't be running after Delia."

"He probably misses his dawdy haus." Laura was used to being the peacemaker and the problem solver. With age came wisdom. Or confusion. Or silence. Lots of silence in the middle of the night. Zechariah knew about that too. His wife, Marian, passed two years earlier of female cancer of some sort. If anyone understood this loneliness, Laura did. "I'm sure he's just getting used to the idea of living here. He'll adjust."

"Ach." Rosalie trudged to the table. She gripped the back of the closest chair. Her knuckles turned white. "This feels wrong. Something's not right."

Iris crossed the room in two quick strides. She rubbed her friend's shoulder. "What do you mean it feels wrong?"

"It's too early. I'm not due for another five weeks." Rosalie's shoulders hunched. She closed her eyes and rocked. "It feels

27

like labor."

"You probably overdid it a bit today." Iris, who'd taken a hiatus from delivering babies when Thomas was born, guided Rosalie toward a hickory rocking chair by the fireplace. "Take a load off those swollen feet. Rest. We'll clean up and take care of the little ones."

Hand on her hip, Rosalie trudged toward the chair. *"Nee, nee, nee."* She jerked to a halt. Her mouth opened and her eyes closed. She sighed. "My water broke."

TWO

Babies come when they're ready. Laura plumped Rosalie's pillows and smoothed the sheets on her bed while Iris checked to see how far labor had progressed. An icy draft swept across the bedroom, but the hard work of having two babies would warm Rosalie. She leaned back and closed her eyes. Her fingers rubbed a spot on the bridge of her nose as if she tried to ward off a headache.

Iris's forehead wrinkled. A concerned look flitted across her face. She quickly shuttered it. Laura lifted her eyebrows. Iris shook her head. She nodded toward the door and the hallway beyond.

"I'll get you a glass of water and a warm washrag for your face." Laura patted Rosalie's cheek. "You rest up. You have work to do."

"Will you deliver my boplin, Iris?" Rosalie lifted her head. Sweat shone on her pale

29

skin. "Or do you think Theresa will get here in time to do it?"

"Bess and Mary Katherine went for her." Iris smiled, but her blue eyes held worry. She smoothed back a wisp of honey-blonde hair and tucked it in her kapp. "Jennie went to get Ben."

A question not answered. Laura headed for the hallway. Iris followed.

"What's it look like?"

"Her placenta is presenting first." Iris chewed her lower lip. "She needs to go to the medical center in Chillicothe. Theresa told me she tried to convince her to have the babies at the birthing center and she said no. This is two babies. They're premature. I don't want to take any chances. We need to call an ambulance."

"I'll tell her. You meet Ben at the door and talk to him. He can run out to the phone shack."

"Say a prayer?"

"I will." Laura took a breath and marched back into the bedroom. It wouldn't be the first time she'd delivered this kind of news, but it was never easy and she had thought herself done with it. *Gott, put Your protective hand on these little ones and give Rosalie the strength and peace of mind to weather any storm that comes. You are the Great Physi-*

cian. *These are Your babies. Thy will be done.*

That last part troubled her the most. *Thy will be done.*

A hard phrase for someone who might lose a baby. Or two babies. Or who lost a husband too soon. Or a wife.

"What is it?" Rosalie threw her legs over the side of the bed and sat up. Her curly brown hair framed her face and straggled down her back. "What are you two whispering about out there? You act like I've never had a baby before. I know how to do this. It's not that hard."

"It's different this time." Laura sat next to her and patted her knee. "You have placenta previa. Do you know what that is?"

Rosalie's hands went to her stomach and began to rub in a soft, circular motion. "The placenta is in the way. My boplin will have trouble getting out."

"That's right. Because of that and the fact that they're early, we feel it would be best to deliver at the medical center. The boplin may need some help with oxygen and such that we can't give them here."

"I've never been in the hospital." Her brown eyes wet with tears, Rosalie's face crumpled. "I want to wait for Theresa, see what she says."

"Theresa already told you she thought it

31

would be best. She knows other Plain women have delivered at the medical center, like Millie Mast. It happens sometimes, and we always want to do what's best for the baby."

Plain folks preferred as little intrusion from the English world as possible, but they also knew what it meant to be good stewards of the gifts God gave them. That included babies.

"Doctors and machines and strangers. How can that be what's best?" Rosalie swiped at her nose with her sleeve. "I'm a grown woman. Is it silly that I'm afraid?"

"Not silly. We're all afraid of the unknown. But we trust in Gott's plan for us. We set our worry aside. That's how we show our faith." Laura stood. Spouting the words was easy. Following her own advice much harder. But Rosalie didn't need to know that. She needed a strong, faithful friend right now. "Lean back and rest. I'll pack a bag for you. We'll be ready when the ambulance comes."

"Ambulance? Why can't we drive?"

"It would take too long in a buggy. The ambulance will zip right out here and get you to the medical center fast."

"It'll scare the kinner."

"Mudder?" They turned to see Samuel, his

chubby face crinkled in a scowl, standing at the door. The five-year-old scampered to his mother. "What's wrong? Are you sick? Delia's crying."

"I'm having the boplin." She hugged him and kissed his mop of curly blond hair. "There's a change in plan. I'm going to town to have them. You need to take care of Delia and Groossdaadi for me."

Samuel's expression grew even more serious. "Can I make them eat their carrots?"

"Delia, jah, but I doubt anyone can make Groossdaadi do something he doesn't want to do." Rosalie's chuckle sounded weak. "Your daed will come back later and tell you if you have new brothers or sisters. Or maybe one of each."

"Two boys. I'd rather have *bruders* to play with. I'll tell Christopher when he comes in with the wood."

"I'll see what I can do about filling your order."

Grinning at being the bearer of good news, he skipped from the room without a backward glance.

"Ach." Rosalie put both hands on her knees and panted. "I'm selfish. I don't want to go by myself. I want Ben to go with me."

"He will."

"But what about the kinner? Who'll make

supper? Zechariah's hands are too shaky. I can't leave them with him. He'll burn the house down trying to keep the fire going."

"I'll stay with them. Don't worry about a thing."

"I can't ask you to stay here with Zechariah."

"You didn't ask. I offered. He's not such an ogre."

"Says you."

Zechariah didn't scare Laura. Never had. He and Eli ran around in the same gaggle of teenagers, hunting, fishing, swimming, and going to singings in their courting days. Memories of his toothy smile swam to the surface amid a sea of images. Icy wind burning her cheeks as she skated on a frozen pond in winter, the taste of fresh apples and the feel of juice running down her chin under a brilliant summer sun. The aroma of frying fish on the Coleman stove at Stockton Lake. In those days Zechariah had a quick smile and a kind word for everyone. Times changed. If anyone knew that, she did.

Swallowing a lump that made her throat ache, Laura packed a fresh nightgown, underwear, and a change of clothes in Rosalie's canvas bag.

She handed Rosalie a clean kapp. "Christopher is eight. Old enough to act as chaperone."

"As if you would need one with that crotchety old man." Rosalie smiled for the first time. "I don't mean to be ugly. It's just been hard since he came to live with us. Everything is topsy-turvy. For him and for us. He doesn't make it easy. I try to be nice. He mumbles. He never smiles. He doesn't eat anything I cook." Her smile collapsed and tears trickled down her cheeks.

"Ach, honey, one thing at a time. Right now, save your strength for the boplin. Everything else will take care of itself."

And Laura would have time to straighten out one crotchety old man before his great-grandsons or -daughters came home from the hospital.

THREE

A siren scream broke the silence. Startled, Zechariah dropped the hammer on his foot. "Ach."

He hopped backward, teetered, lost his balance, and toppled on his behind in the hay and dirt on the barn floor.

What could a bunch of ladies gathered for a frolic to make Christmas presents do that would result in the need for an ambulance? The need to scare the pudding out of him?

Gott, is this what I've come to? Falling all over myself at a siren?

Zechariah rubbed his aching wrists with dirty hands. Despite his thick, black work boot, his toes hurt from the blow. His breaths came in white puffs. *Why not take me now? Why not take me instead of Marian two years ago? She had so much love to give to those kinner in there.*

Zechariah had no business questioning God. He would never do it aloud. But the same unanswered questions wormed their way into his thoughts no matter how often he reminded himself: obedience, humility, patience, discipleship, the foundation of faith.

Thy will be done. Even if I can't understand it after seventy-five years on earth.

God's will did not include feeling sorry for himself or throwing a pity party over a simple fall. "Get up, old man."

He confined talking aloud to himself to times when he was alone. He crawled to the nearest stall post and dragged himself to his feet. With trembling legs he staggered to the stout hickory cane his son Ivan had given him for Christmas the first year after his diagnosis, only months before doctors pronounced Marian's cancer diagnosis.

Reminding himself to walk slowly, he gritted his teeth, shuffled to the doors, and slid them open. A Daviess County ambulance skidded to a stop in front of the house. The siren faded and stopped, leaving blessed silence.

One of the paramedics, looking young enough to be a grade school kid, dashed into the house. The other tugged a gurney from the ambulance.

Zechariah tottered to the porch and slipped through the door the medic left open. His great-grandson looked up from his wooden blocks scattered on the pine plank floor in front of the blazing fireplace. "Do you like my barn?"

"It looks gut. What happened? Is one of the women hurt?"

"Mudder's having the boplin."

"Why an ambulance?" Why ask a five-year-old this question? "Never mind. Keep playing, little one." He started toward the hallway and the bedrooms.

Laura Kauffman trotted from Ben's room. What was she doing? She retired from delivering babies long ago. Zechariah stepped into her path. "Why didn't someone tell me about the boplin? Why the ambulance?"

"Believe it or not, not everything is about you."

Laura's voice was as tart as green apples, but her smile remained sweet as maple syrup. Just as it had been a hundred years ago in school. Why were those memories so bright and the ones of his own Marian fading so fast? Laura had once been a fully rounded woman, like Marian, but now her dress hung on her and she stooped a bit — like he did. However, her green eyes still blazed behind silver wire-framed glasses.

38

She had much in common with a snapping turtle.

"I know that."

"I'm sorry. I didn't mean to snap. I'm just . . . concerned." Her gaze shifted over his shoulder. It seemed she, too, saw other days long gone. She shrugged and made flapping motions with her gnarled hands. "There're complications. They'll carry Rosalie to Chillicothe. Best stay out of the way."

Plain women didn't usually talk to Plain men this way, but her worry for her friend explained it. She cared about Rosalie and the babies. Zechariah leaned on his cane and eased from the hallway. "Are the boplin in trouble?"

"Nothing that can't be handled in a proper hospital."

Gott, please let that be so. Ben and Rosalie have enough burden with me. If it is Thy will, let them care for Your boplin. They'll raise them up right. You know they will. You have my Robert and my Martha. Let these two be.

Not a fair request. Robert had been in his fifties when a heart attack took him. Marian and Zechariah had known from the beginning that sweet Martha, their special girl, would have a short time on earth. Always thin and frail but always smiling. Pneumonia

39

had taken their girl at twenty-eight. Her little hand held his and her feverish smile never wavered in those last moments before she slipped away.

"Prayer is best."

Laura's words penetrated the thicket of memories, startling Zechariah. Laura had a way about her. She knew what people thought almost before they thought it. "You're right."

"It can be easy to forget. We like to think we can solve all the problems of the world." She smiled, but her expression filled with a sweet sadness that Zechariah recognized. Longing for that which one could no longer have. "Gott's will be done."

It always was, whether they liked it or not.

Hollering his children's names in his deep bass, Ben strode down the hallway. He jerked his head toward the back. Laura hustled past him and disappeared into the bedroom.

The boys, with little Delia piggyback on brother Christopher's shoulders, appeared in the front room. Silent, their woebegone faces expectant. "What's the matter with Mudder?" Christopher, as the oldest at eight, spoke first. "Why is she going in the ambulance?"

"It's what they call a precaution." His

40

hands gripping his suspenders, Ben hesitated. He glanced at Zechariah. His Adam's apple bobbed. "Like when I call the vet to come because the horse is having trouble foaling. Horses have babies all the time, but sometimes they need help. Only your mudder is going to the hospital, instead of the doctor coming here. Just to make sure your little *schweschders* or bruders come into the world safe and sound."

Nodding, Samuel crossed his arms over his chest. "It's best then." He tilted his head. "I should go too. Mudder will feel better if I hold her hand."

"That's kind of you, Samuel." Ben's smile was genuine this time. "Mudder would like that, but I need you to stay here with Great-Grandpa. I'll go with your mudder."

In unison they turned to look at Zechariah.

Nothing like the stares of three unbelieving children to strike terror into an old man's heart. "We'll have popcorn and play Farm Animals." He offered the first thing that came into his mind. Could he make popcorn? Rosalie had been adamant about him not touching her stove. "You can help with the popcorn."

"It's called Life on the Farm." Christopher sounded doubtful. "Have you ever played?"

"Sure, sure, when I was your age."

Sixty-five years ago. Maybe a few times since then.

"*Danki.* I'll be back as soon as I can." Ben's tone said he knew Zechariah would not like what came next. "Laura will be here to make supper, and she can help with the popcorn. She'll stay until I get back."

"Nee, there's no need for her to stay." Pride and shame shook their heads from their perches on Zechariah's shoulders. Ben thought his grandfather needed a babysitter. A babysitter as old as Moses' wife. Like his groossdaadi but still able to walk and talk like a normal person. "I can watch the kinner for one night."

The paramedics rolled the gurney carrying Rosalie toward them. Theresa Plank scurried alongside her, murmuring something about breathing. The children rushed to their mother's side. She patted their heads in quick succession.

Ben shook his head at Zechariah. "Laura cooks. You don't. She can clean up and make sure the kinner wash up before bed. You've been sick. You need to rest. Besides, I don't know if it's only for one night."

Zechariah had been resting for years now.

If anything, he was sick from resting so much.

"I'll be back soon." Ben gripped Zechariah's arm and let go as he passed by.

An eight-year-old in charge of the outside. An old woman in charge of the inside. "Don't worry about anything. Just get your *fraa* to the hospital." He swallowed his pride, dry as a thick loaf of unsliced, week-old bread, and nodded. "We'll be fine. We'll be waiting to hear the gut news."

Then they were gone. Laura padded down the hallway with a load of dirty sheets and towels in her arms. "So much excitement. I think I'll make a cup of cinnamon spice tea. Would you like some? Rosalie said you'd been down with the flu. Hot tea is good for what ails you."

"Nee. I have a mess to clean up in the barn."

"It's cold out there and the sleet has turned to snow."

"I'll not rust or melt."

"Nee. Maybe you'll find your good humor while you're out there."

Mouthy woman. Still, her tart tone made him want to smile. "My humor's fine."

But she'd already whirled and sashayed into the kitchen.

All Zechariah wanted was peace and

43

quiet. The barn had plenty of that. He shuffled the other direction.

FOUR

Laying the last freshly washed pot on the drain by the kitchen sink, Laura did a quick check of the room. Rosalie kept a neat kitchen. Dishes stacked in an orderly fashion on open shelves on one wall. Pans hanging from hooks on the gray wall across from the stove. A well-organized pantry and the laundry room beyond were spic-and-span.

Bess and the other women had gone home to their families with the promise that Mary Katherine would stop by Ruby's to let her know Laura would be staying at Ben and Rosalie's. Her first supper in Rosalie's absence had consisted of chili and corn-bread followed by the pumpkin cookies. It went over well with everyone but Zechariah. He crumbled the cornbread into the bowl of chili, then left both to turn cold.

Rosalie had been right about one thing. The man mumbled. He used to have a booming voice. Now it was so soft, Laura could barely hear him. Or maybe she was going deaf in her old age. Strange, she hadn't noticed it before.

"Are you done in here?"

She turned. The subject of her musings stood in the doorway, one hand on his cane, the other on the door frame. His thin shoulders hunched, his russet eyes squinted against the light of the kerosene lamp. Laura summoned a smile and nodded. "All done."

"You should go on home then. No need for you to stay."

"I told Rosalie I would stay until she and Ben returned with the boplin." She hung the towel over the back of a chair to dry. Zechariah wanted her gone, but more than that, he wanted to be seen as independent. No matter their age, men were like that. "Besides, I'm anxious to know how things went. How the babies are."

"They'll be home in the morning, I reckon." He smoothed his unruly silver beard. "You only live down the road. Someone will carry the news to you then."

He didn't know a thing about giving birth to premature twins with the added challenge of placenta previa. Rosalie would not be home tomorrow. Worrying him served no purpose. "Trying to get rid of me then?"

"The kinner are playing Life on the Farm.

46

They're fine." His voice grew raspier with each word. "No need for you to stay."

"You'll get up with Delia during the night then when she has to go potty?"

If looks were stones propelled by a sling-shot, Laura would be knocked senseless on the floor. "I'm not feeble. I'll do what is necessary."

"Nee, but you are a man and most men don't take to the idea of babysitting." She picked up the teakettle and set it on the burner. Even with the fire crackling nearby, she had a chill. A cup of tea was in order. "Even their own kinner."

"Most men don't sit around all day doing nothing. It won't cost me much to get up with her." He closed his mouth. His pulse jumped in his temple. "You should go home. We'll be fine."

Laura was caught between a rock and a hard place. Usually she would do as a man like Zechariah insisted, but in this case, she simply couldn't. She had a responsibility to Rosalie, Ben, and their children. "Why don't you play the game with the kinner? They'd like that. I'll make some popcorn and bring out a pitcher of water."

His face a block of cedar, he held up his free hand. It shook. "I knock things around the board. It annoys them."

47

"They should learn to have more patience."

"They're kinner."

"That's no excuse."

He ducked his head. "You're changing the subject. You're as bad as Rosalie. I don't need your help."

"I noticed you didn't eat much." Another subject change. Do it enough times and maybe he would get the point. Laura wouldn't leave. She couldn't. "Don't you like chili?"

"I do. My belly doesn't like much of anything right now. No offense."

"None taken. I could make you some toast with peanut butter spread."

"Not necessary."

"I'm trying to help."

He rolled his eyes like a teenager. "There's a lot of that going around."

She, too, had noticed the propensity of people around her to take her arm on the steps or hold the door or even pat her head a time or two. As if she were in her second childhood and just learning to walk on her own. Finally, something they could agree on. "It's odd, isn't it, how our children become our caregivers? They forget we first taught them to walk and use a spoon and diapered their behinds."

"Indeed. I'm not ready for a diaper yet."

"Nothing wrong with being independent." Laura plucked a mug from the shelf and set it on the counter next to a tin that held an assortment of teabags. She would have that cup of tea and shoo the children to bed. "At least I have my own space in the dawdy haus. You must miss that."

"I do." His voice softened. He shrugged. "I try to see it as Gott's will."

"It can be hard, I know —"

The back door flew open and Ivan Stutzman stomped into the kitchen. He brushed snowflakes from his black wool coat and wiped his rubber snow boots on the rug. "There you are." His glance encompassed Laura. His bushy gray eyebrows rose. "And you, Laura. I hadn't heard you were here. I thought Rosalie's sister was coming."

"Her youngest has the flu. They didn't want to spread it around."

"Of course, of course." He wiped melted sleet from his face with his sleeve and headed for his father. "Ben's not back? Have you heard anything?"

"Nothing." Zechariah's tone was testy. "It's kind of you to come, but it's not necessary for you to ride over here in the sleet and the dark to make sure I haven't burned down the house. We're fine. I'm fine."

"Whoa, whoa, I just came to talk to you."
Ivan patted his dad on the shoulder. He
towered over the older man, but russet eyes,
long nose, and wild silver beard made him
the spitting image of his father. "Come sit
by the fire. You look tired."

His eyebrows raised as if to say, "See what
I mean," Zechariah shot Laura a rueful
smile. She shrugged and smiled back. The
son's attitude reflected his love and respect
for his father. Zechariah could see that, even
if it could be a trifle annoying. She saw it in
her own children. A desire to help her as
she had helped them.

"I'm not tired —"

"Well, I am. And cold." Ivan disappeared
through the doorway. Zechariah shrugged
and followed.

"I'll get the kinner to bed," Laura said to
no one in particular. "In case anyone was
wondering."

Another busybody. Hoping he hadn't said
those words aloud, Zechariah glanced at his
son. Ivan was busy tickling his grandchildren and laughing at Samuel's efforts to
escape his hugs. The children loved to play
with their grandfather. Once, Ben and his
brothers and sisters had been the same with
Zechariah.

Now they were grown and had their own kinner. Life passed in a flash of rainbows, lightning, and sparkling sunlight one after another. Other days were dark and dreary. They smelled of medicine dripping into an IV and bleach. The sound of clods of dirt thudding against a casket filled the air. He settled into the rocking chair by the fire close enough to feel the heat seep into his brittle bones and warm his aching toes.

"Go get ready for bed." Ivan kissed Delia's forehead and rubbed his beard on her cheek. The three-year-old squealed. He grinned and let her toddle off to Laura, who stood in the hallway, arms crossed, looking like an elderly schoolteacher. "Laura will tuck you in."

"I want Mudder." Delia frowned and dug in her heels a few feet from Laura. Tears materialized, from sunny to rainy in a few seconds. "Mudder, Mudder, Mudder."

Laura knelt, swept her up in her arms, and hugged the girl to her bosom. "Mudder will be home soon. In the meantime, how about I tell you a story before you go to sleep."

"I want a story." Samuel, his face crinkled as if considering tears as well, edged toward the hallway. "About a bear."

"Or a lion." Eight-year-old Christopher wasn't immune to the joy of a good story, it

51

seemed. "Can I have a story too?"

"I want a story." Tears forgotten, Delia chimed in too. "About a little girl."

"Of course." Laura smiled at the men. "I can make you some tea after they're in bed." She followed the small stampede from sight.

"That woman and her tea."

"Now you object to tea?" Ivan slid his wide-brimmed black felt hat from his head and slapped it onto his lap. "She's trying to help. At least try to be sociable."

"I can make my own tea."

"Rosalie doesn't want you messing with the stove." Ivan blew out air. He surely counted to ten in silence. This conversation had been repeated several times in the two months since Esther and her husband Joshua decided it was time for Zechariah to move to Ben's. No talking it over with Zechariah. Just packing his stuff one day. Moving him around like a special child. "You're too shaky. You almost burned down Esther's house."

That was an exaggeration. Wood had fallen from the cookstove and lit a rug on fire. Zechariah had extinguished it in a matter of minutes. It would only get worse. The doctors said he was in stage three or a mid-stage of the disease. The fact that it could and would get worse nipped at his heels from the time he woke up until he went to sleep. "What did you want to talk about?"

"Are you taking your medicine?"

It made him nauseated and took away any appetite he might have. "Jah. You came all the way over here to ask me that?"

Whatever it was, Ivan couldn't seem to spit it out. His expression darkened. He didn't meet Zechariah's gaze.

"It's about Micah and Dillon."

Ivan's two middle sons. Ben was the youngest. "What about them?"

"They've made the decision —"

"To go to Indiana? Nee. It's a bad idea."

"Jah. To Nappanee. Robert's wife is up there with her new husband. She's filled their heads up with how good things are at the RV factories." His face carved with sorrowful lines, Ivan stared at the fire. "If Robert hadn't died, none of this would've come up."

It had been five years since Zechariah's oldest son died unexpectedly of a heart attack. The pain might lessen with time, but it never subsided completely. The loss of his wife, mother of his seven children, three years later only added salt to the wound. For Ivan too. His older brother and his mother and years before, his sister Martha. "If onlys serve no purpose. Running off to

Indiana and leaving behind family serves no purpose either."

"You have to see it from their perspective. There's not enough farmland to go around here and what we do have isn't making much money." Ivan's words came automatically. This debate was a rerun of many before. That didn't make the arguments any more palatable. "They can't afford to buy their own farms. Who can? They have families to support now. Karen says there's plenty of money to be had. All the Plain men up there are working in the factory. They can go in early, make their quota, and go home early if they're good workers."

"They spend their days in an *Englisch* factory with Englisch men, instead of at home, working the land with their kinner. We were meant to be close to the land and our families."

"Times have changed." Ivan leaned back in his chair and sighed. "I don't like it any more than you do, but I can't see how I can stop them. They need the work. We have family in Nappanee. These recreational vehicles are selling like hotcakes."

For now, they were. While retired English couples had the wherewithal to pay for them. "I don't know that Karen is family. She married again only a year after Robert passed."

"She had five kinner to raise. *They* are family. Besides, she did what was expected of her. You know that. And Mark is a decent man. A gut daed to Robert's kinner. Don't be small-minded. They could've become *Mennischt*."

A real possibility right here in Jamesport. Another district had evolved into a less strict New Order *Gmay* over the past several years. Some members had gone on to embrace the Mennonite faith.

"It's not our place to judge others." By the same token, because others chose to part from the basic tenets of their forefathers' beliefs, that didn't mean Ivan and the grandsons should do the same. "We need to tend to our own business and our own faith."

"What Karen did was no different than Bess courting Aidan after only a year of being a widow."

"Maybe not, but she's still here. They both are. They didn't abandon family and friends for a factory." Two years after her first husband's death, Bess married Aidan Graber and settled down a few miles from her first father-in-law and his new bride. "Aidan is a chicken and hog farmer. He works the land the same as his daed did. You must tell them no. Money and material goods are not the goal. Staying close to Gott's earth, family, and faith — those are the important things."

Ivan scrubbed at his face with the back of a callused hand. "Food on the table and clothes on the kinner's backs are important too."

"We share what we have. We grow what we need. We make our clothes."

"Those were different times. Surely you remember what it was like to chomp at the bit to make your own way."

Zechariah still chomped at the bit. Why couldn't Ivan see that? "What happens if the Englisch economy falls apart again and those factories start closing? All the Plain men will lose their jobs."

"It's a chance they're willing to take. They can always come home."

That they could. Zechariah didn't wish that sort of failure on his grandsons. "Have you talked to Freeman about it?"

"Not yet. I wanted to let you know first. Then I'll talk to Freeman, Solomon, and Cyrus."

A small bow to Zechariah's place as the family patriarch ahead of the bishop and the other elders. Ivan would know how much that meant to him. "To tell me or to ask me?"

"They didn't ask me. They told me."

"At least let me try talking to them."

"You can try."

"You don't sound convinced."

"They respect your opinion but —"

"They think I'm too stuck in the old ways. Horse power." The blazing summer sun on his face as Zechariah guided the team of horses through the fields touched his cheeks again for a second. It felt good. Work felt good. "They forget I'm the one who went up to the Horse Progress Days every summer, wherever it was that year, to find new ways to repair our plows and make our equipment work better and improve our harvests."

"They haven't forgotten, but better equipment isn't enough anymore. The megafarms are taking over."

"Small farms support the local community. Jamesport will always be a farming town."

"We have more folks working in tourists' stores than on farms." His expression grim despite his placating tone, Ivan leaned forward and poked at the logs in the fireplace. The flames leaped. "Jamesport is a tourist town now as much as a farming town. Do you know how much horse-worked farms are going for these days? I read an article that said a farm in Lancaster County is going for $8,900 an acre, depending on where the land is. The average price for a farm is $334,876."

"We're not buying a farm in Lancaster County." Zechariah steepled his fingers, keeping them steady in his lap. "That Dunleavy property off Granite Road sold for $4,677 an acre. Way cheaper."

"The total sell price was almost a million-three for 320 acres. We don't have that kind of money, but the folks who are coming west looking for cheaper land do."

"Cheap is a relative term."

"My point exactly."

"My point is I'd like to talk to them before they pack up and move across the country."

"I get your point." Ivan stood. "I have to get back. We're celebrating Kimberly's birthday on Saturday. Someone will come by for you."

Ivan's granddaughter was a shy little thing. Still, what little girl didn't like a birthday party? "It's your birthday too. Don't think I've forgotten."

"At my age, I'd like to forget. Like I said, someone will come for you."

"I can drive myself."

"We've had this talk."

58

Take away a man's buggy and any semblance of independence disappeared with it. Memories bright as blue jays assailed Zechariah. He had been eight. He hitched his Shetland pony to a small wagon and hopped in. He and Carmel carried the wicker basket to the field. Ham sandwiches, fresh peaches, cookies as big as his hand, mason jars filled with lukewarm lemonade. He sat on the back of the hay wagon, dirty bare feet swinging as he ate two sandwiches.

"You are a growing boy." Daed clapped him on the back and handed him the cookies. "Mudder knows oatmeal raisin is your favorite."

"She sent peanut butter pecan for you."

He smelled horse manure and fresh-cut hay. His daed's sweat. Flies buzzed in his ears.

"Daed? Daed!" Ivan's face filled with concern as the memory faded into the night. "You should go to bed. You're tired."

"I wish people would stop telling me what I should do and how I feel."

"I made tea." A brown ceramic mug in each hand, Laura bustled into the room. The fragrance of chamomile and honey sweetened the air, mingling with the hickory of the fireplace. "I added honey, but I couldn't find any lemon."

"I'm sure he'll find fault with that too." Ivan brushed past her. "I'll be back tomorrow to check on the livestock."

"No need. I can —"

"Take care of it." Laura and Ivan spoke in unison. Another person teamed up against him.

Ivan tugged the brim of his hat forward. "Let's not argue. See you tomorrow."

He was gone.

"Don't you love how fresh chamomile smells? It reminds me that spring will come again." Laura held out the tea mug. "I guess you don't need any lemon. You're sour enough."

Trying to come up with a retort that didn't sound childish, Zechariah sputtered, "Am not."

She sipped from her mug and swallowed. "Hmmm. Are too."

At least she sounded as childish as he did.

FIVE

Taking care of small children was not for the faint of heart. Laura rubbed her eyes and settled her glasses back on her nose. She grabbed the coffeepot from the stove, poured the fragrant, steaming liquid into an oversized mug, and took a sip. She needed straight fuel after her first night alone with the Stutzman children. As if two trips to the bathroom with Delia hadn't been enough, Samuel's cries had sent her scurrying down the hall at three a.m. Poor thing had a nightmare. Something about a bear and a wolf fighting over him. She would rethink the bedtime stories tonight. Poor baby had been shaking.

The interruptions hadn't really been interruptions. She spent most of the night staring at the dark above her and listening to the tree branches blow in the wind. The sound soothed her and reminded her of Eli. At night, in the dark, everything reminded her of Eli. Whether in the dawdy haus, whether awake or asleep, she thought of him. And relived old memories. The elderly seemed destined to do that. Relive old memories instead of making new ones.

The day she married Eli. Sitting at the *eck* during the reception, filled with a kind of anticipation like no other. The day she gave birth to her firstborn son, Luke. The day she and Eli buried him. Parents should always go first. A whole life lived. Yet she lingered. Surely, God had His reasons. He still had something for her to do. Otherwise, why leave her on this earth?

She was being prideful. What made her think God had some grand task for her to do? His plan was His plan. A small task, perhaps, in the bigger scheme of things. Something to make life more livable. Something far beyond anything her pea brain could fathom.

She blew on her coffee and took another sip. Heavenly.

The thought made her smile. Would there be coffee in heaven? Would there be pineapple upside-down cake? Watermelon? Chocolate chip ice cream? Mary Katherine's spice cake? If Laura had her way, she'd bake them all and her fingers would work again so she could sew to her heart's content. Scripture said there would be no pain in heaven. She could hop, skip, jump, and run again. Skate on the iced-over pond in the winter and swim in the summer.

The image of her old body peeling away to reveal the young, healthy body of her youth like a butterfly from its cocoon made her chuckle aloud. She should become a writer like Mary Katherine.

Such foolish thoughts came from interrupted sleep. Bacon sizzled in the pan. The aroma made her mouth water. The fluffy scrambled eggs were ready. Warm up the biscuits or make toast?

She trudged to the counter. Biscuits with butter and sorghum sounded good on a frosty December morning. She took another sip of coffee and glanced out the window. Yesterday's sleet mixed with snow was gone, but not the chill in the air. Movement caught her gaze. A visitor so early in the morning? No. Zechariah wielded an ax next to the barn. Chopping wood. The ax wavered over his head, then slammed onto the chopping block. The log splintered and pieces fell to the ground.

He stopped, teetered, grabbed one log, and managed to toss it onto the wood stack.

No cooking, no driving a buggy. Surely no chopping wood had been on the list as well.

63

Laura moved the bacon from the flame and put a lid over the skillet. She grabbed her wool coat from the peg by the door and wrapped it around her as she headed out. The fresh, crisp air welcomed her on the back-porch steps. She raised her face to the sun. What a beautiful day. Even at a distance, Zechariah's scowl was evident. What a pain in her side.

"The woodpile is plenty big." Laura halted a few feet from Zechariah. Despite the wintry breeze, drops of sweat adorned his forehead. He grunted and smacked the ax into the wood. "Christopher brought in a stack last night."

"Won't last more than a day. The temperatures have been dropping all week. Thermometer said twenty-two when I got up this morning. And that's without the wind chill." He wiggled the ax until it broke free of the oak. "Besides, Christopher is too small to be cutting wood. He'll chop his foot off."

Some might say the same of Zechariah. He wasn't a big man and time had whittled his shoulders into a slump. His arms and legs were toothpicks. His pants hung down around his hips despite his suspenders. Even his hat seemed to sit loosely on his bald head.

However, he seemed to have become the

resident weatherman. "The sun is shining. It'll be forty by noon."

"You have some kind of pipeline to the gut Lord?"

"Nee, but I have eyes that can see and a body that can feel the glorious warmth of the sun." If a man could argue about the weather, he could argue about anything. "I'll carry some wood in."

"I can do it." Zechariah buried the ax's head in a huge log. "Shouldn't you be making breakfast for the kinner?"

"It's made. Come eat. Do you prefer biscuits or toast with your eggs?"

"I'm not hungry. Should you leave those little ones alone in the house?"

So now he would get on his high horse and tell her how to care for the children. "Samuel is helping Delia get dressed. They'll be waiting in the kitchen." Laura breathed, the warm air white puffs in the chilly wind. *One, two, three, four, five . . .* They were good children, well trained by their mother. Not nearly as contrary as Zechariah. "You have to eat."

He shook his head. "You're not my mudder or my fraa."

The image of Zechariah sitting by her fireplace while she darned his holey socks assailed her for one fleeting second — long enough to make her thankful for forty-five years with Eli. He was no saint, but at least he had a sense of humor. "Gott is gut."

Zechariah stomped over to his puny pile of wood, knelt, and scooped up a few logs. "Very funny."

It was funny to think they'd known each other since first grade, lived in the same community all their lives, and now couldn't exchange a few sentences without arguing like an old married couple. "I could make oatmeal if that would suit your stomach better."

"I don't like oatmeal."

She had no way of knowing what he liked or didn't like. That was part of getting to know a person. Something he didn't seem to have any desire to do. Perhaps he believed he didn't need more friends. He and Abel Danner huddled together at most meetings and frolics. They'd been best friends as far back as Laura could remember.

'Course Abel still had his wife, Jessica. He couldn't always be running around with Zechariah. A sad state of affairs. When a man's wife was gone and his children grown-up, he could use a load of friends. Like she could depend on Jennie or Bess when Mary Katherine was caught up in the bookstore or Mary Katherine when Jennie couldn't get away from the Combination Store. Zechariah seemed more suited to hanging around Laura's great-grandson Jasper when he had the grumblies. Only not as cute or cuddly.

Although Zechariah did have a certain something in those rich russet eyes when he wasn't frowning. That same "don't-mess-with-me-unless-I-say-so" something Eli used to have when she got in his way in the barn.

Get a grip, woman.

Zechariah stood, teetered, righted himself, and took a step. A second later he lost the battle and keeled over backward. His arms flailed. His hat flew off. His head smacked the woodpile.

"Ach!" Laura rushed to his side and knelt. He wouldn't want her help. He wouldn't want her to see him like this. She would feel the same if she fell in broad daylight in front of a man. Regardless, the helper in her heart couldn't turn her back on a hurting human being. "Let me see your head. Are you dizzy?"

"Get away from me." One hand on his neck, he rolled to his side, his back to her. "Just get away. Get away."

"Let me help you up."

"Nee. I don't need your help."

67

"It's not a shame to need help."

"I don't need your pity either."

"Who says I pity you? I'm more irritated than anything." He would prefer irritation to pity. Laura could at least give him that. The way he rubbed his head said he was hurting. He still had a thick fringe of curly gray hair along the bottom, but a red knot stuck out above it. His fingers touched the spot and withdrew. A half-stifled groan followed.

Laura gripped both hands in her lap to keep from comforting him. He wasn't Eli. He wasn't one of her sons or grandsons or great-grandsons. He was a man who didn't want her help. "It's hard to find and accept our limits as we grow older. Gott knows that."

No answer.

Teeth gritted, he struggled to sit upright. Laura stood and anchored her hands on her hips to keep from helping him. He rolled over to his knees and crawled to the wood-pile. There, he crept to his feet. Leaves and dried, dead grass decorated the back of his coat and his pants. Mud stained his knees and his coat sleeves. Unable to help herself, she scooped up his hat. "Here."

His face red with fury and exertion, he turned and faced her. He accepted her offering. "Danki." The two syllables seeped through clenched teeth. "Go now."

"You hit your head. Come inside and warm up. I'll take a look."

"Are you deaf?"

The soft, weary tone of the previous evening had disappeared, replaced with a thunderous shout filled with the same emotions that kept Laura awake at night.

Shame at her weakness, anger at her loss, bitterness, loneliness, bewilderment, confusion.

All the emotions she'd experienced when God took Eli home and left her to carry on after forty-five years of often-joyful, occasionally painful, but always shared marriage. "My hearing's fine. I'm only trying to be helpful."

"I said I don't need your help. Go inside. The kinner need you. Not me. I'm a grown man."

"As I said before, there's no shame in needing help, grown-up or otherwise."

His hand went to his forehead. He closed his eyes. A second later, he opened them. "Biscuits. The kinner like them best." The thunder had dissipated, replaced by soft contrition. "They'll be starving by now. I'll be in to wash up in a minute."

Laura nodded. This man needed help in

ways that had nothing to do with his disease. A person had to want help, though. It couldn't be shoved on him willy-nilly. She trudged toward the house.

The familiar *toot-toot-toot* of a horn filled the air. Laura looked toward the muddy dirt road that led to the house. Her favorite driver's powder-blue-and-rust minivan lumbered toward them, its engine whining. Ben.

The babies.

SIX

Laura waved as the van pulled into the yard next to the porch. Ben waved in return and exited the passenger side as soon as Dineen stopped the minivan. Everyone moved double-time, yet the minutes seemed to drag by. *Good news, Gott, please good news.*

Ben spoke first. "Where's Christopher? He should be doing the chores."

"He's feeding the horses." Zechariah spoke up. "And Rosalie?"

Ben's craggy face contorted. The van's engine ticked in the pause that followed. "I only came for a change of clothes."

"What happened?" Laura moved closer. Feeling unsteady herself, she stuck her hands on the van's warm hood and let it hold her up. "The boplin?"

"The boplin are fine. Two beautiful girls born at five thirty-eight and five forty yesterday." His voice cracked, but he managed a smile. "Mia and Mary. They're small, but the doctor says they're healthy. They're giving them oxygen."

"And your fraa?"

Ben's gaze bounced over Laura's shoulder to the house. He rubbed his gloved hands together as if to warm them. He had his grandfather's brown eyes, like his father, but also Zechariah's slight build and small stature. "There were complications. They did a caesarian section. There was bleeding and her blood pressure dropped."

His lips trembled. "It was touch and go for a while." His voice dropped to a whisper. He swiped at his face with his coat sleeve. "I thought we might lose her."

"But she's okay?" Zechariah's hand came up as if he would touch his grandson, then dropped. "She'll be all right?"

Ben cleared his throat. "She's better this morning. She was awake and talking to me. Asking for the boplin. She wanted to hold them and feed them, but she has a lot of pain. We took her in a wheelchair to the NICU — that's where they keep the new babies with problems — so she could see them."

"That's a good sign." Laura longed to give the boy — she remembered when Marian took him from his mother and rocked him at the canning frolics — a hug. "Let me fix you some breakfast before you go back."

"I had kaffi at the hospital cafeteria."

"A real breakfast. I make a gut cup of kaffi, if I do say so myself." She started for the back porch. "My biscuits aren't too bad either."

"What happened to you?" The concern in Ben's voice turned accusing. "What were you doing out here, Groossdaadi?"

"Everybody get washed up," Laura interceded. "The kinner are waiting for your news, Ben. They'll be tickled to see you."

A growl indicated what Zechariah thought of the conversation. "I'll tell Christopher you're here and breakfast is ready."

"I'll do it." Ben's gruff voice rose. "You go inside."

"You're tired. You were up all night. I'm just old." As if to punctuate his words, Zechariah smacked his cane on the ground. "Don't argue with your elders."

Ben turned and stomped toward the house. He let out a gusty sigh as Laura caught up. "Dineen will take me to my sister-in-law Jean's after breakfast. She said her daughter Millie can stay with the kinner while Rosalie is in the hospital."

"No need. Let me do this for you." Not just for him and Rosalie. Being able to help was a good feeling, one Laura hadn't had in a while. Cooking, cleaning, and taking care of the children made time fly the way it had when she cared for her own children. Old memories came to life. Like finding a long-lost, much valued heirloom. She didn't want to give it up just yet. "I can watch the kinner, cook, and do the washing. Your daed will take care of the chores. He came by last night and said he'd be back this afternoon."

"You're not working at the store anymore?" Ben held the back door open for her. The smell of bacon wafted through it. Everything would need to be warmed up. "They were shorthanded after Mary Katherine opened her bookstore with Dottie."

"I fill in once in a while, but not recently." Laura hurried to the stove and set the bacon and eggs back on the flame to warm them. Ben didn't need to know that standing in the Combination Store, waiting on customers, caused Laura so much hip and knee pain she couldn't sleep at night. "Jennie's girls are old enough now to help out, and they hired a couple of other young women who aren't married yet."

Samuel and Delia had crawled onto the bench at the prep table where they shared a piece of bread they'd stolen from the basket. "I'm hungry," Samuel announced.

"Me too." Delia nodded and stuffed

another chunk of bread in a mouth already so full her cheeks puffed like a squirrel that'd stowed acorns there.

She wore her dress backward, and her hair needed to be braided and tucked under her kapp. Samuel had neglected to tuck in his shirt and put on his suspenders. Still, they hadn't done a bad job of dressing themselves. Laura would finish up after she cleaned the kitchen. She felt like humming her favorite English hymn. "Breakfast coming up."

"What about Groossdaadi? He's a handful." Ben glanced at the children and lowered his voice. "He's not himself. We can't ask you to deal with his problems too."

"You didn't ask. I offered." She smiled and flapped her apron at him. "Sit. Sit. Tell your kinner the gut news."

"Are the boplin coming home?" Samuel crawled from the bench and launched himself at his father. "Is Mudder coming home soon?"

Ben winced and tugged his son into his arms. "Not today, but as soon as she feels better."

He settled Samuel back on the bench and plopped down next to him. Delia crawled into his lap. His gaze traveled to Laura and seemed to ask for her help.

"Your mudder is tuckered out after having two boplin all at once."

"Bruders? Did I get bruders?"

"Nee. I'm sorry to disappoint you, *suh.*" Ben smoothed Samuel's curly blond hair. "Girls, both of them. Mia and Mary. Little schweschders for you to take care of."

"To boss around. Mia and Mary, Mia and Mary." Samuel made a song of the names. Delia mimicked him. "Mary and Mia. Mary and Mia."

"We'll see who does the bossing." Laura set a plate of eggs and bacon with two biscuits in front of Ben. Samuel immediately swiped a piece of bacon. "Hey, yours is coming, little one."

The back door opened and Christopher hurled himself across the room. "Daed, Groossdaadi said they were two girls. More girls. How come we couldn't get boys?"

Laura chuckled. Ben's smile seemed peaked. "It's not like an order of pancakes, suh. Where's your groossdaadi?"

"Cleaning up the barn." Christopher squeezed in next to Ben and stole another piece of bacon. "He says to tell you he's not hungry."

Laura dished out breakfast for the kinner and busied herself cleaning the skillets. She waited until Ben stood and moved toward the door to approach him. "Is there something else you're not saying?"

He shook his head, but his eyes were wet with tears. It was heartbreaking to see little ones cry, but especially boys because they tried so hard not to do it. "What is it? I may be an old lady, but I was a midwife for many years. I kept my patients' medical issues to myself. You can trust that."

His Adam's apple bobbed. He faced the door, away from the kinner. "There won't be any more bruders or schweschders."

"Ach." An aching lump swelled in Laura's throat. She managed a quick nod. No trite words of comfort would help or were necessary. God's will could be hard to understand, but there was no point in questioning it. Ben and Rosalie had five healthy children. They were blessed. "I'll take care of these three and Zechariah. You be with Rosalie. She'll need you right now."

"They look like her. Little spikes of curly brown hair. Brown eyes. Same chin."

"I reckon they have some of their daed in them too."

He stared at his boots. "The doctor said they'll keep the boplin until their lungs are stronger and they put on some weight. That will give Rosalie a chance to start nursing."

"I'm here as long as you need me."

Being needed was the best medicine for an old woman.

"The kinner will be easy. Zechariah is hard." With a soft sigh Ben shrugged on his coat and opened the door. "I'll talk to him before I go."

"If you want. Then leave him to me. You have enough on your plate at the hospital."

An old woman might be the best medicine for an old man.

Either way, Zechariah had met his match.

SEVEN

Brownie. Zechariah's chuckle echoed in the empty barn. That was what happened when a man let his children name a horse. Brownie was a chestnut gelding. Zechariah brushed the horse's warm flank and inhaled scents of horse, hay, and manure. Comfortable smells. The barn held more comfort than the house did with Laura zipping in and out of rooms and talking, talking, talking. She never sat still. She hovered. She offered tea. She dusted, swept, mopped, and talked. She baked cookies and pies and biscuits.

And talked. Going on three days of nonstop talking now.

The cookies smelled good. The chocolate cream pie melted in his mouth.

She was decent company. Good company, really.

He would get used to it and then she would leave. Not to feel sorry for himself.

No. Simply the facts that became apparent as a person grew older. And older.

Brownie tossed his head and nickered.

"You're right about that. Nothing wrong with wanting a little peace and quiet." Brownie probably wondered why Zechariah continued to brush long after he'd finished the job. The horse's coat gleamed. His buddy Butterscotch needed a turn. "Just so you know, I haven't become crazy in my old age. I've always talked to my horses."

"Eli talked to his horses too. He said they always agreed with him. Unlike his fraa."

Talking, talking, talking in the barn now. Laura had a pleasant voice, if truth be told. Zechariah didn't turn at the sound. Apparently, his hearing was going now. He had been so engrossed in his task, he hadn't heard the barn doors slide open. He kept brushing. "What are you doing out here?"

"I came to tell you supper will be out of the oven and on the table in about ten minutes."

"You could've sent Christopher to tell me."

"The exercise is gut for my arthritis, and the fresh air is gut for my lungs."

"A man might think you were a doctor or something."

The swish of her long skirt told him she

approached the stall. "If you don't stop soon, you'll brush off any coat he has left."

"He likes it." Zechariah leaned his head against Brownie's shoulder and breathed in the horse's smell.

A flash of pale memory, a cloak faded by years, made the knot ache behind his ribs where his heart once resided. The horse's name was Jake. Zechariah nearly wore him out that winter after he turned sixteen. Church. Singings. Sometimes he rode him with a saddle. Sometimes he took the two-seater, especially when he started courting Marian. She liked the furry comforter he pulled over their legs. They sat close, their legs touching. For warmth, she said.

Jake was a black gelding, full of patience and sometimes a little vinegar. Long ago that described Zechariah. That's what Marian liked about him. Or so she said when they huddled under the comforter, letting the snowflakes fall where they may. They kissed for the first time and her lips were cold, wet, and soft. Zechariah warmed them for her.

Marian hadn't been a talker, but their silences were filled with the confidence that he knew what she was thinking, and she knew what he was thinking. As the years passed, they started finishing each other's sentences. She knew him better than anyone ever had or ever would.

Zechariah inhaled a long, painful breath.

Laura chuckled.

He reached for a neutral tone. "What's so funny?"

"You. Hiding from me. If I talk too much, just say so. I'll shut up." She reached over the stall gate and patted Brownie's muzzle. The traitor tossed his head and edged closer. "I know my place. I also know I can be irritating. Eli used to tell me I talked a lot, even for a woman."

Zechariah snorted.

"Supper is tuna noodle casserole. It's easy on the stomach."

He liked tuna noodle casserole. His stomach growled. "Fine."

"Fine." She swished away.

He began to hum.

"I like that song."

"What song?"

" 'How Great Thou Art.' "

"I wasn't humming a song."

"Of course not. Come wash up. Samuel claims to be so hungry he could eat a bear. If you don't hurry, there may not be any casserole left." She opened the doors and slid them shut with barely a sound.

The children were traitors. They must've

told her he liked tuna noodle casserole.

The doors slid open again. "By the way, Elijah and his fraa are here. They'll eat with us."

With us. Like she was family. Or his fraa. He hardly knew Laura. She attended those same singings, but she had eyes only for Eli Kauffman. He was tall, strong, a hard worker, and the oldest son so he oversaw the family farm when his father retired to the dawdy haus. A good choice for a husband. He had a so-so singing voice that carried through the barn. Laura, at least, had been mesmerized by it. Seated on a wooden bench, her eyes dark green in the lantern light. A pretty woman. Beautiful even.

He kept stumbling into these recollections. A symptom of old age. More memories in the past than hopes for the future. Better to cling to the present. Son number four checking up on him, fraa in tow to make it look like a regular visit. "We don't need them checking up on us. I'm fine."

"Not everything is about you."

So much for talking less. "Your casserole will burn. I'll be right in."

The doors shut with a bang this time. Why hadn't he spoken to her in those early days at the singing? A vague recollection of her laugh, high and sweet, flitted by like a moth drawn to the lamp. The Ropps' barn. Rain pelted the roof. Heat from the lanterns. She had been a little fluffy around the edges. A figure made for having children. He had been busy trying to catch Marian's eye. Marian didn't talk as much or laugh as often, but something about her bent head and shy smile suggested her still waters ran deep and were worth traversing.

Why could he remember some things and not others? His mother's face had disappeared into pages long ago turned. His father's a vague hodgepodge that might be David, Robert, and Ivan's melded with strokes that seemed less and less sure. Zechariah laid the brush next to the tack. His hands trembled. His arm moved of its own accord. Odd, jerky movements. The specialist in Kansas City said the medicine caused it. Nothing like the side effects being worse than the disease itself. He gritted his teeth and held his arms close to his body. They jerked anyway.

The doors slid open yet again.

"I told you I'm on my way."

"With that attitude don't bother."

He turned. Elijah stood in the doorway. The spitting image of the man Zechariah used to see in the mirror when he combed his hair and brushed his teeth.

"I thought you were Laura."

"Probably best not to talk like that to the woman doing the cooking. Come on, it's time to eat."

Zechariah shuffled from the barn. With his long legs, Elijah probably found the slow pace painful. "You don't have to wait for me."

"I like to walk with you."

"I'm a slowpoke now." Zechariah struggled to force his legs to move faster. They refused. "Are you checking up on me?"

"Nee. Checking up on everyone. Ivan told Ben we'd all take turns. June will help Laura with the kitchen and putting the kids to bed."

"And you?"

Elijah shrugged and grinned. "I'm here for the conversation."

It would be like this from now on. A steady, rotating stream of people checking on him — them. They were family. They cared. So why did that caring seem to strip a man of his last vestiges of usefulness? Maybe that was his fault, not theirs. He needed an attitude adjustment.

Zechariah cleared his throat. "Your boys don't have that cockamamie idea in their heads about running off to Indiana, do they?"

"Nee. They're not boys, though. They're grown men with families. If they decide to move to Alaska, that's their business and Godspeed. At least they're not deciding to drive cars or get their pictures taken."

On that Zechariah agreed. His district walked a careful line, reviewing each potential change, accepting some things like phone shacks and propane ovens, while rejecting others that would bring their community too close to an ever-evolving, technology-filled outside world. Freeman, Cyrus, and Solomon had done a good job in leading the small Gmay. Still, Zechariah hated to see family spread to the four corners of the country.

"It's one thing to find cheaper land in Montana or Colorado. It's another to work in a factory. It'll take them away from their families every day. They'll be neck-deep in the world five days a week. Cars, computers, and photos are bound to follow."

"You and Ivan had this conversation." Elijah's expression said he had his own concerns, but his words reflected his respect for his older brother. "We have to seek balance. We may only be able to preserve our faith and family by allowing this change. Farming isn't enough."

"My parents and great-grandparents

worked hard to preserve this lifestyle. Back then folks went to the Englisch courts to keep the right to school kinner like me in our own schools. I was one of the farmers, along with many others, who refused to participate in Social Security. When you were young there was another court battle — to keep from being required to send you to Englisch high schools. Do you know why?"

"I've heard all these stories." Elijah released the long-suffering sigh that said he sought patience for old folks and their penchant for living in the past. "To keep us apart from the world so we wouldn't become of the world. The Englisch judges decided we had a right not to be modern. They also thought backward farmers had no need of schooling."

"We wanted the right to educate our kinner as we saw fit. There's nothing backward about that."

"I know. But this is about changing times. Small farms are a losing proposition." Elijah blew out a second gusty sigh. "It's a done deal. Right now, we want to make sure you're okay and Ben's kinner are okay."

Ivan would've vented to Elijah and David. His sons were close. Especially since Robert's death. Something about losing their older brother had cemented their friendship as adults. They put their heads together to decide what should become of Zechariah at every turn. "I suppose you two have figured out what to do with me now."

"Nothing has been decided. Not until we see what Ben has to say."

"He says his fraa has some mending to do, but Laura's here for that."

"We'll see."

Exactly what *he* used to tell *them* when they were children and wanted to go fishing or spend a week at Stockton Lake or make ice cream.

We'll see.

"By the way, did you see that pile of brush in the front?" Elijah clomped up the steps to the back porch. "It looks like someone trimmed their trees and dumped the branches in Ben's yard. I'll clean it up before we leave tonight."

"That isn't a brush dump. I put those there." Elijah obviously wanted to change the subject, but he'd chosen the wrong topic. Zechariah tapped down his impatience. Birding brought him joy as it did so many people. "The evergreen branches attract the birds. They can hide in there when the hawks start hunting them. It's a way of making them feel at home. They'll eat there and sleep there."

"That's all well and gut, but it looks trashy. Ben might not like it."

"Ben has other things on his mind right now."

"All the more reason to keep things spic-and-span for him."

"Rosalie likes the birds." Zechariah might not know about much, but he did know about birds. Their colors brightened the landscape, and they sang happy songs that made folks feel better. Even in the dead of winter, birds brought solace that could only be provided by God's natural beauty. "They'll brighten Rosalie's day when she comes home."

"Maybe so." Elijah, stubborn as dandelion weeds, always wanted the last word. He was determined to have it. "But it's Ben's yard."

Ben's yard. Ben's house. Ben's wife. Ben's children.

Zechariah missed the days when he could call a place his own.

His place would always be a welcoming home for birds.

EIGHT

The challenge of shopping with small children seemed to have grown with the years. Or maybe Laura's age contributed to her discomfort. She switched Delia from one aching hip to the other. Despite a bitter cold December wind that impeded her forward progress, sweat dampened her face. Delia fought taking a nap at home but decided to pass out in the buggy just as they reached Jamesport city limits.

A bright afternoon sun did nothing to take the icy nip from the air. Even so, Samuel dawdled along behind her, stopping to look at every person, rock, trash can, and bench. In a nod to good parenting, he kept his gloved hands behind his back when they entered the Sweet Notions Store. Not that the bundles of broadcloth, poplin, denim, muslin, and wool held much interest for a five-year-old. The rack of snaps, fasteners, and spools of thread in many sizes and a multitude of colors did seem to call his name.

"Stay with me, Samuel." Laura cocked her head toward the bolts of black denim. "We need material to make you some new pants. Yours are getting to be high-waders."

"High-waders." He giggled. "I can cross the creek."

"Too cold." She studied the signs. Delia needed dresses too. Laura could handle a treadle machine long enough to make small dresses and pants. Fewer tasks for Rosalie to accomplish while trying to heal and take care of two new babies. Ben said she was in less pain now. The boplin had started to gain weight in the four days since their headlong dash into a new world. "The broadcloth is on sale for two-forty-nine a yard. Poplin is two-sixty-nine. Denim is more expensive."

Looking wise beyond his years, Samuel nodded. "Daed says we have to be careful with our pennies."

"Your daed's right."

She moved down the aisle, stopping to look at pretty crepe — far too expensive. Familiar voices rose a few rows over. "She's staying there at the house with Zechariah while Ben is at the hospital with Rosalie."

"The kinner are there, but still. They're so

old that no one thinks anything untoward is going on. Besides, Zechariah is meaner than a one-eyed, mangy, starving coyote."

Mabel Plank and Jolene Mast. Laura had delivered babies for both of them. She cleared her throat. Both women jumped and looked over their shoulders. Mabel's face reddened, but Jolene simply smiled. "Laura! You have your hands full today. Can I hold Delia for you while you pick out your material?"

All the better to pump Laura for more information about the goings-on at the Stutzman house. Laura shook her head. "She's tuckered out. I'm trying not to wake her."

"You should've brought the stroller." Jolene tutted and shook one index finger at Laura. "You're out of practice. I know Rosalie has one. She'll need a double now. How is she? How are those new babies?"

A Plain community was only as immune to the grapevine as its strongest vine. "Ben stopped by yesterday for a few minutes. At that time she was doing a little better. The twins are healthy."

"That's a blessing." Mabel patted Samuel's hat. He skooched closer to Laura and grabbed her apron with semigrubby, plump fingers. "You'll be wanting to get back home, what with everything that's going on with Tamara."

"What do you mean?" The question slipped out before Laura could lasso it. She didn't want to feed the vines — especially when it came to her grandchildren. "I'll be at Ben's until his fraa is able to care for the boplin herself. It'll be at least a month, maybe six weeks."

"You haven't heard?" Jolene's saccharine tone matched her candied smile. "Tamara announced to her parents that she doesn't plan to be baptized at Easter. Ava told me."

At twenty and an old married woman, Ava should know better than to speak out of turn about her family's affairs. Her older sister's decision to wait on baptism was a private matter. "If she's not ready yet, then she should wait. Baptism isn't something to be taken lightly."

"She's twenty-two. She's waited plenty, but now she's decided against it." Mabel volunteered this tidbit with great enthusiasm. "She wants to be a doctor. She told Ruby she got the idea from you."

Laura opened her mouth. Then closed it. A memory from the locked closet of her youth burst through the door. She'd been six when her sister was born. She held Mudder's hand and patted her face with a damp

93

washrag while the midwife coaxed the tiny baby from her mother's warm womb. So sweet and little and lungs befitting an auctioneer.

She'd known then she wanted to be a midwife. It wasn't until four years later, when her brother came into the world only to leave minutes later without even a whisper of a cry that she'd been certain she would be more than a midwife. She would do more. She would help more.

Midwives could only bring babies into the world. They couldn't really save them or their mothers when something went truly wrong.

She wanted every baby to live. Every mother to hold a healthy, crying, suckling, wiggling baby. She needed to become a doctor.

Once, after a difficult birth ended with mother and baby son taken to the Chillicothe hospital by ambulance, she had sipped tea with shaking hands and told Tamara, then sixteen, this story.

It hadn't been her intention to influence her granddaughter in any way. It had simply been a shared moment from her past. Could Tamara have seen it differently? As an invitation to think about a different future for herself?

Delia chose that moment to raise her head. She took one look at her surroundings and screeched, "Mudder, Mudder, I want Mudder."

"Shush, bopli, shush." Glad to be called from the far, yet so vivid, past, Laura rubbed the girl's back. "You're fine. Mudder will be back before you know it." She offered the two women her best frosty take-no-prisoners smile. "I better get the material I need and get her snack for her."

Aware of Mabel and Jolene watching her every move, Laura made quick work of her selections and paid. Samuel insisted on carrying a bag even though it weighed almost as much as his small body. They deposited them in the buggy, she tightened Delia's wool jacket, and they walked the block to her second stop, The Book Apothecary.

Tamara would not think of those days when she had held her secret tightly to her chest, knowing how it would hurt and shame her parents. Knowing she would no longer be able to see them. No *Meidung* because she hadn't left the faith after baptism, but no marrying in the faith and raising a family close to her parents and grandparents, brothers and sisters.

A person was either in the community of faith, or out of it. There was little gray

95

between the black and the white.

A lonely existence and not one Laura wanted for her sweet granddaughter. Truth be told, Tamara was her favorite. If one dared admit to such a thing. Laura loved all her grandchildren, but Tamara was so like her. So independent, yet so caring. So sure of what was right. She was an obedient child of God. How could she step away from her faith, her family, and her community?

She couldn't. Laura would convince her of that. She could nurture her own babies. She could deliver babies and apply her knowledge, albeit limited, to bringing those babies safely into the world. That's what Plain women did.

Plain women needed a little bit of help having their babies. Tamara could be that help, and it would be enough until she had her own children to nurture. Her own husband.

It had been enough for Laura.

She had been determined it would be enough. Eli had made it so.

That was the problem. Tamara needed her own Eli.

Inside the bookstore's blue-and-red-painted wooden double doors, co-owner Dottie Manchester waved from behind the counter where she took care of an English customer. Mary Katherine met them in the foyer, but she swept past Laura and made a beeline for Samuel. "Did you come to our story hour?"

Samuel's longing gaze went to the picture books that lined a low shelf under one window. A small wooden table and two chairs — they looked like Jennie's husband Leo's work — sat next to it. *The Little Engine That Could, The Gruffalo, Three Billy Goats Gruff, Llama Llama Red Pajama,* and a dozen more books lined the shelf. "Can I look at books?"

"Story hour first." Mary Katherine pointed to another corner where she'd set up three rows of small wooden chairs in a horseshoe shape around a rocking chair. Most of the seats were already taken by preschool-age children, many of them Plain. Their mothers milled around in the back, chatting. Bess and Iris waved. "I'm reading *Noah's Ark* today."

Clutching her doll to her chest, Delia wiggled. "Can I get down?"

Her mind still muddled with the Tamara dilemma, Laura released Delia. The little girl followed her big brother to the story-hour gathering where they greeted Bess's Joshua and Leyla and their other Plain friends in that enthusiastic yet shy way small children have.

Enchanted by their sweet embraces, Laura glanced at the women who gathered like a flock of mother geese nearby. She had delivered many of them. Determined, she turned to Mary Katherine. "Do you have to start right this minute?"

Mary Katherine glanced at the Dr. Seuss Cat-in-the-Hat clock near the front counter. "Two more minutes. We always have stragglers and I hate for them to miss the beginning of the story. But don't run off. I need information from you."

"You too?" She told Mary Katherine about her encounter in the Sweet Notions Store, leaving out the part about Tamara wanting to be a doctor. "What is wrong with people? Do they not have enough of their own business to take care of?"

A storm gathered in Mary Katherine's plump face. "I'll have a word with Mabel's mother. We're second cousins, you know."

Laura didn't know, but it didn't surprise her. Practically everyone was related somehow in their community. It could present a challenge when it came to courting. "When you submit your next report to *The Budget,* can you request a card party and fundraising for Rosalie and Ben? He didn't say a word, but I'm afraid their medical expenses will be catastrophic."

"I will as soon as I finish my shift today. The Gmay will help and the elders will spread the word to other Gmays as well." Mary Katherine grabbed a dog-eared composition notebook from the counter, tugged a number two pencil with no eraser left from behind her right ear, and scribbled a note. "What about the babies? I want to include them in the report."

Laura recited the pertinent information. Mary Katherine scribbled it down. Two children began to squabble over a book of animals. "Got to go. The natives are restless."

"We have to talk after." Laura needed Mary Katherine's undivided attention and keen problem-solving techniques for her problem. "Just you and me."

"No problem."

Laura enjoyed the story hour almost as much as the children. Mary Katherine was a gifted storyteller. She did all the voices and the animal noises, then encouraged the children to join her.

Afterward there was a flurry of book buying among the mothers. Even Bess splurged on the *Noah's Ark* book that so entranced Joshua.

"You look like you need a cup of kaffi."

Bess stuffed her receipt in her bag and scooped up Leyla before she could remove every book from the bottom shelf in the travel section. "Can I watch the boplin while you rest?"

"That would be a lifesaver. Just for a few minutes. I have to get back and cook for Christopher and Zechariah after this."

"How is Zechariah doing?"

"Suitably cantankerous for a man his age."

Bess chuckled and grabbed Delia's hand before she helped herself to a plate of oatmeal-raisin cookies. "One or maybe half of one. You're sweet enough as it is."

"She probably needs to go potty."

"Got it covered."

Leaving Bess to the all-encompassing task of keeping four toddlers from destroying the children's section, Laura followed Mary Katherine behind the counter and into the back room.

"Dottie delights in taking the money." Mary Katherine plopped into a chair on wheels in front of a rolltop desk and scooted around to face Laura. She pointed to a second desk chair. "Take a load off and tell *Aenti* Mary Kay all about it."

"All about what?"

"You look perturbed. There's more to your story."

"It seems Tamara's decision is my fault. Or so it's been reported."

"You were baptized a hundred years ago. You never miss services. All your children were baptized. How could it be your fault?"

"Mabel says Tamara wants to be a doctor and it was my idea."

"Was it?"

"Of course not."

"Then?"

"I encouraged her to consider being a midwife. Maybe that made her start thinking about what she could do with more learning about medicine."

"You've taught more than a few girls to be midwives in your time. They didn't all rush out to be doctors." Mary Katherine flung both hands in the air and raised her shoulders in her most elaborate shrug. "Tamara has a mind of her own. If she chooses this path, she chooses it alone. It's not the only thing she's shrugged off. I hear things. I'm *The Budget* scribe —"

"Not the sort of thing you put in *The Budget.*"

"Of course not." Sarcasm dripped from Mary Katherine's words. "As I was saying, I hear things. Cyrus, Solomon, and Freeman encouraged her to consider teaching — after she's baptized. She dragged her feet about it. Ruby doesn't want her working in town, because she seems drawn to that world. She took your advice and started following Rachel around, learning about midwifery."

Laura stifled a chuckle at her friend's admission. She certainly did make it her business to *hear things.* "I hadn't heard that."

"Maybe Rachel thought you would be sad you didn't get to teach her your vocation."

"Not at all. But you're right, lots of girls become midwives. I did." Laura studied her hands. She had never told her closest friend about her dilemma as a young girl. She wanted to do more, but she hadn't — praise God. "I didn't leave the faith and try to become a doctor."

"Elijah Stutzman's daughter's baby girl died a few months ago."

"I know. That's part of the reason Rosalie and Ben were more worried this time than they normally would be. Everyone in the family was concerned."

"Tamara wants to be a baby doctor so that doesn't happen."

It happened to doctors too. Sometimes nothing could be done. A hard lesson for a young girl to learn. "She's not so prideful that she thinks she can stop it all by her lonesome?"

"Nee. But she wants to know more of the medicine and the science."

"Have you been talking to her?"

"Nee. Evelyn came in looking for a present for her schweschder's birthday."

Evelyn again. The woman had too much free time if she was spreading gossip far and wide.

"Not gossip. Concern." Mary Katherine had a way of knowing Laura's thoughts that irked her. "She asked for prayers."

"That is something." Laura rubbed her aching fingers, but to no avail. The cold and old age made pain her constant companion. "Have they talked to Freeman?"

"Not yet. Freeman has been under the weather. Maybe you should talk to Tamara first. Maybe it won't be necessary to bother Freeman or Cyrus and Solomon with this."

Freeman's father had passed the previous year. Since then, he'd been missing from a few church services as well. Even bishops had bouts of bad health on occasion. "Tamara's as stubborn as a stump. She reminds me of Eli."

"She reminds me of you. She even looks like you when you were that age."

"Nee, she looks like Ruby at that age."

"Which is to say, like you."

Laura couldn't contain a sigh. "I'm not

sure when I'll be able to see her."

"I'll stop by Ruby's on my way home and tell her to send that wayward girl your way." Mary Katherine's wrinkled face softened. "It's not your fault. Kinner get ideas in their heads, especially in this day and age. There's so much worldly influence bearing down on us from all sides."

"It's our job to show them, through our teaching and our actions, the way they should go."

"But ultimately, it's in Gott's hands, not ours." Mary Katherine sprang from her chair — there was no other word for her friend's spry steps since marrying for the second time — and enveloped Laura in one of her famous hugs. When Mary Katherine hugged, a person knew she'd been hugged. "You know that as well as anyone."

Laura sucked in air. "I do. That doesn't mean I have to like it."

"Now you sound like a crotchety old woman."

To match the crotchety old man at Ben's.

The errant thought knocked Laura back a mile. No match existed. Zechariah was grumpy. He didn't like to talk. He didn't like to play games with the kinner. He didn't like her chili. He didn't even eat the pumpkin cookies, her favorite.

Yet, his glances were wistful.

She was sure of it. Especially when she played checkers with Christopher.

"What? You look like lightning just fried your hair." Mary Katherine giggled the same happy giggle she'd had since they shared a hay bale at singings way back when. "Spill the beans, *freind.*"

"Nothing. It's nothing." Laura hustled toward the door. "I better go rescue Bess. Delia puts everything — and I do mean everything — in her mouth. Especially when she hasn't had her dinner."

"Tell Zechariah I said hello."

Mary Katherine's teasing voice floated around Laura like smoke that hinted at a fire in the distance.

NINE

"You better watch out or your face will freeze like that."

Remorse for the remark immediately blew through Laura as she approached the front porch. The cold wind cut through her. Exhaustion, the children's bickering on the ride home, or hunger served as her flimsy excuse for being mean to Zechariah. Even all three combined couldn't be allowed to excuse her attitude. Day four of her mission to soften him up and she was the one being cranky.

He didn't respond. He simply continued to hull pecans from a large sack that sat on the bench next to him. He had pulled up a short wooden table to hold his tools. He took turns using side cutters, pliers, and then a skinny screwdriver to pick the remaining shells out. His gloved hands occasionally jerked and sent pecan meat flying, but he didn't seem to notice.

Or notice her and the children for that matter. Too busy scowling and cracking. Cracking and scowling. It wasn't just his face that would freeze like that. His whole body would freeze. The afternoon sun sought the horizon and the wind continued to huff and puff. Gathering gray clouds, like dirty wool, threatened sleet or maybe even snow. Zechariah wore a woolen coat, thick pants, and boots. His black winter hat didn't cover his ears, however, and his nose was bright red, his lips chapped, and his breath came in white puffs.

Why not hull the pecans at the kitchen table or by the fire in the front room? Sheer stubbornness came to mind.

Laura took a long breath of cold air and set Delia on her plump legs. She shifted the weight of the packages between both arms. Surely Zechariah hadn't descended the steps into the basement. "Did Christopher bring that bag up from the basement?"

Zechariah's arm jerked. The pliers flew from his gloved hand and pinged against the porch railing.

He growled. The scowl transferred from the pecans to Laura. "Don't sneak up on a man like that."

"I didn't sneak. Didn't you hear me talking to you?"

"I was thinking. I had a hankering for pecan pie."

As if that explained everything. Still, it was a tiny half step in the right direction. "I've been told my pecan pie is decent."

"No rush."

"Are you sure —"

"Hand me the pliers."

"If you don't take my hand off with them."

"I promise not to inflict any harm."

She let go of Delia's hand and started up the steps.

"I want nuts." Delia scooted up the steps on her hands and knees like a kitten. Dried leaves stuck to her brown mittens. "Nuts, nuts."

"I'll tell Christopher we're here." Samuel raced past his sister. "I can help him unhitch the horse."

"Pick up the pliers first for your great-grandfather and be sure to wipe your boots on the rug."

Samuel did as he was asked, but he didn't waver in his determination to share his adventures in town with big brother.

"Don't slam the —"

The door slammed.

"You want a pecan, do you, Delia?" Zechariah made a big show of studying the half-full orange plastic bowl. "I see one here that has your name on it."

Eyes wide, Delia stared at the bowl as if trying to see what her great-grandpa saw. He selected a small piece and held it out.

Delia's lower lip protruded. She eyed the pecan and then her great-grandpa. Zechariah wiggled his fingers. He popped the meat into his mouth and made a big show of chewing. His eyes rolled back and he rubbed his stomach. "That some gut eats."

Delia squealed and jumped up and down. "Mine, mine. I want nuts."

Zechariah obliged by holding out another pecan. "Better hurry or I might eat this one too."

"Nee, mine." Delia shook her head and plucked the pecan from his gloved fingers. "It's gut."

"Gut."

The two nodded at each other as if in cahoots over something valuable that only they could understand.

"More, I want more." Delia held out her hand a second time. "Nuts."

"One more." Laura didn't want to sever the sweet connection between the two. "If you eat them all, I won't be able to make pie. Do you like pie, Delia?"

The little girl nodded. "Mudder's apple pie."

It always came back to the center of Delia's world. Mommy.

"You can help me make the pie." She offered a smile to Zechariah. "If Zechariah will let us have the pecans he's hulled."

He returned the smile with one of his own. "Help yourself." He held up the bowl.

Astonished, Laura opened her mouth and then shut it. Zechariah had a beautiful smile with a set of even teeth that surely were still his own. A lot to be said for that in a man his age. Now she remembered what Marian saw in young Zechariah.

If looks counted for anything, which, of course, they didn't.

After a few seconds, his eyebrows shot up. She remembered to shift her packages so she could take the bowl. She managed not to spill the pecans. Aware of sudden heat on her cheeks, she hurried toward the door, Delia her little shadow.

"Your hands are full." Zechariah stood and opened the door for her. "One of your grands is here. She's been waiting awhile. She said she didn't mind."

His neutral tone told her nothing of what he thought of this visitor or her decision to wait.

Tamara. She'd saved her old grandma a trip to Ruby and Martin's farm.

The sound of squeaking buggy wheels and horse hooves thudding made her stop and swivel. Zechariah still held the door but he, too, looked back. A buggy with some of Zechariah's sons on board halted by the front porch.

"Visitors for you." Laura was pleased at the idea, but Zechariah didn't seem happy. "Be sure to invite them to supper. There's plenty."

"Elijah and Michael checking up with me." He grunted and pulled the screen door wider. "Looks like Ivan is with them. I'm surprised my *dochders* didn't show up too."

"I'm sure it's more to help out with chores for Benjamin than it is to check on you." She didn't bother to try to keep the tartness from her voice. "Don't forget to invite them to eat supper with us when they're done. I'll make hot kaffi to warm them up. And start the fried chicken."

Not everything was about Zechariah Stutzman, even if he did seem to think it was.

How many men did it take to water and feed horses, pigs, chickens, and a couple of milking cows? His cane secure in one hand, Zechariah trudged down the steps to Elijah's buggy. His grandson Michael, one of the few blond, blue-eyed offspring in the Stutzman family, waved and slipped from the back of the buggy. Ivan hoisted himself from the passenger side. None of them spoke.

"What brings you out here so close to dark?" Zechariah had a suspicion, but he kept his tone light. "Not enough work at your places?"

"I told you. We all told Ben we'd give you a hand. David's down with the flu or he would've taken a turn tonight." Elijah stomped his feet, rubbed his hands together, and then blew air on them for good measure. "It's a mite cold for so early in winter."

"It *is* winter." Zechariah stalked past them. With God's help he wouldn't fall flat on his behind in front of them. "I've got work to do."

"Did Christopher feed the chickens?"

"I reckon."

"I'll chop some more wood." His tall, thin frame bent against the wind, Michael headed that direction before Zechariah could speak up. "It looks low."

Not really. He'd just restocked the day before. Never mind. "Laura says to stay for supper. She's making fried chicken."

"Sounds gut." Ivan shoved the barn door open and led the way inside. The corners

112

were beginning to get dusky. "We'll earn our keep first."

"No need. What's on your mind?"

Elijah grabbed the pitchfork and tossed hay into the horses' stalls. He did it with such ease. He'd been a skinny boy who ate like a horse. Now middle-aged, he was broad through the chest and had the beginnings of a paunch. His hair had gone white far sooner than his older brother's. Both had Zechariah's brown eyes, but only Ivan had resorted to glasses — so far.

"Nobody wants to go first?"

Ivan snapped up a strand of hay and chewed on the end. "Me. I'll go first."

"Then do it. I'm old. I don't know how much longer I'll be around."

"It's words like that —"

"He's just trying to get your goat." A light sheen of sweat shone on Elijah's forehead despite the winter air. "We've been talking with David, and we think you should move in with Michael and his fraa."

Zechariah inhaled the comforting scent of hay, dust, horse, and manure. He had been in Ben's house for nine months. Before that, Esther's for six months. Seven months on his own after Marian's death. His symptoms during her illness had been kept from her. She knew he had Parkinson's but not that it had progressed toward the end of her illness. She had enough challenges of her own. His children decided — not him — that he shouldn't be alone as the symptoms continued to progress. They went with him to the doctor. They convinced him he could no longer take care of his daily needs on his own. "I won't be moved around like a piece of furniture or livestock."

"That's not our intent." Elijah handed the pitchfork to Ivan, who pitched hay into the next stall with even less effort than his younger brother. If it was their intent to add insult to his injury — which it wasn't — they were doing a good job. "Ben and his fraa have their hands full. Rosalie is coming home in a few days with the boplin. She can't lift anything heavy. They've already got the three little ones."

His sons weren't adding up the entire equation. They'd failed to include Laura. Laura with the sharp gaze and crackly laugh. With her obsession with tea. The maker of biscuits so flaky they nearly floated. The owner of sharp, green eyes.

Zechariah grabbed the stall railing to steady himself.

"What? Are you all right?" Ivan laid his hand on Zechariah's shoulder. "We don't mean to upset you. We want what's best. We

114

want to make sure you're comfortable."

"I haven't outlived my usefulness yet. I need to work. I can work. You seem to think I'm an invalid."

"No one thinks you're an invalid." Elijah's soothing tones said exactly that. "We know Mudder's time had come. Even so, we know you miss her. And with Robert passing too —"

"No need to dig up the past." He forced the words past the knot in his throat. He never talked about Robert. A father should not outlive his children. But the longer a man lived, the more loved ones went on before him. His wife. His oldest son. Sweet special daughter Martha. His three older brothers gone. His two older sisters. His parents. Life often seemed a series of births, weddings, and funerals. Until they became an indistinguishable blur. "I'm no different than I was before. Gott will take me when He is gut and ready. In the meantime, I can't keep moving every time there's a hardship."

Both men were silent. Brownie shook his head and whinnied. Another country heard from. Elijah tugged at his beard. Ivan wrinkled his nose and rubbed his forehead. They wanted to confer, it was easy to see, but didn't want to talk in front of him.

"Don't forget Laura's here."

"True, but she's . . ." Elijah's voice trailed away.

"Old too?"

"I think we should ask Ben about it." Ivan hitched up his pants. "Why don't you get some oats for the horses? We'll give them a treat to go with the hay. How are the pigs doing? Enjoying the cold weather?"

"So you haven't asked Ben if he wants me to go?"

"Nee, he won't ever say that. He'll do his part. He never complains."

"You're right about that. But I don't want to be a burden to anyone. Let me move into the dawdy haus."

"That won't work. But you can check on the pigs if you want. Or feed the chickens."

Grunting like an old pig, Zechariah dunked the bucket into the bag of oats and gave the horses their treats. Let the boys check on the pigs and feed the chickens.

He needed to stay in one place. He needed a home.

TEN

The girl waiting in the kitchen wasn't Tamara. Hannah, great-grand number ten, had a way with words and loved to tell stories since she was a first grader on Laura's lap on cold winter nights. She was also the spiker everyone wanted when they chose sides for volleyball teams.

When Laura had settled the pecans and her packages on the table, Hannah had been washing dishes at the kitchen sink. In the twenty minutes since then, she'd talked about everything under the sun — how big Delia was getting, how cold it was, how were the twins, and how good the pumpkin cookies smelled — except why she stood in Rosalie's kitchen washing dishes.

Laura handed Delia another piece of white construction paper to draw on and patted her silky cheek. "Now draw me a picture of your kitty cat."

Delia nodded enthusiastically, as she had

117

done when asked to color a cow and a horse, and went to work. It would last about two more minutes. Then the crayons would be on the floor and Delia on the run.

No answer from Hannah, who still faced the sink. "Don't you get enough dirty dishes at home?"

Hannah's shoulders sagged. She sank against the counter, her back to Laura. A sob burbled in the air.

"What's the matter?" Laura trotted to her. "Ach, *kind,* tell me what's going on."

Hannah darted into Laura's arms with such abandon she had to take a step back. "I'm so glad you're here. Where have you been? I needed to talk to you."

Had she forgotten she had a visit from Hannah on her calendar at the dawdy haus? Did Hannah share some terrible problem with Laura that only a seventeen-year-old could have? A problem Laura now couldn't remember?

Hannah was the granddaughter of Aaron and Deborah, daughter of Seth and Carrie, a carrot-topped Englischer who'd joined the faith many years ago before marrying Seth. Truth be told, Laura kept a genealogy tucked in her German Bible on the kitchen table so she could keep them straight. Right next to the list of all the babies she'd

118

delivered. Her memory wasn't what it had once been.

No shame in that. Seventy-three years on this earth called for a lot of memories tucked into boxes and baskets of her old attic of a brain. Some flew away on the night wind, but others were too precious to be released.

"I have to get supper." She nudged Hannah back so she could examine the girl's blotchy face. Acne mixed with her freckles. Her blue eyes were red rimmed. "But you're welcome to stay and help. You can eat with us. Zechariah has a hankering for pecan pie. I thought we'd have fried chicken and mashed potatoes and gravy. You can bring up a jar of corn from the basement."

"Okay." Hannah wiped at her face. "But I'm not very hungry."

"I'm hungry." That from Delia. "I want a cookie."

"No cookies. Color."

Hannah did look a little green around the edges. Concern rolled through Laura. "Don't tell me you have that flu that's going around. I don't want the kinner to get it with the babies coming home one of these days."

"Nee. It's not that." Hannah's cheeks flamed red. Her gaze slid to the floor.

119

"Mudder and Daed are mad at me."

"About what?"

Hannah went to the table and opened the first bag. "I like this material. I thought you weren't sewing anymore."

"My dresses." Delia took a swipe at the material. Hannah shook her finger at her and returned the material to the bag.

So it was like that. Laura turned to the cabinet and gathered the ingredients for the piecrust. "Why don't you start on the pecan filling while I make the crust?" Sometimes it was easier to talk without eye contact. "Once it's in the oven, we'll start on the chicken."

The sound of her rubber soles on the wood floor said Hannah had consented to the plan. She came to the counter and picked up the pecans. She didn't speak.

Laura measured the flour, salt, and lard. She went to work cutting the lard into the flour and salt. She sprinkled in a tablespoon of water and tossed the mixture with a fork. Another tablespoon. She didn't want it to be too dry or too wet. Just right, like the bear's porridge. Flaky piecrust was her specialty.

It should be after sixty-five years of making it. Her mother's scent of lavender floated in front of her nose. The scenes rolled through her mind, her mother showing her how to use the rolling pin. Her mother teaching her to knead bread. Her mother clapping in delight when Laura's first cinnamon rolls came from the oven puffy and fragrant. All those lessons all those years ago.

"I can't believe your daed and mudder are mad at you." Laura rolled the dough from the bowl and laid it on a floured cutting board. She gently flattened it with a rolling pin. "Especially during your *rumspringa.*"

No one spoke of those rumspringa activities.

"This one can't be forgiven." Hannah's voice quivered, rose, and broke. "I've brought shame on myself. I've shamed them."

"All can and must be forgiven." Laura stopped rolling. "Ach, *kind,* tell me." She moved to Hannah's side and stilled her hands. "Tell me."

Hannah's face crumpled. Her hands went to her flat belly. "I can't. I can't say it."

The truth of the matter hit Laura with a force that sent her breath reeling from her lungs. "Ach, *kind.*"

Hannah ducked her head and sobbed.

Delia skipped over to Hannah. "Don't cry,

Hannah." She patted her hand. "It's okay. My mudder is coming back. I have two baby sisters."

The sobs grew louder. Laura picked up Delia and took her back to the table. "Why don't you color a picture for Hannah? It'll make her feel better. We'll turn it into a card, and I'll help you print your name on it."

"I can color pretty."

"Jah, you can. Can you draw a *D* for Delia under the picture?"

"D for *Daed."*

"Jah, *D* for *Daed* too."

Her mind running in six directions, Laura went back to Hannah. A public confession before the Gmay was in order. She and the baby's father would be shunned for at least six weeks. A small, quiet wedding would follow. Their disgrace would mean fewer guests, a smaller reception. It would need to be soon. "Have you and your special friend spoken to Freeman?"

More sobs. "Daed talked to Cyrus. Freeman is sick. He's not seeing anyone right now. We're waiting."

"And the daed?" Laura had no idea who her great-grandchildren courted. Only that they did. "Why hasn't he spoken up? You'll take your punishment together."

Hannah covered her face with both hands. Laura peeled her fingers away. "You'll make your confession. You'll survive the *bann.* Then you'll wed. The Gmay will forgive you. Gott will forgive you. Your family will forgive you."

Hannah collapsed against Laura's chest and hid her face like a child. "He doesn't want to marry me."

Worse. She'd sinned with an English man. "He's not Plain?"

"He's Plain. But he's leaving. He's decided to go up north with the others to work in the RV factory."

A Plain man should recognize his responsibility and step up to it. This boy, whoever he was, intended to take the way of a coward.

It said much about his character. He would not make a good husband for Hannah. Marriage was for life and not to be entered into with someone unable to accept its responsibilities.

Hannah's friend was not special. He'd taken a gift from Laura's great-granddaughter and not given one in return. He hadn't given his heart with his body. The two were godly gifts entwined as to never be separated.

Laura inhaled and exhaled. She gritted

123

her teeth. *Breathe, breathe.* Her stomach roiled.

To stumble like this was human, but she held high hopes for all her children. She'd been happy when each of her nine joined the church, when they married, and when they produced grandchildren for her. In that order. As was expected in every Plain community. While this sin brought disgrace on Hannah, it would be forgiven. This child would be welcomed and loved. How Hannah handled her mistake would have enormous bearing on how she lived out the rest of her life in the Gmay.

Laura led Hannah to the table and went to get her a glass of water. She set it in front of her and took a seat. Her stomach calmed. "Your daed can talk to the boy's parents."

"Nee. I don't want him to marry me out of obligation."

Although Laura agreed with that sentiment, the decision wasn't necessarily Hannah's. The Gmay would decide. Freeman, Cyrus, and Solomon would meet with the couple. And with the parents. They would weigh the circumstances against the likelihood that the two could make a successful marriage. Unlike the rest of the world, Plain folks didn't divorce. The question became whether Hannah and her special friend could finish what they'd inadvertently started. "It's a responsibility. That he feels none doesn't say much for him."

"We made a mistake. I made a mistake." Hannah gulped water. Laura offered her a napkin and she blew her nose. "I'm so sorry, *Groossmammi.*"

"I'm not the one who needs your apology. Your disgrace touches everyone in the Gmay. Your parents taught you better."

"I know. I was weak. Thaddeus knew too. I could tell from the disgust on his face and the way he avoided looking at me. He turned away from me. I felt so alone and so ashamed."

Laura's heart broke. What should've been a special, sacred moment, a memory Hannah would carry in her heart forever, had become a dark burden she would carry on her shoulders until that day when she met and married her true soulmate — if she did.

Great obstacles littered the road to such a happy ending.

"You need only ask to be forgiven and you will be." Laura cleared her throat, tight with unshed tears. "Gott understands our weakness. His grace is unending. He loves you no matter what you do. Never forget that. There will be hard days ahead, but never forget that you are God's child. He has a plan. Trust Him."

"I've prayed and prayed."

"Then you are forgiven. Hang on to that each day from now on. Take your punishment and keep moving your feet forward. One step at a time. You're not the first and you won't be the last." Which was no excuse, but done was done. It was best to focus on the next steps. "Your parents know about his decision?"

"They want me to give the bopli to a family who wants him." Hannah rubbed her red eyes with the sodden napkin, which only served to make them redder. "I don't think I can give up my bopli."

Her hands went to her flat belly again. She gazed at Laura as if she had all the answers. Laura longed to have them. A good home for the baby was the most important concern. Not Hannah's wishes or desires. She was barely a woman herself, but she had been raised to be a wife and mother. As a midwife Laura knew better than most how much couples wanted children and how content they were when they held their new baby in their arms. "Some couples can't have boplin and would be gut parents."

"But it's my bopli."

Now Hannah sounded more like a child than a woman. "This isn't a pair of shoes or a new dress or a kitten."

"I know. I help with my bruders and schweschders. I've been in the room when boplin are born. I change the diapers and rock them to sleep."

But it would be different when the baby belonged to her. Especially for Hannah, with no husband to share in the responsibility and the joy. "You bring this bopli up on your own, you will see other consequences."

"You mean no Plain man will want me." Her eyes closing, Hannah laid her head on the table. "That will be true, either way."

Her voice was muffled, but the words touched Laura's heart anyway. "The right man — the man Gott intends for you — will accept your past transgressions just as you accept his."

Hannah raised her head. Her expression turned fierce. "My bopli will love me no matter what."

"That's true —"

"Groossmammi, can I have a cookie? Two cookies?" Samuel dashed into the room. He carried his burlap sack that held his favorite toys — a dozen or more carved wooden horses and cows. "Tulip wants one too."

Tulip was a cow.

"It's too close to supper."

"I want a cookie too." Delia's whine

reflected the late hour and her desire to have whatever her brother had. "I want two cookies."

"Play with your schweschder while I get supper." Laura gave Samuel a hand up to the table and brushed brown, dried leaves from his hair. "I guess you found Christopher."

"We wrestled. Then he went to check on the piglets."

"Very gut."

"He's coming in to paint his horseshoes in a minute."

"His horseshoes." That was a new one. "Do the horses like their shoes painted? Pink? Blue? Or maybe purple."

Samuel giggled. Delia joined in although it was clear she had no notion as to why. "He paints pictures on them and sells them. The Englischers like them. Daed says he can have them at the produce stand in the spring. And the craft fair in the summer."

"What a good way to make money." Everyone in the family helped make ends meet when they got old enough. "Do you paint too?"

"Nee. I help pick the strawberries."

"Gut for you."

Hannah got up and hugged Samuel.

"What was that for?"

"Because you're a gut boy."

"I'm gut girl," Delia chimed in. "Hug me too."

Hannah swooped her up in a big hug that made the little girl chortle. Tears coursed down Hannah's face.

"Don't cry, Hannah. My mudder will be home soon. She'll make you feel better."

Hannah cried harder. "Sorry, Delia. I don't think your mudder can help."

"You have to help yourself on this one. Let's make supper." Laura went to the propane refrigerator and brought out two chickens that still needed to be cut up. "Help me. Finish the pie."

Hannah settled Delia back in her chair. She wiped her face with a fresh napkin and blew her nose again. She looked green around the gills. "My stomach feels terrible."

"How long have you known?"

She shuffled to the shelves and picked out the sugar and corn syrup. She laid them on the counter and then added the eggs she found in the refrigerator.

Meanwhile Laura counted to ten and recited the Lord's Prayer in her head. *Give the girl time. This is hard. It will get harder. Lord, I lift her up to You. She has sinned. She's sorry. Gott, forgive her.*

No excuses were needed and none should be offered.

"It was only once."

How many teenagers had said those words since the beginning of time? "It only takes once."

How many parents had responded with those same words?

"I didn't think of it until I started to feel sick. I thought maybe it was the flu or something I ate." She mixed softened butter with the sugar, corn syrup, a little salt, and three eggs. Her forehead wrinkled in concentration as she beat the ingredients, and she stumbled over the words. "But every day it came back. Then one day it hit me."

Hannah ducked her head. "You know what I mean?"

"I do. How long ago was that?"

"A month."

"You waited a month to tell your parents?"

"Wouldn't you? I wanted to convince Thaddeus that we could get married and have a family before I told them. But he wouldn't agree to it. He said it was the wrong reason to get married. That he's not ready."

Ready for some things, but not others. A convenient thing for a man. The woman couldn't escape the error of her ways so easily.

"Why did you come here?"

"Because I thought you could tell me what to do."

Laura slid the knife through the cold, clammy chicken skin and sliced a thigh and drumstick from the breast. Then again on the other side. Then the wings. She'd cut up chicken hundreds, maybe thousands, of times. Now it required her complete concentration. Aaron, Hannah's grandfather, was Laura's youngest son. The one least like Laura. Or Eli, for that matter. He was the spitting image of Eli in looks, the way he walked, and his mannerisms. But he opened his mouth and another man appeared. One who followed the rules and never deviated. With a firm grasp on his way of life. A good man. A good father. A good husband.

It wasn't clear why he wasn't Laura's favorite. A mother shouldn't have favorites. He simply rubbed her the wrong way.

His wife, Deborah, on the other hand, employed a hug that could break a rib. The thought prompted Laura to slice the breasts from the back and ribs. She made quick work of the final pieces. One chicken down, one to go. "Do your grandparents know?"

"They went to talk to Groossdaadi before

131

I left the house."

Laura trotted to the shelf and retrieved the flour. "They know you're here then?"

Hannah wrinkled her nose. She poured the pecans into the mixture. Her sigh filled the room. "Nee. They told me to stay in my room until they came back."

"Instead you took a buggy and came here."

"A horse. Not a buggy."

"Hannah Kauffman."

"I know."

"Such disobedience is salt in the wound." Laura dumped salt and pepper in a bowl with flour. "Adding insult to injury and so on."

"I needed to talk to you."

"You waited this long. You could've waited until tomorrow or the next day."

"I couldn't wait anymore. They'll make decisions, and I'll have to live with them."

"Talking to me won't change that."

"I needed you."

How could a great-grandmother argue with that? Laura needed to be needed. She wanted to be useful. Her body might be failing her, but her mind remained as sharp as Eli's ax all those years ago. What would Eli say?

He'd say make the best of it.

She dropped the first piece of chicken in the bowl of flour and spices and coated it. "We'll eat and then you'll go home."

"Are we having supper tonight?"

At the sound of Zechariah's soft inquiry, Laura swiveled. "I'm sorry. I've gotten behind, but there will be supper. Can I get you a snack in the meantime?"

"Me want a snack." Delia dropped a fat crayon on the table. It rolled across the expanse of blue tablecloth and disappeared over the edge. "Cookie. Two cookies. And milk."

She climbed down from the chair and went to Hannah. "Don't cry. We have snacks."

Zechariah's gaze went to Hannah. His bushy eyebrows lifted. "It doesn't need to be a big spread. Everyone is tired. We had ham a few days ago. There's probably leftovers in there. We could have sandwiches. Or BLTs." He leaned on his cane and cleared his throat. "Why don't we have the pie tomorrow?"

"Hannah's making the pie, and I've started the chicken. It doesn't take long to fry it."

The back door opened. In tromped Seth and Carrie. Laura opened her mouth to greet Hannah's parents. Seth's scowl and

133

Carrie's worried face made her shut it again.

"What are you doing here?" Seth's fury ringed the words with fire. "You weren't to leave your room."

"I needed to talk to Groossmammi —"

"You should've sent her back home as soon as she got here." Seth turned the fury on Laura. Carrie put her hand on his coat sleeve. He shook her off. "This girl can't be trusted gallivanting around the countryside. Did she tell you what she did? Did she tell you?"

"She did." Laura kept her voice soft. "We have kinner in the room."

Seth's gaze went to Delia and Samuel, who stared up at him with unabashed curiosity. Delia's face crumbled.

"I shouldn't yell."

"You shouldn't. It doesn't accomplish a thing." Laura waved a floury drumstick in the air. "We'll eat. Then we'll talk."

"No need to feed us."

"The more the merrier."

His thunderous expression said there would be nothing merry about it.

ELEVEN

If the lack of talking was any indication, the fried chicken, mashed potatoes with gravy, corn, and homemade bread were a big hit. Hungry after a long day of shopping and fending off gossipers, Laura focused on filling her empty stomach. Forks clinking on plates, chewing, and the occasional "pass the corn" filled the silence at the dining room table. Fine by her.

Zechariah ate better than he had been. Maybe the cold air gave him an appetite. Or he wanted to show Ivan and Elijah they needn't be concerned about him. Whatever they'd talked about while doing chores hadn't set well with any of them. They stared at their plates and ate fork to mouth as if it required great concentration.

Like they'd never eaten fried chicken before.

Hannah picked at her food. Carrie did the same. Seth inhaled his food like a man who hadn't eaten in days. Then he leaned back and sipped his coffee with his gaze riveted on his oldest daughter. She squirmed and dropped mashed potatoes to cover the corn she hadn't eaten.

This was ridiculous. Even the kinner seemed overtaken by sudden shyness. Their drooping heads suggested bedtime would come early as darkness did this time of year.

With the dearth of conversation, it didn't take long to finish. The pie came out of the oven in time to be enjoyed hot, sweet, and steaming, with equally hot kaffi. The belches and sighs of contentment also signified satisfaction, even though no one commented.

Laura didn't need compliments. She preferred conversation.

They were hurting and Laura couldn't fix it. She might have words of wisdom, but they didn't change the fact that Hannah had disgraced her family. Her life would never be the same. She would be forgiven, but she would be the woman with the baby and no husband. Or she would be the woman who gave up her baby.

"Hannah, why don't you take the kinner down the hall and get them washed up." Laura smiled at them. "You can help Delia into her nightgown and read her a story.

Make sure she says her prayers."

Laura took Samuel's and Christopher's plates. "You two know what to do."

"What about the dishes?" Her tone eager, Hannah laid her napkin by her still-full plate. "I don't want to leave you with the mess."

She was a good girl. Laura made shooing motions. "I'm sure Carrie will help me."

And they had things to discuss out of her earshot.

Ivan scooted back his chair. A second later Elijah did the same. After some meaningful glances, Michael did as well. "How long do you plan to help out here?" Michael laid his napkin by his plate. "I mean, are you staying after Ben's fraa comes home?"

"Jah, if that is what Ben wants." Laura added the three men's plates to her stack. Carrie began to gather up silverware. "She'll not be able to be on her feet all day doing laundry and cooking and cleaning. I can help with that while she concentrates on feeding those babies. Two are more than a handful with a toddler running around to boot."

Carrie nodded. "I had mine two years apart three times in a row. At times it felt like twins, but it's not the same as trying to feed two in the middle of the night."

The men shifted in their chairs. Their gazes went from the table to the ceiling and back. Sometimes Carrie still sounded English. Laura smiled. "Why do you ask?"

Ivan's gaze went to Seth rather than to Laura. "Ruby and Martin are gut with that?"

Seth's eyebrows danced. "As far as I know. Groossmammi is a big help at the house, but everyone knows she helps out where she can, even if she's not at the store anymore or delivering babies."

Carrie's grim smile matched his. "We're thankful she has a calming effect on some of the more rambunctious kinner." Her gaze wandered to the doorway through which Hannah had disappeared. "Although some still manage to get themselves into messes."

"It won't be too much for you?" Elijah frowned at Laura. "Rosalie's sister could come up from Seymour."

Zechariah's snort could hardly be called polite. Did he want her to stay? It didn't seem likely. Something was going on here. The three younger men were not in his good graces. But it didn't take much to get in Zechariah's bad graces.

"No need." She did need help. The trip into town earlier in the day had taught her that. But no need for Rosalie's sister to leave her own children to come up. Laura had a plethora of grands who needed something to do. And one in particular. Tamara. *Gott, You are so smart and so wise.* Laura ignored Elijah's perturbed expression. "I have someone in mind to help."

"Who?" Seth's lips pursed. "What are you up to?"

"Not a thing."

"Then we'll get going. Dawn comes early." Ivan tucked his hat on his head and nodded at Zechariah. "We'll get back to you on that other thing."

"You do that." Zechariah waited until the men cleared out before he picked up his coffee cup and stood. "A new book came in the mail today. I think I'll take a look at it by the fire while you discuss your family business."

"We'll be out of your hair in a bit." Seth cocked his head at Carrie. "We have plenty to do at home."

Laura waited until Zechariah made his way from the dining room. She turned to Seth. "What did Aaron say?"

"He's sick about it. Ashamed. Sorry. Sad. Worried about how Hannah will do without a *mann.* How she'll do during the bann. He said to go to Cyrus if Freeman is sick. Not to wait. The longer we wait, the worse it'll be."

"He's right about that."

Seth rose and stomped from the table to the stove and back, his heavy boots thudding on the wood. "I can't believe this has happened. I can't believe she did this to us."

"To you?" Laura wrapped her hands around her coffee mug and tried to smooth the irk in her voice. "Is that what you think she did?"

"He knows she didn't do it on purpose." Frowning, Carrie plucked a lemongrass teabag from her cup and laid it on the saucer. She squeezed in enough honey for three cups and set the plastic honey bear down with a thump. "No teenager does, but we taught her better. She knows better. She's seventeen. She knows the difference between right and wrong. She knows the consequences."

"When it comes to these matters, it has nothing to do with what you know, only what you feel." Laura grappled for words that would be acceptable for a woman — a grandmother — to utter in the presence of a man — her grandson. "You're not so old that you don't remember. I'm seventy-three and I remember."

"Groossmammi!" Seth frowned. His

bushy eyebrows got a workout. "We don't speak of these things."

Which was why it was so difficult. Biting her lip to keep from telling Seth so, Laura stared into her mug. No one talked about it. Folks tried not to even think about it. They prayed their children would do the right thing and avoid temptation. They hinted about it. They hemmed and hawed about it but never came out and asked if there were any questions. There had to be questions and concerns and worries and uncertainty about what exactly was wrong and where to draw that line between sweet and forbidden.

The more forbidden, the more enticing.

Maybe Seth and Carrie had forgotten, but Laura hadn't. Eli with that come-closer smile and those brilliant blue eyes. Soft, wavy blond hair over a face tanned from working in the sun every day. Dimples. Strong, farmer hands. Broad chest. Not an ounce of fat on him. Muscles built through hard work.

But it wasn't his looks — granted they didn't hurt — that made him so desirable. When he smiled, the world slowed and disappeared. When he spoke with kindness, tenderness, and a touch of laughter in his deep voice, he made her feel like no one else in the world could.

He was The One. Her Only One. There might be more than one for her friends Bess and Mary Katherine and Jennie, but for Laura, God had chosen only one. Eli Kauffman, father of her nine children and owner of her heart, lock, stock, and barrel.

His touch sent a current through her that vibrated from her head to her toes.

She'd never told a soul, but there was a reason they'd married at twenty. They were afraid if they didn't, something untoward would happen. They didn't want anything to sully their bond. So they married and never looked back, never looked left or right.

"Laura? Laura!" Carrie's voice startled Laura from her reverie. "Where did you go? We're trying to strategize here."

Carrie talked like that. Strategize. She might be Amish now, but she had been English for the first twenty-two years of her life. Until she met Seth. She insisted she wanted to embrace the Plain way of life because of her faith, but Laura suspected it had much more to do with Seth's blue eyes and dimpled cheeks and broad chest than the articles of faith.

Still, Carrie had never given them reason to regret welcoming her into the faith and the community.

"It's hard to strategize, as you call it, without talking about it. We tiptoe around the subject. Maybe that's part of the problem." She managed to meet Carrie's gaze but drew the line at looking directly at Seth. "We don't talk about it and how to ward off temptation."

Carrie smiled for the first time. "I turned myself inside out and upside down because of that feeling of being in love and all that goes with it. I love being Plain. I'm content and happy and where I must be. I love this faith that I have now. But it all started with the feelings you're talking about."

She glanced toward her husband, who growled and made another trip to the stove and back to the counter. "Women," he muttered. "Always talk too much."

"Laura's right. Sometimes talking helps straighten things out before they get out of hand." Carrie shrugged and patted her nose with a tissue. "It could have saved us a lot of heartache."

"It doesn't need talking about." Seth smacked his hand on the counter and stared out the window over the sink. "We do too much talking around here. Hannah will do her freewill confession of *Fehla* to Freeman, she'll be under the bann for a few weeks, and then she can do her kneeling confession at a meeting. She'll be done."

"Except for the bopli." As the mudder of eight children, Carrie could envision how this part would go too. "That will not be done."

"She should stay in the dawdy haus at Ruby's until her time is done." Laura wanted Hannah close. She was barely a woman. She shouldn't go through this alone any longer than necessary. "I'll be here for a few weeks at least, maybe longer. Ruby can keep an eye on her from the main house."

"If the Gmay agrees."

"Do you intend to talk to the boy's parents?"

"He's not a boy. He's a man." Seth turned and leaned against the counter. He crossed his arms. His scowl burned a hole between Laura's eyes. "We'll do what Freeman tells us to do."

"Do you think he's told them?"

"I don't know." Carrie shook her head. "Word will travel fast. His family will hear of it if he doesn't tell them first. But that won't stop him from going to Indiana or wherever with no burden to bear. It's always been that way with men."

"Don't be throwing us all into the same corral. I would never do what Thaddeus intends to do."

144

Carrie hopped up from the chair and scurried across the room to her husband. "I know that. I didn't mean to imply such a thing. Forgive me."

She was a good wife.

"I can't believe this is happening." Seth sighed. "She was such a gut girl. A gut helper. Kind to her bruders and schweschders."

"She still is all those things." Laura swallowed the lump in her throat. The memories overwhelmed her. Huddled in a rocking chair, she held the tiny bundle of bones with a big cry who arrived early and cuddled her after her long, fierce battle to see the world. A cold winter wind blew outside the window. Branches dipped and scraped the roof. She kissed the damp curls and sang "Amazing Grace" over and over until the newborn slept. "We'll forgive her and move on."

"Alone with a baby."

"With us to help her."

"But not a mann."

"One thing at a time."

"I think she should give the baby up for adoption." Carrie stuttered the words. She hugged Seth's arm to her chest and eyed him with trepidation. "Then she could start fresh."

"No one will forget she's had a bopli."

Seth tugged his arm from her grasp. "This bopli is our grandchild."

Therein lay the crux of the matter. Despite the circumstances, this baby would be welcomed and loved and grow up just like any other member of the family. A baby was a gift from God to be loved and cherished. No matter the difficult circumstances. The Gmay would forgive Hannah and welcome her back into the fold, if she recognized her failure and accepted her punishment as deserved.

"I agree with Seth." Laura sought to pluck the words from the mire of her thoughts. "But we must make sure this is what Hannah wants. She is the bopli's mudder. She will raise him. There will be consequences for her, with either choice."

Seth nodded, but the pain that etched his face made him look much older. So much like his father, Aaron, who looked like Eli. How would Eli have reacted to one of their children in this situation?

Like a hurting father who wanted to fix it but knew the child must face the consequences of his or her actions. Grow from the mistake and move forward. Forgiven.

Forgiving was easy. Facing the consequences much harder. For Hannah and for her parents.

TWELVE

Odd shadows from the firelight mingled with those thrown by the propane lamp's wispy shadows. Zechariah held a new book that had come in the mail — *National Geographic Complete Birds of North America* — in his hands, but it rested in his lap. Either lamps weren't throwing as much light as they used to or he needed a new pair of reading glasses. Or maybe King Eider and northern bobwhite quail held no sway over him when he was tired after all the company for supper — and the obvious tension among those at the table. He relaxed against the rocking chair pillow and let the fire's heat seep into his bones. It felt good. Not moving, except for the occasional twitch, felt good.

This room felt as much like home as any place since Marian died.

His sons could decide his fate. Two of his grandsons could decide to bail out of their

Gmay and move to Indiana to work in a factory. That much he knew. *Gott, take me home. I'm ready. I know it's on Your time, not mine, but I can't help but ask. With humility. I try to be obedient but I'm tired. If I sound whiny, I apologize and ask for forgiveness. I'm in my second childhood, according to my kinner.*

Laura's quick, light step in the hallway signaled her impending arrival. Zechariah straightened and tugged at the book. It fell open to page 73, which featured the loon and how to identify it in flight. For some reason this made him laugh the crazy laugh of a loony man.

"What's so funny?" Laura pulled the other rocking chair closer to the fire and sat. Her joints creaked in a familiar, achy sound. "I thought maybe you were asleep by now."

"Did you know the loon's song is loud, mournful, eerie, and far carrying?"

"I did not. I feel like a loon after this day." She tilted her head from side to side, making her neck pop. "It's hard to believe it all happened in one day. I just went to town for sewing supplies and *boom,* life happened."

At least he wasn't the only one. Of course, her children didn't pass her around like a horse that could no longer pull his own

148

weight. Put out to pasture. "As it tends to do. Everyone down?"

"Kinner asleep and company gone." She leaned forward and held her hands near the fire. "It's chilly. The fire feels gut."

Small talk was fine, but life was short. "I gathered all is not well. Not that I was listening."

"You really had no choice, I suppose." Laura let her hands rest in her lap. She leaned back. Her eyelids drooped. She might drift off in front of him, and he could sit here next to her in silence, secretly enjoying company that required nothing of him. She stirred. Or not. "I guess you gathered that my Hannah is in a family way."

It wasn't a topic for mixed company, but Laura had become one for directness since her husband passed. As if she had no reason to care. Or thought she'd be going along soon herself and didn't have time to meander. Like Zechariah. "They'll do their punishment as Freeman and the others see fit. It's not the first time and it won't be the last."

"The boy wants to leave. He doesn't want to marry her and well he shouldn't if that's the way he feels." Sadness laced the words. She was a good grandma who hurt for these young folks who had sinned in such an egregious way. "My grandson and his fraa are beside themselves with shame, but we can't always control what our kinner do. And at a certain point, they become responsible for their own actions."

"Fornication is a biblical sin. They have to take responsibility for it."

"She shouldn't have to do it alone." Her retort matched a glance as hot as the fireplace flames. "The daed shouldn't be able to walk away unscathed."

"No one who commits a sin and fails to repent walks away unscathed."

Her scowl died. "You're right."

"That must've hurt."

"What?" She frowned, but the fire had dissipated. "What are you talking about?"

"Admitting I'm right about something."

She laughed and began to rock. He did the same.

The quiet didn't feel as empty as it had before.

"Your Marian was a gut woman, a gut fraa. We had gut laughs while we canned and sewed and planted."

"She was." He tried to conjure up Marian's face. Soft, dimpled cheeks, full lips, caramel eyes, pink skin in summer, never brown, never tanned. "I had no complaints."

"Me neither. With Eli, I mean." She

rocked harder. "We were twenty when we married."

"Me too. Marian, nineteen."

"We were in a hurry."

"Us too."

"It went so fast. Those forty-five years."

"Gut years do."

"How is it possible? Eli's been gone eight years this Christmas Eve."

"Time is like that. I have trouble remembering what Marian looked like and she's only been gone two years." When folks got to be their age, they often watched as family members and friends were laid to eternal rest. Still, it didn't seem right that sons would go before their parents. "What she looked like doesn't matter. It's who she was and how she . . ."

"Made you feel." Her gnarled fingers moved in her lap, restless, plucking at her apron. "I look at my suhs and see him. My suh Luke has been gone three years and I see him in his suhs. I reckon that is Gott's intent."

"It's been five years for Robert. Two for Marian."

"I should remind you that their days were done." Laura managed a soft smile. "That Gott knew how many days they had from the very beginning. That kinner are gifts

151

from Gott and He takes them home on His schedule, not ours."

They shared a bond no one wanted. Parents who had watched their children be buried. He could understand as no one else could what that felt like. "But you won't because you know it was cold comfort when they stuck Luke's body in the ground."

"He wasn't there. I know that. But it was so cold that day. Just as it was when we buried Eli." Her gaze shifted and examined the fire as if seeking its warmth to banish the cold she felt in remembering those dark, frigid winter days. "I wish to be absolutely without doubt that they were home and warm and not wanting for a single thing, not even me, but I know that it is impossible to be thus."

"So we just do the best we can and keep our lips buttoned up."

She nodded and smiled. Her gaze veered from the fire and met his head-on. She had a spark in her eyes that reminded him of what it was like to be young and full of passion. Keeping her lips buttoned up would be a difficult task for a woman like Laura. Eli had his hands full.

Eli was blessed.

Laura stopped rocking. She leaned forward, her face intent, her frame bent by old age, tense and still. "You are not used up, Zechariah. Nor a child. No one babysits you."

The agility of a mind that made such a leap and so quickly. "Then what are you doing here?"

She stood and tugged at a small table until it sat between them. It held a set of checkers scattered across the board. "I like to play checkers. It's hard to do at the dawdy haus when I'm all alone. Here, I have an opponent."

"They want to move me again."

"You have a say in it. Don't let them tell you that you don't."

"I said as much. Then I felt selfish. They say Ben and Rosalie will have too much on their hands with the twins and Rosalie not being well. They can't take care of me too. They don't see that it can be the other way around."

"Then make them see it. I'm here to help with Rosalie and the babies. I'm here to help, period." She began to arrange the checkers in their proper spots. "Let's play."

She would pick something that required a steady hand. Zechariah's body tensed and then jerked at the mere thought. "I'm not good at games."

"Afraid you'll be beaten by an old

woman?"

She didn't know what it was like not to have control over your arms and legs. Never knowing when one or the other would decide to jerk. He studied his boots. They were scuffed and worn. Even though he did no work. Dragging his feet was no doubt hard on them.

"It doesn't matter." The words were gentle, her tone soft. "I don't care. It's just you and me and these four walls. Who will know if you fling a checker at me? I might fling it back."

He swallowed against a sudden lump in his throat. A tone as soft as peach fuzz. A caring that soothed aches and pains with a simple word. He missed that too. "Fine. I'm red."

"Fine, be red. I'd rather be black anyway. And I get first move."

The first move and the last word, no doubt. "Sure you do. I prefer it that way."

"Sure you do."

The crackle of the flames and the hiss of still-damp wood filled the silence as they arranged their checkers. Warmth filled the room, followed by a semblance of peace. It felt nice and strangely nostalgic. "I miss having my own place."

"I understand that." Her head tilted,

Laura studied the board. Then she looked up, her eyes bright. "Sometimes it's hard to understand why things turn out the way they do."

"Yet who are we to question?"

"Exactly." Laura nudged her first checker onto its adjacent block. "My older schweschder and her mann got married in a rush."

Somehow her thoughts were connected. "It's happened since the beginning of time, I reckon." He stifled a chuckle. Typical first move of a checkers neophyte. Either that or she was going easy on an old man with nothing better to do but hull pecans, argue with his kinner, and sleep in a rocking chair by the fire while pretending to read a book on birds. "Unlike the Englisch world, we don't look at it any differently now than we did fifty or sixty years ago. Our grandparents and great-grandparents would be happy that we still stand by our biblical principles and the articles of faith."

"More importantly Gott sees and Gott knows."

"Jah."

"She miscarried. But she never regretted marrying Jonathan." Laura snickered softly at his move and shoved a black checker into the next spot. "They were married almost

155

fifty years when she passed. Jonathan went a few months later. Irene never once spoke about it — not even to me."

"It wasn't something we jawed about then."

"Or now. Maybe that's part of the problem."

"There's altogether too much talking going on, in my way of thinking." He jumped two of her pieces and landed within spitting distance of the last row and his first king. "Some things are wrong. We know they're wrong. No point wasting air and discussing them."

"Are you telling me I should talk less and think about my moves more?" She did her own double move. "Believe me, I can talk and think at the same time."

She had a nice laugh. Sort of a merry tinkle. Not like Marian's low, breathy laugh. His gut tightened. His fingers twitched. *Not now. Breathe. Breathe.* He tried to lift his arm and move it toward the piece on the edge of the board. One more move and he'd have a king. *Smooth. Smooth.* His arm flailed, his hand flapped, and his fingers hit the edge of the board. Pieces sailed into the air. One landed on her black, thick-soled shoe. Another on the piece rug next to the fire. A third in the dwindling woodpile.

"Ach. Grrrr." Gritting his teeth, he stood. "Looks like you won."

"Don't growl like a grouchy old bear. You're not getting off so easily." She scooped up the pieces on the floor. "I have a photographic memory. I know where each piece was."

"You do not."

"Do too." She sashayed over to the woodpile and plucked the third piece from its resting spot. "Ask anyone in my family. I have a memory like an elephant. I never forget. At least not important stuff."

"Like where checker pieces go. I wouldn't put it past you to cheat. Put those pieces back exactly where they were."

"I never cheat. I'm a gut Christian woman. Just like I never forget how to make piecrust so it's tender and flaky. Or how to can blueberry jam." She sat and reassembled the pieces. It seemed obstinate not to join her, so Zechariah eased back into the chair. Her grin was self-satisfied. And irritating. At least she had all her own teeth. For a woman of her age, that was saying something. "Want to know a secret?"

Feeling like a schoolboy — he hadn't felt young in fifty years — he nodded.

"I keep lists."

"Lists?"

"I have a family tree in my Bible. It's gotten so long, I have to fold it out two folds. It has my entire family from my groossmammi and groossdaadi, all the way down to my great-grands." She leaned forward and cupped her hand as if she were telling him a secret in his ear. "I have another one with all the boplin I delivered and their parents. I'm afraid I'll forget."

"Does it help?"

"Loads."

"Maybe you can make one for me."

"Sure. I'll see how much I can do from memory. It'll be gut work for my brain. Then you can fill in the rest. That'll be gut for your brain." The lines wrinkled around her mouth and her green eyes when she laughed. Which seemed often, now that Zechariah thought about it. Her chest heaved with the force of her mirth and her shoulders shook at her secret. "I also kept a planner when I worked at the store. Who knew an old woman like myself would need a planner? It had big spaces for each day of the week. I wrote down my shifts. When the frolics were. When I was to go to the kinner's house for supper. I used to remember all those things. Not anymore."

Zechariah didn't need a planner. He mostly sat in a chair and read or puttered around in the barn. Ben didn't let him do much more than feed the chickens or curry the horses. His highlights were going to town for coffee with Abel, bird counts, cleaning the birdhouses, and feeding the birds. What would he do without the birds? He should be thankful for this God-given love of nature. "That's why you thought you'd forgotten a date you'd made with your Hannah today?"

Her face clouded. The smile was replaced by sadness. The room seemed darker. "Nee. I thought it was Tamara."

"Which is she?"

"She's Ruby's youngest. Ruby is my youngest."

"She's the one who looks like Eli."

"You remember what Eli looked like?"

"Tall. Blond. Like a giant among men."

"That was my Eli."

"No one had a chance with you once he offered you a ride."

"No one else was interested, least ways that I noticed."

"You wouldn't have noticed. You had eyes only for Eli."

She nodded, the sadness replaced by an even more painful wistfulness.

Zechariah had seen that look on his daughter-in-law's face after Robert died.

Maybe that's why she moved away, taking his grandchildren with her. So she wouldn't be reminded of her loss. "Why did you think it was Tamara?"

"She's leaving the Gmay. She has decided not to be baptized. Or so she says. I thought maybe she would come talk to me about it. Get my thoughts on it." Laura cocked her head toward the board. "All fixed. It was your move."

"Move my piece over there." He pointed at the black checker that had been returned to its rightful spot — as far as he remembered. "You're patient."

"I'm seventy-three and moving slower every day. I have no choice but to be patient."

"You're helping out Rosalie, taking care of kinner, cooking and cleaning."

"It makes me feel useful." She lifted her gaze to look directly at him. And caught him staring at her green eyes. Heat billowed through his body. No harm in looking at an old woman. He was too old for it to mean a thing. Too old and feeble and jerking around like a man with his finger caught in a skill saw. He hadn't been alone in a room with a woman in years. That was it. Nothing more. Laura smiled. Which didn't help in the least. "It's what we all want. To feel useful. To have a reason for still being here."

"Why did it bother you that it might be Tamara?"

"Because I still hadn't figured out what to say to her. I needed time to think."

"Why do you have to think about it? It's wrong. She must stay. She must be baptized."

"Not if she can't be baptized in gut faith that she plans to remain Plain the rest of her life and follow the *Ordnung.*"

Her hand hovered over the board, then dropped back in her lap. Her head drooped in a dejected air Zechariah had not seen before. The desire to touch her cheek flickered through him, a flame that grew by the second. He hadn't touched but one woman in his lifetime. Marian. When she died of cancer, he put such thoughts and feelings aside. A man his age didn't ask for lightning to strike twice. Didn't need it.

He could barely walk on his own. He shook like a leaf in a tornado. He had little to offer a woman like Laura, still vibrant and strong and mouthy after all these years.

Only Marian would understand. Only Marian would accept the man she loved all those years. They could've declined together. Now, the bed was cold and the nights long, but the days were longer. At

161

least at night he slept and forgot. The days stretched endless and empty of the small conversations and the laughs over shared jokes that were only funny to them. He missed the crinkle of her nose when she didn't like something he did or said. The way she rolled her eyes but held her tongue until the words burst out in a singsong tirade that had him gasping with laughter. Soon, she laughed with him, but she always got her way.

He cleared his throat and banished the memories. Why tonight? Why when a living, breathing, sassy, contrary woman sat across from him looking as if she'd just lost her best friend. She wasn't at fault that a young woman had made such a heinous mistake.

He bit his lip and held his peace. She would tell him what was on her mind in her own time.

"She told Ruby that it was my idea."

"Was it?" Stupid question. "Of course it wasn't."

Laura nudged a piece across the centerline. Zechariah had her right where he wanted her. He did a double skip, hop, and jump. "King me."

"You distracted me."

"You said you could think and play at the

same time. You said you could talk and play."

Laura laid a checker on top of his and proceeded to hop her way to a king on his side of the board. "So there."

"You sound like Samuel."

"He's a gut boy and smart."

"Why did Tamara tell Ruby it was your idea?"

"She's leaving because she wants to go to medical school and become a doctor. I encouraged her to become a midwife. She followed me around when she barely reached my waist. Then she followed Iris and Rachel around. She would make a good midwife. She's never courted. They were thinking of asking her to teach at the school after she was baptized."

"No boys following her around?"

"A few have tried, but none seem to stick."

"She hasn't met the right one yet."

"Time is running out. If she leaves and goes off to college, she'll love the choices and the freedom and be so busy soaking up knowledge that she won't notice that she's filling up with everything except God and family. She'll be alone."

"Or she'll meet an Englischer."

"Whose side are you on?"

"Gott's side." He hoped. If it weren't too

prideful to suggest it. He moved his king in position for another jump. This game had gone on long enough, but he didn't want it to end. He wanted the conversation. He liked being treated like an adult and not another child to be questioned about medicine and brushing his teeth and "isn't it past your bedtime, Groossdaadi?" type questions. "He knows what's best for her and we need only pray and let Him do His work."

"That doesn't mean we shouldn't be gut stewards of the children He's given us, the gifts He's given us. Tamara would make a gut mudder and a gut fraa. She belongs here with her family and her community, where she can go to her eternal Father when the time comes with a clean heart and a clear slate without any of the worldly sins she'll encounter if she leaves."

"Agreed."

"Then why argue with me?"

"Who's arguing with you? She'll have to finish school and get into a college and find a way to pay for it." Zechariah leaned back in his chair, suddenly so tired his bones felt heavy in his body. "Then she has to get into medical school. Our education, while exactly what is needed for our kinner, doesn't prepare a student for the rigorous entrance exams and the science and math those students need to succeed in medical school."

"So you think she'll fail and come home? How happy will she be here then?"

"I don't think anything. I read a lot." It filled the hours and the days. "I see what's happening in the world. I would hope she would come to her senses and recognize the void in her that can only be filled by Gott, faith, community, and family. We can't do that for her."

"I'd like to take her to the woodshed and smack some sense into her backside."

"That stops working when they're about eleven or twelve." He sighed. "You heard that two of my grandsons want to move to Nappanee to work in the RV factory?"

"I heard. My letter circle includes a friend in LaGrange. She says more than half of the Plain men there work in the factory. Including her mann and two of her suhs. The money is gut. They bought a big boat."

"There's the problem in my way of thinking. Easy cash." Life made too easy. Too comfortable. "Instead of hard work with their family every day on the farm. What happens when the Englischers don't have money to buy the RVs? It happened once before."

"They'll come back to the farms."

"There will be no farms to come back to."

Her smile returned, this time rueful. "You're pretty smart. I guess there's something to be said for the combined years in the room. If someone would listen to us, they'd know we're right about some things."

Enough whining. "Gott will prevail."

"He always, always does. So why do we worry and natter on about it?" She stood. "I'm tired. We'll finish the game tomorrow night."

The words sounded like a promise. They had a nice ring about them.

He nodded.

"Shall I put out the fire or will you?"

She offered the question as if she spoke to a man who had all his faculties. He liked that about her. "That's on the list of things I'm not allowed to do."

"I never liked putting out the fire myself. I wouldn't mind not having to do it."

He'd never looked at it that way. "That's a smarty-pants ploy."

She grinned. "Don't you ever ask them to add things to the list that you don't want to do?"

He laughed — something he never expected to do about his disease. "Nee, I feel like my world keeps getting smaller and smaller. Work is what makes life worth living. Work is what we do for fun. And now I'm not allowed to have fun."

A wicked twinkle sparked in her eyes. "We shall see about that."

This time there was no doubt. Her words held a promise.

THIRTEEN

Two heads were better than one. Three had to be a problem-solving triple threat. Laura plopped onto a chair between Bess, who was knitting a beautiful shawl for her mother, and Jennie, who'd taken the morning off from the Combination Store to work on her quilt. Mary Katherine couldn't make it — one of the girls scheduled to work at the bookstore was sick today. With Samuel and Delia settled in with the other children, Laura could spend some time picking her friends' brains before approaching Tamara, who was in the kitchen helping her sisters make sweet-smelling candles and sachets for quilt chests.

Keeping her granddaughter from making a horrible mistake was the order of the day. The thought gave Laura renewed energy despite a night of broken sleep with Delia's trips to the potty and Samuel's nightmares. The children missed their mother and

Laura was a poor substitute. She didn't have the energy she once did. Until it came to this moment of convincing Tamara that her eternal salvation and her happiness lay in Jamesport with her family and her church. She couldn't lose another child. She'd already lost a son to death. His days were done. But Tamara had a choice. Luke had not.

"Are you getting enough sleep? You're not used to getting up with little ones during the night." Jennie stabbed her needle into the burgundy material. "You look tired and not at all happy."

Jennie was almost as good at reading faces as Mary Katherine. Laura composed hers. "I enjoy watching over the kinner. It makes me happy. I feel useful. Besides, it's been almost a week and I'm getting used to it."

"You feel happy watching over Zechariah?"

Her knitting needles clacking in a steady staccato, Bess giggled. "How could such a sourpuss make anyone happy?"

His defeated expression when Laura walked into the front room the previous evening flashed in her mind. The checkers and the conversation had left her feeling better somehow. He felt better, she could tell. He'd laughed and sat up straighter in the chair. Asking him his opinion about Tamara made him feel valued. She understood the need for that. Leaving him to put out the fire showed she trusted him. At the time she hadn't thought it through, but now she could see the groundwork being laid.

For what?

Friendship? She could always use a new friend. She'd never had a man friend. At her age she couldn't — wouldn't — ignore a chance to have one more. Especially one so in need of the return favor. Especially one who had enough years under his belt to understand how she saw the world, because he saw it the same way.

He had a nice smile and enormous russet eyes that had seen so much. She had gone to bed wondering what else went on behind those eyes.

Bess was too young to understand any of this. She had been through a lot in her short twenty-some years, but not the vastness of experience that came in a lifetime.

"He's not so bad." She sought words in Zechariah's defense that wouldn't give away her own thoughts. They were too new and too strange to be shared yet. A woman having a man as a friend at her age might be hard for the younger women to understand, especially Jennie, who'd experienced such pain and hurt at the hands of her first husband. "Not only does he have the aches and pains that come with age, he also has a disease that's taking away his independence. That's hard for all older folks, but especially men."

"So Mary Katherine was right?" Jennie laid down her needle and stretched her arms over her head. "You are interested in Zechariah. That's why you were so anxious to stay and take care of Ben's kinner."

Had she been interested in Zechariah before the twins' birth? The bird books. Reading up on Parkinson's disease. Only as a friend who'd known the man since childhood. Surely.

Laura shook her head. "I've known Zechariah all my life. I remember how sweet he and Marian were together. He was the light of her life. That speaks to what kind of mann he was. He was a hard worker and a gut father too. The grouchiness is a new thing, brought on by the death of his fraa and two kinner followed by an awful disease I wouldn't wish on my worst enemy."

"Well, I guess you told us." Bess held up her needles as if in surrender. "Sorry, I didn't mean to speak ill of your special friend."

"He's not my special friend." Heat burned

171

Laura's face. So much for keeping her feelings to herself. Her friends knew her far too well. "We played checkers and drank tea. That's all. We didn't even finish the game."

"This does sound like something is simmering at Ben's house that has nothing to do with babies or cooking and cleaning." Jennie went back to her quilting, but her expression held obvious mixed emotion. "We want you to be happy, my freind, but be careful."

Even a blissfully happy second marriage couldn't keep caution from Jennie's every move. Ever the nurturer, she didn't want others to experience what she had with Atlee.

"You're putting the cart a hundred miles before the horse. We played checkers because I'm there taking care of the kinner. That's all." Laura picked at the bits of oatmeal on her apron. She couldn't deny the thought of a man replacing Eli had crossed her mind a time or two over the years, but it was always followed by the assurance that no one could replace him. Nor did she need a replacement. She lived a life filled with kinner and friends and faith. It was just dark winter, filled with short days of little sunshine, long evenings, and cold nights that made a person start to think about such silliness. "I remain content with what Gott has given me."

"Maybe He's planning to give you more. Ever think of that? Maybe Gott is waiting for you to get up and get moving on His plan." Bess's needles paused. "I hear Joshua fussing at Delia. He is not gut at sharing. He has to learn."

She settled her partially completed pale-blue shawl and skein of wool onto her chair and bustled across the room. Her expression thoughtful, Jennie watched her go. "If it's not Zechariah, what is bothering you? If it's the gossip about Tamara, don't worry about it. Mary Katherine talked to Ruby. She'll talk to those gossipers, count on that."

"It's Tamara — whom I intend to speak to today if I have to tackle her — and then there's Hannah —"

"I heard. I tend to hear everything at the store. If I don't, Leo does. He often forgets to tell me, or I have to drag it out of him, but between the two of us, we hear just about everything." Jennie made a *tsk-tsk* sound. "Every time one of the women delivers their goods to the store, a little more of the story gets told. Of course, I don't believe everything I hear, and I surely don't repeat it."

"I can't believe the grapevine got a hold

of her already."

"Her, but not the daed. They're saying she's leaving the Gmay to live with some Englisch man."

"Not true." Nausea bucked in Laura's stomach at the thought of people gossiping about her sweet Hannah. The bacon and biscuit she had for breakfast rose in her throat. She swallowed. "What possesses people to make it up as they go along?"

"Nothing better to do, I reckon."

"I know it's a sin to worry, but I think of her being banned for a month or six weeks or even longer, on her own." Laura cleared her throat. She plucked her glasses from her face and made a show of wiping them on her apron. Hot tears welled, but she whipped them back by sheer force of will. Jennie squeezed her arm. Laura breathed. "She's a sweet girl who made a terrible mistake. We'll love her and help her raise her bopli, but there's so much hurt and pain in between."

"If she's truly repentant, she'll do fine." Jennie wiped at her cheeks. She was a good friend who had her share of experiences raising teenagers, especially her son Matthew, who had suffered lingering effects from his dead father's anger issues. "We love our boplin, no matter their ages, but we also

174

have to let them suffer the consequences of their actions. It's the only way they can grow up and become Gott-fearing adults who raise gut kinner themselves."

"We all make mistakes. Sometimes we teeter on making grave errors, but somehow, we pull back from the cliff or someone or something pulls us back." Like Eli's offer to give her a ride home one night after a singing. Those simple words, "Will you take a ride with me?" changed her life. "Didn't you ever come close to making a mistake as grievous as Hannah's?"

"Atlee swept me off my feet, for sure. I'd never been kissed before. He took my breath away." Jennie's voice faltered. Her cheeks turned as red as a fresh tomato. "I was all mixed up. I thought it was love. I thought this was what grown-ups did."

"So when he asked you to marry him, you said jah."

She wiggled in her chair and ducked her head. "I did. It didn't take long for me to realize lust and love are not the same thing." Her needle paused in midair. "Leo is different. The two are bound so tightly — we're bound so tightly — there's no unraveling where one ends and the other begins."

"I don't think I need to hear about this."

They both laughed, the embarrassed

chuckles of two old women. Jennie rolled her eyes. "It's not only the young who are tempted by pleasures of the body. I'll leave it at that."

"Danki."

They were silly old ladies who couldn't hold their emotion any more than their tea. Jennie stuck her needle in the material. She leaned back and folded her hands in her lap. "What will you say to Tamara?"

"I'm praying for the right words."

"You're never at a loss for words."

They both laughed again. Laura wiped at her face with her sleeve. "So much is riding on the right words."

"Gott is in charge. He'll give you the words. He knows the outcome, so there's no reason for you to get all tied up in knots over it."

The older Jennie grew, the wiser she became. Soon she would overtake Mary Katherine and Laura both. Her words were as bracing as cold water splashed on Laura's face on a winter morning. "Time to wade into the fray."

"I think she's been avoiding you."

"I know she has, but I'm spryer than she thinks."

"There she goes to talk to Ruby." Jennie cocked her head toward the other end of the room. "You know more than she does about life. Never forget that. I don't."

FOURTEEN

One zig, two zags, and Laura had Tamara cornered between Ruby's quilt rack and the circle of chairs where smaller crib quilts in various stages were being finished. Or she thought she did. Tamara simply squeezed past her and trotted toward the kitchen.

"Tamara! I've been looking for you."

Ruby, caught in the middle between her mother and her daughter, smiled, but sadness deepened the lines around her eyes and mouth. "That's what she does to me every time I try to talk to her." She stabbed her needle into a purple-and-yellow Double Star baby quilt that surely would be a Christmas gift for her daughter Cassie, who was expecting in the spring. "My mann won't even look at her anymore."

"She can't do that with me. I'll run her down, don't you worry." Laura marched into the kitchen, where the scent of cinnamon rolls mingled with lilac sachets and

178

vanilla candles in various stages of production. Tamara stood at the table where her mother had arranged platters and bowls of food brought to the frolic. She picked up a plate. Laura did the same. "How have you been?"

Tamara laid a peanut butter spread sandwich on her plate, then added two molasses cookies and two walnut cookies. The girl had a sweet tooth. She sighed and held her plate out to Laura. "Would you like a cookie? Mudder made the molasses ones. They're so gut."

Knowing what a good baker Ruby was, Laura took one of each. She had her own sweet tooth. "Let's take a walk."

"It's too cold. And we have work to do."

"We still have time. Christmas is three weeks away. Besides, the wind has died down." Laura wrapped the cookies in a paper napkin and laid them on the table. She tugged on her favorite mittens knitted by her granddaughter Jana for Christmas the previous year. "I could use a breath of fresh air."

She told the truth. The smoke from the fireplace, mixed with the crush of women chattering and the perfumed potpourri scents had given her a headache.

"You'll bend my ear. I know it." Tamara's

cheeks reddened, but her gaze didn't waver. She set the paper plate on the table and picked up her sandwich. "My mind's made up."

"Not here." Laura slipped her arm through the crook in Tamara's and propelled her toward the back door where they grabbed coats from the hooks. "This is a private conversation."

Outside, she took a deep breath of December air and exhaled. The white puffs lingered a second, then dissipated. Gray clouds covered the sun, but the air still felt crisp against her skin. She could think more clearly despite her fatigue and concern. She needed to think clearly to convince a smart girl like Tamara, who was always sure she was right. Just like her grandpa Eli. Only not as smart as he was. "Much better."

"Better for what?" Tamara tugged away and clomped down the steps. "I don't need anyone else to bark at me."

"Bark at you? Is that what you call it when your mudder and daed talk about how concerned they are for your eternal salvation?" Laura followed her. Tamara looked like her mother, which meant she looked like Laura when she was young. Except her eyes were cocoa colored, not green. Over the years, Ruby had suffered through many

180

heart-to-heart talks with Laura, but never one like this. "Is that what you call it when they want you to know how much they'll miss you? How their hearts are broken?"

Tamara's face flushed scarlet. She tossed her bread to the birds gathered under her daed's bird feeder. "I'm not a mean person." Her pace picked up to match her agitation. "I have to do what's right for me. It would be wrong to be baptized if that's not what's in my heart. You taught me that."

The boisterous laughter of more than two dozen children playing hide-and-seek among the buggies and farm equipment seemed out of place as a backdrop for this discussion. Laura gritted her teeth and sallied forth. "You told your mudder I gave you the idea of leaving Jamesport and becoming a doctor. I figure *I* have a say in this."

"I didn't put it quite like that. I said watching you gave me the idea."

"Watching me deliver babies made you want to leave your faith and your family to become a doctor." Laura understood the desire. She'd felt it herself. But her faith and her love for a good man had kept her from taking that road. Tamara had decided to put this desire for her vocation before her faith. And she hadn't found her Eli —

not yet. "Help me understand."

Tamara veered left and came to a stop between two buggies. The horses had gathered around a pile of hay left there by her father for that purpose. They chewed with a contented air. She ran her long fingers through the ginger mare's mane and began to braid small pieces of it. "I don't know if I can explain it. Martha's baby died."

"Jah."

"And I felt helpless watching. Rachel was helpless."

"Rachel did what she could. Even if Rachel were a doctor and the bopli born in a hospital, she would've died."

"I'm not sure of that. You weren't there and you can't know either."

"I know Rachel would do everything she could to save a bopli. I know the rest is in Gott's hands. So you are smarter than Gott?"

"Nee. I would never say that."

"You're Plain."

Tamara laid her head on the horse's neck and whispered sweet nothings in her ear. She sniffed. "I hate breaking Mudder's heart. I hate making Daed look sad and mad at the same time. He's never been mad at me before. Ever."

"You are a gut and smart girl. He knows

182

that." Laura leaned against the wooden fence. Her legs were tired, but her mind was more tired. "He has a plan for you that has nothing to do with brains and everything to do with heart and soul."

"I have no special freind. You know that. I have no one to love, and I like the idea of learning more than I like cooking or sewing."

"You've got this all figured out."

"I talked to Dr. Reeves." One of Jamesport's family doctors. "I have a plan. I'll take the GED — that's the General Equivalency Development test — and get my high school equivalency diploma. She thinks with the extra reading and work I'm doing I can pass. But I don't know if I have enough science and math. Especially math."

The cold air had nothing to do with the red on her cheeks now or the way her dark eyes sparkled with enthusiasm. Everything about her changed. She stood taller. She spoke with more confidence. She was a smart girl. If anyone could pass this test, she could.

Which scared Laura. "Maybe you need to study more before you give it a try."

"You're trying to delay the inevitable."

A smart girl, indeed. "I'm more worried about your spiritual smarts than your book

183

learning."

"I can still worship Gott and believe everything you believe. Plain folks aren't the only Christians in the world."

"No one likes a smarty mouth."

Tamara abandoned the braid she had been attempting in the horse's mane and stalked toward the dirt road. A fine mist of sleet mixed with snow began to fall. It sparkled against the dark of her wool coat. Like the ideas that sparkled inside this too-smart-for-her-own-good girl.

Another girl just like Tamara stalked along the road with her. The one Laura had been at nineteen. So sure of herself. The girl who longed to do more and be more. More than a wife and mother. Laura had wanted to be a doctor once. She'd been certain she would never be happy unless she became a medical doctor. The struggle between her faith and her calling had kept her awake night after night.

Then God revealed His plan to her. She met Eli. Her plans fell away like a house built on the sand. One kiss and the desire to know the world had faded away in the happily ever after of being the wife of a man who could sweep her off her feet without touching her. She could be a midwife, remain with her family and her faith, and find happiness.

Tamara whirled around and walked backward with all the confidence of a woman who had eyes in the back of her head. "I'm waiting until after Christmas."

So little time to convince her. Or find her a special friend. Matchmaking was not Laura's favorite activity. But anything to derail this plan. "So you can spend one more of Jesus' birthdays worshipping with family?"

"Jah, that too. But also because the new semester begins in January. Dr. Reeves is helping me fill out the paperwork for financial aid and admissions at the community college in Trenton."

That answered the question of how she would pay for it. Trenton was only thirteen miles from Jamesport. But once Tamara made good on her intention to get a college education, it might as well be five thousand. She hadn't been baptized so there would be no official Meidung. Instead, she simply would lead a different life, one that didn't involve her family. She would wear English jeans and T-shirts and likely learn to drive. She'd talk about current events at coffee shops and spend all night in the library with other students intent on saving the world while they lost their souls.

"Community college is gut enough to get you into medical school?"

Tamara lifted her face to the ping of the sleet. Her damp cheeks and clothes didn't seem to bother her in the least. The cold invigorated her, it seemed. Or maybe it was her plans for a future that didn't include Ruby and Martin and her eight brothers and sisters. "Nee, but it's a long road. I'll transfer from community college to the university in Kansas City or St. Louis in two years. I need a four-year premed degree with perfect grades and great recommendations. Then I apply to medical school."

"It sounds expensive."

"It is. But we're poor as church mice compared to most Englisch students and once I'm kicked out of the Gmay, only my income counts for financial aid and I don't have any. Dr. Reeves has a sister in Trenton who rents rooms to students cheap. I'll get a job."

Dr. Reeves had lived in Jamesport most of her life. She knew what she was doing when she interfered in a Plain girl's life. Good intentions or not. Laura added a visit with the doctor to her to-do list.

Not that it would help now. Tamara had such a blithe attitude. And how had she accumulated so much knowledge of this world so quickly? "You've been thinking about this and planning it for a while."

"Since I turned eighteen."

Four years. "You've been studying this whole time."

"I knew I couldn't compete without learning a lot more than I did in a one-room schoolhouse and an education that ended at the eighth grade."

Compete. Not something a Plain person did. They competed with no one — not with each other or the Englisch. Without a word to anyone, Tamara had plotted and planned. "You want to be better than others. You want to show them up. Have you learned nothing of *Gelassenheit*?" Laura's body heated despite the cold air. Anger burned and sparked like dry kindling suddenly lit with a match. "Have you no respect for our belief in surrender, in resignation, in humility, and sacrifice that honors Gott? We have no need to show off to the world. We have no need of science or years of study. We know what we need to know. That Gott is in charge. We need only surrender to His plan."

"Weren't you ever tempted?" Tamara's voice rose. "I know you were. You just don't want to admit it."

Lying would be a sin and not one Laura

187

intended to embrace in the middle of a tirade about the virtues of Gelassenheit. "I was, but Gott showed me His plan and I'm so thankful and so blessed to have had a life as a fraa and a mudder and a midwife. I would've missed all that if I'd run away from this life."

"I'm not running away from this life. I'm embracing a new life."

They were getting nowhere. Tamara was as stubborn as her father. They got that from Eli. "If Freeman or Cyrus or Solomon hear about this, they may make you leave before Christmas."

"I know. I'll go to Trenton early and get a job. Get situated."

"You have no regrets?"

Her smile flew away on the achingly cold wind. "Of course I do. I care about Mudder and Daed and my bruders and schweschders. I've thought about what it'll be like not to be with them." Her voice quivered for the first time. "Holidays and birthdays and not having family. But this is what will make me happy."

"Sometimes we sacrifice in order to have another kind of happiness."

"You mean *lieb.* I don't think that'll happen to me."

"But you don't know. You have all the

qualities of a gut fraa."

"Maybe my mann is out there in the world, waiting for me."

A knot lodged in Laura's throat. "You've thought of everything."

"I've thought about how it will affect my family and I'm sorry." She skidded to a halt, her sneakers squishing in the wet earth. Tamara threw her arms around Laura and hugged tight. Her breath was warm on Laura's cheek. She smelled of peanut butter. Her voice held bravado, but also a trace of uncertainty for the first time. "I'm sorry to hurt you and make you worry. Don't worry. I'll be fine. I'll never be more than a car's drive away. I'll peek at you in Sweet Notions and make it a point to run into you in The Book Apothecary and I'll take pictures from afar and put them on my refrigerator with magnets. Don't you see, Groossmammi, I was meant for this?"

"Nee, I don't see it." Laura returned the hug and let her forehead rest on Tamara's shoulder for a second. The wool was scratchy. She took a deep breath and raised her head so she could look Tamara in the eye. "I see a woman who is fleeing from Gott's plan. He put a bopli in the arms of a Plain woman who raised her with a Plain man, who taught her everything she needed

189

to know to be a Plain fraa with a Plain mann. Her mudder taught her to work hard and love the work. Her daed taught her to go to services and believe Gott knows better than she does. He taught her to be humble and obedient, to keep herself from the world so she doesn't fall into the world's ways."

Laura sucked in air. She talked a lot, but never this much. Never something so important as her granddaughter's eternal salvation.

Tamara shook her head and patted Laura's cheeks with her mittened hands. The look on her face was so like Eli's. He was always right, bless his pea-picking heart. Always. "You're so sweet. I lieb you."

Not something Plain folks said to each other much. Laura had to clear her throat again. Her joints and bones ached from the cold. Standing out here in the sleet and snow, she might be coming down with something. "I have an idea."

"You are a sly one." Tamara eased away from Laura and began to walk again. "I won't be tricked into changing my mind. It's done. I'm going."

"It's not a trick. I need your help. Rosalie and her twins are coming home later this afternoon. Come take care of them with me.

I'll do the cooking and cleaning. You can help Rosalie with her dressings and with the boplin."

"It should be the other way around. You're —"

"Old? I can still hold my own with a mop and a wringer-wash machine."

"And old men, I hear."

Laura slipped in the mud. Her arms flailed. She bit her tongue and caught her balance before it flew away entirely. "Ach, ouch. What did you hear?"

"Just that you were whipping folks into shape at Ben's house."

"I don't know about that." The warmth of the fire flickered inside her. The checkers. The conversation. The scent of cinnamon-spice tea. The sense of shared joys and suffering. Lives lived on parallel lines now intersecting. "I'm taking care of the kinner and cooking."

"Is taking care of Zechariah like taking care of kinner?"

"You shouldn't listen to gossip about me or Zechariah any more than I listen to the gossip about you."

"Fair point." Tamara entwined her arm in Laura's and guided her around so they walked back toward the house. "I'm leaving in January."

"So help me until then."

Tamara didn't speak for several yards. Laura waited. She'd spoken her piece. Nothing more to be done at this moment.

"I'll do it if you promise me one thing."

"What one thing?"

"To not try to chip away at my resolve forty times a day every day. You won't change my mind."

Yes, she would. Everything depended on it. "You promise to play checkers with Zechariah now and again and take Delia to the potty at night, and we'll see what happens from here."

"Fine."

"Fine."

Tamara let go of Laura's arm and ran up the steps to the door. She looked back, smiling, her eyes lit with certainty and laughter. Like Laura more than fifty years ago. No one could convince her to stay either. Until Eli did.

"I will be a doctor."

Laura forced a smile in return. "We'll see about that."

FIFTEEN

Spoon from plate to mouth. From mouth to plate. Zechariah concentrated. For all the effort it took not to fling the spoon across the front room, a person would think he was building a tower of glasses. But the effort proved to be worth it. Homemade vanilla ice cream and chocolate cake with cream cheese frosting. Because he sat by a blazing fire that filled Ivan's front room with the homey scent of hickory wood, Zechariah's ice cream was already melting. He didn't mind. Kimberly, her smile displaying her two missing front teeth, had informed him chocolate was her favorite. At seven, she still had time to come around to carrot cake, which, to his way of thinking, was the best.

His great-granddaughter shared her seventh birthday with Grandpa Ivan's fifty-second birthday, but Ivan didn't seem inclined to go around shouting "Happy birthday to me" at the top of his lungs the way little Kimberly did.

Zechariah's real mission — to find and convince Dillon and Micah to stay in Missouri — went nowhere fast. Neither boy had made an appearance so far and time was running out. Zechariah would have to return to Ben's when Esther decided to go since she had been his ride. She would decide if he could be responsible for Ben's children until Laura returned from her frolic.

Ridiculous.

Donald, his granddaughter Anna's special child, approached and climbed into Zechariah's lap without so much as a by-your-leave. He proceeded to claim Zechariah's spoon and help himself to a heaping bite of the ice cream.

"Hey, that's mine."

"Mine." Donald was eight, with the mind of a four- or five-year-old, and didn't talk much, but he had a smile that would knock a great-grandpa's socks off. He handed the spoon back to Zechariah. "Now yours."

"Are you sure? You don't want a bite of my cake too?"

Donald nodded so hard his hat shook. Zechariah made a show of cutting a large chunk of cake and loaded it onto the spoon.

"Are you sure? It *is* my cake."

Donald opened his mouth wide. Zechariah floated the load into his mouth while making train sounds. Chewing with his mouth still open, Donald grinned and gave Zechariah a big hug. "I like you."

That came from his mudder. Anna always was the most affectionate of Zechariah's grandchildren. She was nothing like her father, David, Zechariah's oldest living son. "I like you too, Donald."

"Donny."

"Donny."

The boy slid from Zechariah's lap and took the bowl of ice cream and cake with both hands. "Mine."

"Mine." Zechariah tugged back. "Go get your own."

"He already had his. Any more sugar and that boy will bounce off the ceiling."

Ivan approached and settled into the walnut rocker next to Zechariah's padded straight chair. He had two unopened presents in his arms. David followed behind. He might be Zechariah's oldest son, but at fifty-four, he looked no older than his brother. In fact, they could be twins.

"Mine." Donald tried to crawl into his uncle's lap. Ivan shook his finger at him. "It's not your birthday, Donny. It's me and

Kimberly's. Go play."

With a grin Donald shrugged and skipped away.

"What a blessing that boy is. Always smiling. Never complaining. A sweet soul. He reminds me of Martha. Even has her smile." Ivan's sad face didn't match the vigor with which he ripped the paper from the first package. A new church hat. The sadness disappeared, replaced with a glimmer of satisfaction. The man needed a new hat. "From my fraa. Only you could look that sour while eating ice cream. Did someone dump salt into it?"

"Have a little respect for your elders." Zechariah raised his voice to be heard over the conversations among a couple of dozen children ranging in age from two to twelve playing games on the floor, running from room to room, and generally providing the festive air to this birthday gathering. "It's gut. Everything your fraa makes is gut."

"Nadia made the cake. Our suhs made the ice cream."

"December is cold for cranking ice cream."

"Stays firm longer."

Zechariah stirred his creamy dessert. "I like it soft. Like Dairy Queen soft serve."

"Where's Abel?" David slouched on the

sofa and rubbed the fingers of his right hand as if in pain. "He never misses the opportunity for free ice cream and cake."

"He got a better offer. It's his granddaughter's birthday. His fraa makes a fine German chocolate cake and strawberry ice cream. His favorite." Zechariah studied his oldest son's face. His skin was pallid and dark circles ringed his eyes. "I thought you were home with the flu. You still look sickly."

"Danki." David grinned and pointed at his younger brother. "I'm fine and I wouldn't miss Ivan's birthday. He's getting old."

"I'll never be as old as you are." Ivan growled and tossed the hat at his brother, who caught it with one hand. "You're the most ancient one."

They both turned to look at Zechariah. "Almost."

They were horsing around to avoid the real topics of the day. Moving an old man around like a piece of secondhand furniture. And Ivan's two sons' plans to move to Indiana to work in a factory. Kimberly would go with her father, Micah. Ivan would miss his sons and his grandchildren. No doubt. Zechariah's hard line softened to a squiggle. "I know this isn't what you want either."

"I like vanilla just fine."

"Don't be dense."

"No point in beating a dead horse." David tossed the hat back to Ivan as if to say, "Your turn." "They're adults."

"I always treated my horses with respect. That's more than I can say for the way Dillon and Micah are treating Ivan or the way all of you are treating me."

"They want what's best for their families. We all do. Look at all these kinner." Ivan's arm swept out toward the room. "All your grands and great-grands. Moving around gives you a chance to spend time with them. That's a gift from Gott. For you. And for them."

When had Ivan acquired such wisdom?

Still, he couldn't read minds. He had no way of knowing Zechariah didn't want to be relegated to the children's table. He still longed for adult company. Even he hadn't known it until the checkers match.

The unfinished game.

The unfinished conversation.

A man could still want female company in his seventies, couldn't he? What would Marian say? She would say it was about time and to get off his keister and stop feeling sorry for himself. But she also would never have done the same. She told him so once. Should God call him home, she expected to live out her life taking care of grandchildren and great-grandchildren. But men needed women more. That was Marian. Always with a theory.

"I can help Ben and Rosalie. I'm not dead weight. Not yet."

"No one said you were, but someone has to take you to the doctor appointments and make sure you get your bath —"

"No need to list the things I can't do. I know."

Raised voices in the kitchen served as a signal that the two traitors were in the house. They sounded jovial and perfectly unaware of Zechariah's intent to bend their ears but good.

"Don't start with them." David shook his finger at Zechariah. "We're celebrating birthdays."

"And in a few weeks, we'll be eating a last meal with them before they drive off across the country." Zechariah set his bowl on the table between them and scowled at Ivan. "Open the other present. I need a cup of kaffi."

Micah appeared in the doorway before Zechariah could make it across the room. He held two more presents wrapped in brown sack paper in both arms. "Where is

199

the birthday girl? I have more booty for both her and Daed."

"I need a cup of kaffi. Come carry it for me. With my shaky hands I'll burn myself." This served as the first time Zechariah had used his disease as a tool. It might come in handy now and again. "Nadia will fix you some food. The venison chili is gut. So is the cornbread."

"Sounds gut. It's snowing again. Or trying. It doesn't know whether to sleet or rain." Micah followed him into the kitchen where Dillon stood talking to Micah's fraa, Jeanie. Kimberly was one of theirs.

Zechariah cocked his head toward the door. "Jeanie, Kimberly is opening presents. She wants you to come look."

Not a lie. Everyone liked an audience when opening presents. Better to *ooh* and *aaah.*

"Don't start." Dillon obviously wanted to get out in front of the argument. He grabbed a bowl and helped himself to a ladle of chili. "We've decided."

"Your daed told you my thoughts on this plan?"

"He tried, but don't blame him for not getting through to us." Micah plopped into a chair and yawned. "I was up all night with a sickly horse, so I'm too tired to have this discussion."

At least he hadn't called it an argument. "Then just listen." Zechariah held out his cup. Micah rose and took it without question. A minute later Zechariah had his coffee. "We're farmers. We've always been farmers. Staying close to the land keeps us close to Gott. And far from the world."

"I will miss farming." Dillon's tone held something akin to grief. "But I must provide for my family. Here, there's not enough land and too many big farmers who raise crops cheaper than we can. I'm not a carpenter or a leatherworker or a shop owner. I have two kinner." His face turned red. He ducked his head. "And another on the way."

Another child Zechariah wouldn't know. Distance would prohibit it. "All the more reason to stay here. Close to family."

"Change is a part of life." Micah returned to his seat. "We go carefully. We go slowly. But sometimes we concede that change is necessary."

"Whether we use battery-operated smoke detectors. Whether phones are allowed in our businesses. How long our beards will be or what color the girls' dresses may be." Zechariah managed to set his mug on the table without spilling a drop. A small victory. "But not working in a factory. That's not change. That's giving up a way of life."

"No one is giving up." Dillon crumbled corn bread into his chili, but he didn't take a bite. "Do you think we're looking forward to spending our days making a quota in a factory? We can go in before dawn, make eight campers or motor homes, and go home to our families."

"And it pays at least fifteen dollars an hour, or more," Micah chimed in. "It's not any different from building boats or cabinets and they've been doing that in Elkhart and La Grange for sixty or seventy years."

"But we haven't. We're farmers." He sounded old and tired. Even to himself. "Since when do we talk about how much we make? What about humility? What about equality? What about family time?"

"There will be more family time because we'll work fast and get home early. Not like working the fields sunup to sundown."

"Here you see your fraas and your kinner for every meal. They work in the fields with you. That won't be the case in Indiana."

"Joshua inherited the farm. He's the oldest son." Micah's tone didn't change, but his expression held frustration — with Zechariah or for their situation or both. "We can't all support our families on one farm. It can't be done. Not anymore."

"You're making it harder." Dillon set his bowl on the counter and went to the window. It was cloudy with condensation. With one callused finger he drew a box house with a smokestack and a sun overhead. Quick, sure strokes. "We'll go to Freeman tomorrow after church to inform him. He'll understand."

"He might, but he won't be at church." Cyrus's bulky frame squeezed through the doorway. Ivan and Nadia followed in his wake. "The announcement will be made tomorrow. Freeman is stepping down."

The words hung in the air. Dillon's mouth slid open. Micah dropped his spoon. It clanged on the floor.

A man didn't step down from being bishop for a puny reason. The drawing of the lots brought a lifetime obligation with it to be shed only in the case of death or debilitating disease. Zechariah remembered to breathe. No one spoke for two beats. The obligation fell to Zechariah as the elder family member and host to Cyrus, their deacon. He sat in the closest chair and motioned for the other men to sit as well.

"Is Freeman ill?" He pointed to his cup. "Have some kaffi. There's chili. Or cake if you're in need of sweets."

"Nee, not exactly. I'll have kaffi and cake."

Cyrus, never one to pass up sweets, shrugged off his coat and hung it on the back of his chair. "He has an eye disease with a peculiar name." His expression perplexed, the deacon studied a knot in the table's wood for a minute. Finally, he tapped on it with his fingernail. "Macular degeneration. That's it."

More quiet. Nadia went to the counter and fixed coffee and a slice of cake for Cyrus. She set them in front of him and left the room. This was man talk and Ivan would tell her about it later.

"An eye disease." Freeman wore thick, Coke-bottle glasses. But then so did Cyrus and Solomon. The bishop, deacon, and minister all wore glasses. They were three overgrown, big-bellied bears. Each with long gray beards, girth, and strong opinions. They worked well together. They'd been the church elders for so long, some of the young folks didn't remember them being anything else. "The middle of his sight is going, but the outside is still there. Eventually he won't be able to see your face."

"But he could see stop signs?" Ivan ventured the question. "Could he still drive a buggy?"

"He could see stop signs but not a car coming right at him." Cyrus sipped the coffee and gave a contented sigh. He picked up his fork. "He could still preach but he wouldn't be able to see the faces of the people in front of him."

They were quiet again, surely contemplating such an odd disease.

"Not being able to see doesn't make him unable to serve as bishop." Zechariah tackled the subject on everyone's mind. "Gott appointed him. He drew the lot."

"He has prayed. We have prayed." Cyrus shifted in his chair. His fingers, covered with wiry, white hair, gripped the fork and cut into the cake. "The Ordnung allows for him to step down because of illness or chronic disease. He believes this is a sign that Gott wants him to step aside. Not being able to see a man's expression, to see how he holds himself when he speaks, that is a problem when it comes to spiritual matters. It's not enough to hear the tone of voice to know the truth of a man's convictions."

"He'll retire to the dawdy haus then?" Micah slid into a chair next to Ivan. "When will we have the drawing of the lots?"

His bigger concern. Zechariah stifled the urge to smack him with a rolled-up newspaper. The young were in such a hurry. The Gmay would not rush such an important ritual.

A painful irritation flitted across Cyrus's face. He felt it too. He chewed and swallowed. Chocolate crumbs fell into his gray beard, but he didn't seem to notice. Taking his time, he slurped another sip of coffee. His lips smacked. "Usually we would wait until Communion, but we just had it in October. We'll have a meeting later this week and then the casting of lots with the ordination a week later if everyone agrees. We want to do it before Christmas."

"We plan to leave —"

"I've heard of those plans." Cyrus shook his fat finger at Micah. "You'll have to wait. The casting of lots is too important. Everyone needs to be here. Freeman will not hear your arguments. He'll leave it to the new bishop."

That new bishop would also hear Laura's great-granddaughter's freewill confession. Did she know yet? He would be a busy man. The names and faces of the men in the Gmay eligible for the lot floated through Zechariah's mind. Sixteen or more. Only five or six would be in the pool for the lot. From young men like Dillon and Micah to older ones like David. Better an older, wiser man. It wouldn't do to have someone like Micah who had one foot in Indiana and who thought working in a factory a good job for a Plain man.

God's hand moved in the Gmay. Human failings and plans would have to wait.

Sixteen

Squeals and shouts of laughter followed by the lusty cries of two babies heralded the arrival of Ben, Rosalie, and the twins. Zechariah settled into the rocking chair in Ben's front room and waited for the hubbub to die down. Laura hadn't returned from the Christmas present frolic. She was missing all the fun here. Maybe she wouldn't return. Maybe she thought her help wouldn't be needed after all or her family needed her more to untangle their issues. No, she wouldn't abandon her duties. Laura wasn't that kind of woman. What kind of woman was she? And what kind of thought was *that*? She was no Marian. For sure.

Zechariah batted the thoughts away like pesky fruit flies in summer and focused on the new arrivals. Grinning from ear to ear, Ben knelt, a baby in each arm, and introduced Delia, Samuel, and Christopher to their new sisters. With a half-stifled groan

Rosalie eased into a rocking chair. She looked wan.

"Welcome home." He lifted his voice over the children's excited chatter. "How are you? Happy to be here, I reckon?"

"Very happy." Rosalie's voice quavered. "It's gut to be home. The hospital is not a place you want to stay for a day, let alone a week."

Looking at her children probably reminded her that she would have no more. God had blessed her with five healthy children. All she needed in the Lord's way of thinking. "I didn't like it much. You'll heal faster at home with gut cooking and your kinner to wait on you."

Hospitals reminded Zechariah of Marian and her illness. Surgery, chemotherapy, and radiation did nothing to stall its forward march toward an inevitable end. Scars marked the spots where she'd once nursed her children. Her long hair fell to the floor in chunks. Her body had been skeletal at the end when she asked him to take her home. Glad to have her with him, Zechariah wrapped her in her grandmother's Log Cabin quilt and settled her on his lap in the rocking chair by the fire. She weighed less than a child. He leaned in to kiss her forehead and heard her soft murmur. Her last words. Something about Robert and Martha and the sun. It had been a cold, blustery November day. The sun hid itself behind a foreboding blanket of black clouds.

That night it rained ten inches and the Missouri River flooded.

"Look, they're here. They're here." Delia ran to Zechariah, tugged at his sleeve, and raced back to Ben. "I want to hold them."

He blinked away tears. A person must hoard happy days, store them up against the hurtful ones sure to come.

"Groossdaadi gets first dibs." Ben stood and offered the squirming, fussing girls to Zechariah. "Can you handle both or would you like to meet them one at a time?"

Zechariah ducked his head, not wanting his grandson to see his face. Daily he measured his lifetime and found it should've ended, but then God came along and gave him an event such as this to remind him he still lived. That he would live on in his children, grandchildren, and great-grandchildren, just as Marian did. They would know and remember him and any sparse bits of wisdom he imparted to them.

He held out his arms. "Let me see Mary first. They might be twins, but they deserve to have a man's full attention, one at a time."

Ben studied the girls in his arms. Rosalie laughed and hoisted herself from the chair. Hand on her puffy belly, she shuffled to her husband's side. "You have to learn. See, this is Mary." Her hand smoothed the blanket tucked around the noisy one in Ben's left arm. "She has that pucker in her chin and her eyes are a tiny bit farther apart. Mia has less hair. Plus Mary is the fussy one. Her cry is different, higher. And she's the oldest, by two minutes."

They both had a full head of dark hair, but Mia's forehead was longer. Zechariah could see that. He made note of Rosalie's words. A person didn't want to mix up twins. Later they would have their own personalities, but for now, they were nearly identical. He took Mary and held her straight out and up so they were face-to-face. Her lips scrunched. Her mouth opened. She wailed.

Her forehead crinkled, Rosalie hovered nearby.

"Don't worry. I won't drop her." Zechariah cocked his head toward the other chair. "Sit down and rest before you keel over."

Rosalie sat, but her gaze stayed on the baby.

"Hello to you, too, fussy one." He tucked

Mary in his arm and began to rock. "I'm Zechariah. I'm an old man. I'm your daed's groossdaadi. You don't have to remember all this right now. You can memorize the names later. I reckon as long as you have a clean diaper, a full belly, and a warm place to sleep, you're happy. So which is it now? Are you tired or hungry?"

He leaned over and sniffed. Her little button nose wrinkling, she sniffed back. "Unless my honker stopped working, it's not your diaper."

With great care he nestled her against his chest. *No arm jerking, Gott, please.* Despite the rocking, her eyes were wide and her face perplexed. One new experience after another. Zechariah tried to grasp the tail end of how that must feel. New to the world. Fresh. Everything big and loud and exciting, moreover frightening. She instinctively knew her mother would take care of her. Mother would feed her and Father would keep her safe. Everyone else was a stranger waiting to be experienced. A life just begun. "She looks like you, Rosalie."

"She looks like me," Delia volunteered. "I can hold her. I can feed her."

Christopher snorted. Ben shushed him. "You can help by bringing clean diapers to your mudder and helping wash the dishes and the clothes and sweeping the floor. How's that?"

"I'd rather rock her like Groossdaadi."

Zechariah stared at Mary, memorizing her tiny face and the way her arms flailed. Kind of like his did. She was a kindred spirit. "Pleased to meet you, Mary. You and your sister will like it here. You'll see. It's not so bad."

Ben laughed. "You would know."

A knot formed in Zechariah's throat. He tore his gaze from the baby and met Ben's head-on. "Did they tell you they want me to leave and go stay with Michael and his fraa?"

"It's not necessary for you to go anywhere." Ben didn't hesitate. His smile disappeared. "I told Ivan that. I told Michael that."

"Even though you have your hands full?"

"You're a help, not more work." Rosalie took Mary and eased back into her chair. "I told them the same thing when they came to visit me. They needn't fix something that's not broken."

Ben laid Mia in Zechariah's arms. Unlike her sister, she saw no reason to fuss. Instead, she stared at him with a serious, owlish gaze. "Welcome, welcome, Mia. I'm Zechariah. It's a mouthful, I know. You'll get the hang of it. No hurry."

Her rosebud lips pursed. She almost smiled. Zechariah was certain of it. He tickled her cheek and murmured sweet nothings. Her head turned and she began to root around his chest. He held her out. "Nee, bopli, you're mighty confused."

Rosalie and Ben laughed. The boys crowded the chair. Samuel tried to crawl onto Zechariah's lap. "You'll have to wait your turn." Zechariah smiled at the boy. "I promise you'll get one."

"Unless you want to go." Ben gathered Delia in his arms and gave her a big, fat kiss on top of her kapp. "Don't feel you have to stay here. The kinner will miss you. So will me and Rosalie."

Zechariah doubted that. "Don't blow smoke, suh."

Ben rolled his eyes just as he had done in his youth. "Where is Laura? She's needed too."

"I'm right here." The woman had a way of making an entry. Not something most Plain women would want. The front door stood open and Laura planted herself on the rug. She had her granddaughter, Tamara Eicher, in tow. "Look who's with me. Tamara's here to help."

The fact that Laura had one hand on the

girl's arm and the way Tamara grimaced told the story. Laura had bulldozed her into coming, and Tamara wasn't happy about it.

A man rocking a newborn baby in his arms was a man after Laura's heart. She tore her gaze from the sight of Zechariah, his face softened with love, cooing to his grandbaby. His trembling fingers smoothed her crib quilt. His soft murmurs of "hush-hush-hush-bopli-don't you cry" were like a lullaby to her ears.

She bent over and worked off her muddy boots. "Ruby sent a stuffed-pepper casserole. We waited for her to finish putting it together, or we would've been here sooner. All it lacks is baking. I'll run it into the kitchen."

"You sit." Rosalie intervened. "Christopher can do it."

The boy hopped up and took the casserole like he'd been given a fragile gift to carry. He was much more agreeable than Tamara.

She would get over it and Laura would convince her she was meant for this life. She had to. But first, Laura had to meet the babies.

"Let me at those boplin." Laura swooped down on Rosalie and held out her arms. She had no choice but to hand over the baby. "Gott is gut. You are a sweet little thing. Which one are you?"

"Mary, the fussy one. She has the higher cry, just so you know."

Zechariah was already an expert. Excitement brought color to his face and a brightness to his eyes. It looked good on him. Laura forced her gaze to the baby. "We'll fix that, won't we, Mary?" She drank in the scent of baby. She missed babies and their smell of milk and innocence. And a diaper that needed changing.

Maybe not that last thing. She glanced back to make sure Tamara hadn't skipped out on her. The girl was stubborn. She agreed to come and then nearly talked herself out of the idea while she packed her bag. The trip to Ben's had been a long one. "Look, Tamara, she's a tiny mite, isn't she? Have you ever helped deliver a baby this tiny?"

Tamara shrugged. "Iris's boy was six pounds."

"Mary is the bigger one." Rosalie leaned back in her chair and sighed. "Four pounds four ounces now. Mia weighs right at four pounds. They had to weigh four pounds in order to come home. I reckon they'll gain faster now that they're home and I'm home."

"Healthy boplin, that's the important thing." Laura cooed and talked as if Mary understood every word. If she didn't, she soon would. Laura squeezed past the boys so she could get a glimpse of Mia in Zechariah's arms. "They're identical, aren't they, except Mary has a bit of a tuck in her chin and her eyes are a little farther apart — just a tad."

"We just went over that." Seeming slightly irked, Zechariah clutched his twin to his chest. "Spend any time at all with them, and you'll see the differences."

Laura offered him a smile. He might not want to share this bounty of baby with her, but she didn't mind. It was a sign he cared, that he was engaged in this homecoming. Seeing him hold his newborn great-grandchild gave her hope for him. And made her heart flutter, something it hadn't done in years.

He could still care, and if he could still care about a baby, he could care about other things.

What things? Her mind did a swirling, dizzying loop-di-loop. About living. About finding a reason for getting up in the morning. For ending the pity party. For finding a reason to employ that lopsided grin in friendship.

Only that. Nothing more.

That and they had a checkers match to finish.

"I'll go unhitch our horse." Ben nodded at Tamara, who still stood by the door. "Shall I get yours too?"

"Jah. We're here to stay." Laura tried out her smile on Zechariah. His eyebrows popped up. Then a fraction of a second later, his lopsided grin appeared. Her stomach joined in the loop-di-loop. "Isn't that right, Tamara?"

"I told you I would help until the first of the year." Tamara's tone hadn't changed. Still begrudging. Who could stay stiff-necked at the sight of such baby bounty? She must've known it, because she paused and forced an unduly bright smile. "I can help you with your dressing, Rosalie, and bring the boplin to you when they're ready to eat and help the kinner with their baths."

"I'm not an invalid. The doctor said I need to get up and walk around. I'll recover faster."

"I reckon the doctor also told you not to lift anything heavier than five pounds." Laura rocked Mary in one arm as she turned to Rosalie. "We've got everything covered. All you have to do is feed the babies and rest."

"I've been resting for the last week —"

"You're not healed yet. I'm a midwife, remember?" Laura cocked her head toward Tamara. "Tamara might be one someday. It'll be gut practice. Now, go on, get yourself into your bedroom and lie down for a while. You look like the trip wore you out. We'll get supper."

Red crept into Rosalie's cheeks. "I really don't need to rest."

"You really do. I'll put Mary down in the cradle and Zechariah can put Mia down."

Zechariah's grin unfurled across his grizzled face. "She's asleep."

"Seems you have the touch. You'll be on twin duty." Laura memorized his face. She would remember it when he decided to be surly and uncooperative. "Especially when one's asleep and the other wants to cry. We want to keep the roar down to a minimum."

She turned to the children. "Boys, you have chores to do with your daed. Run along. You can see your schweschders when they wake up. Delia, you can pick up the toys and put them away. Then you can help me fix supper."

"I want to sleep with Mary and Mia."

"If you're quiet and lie still, you can lie on my bed with me." Rosalie eased from the chair. White lines etched themselves around

219

her mouth. "Let me have one of them."

"Nee." Laura shooed with one hand. "We'll make a little parade. When you wake up, supper will be served. We'll have the casserole, some canned corn, and warm bread. I made some oatmeal-raisin cookies yesterday."

"Anything not made in the hospital kitchen sounds *wunderbarr.*"

Rosalie led the slow-moving procession. It took a good five minutes, but soon everyone was resting. Tamara took her battered suitcase to the remaining free bedroom next to Laura's. It was the size of a storage closet just big enough for a single bed and a chair. All a young woman needed. Laura headed for the kitchen. Zechariah followed.

His expression preoccupied, he stood in the doorway. "Cup of kaffi?" She needed one herself. It had been a long day and there was more to be done. "It only needs to be heated."

"I can get it myself. You look tired." He shuffled to the stove, put the pot on the burner, and turned it on. He tugged a mug from the rack next to it. "It's possible Tamara could take this load and you could go back to your dawdy haus."

"Trying to get rid of me again?"

"Nee, nee." He studied the coffeepot as if

220

it might burst into flames any second. "We have checkers to finish."

"We do. I noticed the kinner moved the board."

"We might have to start over." Even though the coffee would still be cold, he poured a cup, added milk, and dumped in a liberal amount of sugar. Again no jerks. Some days were better than others. *Thank You, Gott, for giving him these gut days.* "But we have time. You'll be here awhile."

"But will you? I heard my suhs talking and it sounds like your suhs want you to stay with Michael."

His bemused expression disappeared. "Don't people have better things to do than gossip?"

"I hope you know Raymond and Aaron have no malicious intent." Even so Laura had scolded them with the same words. "I think they were wondering what they would do if I were sick."

"I'm not sick. I have Parkinson's."

"You won't concede you need help?"

"Would you?" His grin nowhere in sight, he shuffled to the window and gazed out. "I try to reconcile myself to this new me, but I don't recognize it."

"I understand that. Mary Kay and I talk about how we don't recognize the women we see reflected in the store windows in town. It must be someone else with the gray hair and wrinkles."

"You look pretty gut to me."

Laura opened her mouth. She closed it.

He didn't fill the space either.

The room seemed warm. Even a frigid north wind wouldn't cool it.

Stop being a twit. You're no schoolgirl.

The silence grew.

She opened the refrigerator and pulled out the casserole. "I need to get vegetables from the basement."

"I could do it."

"Nee —"

"Right. The stairs."

She opened the basement door.

"I didn't mean to speak out of turn." His hand caught the door and held it. "I don't know what I was thinking. The words just came out."

"I'm not so old I can't recognize a compliment." In her case the words seemed to scatter and she had to chase them down willy-nilly. "I was surprised."

"I'm not so old I can't give a woman a compliment."

Laura couldn't speak for Zechariah, but one thing seemed certain. They were both so old they were surprised they had the capacity to be embarrassed by someone of the opposite persuasion.

Compliments were nice. At any age. *"Pretty is as pretty does. Which is not much."* Her grandmother's words rang clear as a cold morning in her head.

Not that she had much to worry about in that department.

She slipped past him and trotted down the stairs. The dank basement air cooled her burning cheeks. "You're too old for shenanigans, woman."

So old she sometimes talked to herself.

SEVENTEEN

With pressing issues to be decided, no one wanted to wait until after Christmas to ordain a new bishop. Zechariah slid onto a bench in the front near Cyrus's fireplace where the oldest men sat. A unanimous vote at the Gmay meeting after church the previous week had set the ordination for one week with the understanding that everyone would spend the intervening time in prayerful consideration of whom they should nominate to fill the position and for God's intervention in the casting of the lots.

He rubbed his hands together, thankful for the fire's warmth and its scent that reminded a person life went on, no matter what. Icy snow pinged on the windows. Wind whistled in the eaves. The young whippersnappers got the back seats with only their body heat to keep them warm. The ordination would not take long. God would give them His answer.

Which was good because figuring out who to nominate had been a bee in his hive for an entire week. Zechariah swiveled and cast a surreptitious glance at the row behind him. His sons and grandsons began to fill the bench. David and his sons. Ivan and Elijah and their sons. His married grandsons, also eligible to be in the lot, included Micah, Dillon, Carl, Ben, Mark, Seamus, and George. They were quiet. No chitchat today. No ribbing one another about falling asleep during a sermon. Serious faces. Any one of them could walk from Cyrus's house as the Gmay's new bishop.

That didn't mean they were equally good candidates. Each man had his good points and bad, as did all men. Not one was a slug — a lazy man — and all of them were able to make a decent decision. Still, that didn't make him a good bishop. A bishop would officiate at weddings, funerals, Communion, and the foot-washing ceremonies. He would work with the deacon and minister to deal with offenders who violated the Ordnung or failed to keep biblical law. The nominees would have no special training or desire to hold the position. The chosen one submitted to the will of God and figured it out as he went along. It took a certain kind of man to do that.

A man God already had picked out. *Gott, who is it? Who would You have nominated so You can do Your work?*

Another good thing about the Parkinson's — it meant Zechariah was not a candidate.

Abel Danner plopped onto the bench with a grunt. "Long time no see. What's the matter? You look constipated. You know prune juice is gut for that."

As Zechariah's oldest friend, Abel felt obligated to give Zechariah his honest opinion. Even when it felt like salt in an open wound coming from a man who stood tall and broad shouldered. He walked with an easy stride at seventy-three. Except for the snowy white of his beard and full head of hair, he never seemed to age.

Which wasn't his fault. "I feel fine. Where have you been?"

"My fraa insisted I use the bad weather to paint the whole house." A pained expression on his face, he craned his head from side to side and rolled his shoulders. "You don't know how many muscles and joints you have until all of them ache. Simple jobs seem to take longer than they used to."

At two years younger than Zechariah, Abel still had two things Zechariah didn't — his health and his wife. Zechariah would never hold it against the man. God's plan for him was different. "You should've let me know. I could've helped."

"You'd be as much help as a jackrabbit at a coyote hunt." Abel never danced around Zechariah's disease. "Jessica wants the paint on the walls, not the floor and the windows and the ceiling."

"I can slap paint on a wall. It doesn't matter if the lines are straight as long as you get all the spots covered." The less work Zechariah did, the less use his muscles received and the more they turned to gelatin. "You just think you do a better job than me."

"My suhs came over and their fraas. My dochders and their manns. It was a regular family reunion." Abel shook his grizzled head and laughed. More of a bark than a laugh, really. "It took twice as long than it would have if they'd left me on my own. I think they think I'm too decrepit to paint a wall by myself. I might fall over dead. My heart might stop."

His eyes rolled back in his head and his arms flung out, Abel pretended to keel over on the bench.

Not only did Abel have all his faculties, all six of his children were alive and well. Jealousy was a sin. A terrible sin when the man next to him had stood with him by the grave of his sweet special child when she passed of pneumonia. He'd helped build the casket for Robert's burial. He'd been silent but ever present, ready to help with every need at Marian's passing. The most stalwart of friends, he deserved his good fortune. "Sit up, you old coot. You're embarrassing me."

"How are the new boplin?"

"They cry, they poop, they eat, they sleep."

"Gut for them. Sounds like a fine life."

"Do you know who you'll nominate?"

"That's for me to know and you to find out." Abel settled back on the bench and scratched at his voluminous beard as if he had lice. "Why are you looking so grim?"

"Nothing."

"I know you, old man. What's up? Is it that Laura Kauffman? I heard she's staying at the house —"

"It has nothing to do with Laura. Keep your voice down." He glanced back. Ivan glared. He glared back. He scooted closer to Abel and lowered his own voice. "They want to move me again."

"I know they're your suhs, but they aren't the sharpest tools in the shed sometimes." Abel swiveled and added his glare to Zechariah's. Turning back around, he leaned toward Zechariah. "I'm telling you. Come stay with me and my fraa. We'd have a dandy time. Card games, checkers, chess, popcorn, and apple cider every night. We'll drive the buggy, chop the wood, hunt, bird-watch whenever we please. I'll be your cover. You can tell them I'm doing the driving."

It sounded beautiful, enticing, a perfect way to spend his last years on earth if he couldn't spend them with Marian. A perfect plan with one singular flaw. Abel's wife didn't deserve a third wheel hanging around her buggy this late in life. She had one man to whip into shape every day. She didn't need two. Especially one who had trouble walking down the hall to the bathroom and would only get worse. "What makes you think I want to squander my last breaths on this earth talking to an old geezer like you?"

"Fine. You want to be a secondhand piece of furniture on the back of your grandson's buggy, you old booger." Abel's grin remained amiable, which meant the discussion wasn't over. The man knew how to worry a bone until it was crushed like the best barnyard hound. "I think your son David would make a gut bishop."

"Hush." Zechariah stifled a groan. David was a good man. A little too open to change, but thoughtful about it. He was getting ready to settle into the dawdy haus and let his sons Seamus and George take over the farm. He'd always gone his own way, much like Zechariah. They were too much alike to be close, butting heads over every little thing for years. "I don't know if he has the right frame of mind for it."

"His mind is sharp and he's faithful."

"We can hear you." Ivan leaned forward and muttered in Zechariah's ear. "It's best to keep your opinions on this to yourselves."

Zechariah glared at Abel. He grinned back. "Sorry." He was about as sorry as a coyote who chowed down on the first ripe cantaloupe in the garden.

Freeman plopped onto the bench and laid a wooden cane between them.

Another reason to zip it up. His hours as bishop winding down, Freeman didn't look any different. In fact, he looked as contrary as he always did.

"I reckon I better sit between you two old farts or you'll be arguing in the middle of the lot."

A man didn't argue with the bishop, even if he was about to retire. And go blind.

Zechariah nodded. Could Freeman see his nod or had this strange disease already progressed to a place where people were strangers until he heard their voices?

"I can see you both fine."

Freeman's years as bishop had taught him much about the way people thought and acted.

"That's gut. Although I suppose not seeing our ugly mugs would probably have its upside too."

"Speak for yourself." Abel didn't understand the concept of keeping his voice down. The women on the other side of the aisle probably heard every word he spoke. "You may be an old fart, but my fraa says I'm as handsome as the day she married me."

Freeman guffawed. "Maybe I'm not the only one whose sight is going bad."

He hadn't lost his sense of humor, an important attribute for a man who'd been bishop for almost thirty years. Many of the folks in the room didn't remember any other bishop. Of course, he didn't have to be worried. His name would not be in the lot. He could laugh. Zechariah managed a chuckle as well.

He let a few seconds pass, then leaned closer. "I'd like to bend your ear about something."

"No point in it now."

No pity emanated from the words. Freeman might be free of his bishop duties, but he was embarking on a new season in his

231

life. One that would be difficult and dark. Zechariah recognized a fellow sojourner. "Your advice is always gut, whether or not it carries the weight of a bishop."

"I can give you advice." Abel leaned in too, his big ears flapping. "Why didn't you ask me?"

"Hush up, old man, and let Freeman talk. Mind your own business while you're at it."

"I'm not in the advice-giving business anymore." His Coke-bottle glasses and long, gray beard made it hard to read Freeman's thoughts. "It will be for the new bishop to decide if your grandsons are doing the right thing. Truth be told, it's gut to know someone else will wrestle with understanding Gott's will in such situations."

His sonorous voice carried. Zechariah glanced back. Ivan scowled and shook his head. Zechariah shrugged.

That Freeman recognized God's role in the future of the Gmay was a comforting thought. What were God's thoughts on Zechariah's future? Despite himself, Zechariah's gaze swung to the other side of the room. Laura sat with her daughters and their families as well as Ben's womenfolk. Laura held one of the twins, asleep from the looks of her. Laura's head bowed as if in prayerful thought. With fussy newborns in the house, along with a whiny Delia who didn't seem to think the babies were as much fun as she had first thought, Laura had managed to avoid being alone with him again. She bustled about doing laundry and cooking as if it took every minute of her time.

It had been a simple compliment. Why turn it into a big deal?

Tamara cared for the babies and the children like the best of mothers, all smiles as she tried to teach Delia and Samuel to *botch*. Their attempts at the clapping games had tears of laughter running down her face. If he didn't know better, Zechariah would think she was happy in her Plain way of life.

The checkers he'd reassembled to the best of his memory remained untouched. Dark came early and everyone went to bed early.

"Then let me ask you about something else." He kept his voice low and close to Freeman's ear, low enough that it couldn't be heard in the next row back. No doubt Abel's ears worked just fine. Everything about him did. Which shouldn't bother Zechariah. But it did. In the deepest, darkest place in his heart, it did. Another reason he couldn't stay with Abel and Jessica. He didn't need his face rubbed in their healthy, happy marriage. It might — despite his best efforts — sour a lifelong friendship. "Is it truly necessary for widows and widowers to remarry?"

Abel sputtered. Zechariah gritted his teeth and glared in his most menacing manner. Abel stuck his hand over his mouth, but his shoulders shook like a man having a fit.

"That also is Gott's will. If His plan is for a man or woman to remarry, then so be it. Men are meant to have fraas. A woman needs a mann. Kinner need parents." Despite the measured answer, Freeman's nose wrinkled. He shoved his glasses up his nose with his stubby index finger. "Such dilemmas are worthy of prayer, to be sure."

"Even if the man is old and diseased?" Zechariah lifted his arm and his hand shook. "Like me. What use would I be as a mann now?"

"Gott's plan will reveal itself."

A handy answer.

Zechariah subsided. Freeman obviously had moved past his role as bishop to this new place in his life where he wasn't required to offer advice at the drop of a hat.

Better to spend this time wrestling with his nomination. Ignoring Abel's attempts to get more information about the widows in his life, Zechariah bowed his head and closed his eyes. David looked like neither Marian nor Zechariah. Marian claimed he was more like his father, quick to anger and quick to apologize. He had the most heart, according to his mother. He cared deeply and let it show. His rumspringa had proved the most difficult to navigate for parents who could only watch and wait. He waited until twenty-three to marry, then chose Lee-Ann Luther, a young girl of eighteen whose rumspringa had been equally eventful.

Thirty-plus years later, they were the content parents of half a dozen children and several grandchildren.

No bad reports, but nothing that led Zechariah to believe David would make a good bishop.

Ivan had years of wisdom and experience, but he tended toward stubbornness that sometimes resulted in a situation being allowed to progress when compromise would be better. Compromise didn't enter into his vocabulary. He was more like Zechariah than Marian.

What would Marian do in this situation? She would pray and keep her counsel to herself. Zechariah sighed.

Elijah was steady and a hard worker. He had a quiet sweetness about him that made him most like Marian. He also looked more like her with his blond hair and hazel eyes. His rumspringa had been short with no doubt that he would choose baptism. He married June soon after. They had seven kinner. His had been a quiet, uneventful existence — one that honored their way of life. But did it prepare him to be bishop?

Zechariah sighed again.

"Don't make it harder than it is." Freeman spoke as if the conversation had never ceased. "Examine your heart of hearts."

A strange thing for a man like Freeman to say. Zechariah nodded and stared at his boots. His heart of hearts said Laura's son Abraham would be well suited to the position. Calm, smart, well versed in Scripture, a good husband and father. Never a sharp word. Helpful to those in need. Kind. Heedful of the Ordnung.

No one would know who Zechariah nominated. It wasn't a matter of familial relationship. Or not wanting to put new burdens on a son. Or a matter of pride in having a son chosen.

He would not sigh again. Every adult in the room had the same dilemma.

"It's time." Cyrus clomped to the front of the room. "I'll be at the kitchen door to record your nominations. Come by one by one. Keep your voice down. Solomon will record the nominations. As soon as you're done, we'll do the arithmetic and begin the drawing of the lots."

It took about ten minutes to file by the door. Zechariah went third behind Abel and Freeman. Cyrus's expression did not change. He simply nodded.

Minutes later they were done. If a man received two or more votes, his name would be entered in the lot.

The minutes ticked by. Abel wiggled like a five-year-old. Freeman stared at him. He rolled his eyes. A child whimpered. Someone coughed. Another person sneezed. Heads were bowed in silent prayer. The scent of seasoned walnut burning filled the air, mingled with a sense of awe and God's presence.

Solomon and Cyrus entered the front room and went to tables set up near the fireplace. There, they placed a series of *Ausbands* held shut with thick rubber bands.

Zechariah counted as the worn hymnals were laid side by side on the table. Seven. A good number for the lot.

Inside the front cover of one of those books would be a slip of paper containing Proverbs 16:33: *"The lot is cast into the lap, but its every decision is from the LORD."*

Zechariah repeated the verse in his head

again and again.

Cyrus turned and faced the gathering.

One by one they were called to the front of the room. First, Ivan Stutzman. Zechariah's stomach flip-flopped. A tiny gasp from Ivan's wife, Nadia. Her hand went to her mouth. Ivan's stoic expression didn't change as he tromped through the narrow aisle between benches.

Abraham Kauffman.

Laura's son. His wife began to cry. Abraham's stoicism matched Ivan's. A man submitted to the Lord's will.

Aidan Graber. Another good choice. A man who did what was right rather than what came easy. He was younger than bishops usually were, but his nomination signified the respect his church family accorded him.

Silence simmered as he strode to the front to stand next to the other men, who schooled their faces in neutrality. Not a single noise, not even from the babies held in their mothers' arms.

Andrew Miller. He had his hands full with his son Kenneth's cerebral palsy, but a good choice otherwise.

Cyrus cleared his throat and hitched up his pants. "Josiah Ropp." Mary Katherine's son. Not a bad choice. "Thomas Ropp."

Mary Katherine's oldest son. Another stubborn man not capable of compromise. Surely that was it. Two sons from the Ropp family. The odds went up of them having a new bishop in their midst.

This was not about odds. Zechariah forced himself to breathe. *Gott, Thy will be done in all things. Guide us and direct us. Show us Your will.*

Cyrus cleared his throat. "The final name is Ben Stutzman."

Zechariah jerked his head up. Had he heard right? Ben was too young. He had so much responsibility on his shoulders now. Burdens. Other members of the Gmay respected him, no doubt, for how he handled his burdens.

Zechariah respected him. But to add to those burdens now? He peeked at the women's side. Nadia's cheeks were apple-red, her face white. She managed a quivering smile. Her husband and her son. His son and his grandson. The Stutzmans had as much chance of having a bishop in their family as the Ropps.

One Stutzman was sitting on the front bench weighing the results of this lot by how it would impact him, instead of relying on God's plan to do what was best for the entire Gmay.

Thy will be done. Thy will be done. Thy will be done.

One of the twins began to cry. From the sound of it, fussy Mary. Laura's voice gently shushed her.

"You may kneel now."

Cyrus asked each man to affirm his beliefs. That done, the congregation knelt for silent prayer. Grunting, Zechariah eased from the bench, hand on the solid wood, and managed to hit his knees without a mishap. *Thank You, Gott.* So did Freeman, but with a lot more grunting. Abel popped down as if ready to do handsprings.

Gott, we yield to Your will. You hold this Gmay in Your hands. We submit to Your will for its future. And for mine.

Zechariah tacked on that last bit as people scrambled to their feet. They were anxious for the final step. So much rode on it. For the Gmay, for the man God appointed to His service, and for the man's family.

His life would no longer be his own. Weddings, funerals, Communion, every individual problem in the Gmay became his problem. He would preach. He would mediate disputes. He would run meetings. The stakes were high.

Looking as if he'd rather pat a rattlesnake, Andrew's hand wavered over one book, then

240

snatched up the one next to it. Ben didn't hesitate. His expression grim, he took the one directly in front of him.

Then Cyrus started down the row. He opened each book. The naked look of relief on Ivan's face quickly disappeared, hidden behind a solemn look of solidarity for his fellow candidates.

No slip of paper in Aidan's book. An audible sigh of relief from Bess.

Next Ben. A little older than Aidan, but one with greater responsibilities at home.

Cyrus opened his hymnal. He picked up the small piece of tablet paper.

Proverbs 16:33.

A gasp ran through the crowd. Quiet sobs followed.

Of relief, no doubt, from some wives, but also in tearful recognition of the importance of what had just occurred. Zechariah craned his neck to see Rosalie. She handed a twin to Tamara and began the trek to the front of the room as the other men, now free of the ritual, made their way to their seats. She wasn't one to like attention. At their wedding, she had been green around the gills with nerves, not about marrying Ben, but about standing in front of two hundred guests to do it.

His shoulders hunched, Ivan passed by.

His gaze connected with Zechariah's and his eyebrows lifted and fell. What must he be thinking? Relief at dodging the bullet, or a tiny germ of pride that the congregation had seen fit to nominate his son for the position? Pride shouldn't enter into it, but a man was only human. Along with the knowledge that Ben now faced a lifetime of service with no remuneration and no training.

With a solemn face Cyrus ran through Ben's new duties. Ben's shell-shocked face was reminiscent of the one he had the day he came to tell them about the twins' birth and his wife's condition. He could be the last one in the room to think he might end up as bishop of one of half a dozen church districts in the Jamesport area.

"Be faithful to your new calling, Ben Stutzman." Cyrus shook Ben's hand and bestowed on him the holy kiss. "Godspeed."

The flood began. Freeman Borntrager and his wife went forward to do the same, with Rosalie receiving the holy kiss from Dorothy. Solomon Weaver and Diana were next, followed by the other nominees, and then the rest of the Gmay. No smiles, no congratulations, a simple salutation that reflected respect for the responsibilities that now rested on Ben's shoulders.

Zechariah edged toward the front door. A breath of fresh air might blow away the intense sense of sorrow that inundated him.

His steps took him to the porch. A fierce wind blew through his wool coat and froze his ears and nose. To be numb from head to toe seemed preferable to the sense of emptiness that made his body feel hollow.

"Daed."

He turned. His heavy steps thudding on the damp wood, Ivan joined him.

His son's face said it all.

Zechariah's days at Ben's house were numbered.

EIGHTEEN

Even the twins were quiet on the ride home from the ordination. Laura kept one hand on each blanket in their baskets. It warmed her fingers and gave her a sense of comfort in their blissful assurance that someone else took care of them.

Ivan had taken the boys in his buggy, making the silence more pronounced. Tamara went to supper with her parents. Her brother would bring her to the house later. Zechariah sat on the other side of the babies' basket. He leaned back, eyes closed, as if sleeping or praying. Occasionally he shook his head as if having a conversation with someone Laura couldn't see.

It didn't strike her as odd. She often caught herself doing it. That he hadn't uttered a single word during the entire ride bothered her a little more. Was he thinking about his comment that she looked good? She tried not to obsess about it. Surely his thoughts were of issues more substantial. Her thoughts scurried hither and yon, like squirrels gathering acorns before the arrival of a long, frigid winter. She wanted to gather them and examine each one. She wanted her questions answered. Most likely Zechariah did too.

By the time they arrived at the house, Laura's nose felt like an icicle and her toes ached. Anxious for a hot cup of peppermint tea with lemon and the warmth of the kitchen stove while she cooked supper, she hopped from the buggy in the gathering dusk and helped Rosalie down. The white puffs of their breaths mingled in the icy air. The sleet turned to snow clothed the grass, the corral fence, the porch railings, and the windowsills in a lacy, crystalline covering as if God had taken up embroidery.

Rosalie took Mia and Laura clutched Mary to her chest, her crib quilt covering the baby from head to toe. Ben hoisted Delia, who'd passed out the second they left Cyrus's, to his shoulder and trudged along behind them. No one spoke. Rosalie's face reflected the same shock and disbelief as her husband's. Ben was a good man, solid in every way, but this would take adjustment — both mentally and emotionally. And physically. He had to take care of his family and meet his new obligations as bishop. Starting immediately.

His boots making a shuffling sound in the snow, Zechariah brought up the rear.

Laura tried to corral her thoughts. So she had an inside track, staying at the bishop's house. She couldn't take advantage and bend his ear about Hannah's situation. Could she? And then there was Tamara. She might come back. Or she might sneak away to start her new life early. Another thought Laura refused to entertain.

She sighed and tugged the sagging blanket over Mary's cherubic face. The baby's cheeks were pink and her nose scrunched up. Her mouth moved as if sucking. Eating even in her sleep. The girl had a voracious appetite.

Inside the house, it wasn't much warmer. Ben began to light lamps, while Laura and Rosalie headed to the bedroom to put the babies down for the night. Zechariah's footsteps disappeared to parts unknown.

"It'll be all right." Rosalie's words were more a question than a statement. "We'll be fine."

"Of course. Gott makes no mistakes." Laura laid the baby in the cradle next to her sister. "The lot has been cast."

"Ben will be a gut bishop." Rosalie's

round face colored. Her plump fingers fluttered to her lips. "I don't mean that in a prideful way. Just that he's fair and even tempered. He never loses his sense of humor either."

She spread her hands out as if to encompass everything in their world that required a good sense of humor. And a sense of equilibrium. God controlled all things.

"Agreed."

Rosalie slipped from her black wool coat and hung it on the hook next to her small wardrobe of dresses in dark blue, lilac, evergreen, and chocolate brown. "One gut thing will come of it, I reckon. Zechariah will move in with Michael and his fraa."

"What's so gut about that?" The words escaped more sharply than Laura intended. "I mean —"

"I thought you'd be happy." Rosalie's forehead wrinkled. A smile spread across her face, still round from childbearing. "He makes a lot of extra work, but then maybe you don't mind that."

"I don't know what you mean." Laura edged toward the door. "I'll start supper."

"No hurry. The kinner filled up on cookies and peanut butter sandwiches. I think Samuel ate four of them. Zechariah has his moments, I guess. When Ben and I were first married, before Marian passed, Zechariah was the storyteller and could he tell some whoppers. His grands loved it. Ben and I would go visiting and stay past sundown, listening to him fill up the kinner with stories of the whale he caught at Stockton Lake or the five-hundred-pound grizzly bear that invited him to dance. Silliness, but he told the stories with such a solemn tone and straight face, they believed every word."

Laura could imagine it. She'd caught him a time or two with that twinkle in his eye paired with a solemn look that said he was pulling Delia's leg. "I don't know why you're telling me this."

"Because I hate seeing folks alone who could be together, giving each other company in their old age."

"I'm not old."

"That's the part of my statement you want to argue over?" Rosalie chuckled as she folded blankets around the sleeping babies and straightened. "If you don't think it's a gut idea for Zechariah to move, say so."

"It's not my place."

"You're taking care of all of us right now. That makes it your place."

"I'll make the tea and get supper started." Laura trotted from the bedroom like that grizzly bear was chasing her and not because he wanted to dance. Rosalie saw far too much.

Ben stood in the kitchen, a glass of water in one hand and a bottle of aspirin in the other. "Bit of a long day." He tossed two pills in his mouth and took a long draught of water. "Delia went to get her doll. She wants to help make supper."

"It has been a long day. I'll make something simple so everyone can get to bed early." Laura opened the refrigerator door and peered in. She closed it. "We all have faith. You'll do fine."

Ben set the glass on the counter. His back to her, he wiped his mouth with his sleeve. "Gott's will." He turned. His face was lined with doubt. "I'm twenty-eight years old. A lot of years ahead, Gott willing, to figure it out. A man hopes he doesn't make too many mistakes before he knows what he's doing."

"You'll have Cyrus and Solomon to help. They won't leave you dangling in the wind."

"You're right. It's a sin to worry." He burped. A look of pain came and went. "Indigestion. Headache. I think my mind is bleeding over on my body."

"Gott will give you all the guidance you need."

She pulled leftover ham from the refrigerator and a bowl of boiled potatoes. Fried hash for starters.

"I get the sense you might have something to say about it too."

"Not my place."

"That's what Rosalie says right before she jumps in and meddles." The lines cleared and he smiled. "I'm your bishop. If there's something on your mind, get on with it. Time's a wasting."

A good start. Very stern and stout. Smiling, Laura set out the cutting board and began to cube the potatoes.

"Tamara or Hannah?" The sharp nudge in his voice mingled with amusement. "Or Zechariah?"

No doubt, Ben would be a good bishop. He already had his finger on the Gmay's pulse.

Where to start?

"I don't believe I've ever seen you speechless, Laura."

"Not speechless, weighing my words. Each person you mentioned is important to me and important to their families and to the Gmay."

"I know that. Be assured that no snap decisions will be made."

"You know about Hannah."

"Things like that spread like poison ivy in

a community like ours."

"And Tamara?"

"Only bits and pieces, enough to know her life in faith is at risk." He leaned against the counter and crossed his arms. Suddenly, he looked older and wiser than his years, as if the bishop's yoke had wreaked its havoc in a few short hours. "Maybe it's better to talk of Zechariah's future. That decision affects my family and I could use some words of wisdom."

"Even from a woman?"

"Especially from a woman who is of age and who has lost her mann and a suh and knows what infirmity can do to mind and body."

Laura dropped the knife on the cutting board and faced Ben. "Don't make him move. It will only serve to worsen his malaise."

"What is his malaise? He's never been one to shy away from his burdens. After Groossmammi died and he got the diagnosis of Parkinson's, he changed. He shriveled up."

"He feels unwanted, unneeded, and no longer useful. He has nothing to contribute. Handing him around from family to family isn't helping."

"He is wanted. Michael and Robert are arguing over who gets him next."

"He doesn't see it that way."

"He's determined to take the low road. That was never him before. He told tall tales and jokes and played practical jokes on the kinner. Now he's contrary all the time."

"There's a strong spirit under the rust and the corrosion of feeling sorry for himself." Laura diced thick slices of ham and tossed the pieces in a skillet with melted lard. The scent of ham frying made her mouth water. "Give him a job to do. Make him feel useful."

"This isn't bishop business. It's family business." The slightest quiver in his voice gave him away. His grandpa's hurt was Ben's hurt too. "Don't tell anyone this, but Groossdaadi was my favorite. I wanted him here. I argued for it. The decision to move him won't be mine alone."

"But you have no objection to him staying here."

"None, but that may change as his disease worsens and my duties multiply."

"Give it time. You may find he can be helpful around here while you're busy with those duties."

"I'll give it some thought."

A very bishop-like answer. Ben, the farmer, father, and husband, seemed to turn into the bishop before her eyes.

"I reckon you'll give Hannah's situation thought as well."

His expression bleak, Ben smoothed his beard. He shook his head. "Hers is a sin I cannot speak to you about."

Heat rushed through Laura. She ducked her head and dumped the chopped potatoes in with the ham. The stove's heat warmed her face and hands. "I know it's delicate. I only wanted to say that she's welcome to stay in the dawdy haus for the bann that will surely follow her confession. I'm here and if you don't need me here, I can stay with Ruby and her mann."

"Understood."

The pause lengthened. Ben cleared his throat. Laura concentrated on stirring the hash. She added salt and pepper with a liberal hand. "She's not a bad girl."

"Nee."

"The boy is leaving her to face her punishment alone."

"His parents spoke with Cyrus last week. He shared the conversation with me briefly this afternoon. I'll be meeting with them as well."

"You'll do what's best for them and for the Gmay."

"I will do my best."

"I should get some canned corn and green

253

beans from the cellar."

"Do you smell smoke?" Sniffing, Ben straightened. He frowned. "It's getting smoky in here."

Gray, hot smoke rolled through the doorway. Laura inhaled and coughed. Seasoned oak. "The fireplace!"

NINETEEN

Laura bolted toward the door, but Ben's youth won out. He shot across the hallway ahead of her toward the front room.

Acrid smoke choked the living room. One hand over his mouth, Zechariah squatted by the fireplace. He held a poker in the other hand. Flames crackled and popped. Sparks and flames shot embers like Roman candles around him. Some landed on his coat sleeves and glowed as they tried to take hold and burn.

"We need water!" Zechariah shouted. "Get buckets of water. The flue is on fire."

No time for anything. No time to think. *Gott, save this house. The kinner. The boplin. Gott?* The kitchen seemed a million miles away. Water, too far away. Laura grabbed a blanket from the sofa. Everything slowed to a nightmarish pace. Her legs and arms didn't want to cooperate. *Faster, faster.* The young, agile woman inside her screamed in

255

frustration. *Move, move. You have to move.* She stumbled forward.

Ben's big body cut her off.

"Get back, get back!" He grabbed something that looked like a paper-covered log and shoved Zechariah aside. Zechariah fell back and caught himself with one arm. Ben removed a cap, scratched a black button with the cap, and dropped it inside the fireplace alongside the fire. In seconds that lasted a hundred years, the fire subsided, its snarls gone.

Life snapped back into place. Laura would make supper. The kinner would bicker. The babies would cry and Rosalie would shush them.

Miraculous? Or simply quick thinking? No matter. Zechariah was safe. They were all safe.

Danki, Gott. Laura brushed away thoughts of what might have happened and dashed forward. Her traitorous body cooperated now without a hint of mutiny.

She knelt next to Zechariah. Black ashes smudged his hands and face. Red patches of burned skin marred one cheek, his forehead, a spot on his bald head, and both hands. He smelled of singed hair and burned cotton. "Ach. You're burned. You're hurt."

"I'm fine. I don't know what happened." The smoke roughened Zechariah's voice, making him sound as if he had a cold. He coughed so hard he retched. "The fire was down to a bed of coals. I didn't want the boplin to be cold. I added a few logs and boom, it took off."

"We had the start of a chimney fire." Ben whirled and stood over them. The muscle jumping above his jaw said he gritted his teeth. He was trying not to explode like the fire had. "I told you not to mess with the fire. Several times. I take care of the fire. Not you."

His face as red as the burned patches on his hands and face, Zechariah hacked and coughed for a few seconds. "I only added a couple of logs. They're seasoned wood. They should've been fine. When was the last time you cleaned the chimney?"

"I checked the flue yesterday. It was fine." Fear disguised as anger boiled over in Ben's words. He glowered at them both, as if Laura had some role to play in this near disaster. "You have to be careful adding logs to coals. They have tremendous heat."

"I've been taking care of fires for sixty-plus years. Before you were a gleam in your mudder's eyes, young man."

"Accidents happen." Laura grabbed Zechariah's hand and examined the burns. Painful, fiery blisters sprang up across the back and on his palm. "Gabbing about it doesn't help. Let me get some salve on these burns. I think I have some B&W. We can jaw about it later."

"He wanted to put water on a chimney fire. You don't put water on it. We learned that at the Volunteer Fire and Rescue Community Day last year. Don't you remember?" Ben took a long breath. No doubt counting to ten in his head. "That's when I bought the chimney fire extinguishers they recommended. You were with me. Do you remember that?"

A befuddled look on his soot-covered face, Zechariah shook his head. He snatched his hand from Laura's grip. He rolled over and dragged himself to the nearest chair. Propping his forearms on it, he pushed up until he could stand. "It was a chimney fire. That's caused by a buildup of soot that turns into creosote, which is highly flammable."

"You do remember." Ben turned his back. He grabbed the fireplace brush and began to sweep up the ashes and remnants of wood. His shoulders hunched. Finally, he turned to face his grandfather. He seemed to measure his words. "You also remember

— I know you do — that I told you to let me handle the fireplace duties."

"Chimney fires happen all the time." Scrambling to her feet, Laura fought to broker peace. Both sides of the discussion presented themselves to her. "Mary Katherine's dochder and mann had one last week. Remember, they had to call Fire and Rescue. It spread upstairs and into the attic area. They had all that smoke and water damage."

"Which is why I keep the chimney fire extinguisher handy, should the fire spread beyond the fireplace, and I sweep the fireplace regularly." Ben's grim expression didn't ease. "I know how to keep the flue clean."

"I only added wood." Zechariah held his arm to his chest. A look of pain mixed with misery shot across his face. "If you kept the fireplace and chimney clean it wouldn't have happened."

"I know you were trying to help. But you did something I specifically asked you not to do. Your actions put the kinner in danger. The boplin in danger. Do you know what damage smoke could do to their little lungs?" Ben stopped and inhaled. His Adam's apple bobbed. "They were born early with underdeveloped lungs. This is very dangerous."

"I know that. I wouldn't do anything to hurt them."

"You endangered them, Groossdaadi."

"I didn't mean —"

"I know you had gut intentions." Biting at his lower lip, Ben stared at his boots. He raised his gaze level with Zechariah's. They both seemed to have forgotten Laura's presence. "Ivan approached me after the meeting today about moving you to Michael's. I told him there was no need."

He glanced back at the blackened fireplace. "Now, I realize he's right. It's time."

No. Zechariah only wanted to be useful. A young man like Ben couldn't see far enough into the future to know he, too, one day would be old and frail of body, but not mind — God willing. "Don't do something now you'll regret later —"

"Hush, woman. Leave it be. It's his *haus.*" Zechariah tottered to the wall next to the fireplace and grabbed his cane. With an obvious effort he held himself upright and moved past his grandson. His gaze met Laura's. "He has a right to decide who lives in it."

With great dignity he marched from the room.

"That is unfair." Laura clamped her

mouth shut. It wasn't for her to interfere in this family matter. As much as every fiber of her being clamored to meddle. "Can't you see that?"

"I do see it, but I have to do what is best for the kinner, for the boplin." Ben brushed past her and grabbed his coat from the hook. "I need to get up on an icy roof to see if damage was done to the chimney. Life isn't fair. He likes you. Go look after him. Please. Tend to his burns."

He let the door close softly behind him.

Zechariah liked her. That Ben had noticed didn't escape Laura's note. Now was not the time to pick that observation apart. She had to patch things up between Zechariah and his grandson. No easy task. He couldn't move to Michael's. Not under these circumstances. A cloud of smoke and ashes cloaking him. Zechariah would want to lick his wounds in private. Be that as it may, burns could become infected and with nine children, Laura had years of experience tending to them.

Old men too. Eli could be as prickly as a rosebush. But like roses, he was worth the effort.

Zechariah had those same thorns and he was past blooming, but something about him seemed worth the effort.

■ ■ ■ ■

Which burned more? Zechariah swallowed the acrid taste of smoke, anger, and fear lodged in the back of his throat. He stared at the ugly, inflamed patches on his hands and breathed through the pain. It didn't bother him nearly as much as the way Ben had talked to him. The way he'd treated him. Like a disobedient child. Leaning on the knotty familiarity of his birch cane, Zechariah shuffled to the window covered with icy condensation. He pushed the back of his hand against the pane, letting the cold cool the burn. The ice melted, giving him a distorted view of snow-covered trees that glowed in the starlight. Every instinct urged him to leave this place where he was seen as a liability to his own flesh and blood.

Flee. Walk out into the dark and the snow. Trudge through the night until he reached the other side and Marian. Sweet Marian. A hug and a kiss and a good talking-to and he'd be right as rain. That's what Marian would say.

Foolishness. Marian was gone, gone, gone. Long gone. That's what she would say. Get over it. God knows what He's doing. Stand aside and let Him do it.

"Remain in my love." John 15:9
"I am with you and will watch over you wherever you go." Genesis 28:15
"My Presence will go with you, and I will give you rest." Exodus 33:14

In Zechariah's old age, he could only remember short verses now. The longer ones had become wispy shadows flitting around in the corners of his mind, like the lyrics to hymns he'd sung for an entire lifetime.

I'm tired, Gott. Where's that rest You talked about?

"Zechariah?"

Laura couldn't be here. Not in this room. He shifted his weight and turned. "What are you doing here?"

Her gaze danced around the room. Chair. Small table. Lamp. Bed. She flushed and her gaze dropped to the piece rug on the floor next to his narrow, single bunk bed. "I came to fix you up." She held out a woven basket filled with gauze, scissors, a jar of ointment, and a washcloth. "You should put something on those burns right away. You don't want them to get infected."

"I don't really care." Now he sounded like a child. Not surprising that he'd been treated like one. "You can't be *here.*"

Heat ripped across his face. His hands shook. He studied the pants and shirts

263

hanging from hooks next to the table on her left, far from the bed covered with a Log Cabin quilt made by his dead wife on her right. "Don't you see that?"

Laura's eyebrows rose and the ruddy hue of her cheeks darkened. She lifted her chin. "If you don't come out, then I'll have to come in."

"Don't you have someone else's business to mind?"

Laura took one step forward. She now stood in his bedroom. Would lightning strike them both dead? Would their bishop — whom Zechariah had known since he slipped from the womb wailing like he couldn't wait to eat — make them confess their sins before the Gmay?

She nodded toward the chair. "Sit."

"Nee."

She glowered. He summoned his best scowl.

"Ben has gone outside to check the roof." She took another short step forward. Her cheeks turned the color of pickled beets. "Delia's asleep. Rosalie is feeding the boplin in the bedroom. Tamara hasn't come home."

"Not here." Careful to keep his gaze on the unvarnished red-oak planks under his feet, Zechariah brushed past her. "It isn't right."

Her scent floated around him. Spice tea and lemon, maybe. The baby smell of puke. Like a mother and wife. The knot in his throat grew. He stuffed a groan there with it. Gritting his teeth, he stomped down the hallway into the kitchen and plopped into a chair with his back to the wood-burning stove.

The smell hurled memories at him. The fire roared. The wood popped. Smoke roiled like a living, breathing animal intent on consuming him and everyone and everything in its path.

He coughed. His throat burned and itched. He couldn't stop. Fearing he would throw up, he stumbled to the sink.

"Here." Laura's soft voice soothed. She held out a glass of water. Her other hand rubbed his back in a soothing, circular motion. She needed to stop doing that. *Please don't stop doing that.* "Come on, take it. The smoke irritated your throat. I'll make you some tea with honey. But first drink this and let's see to those burns."

To his eternal mortification, tears filled his eyes. He grabbed the glass and slurped the water down in enormous, noisy, embarrassing gulps. "Danki." The word came out in a sputter. "No need to make tea."

"My kitchen, my rules."

"It's not your kitchen."

"You're already feeling better if you want to argue." She scooted a plastic bucket of water toward him. "It's cool, clean water. Stick your hands in it. It'll help take the sting out of the burn."

He did as he was told. Afterward, she patted them dry with the lightest of touches. She pointed a gnarled finger at the chair. "Sit."

Afraid to speak, he sat.

She pulled up a second chair so close their knees almost knocked. Afraid to look at her face, he stared at her white apron's folds. Snowy white but warm, like her hands.

She started with the burns on his bald spot and then his forehead. Her head bent so close to his, he could smell her breath. Sweet peppermint. He inhaled. He probably smelled like coffee. He swallowed and held his breath. She leaned back and tilted her head. "Better?"

"Better." Two syllables that sounded breathless in his ears. "Fine."

She took his hand in hers. Her bony fingers were warm and surprisingly soft. She peered at the patches through glasses that needed to be cleaned. How did she see out

266

of those things? She applied the burn ointment used by Plain families all over the country for all sorts of ailments. Most doctors didn't like the idea, but then Plain folks did a lot of their own doctoring. Cheaper, common-sense doctoring.

The familiar smell of honey, aloe, lanolin, and comfrey root reminded him of his childhood and his mother's soft touch when he burned himself stoking the fire. She never spoke a cross word to him, never. His dad, that was another story, but it seemed so long ago he couldn't remember why his dad bellowed at him.

Laura hummed a hymn as she covered his wounds with gauze and a nonstick tape. The words escaped him at first and then bumped around in his head the way Bible verses he'd known since childhood did now. *"Amazing grace, how sweet the sound that saved a wretch like me."*

That was him. The wretch who had caused a fire and put babies in danger.

"Does that feel better?"

He jumped at the sound of her voice. "Jah, it does."

"Ben was upset and worried." Her fingers smoothed his sleeve, blue against the startling white of the gauze patch. "He didn't mean what he said."

Zechariah concentrated on the feel of her fingers on his skin. The pain receded. Darkness receded. The bitter anger in the back of his throat disappeared. A light danced at the far end of a path of packed dirt cool under his bare feet. Trees shaded the path and the wind blew leaves from their branches. They floated in the air like feathers, twirling and somersaulting until they touched the ground like kisses at dusk. Her touch smelled like lilacs and shoofly pie and fresh-cut grass, each more tantalizing than the last.

"Zechariah?"

He looked into her eyes for the first time. Sweet, sweet caring looked back at him. The enormity of her caring astounded him. It knit the wounds on his heart in tiny, neat, perfect stitches. He cleared his throat. "It feels much better. Much better."

She laid his hand back on his knee. He caught hers before she could settle it back on her side of the great divide. "Not yet."

Her lips curled in a small, bemused smile. "Okay."

Silently they sat, hands clasped between them. With each second their bodies became more and more entangled. Hands, arms, bodies, legs, feet, a heap of humanity. It was impossible to tell where one ended and the other began. Her warmth, her womanliness, her humanness hummed as they flowed into him. Heat seeped into crevices that had been icy cold for years. The dust blew away. Shiny reappeared.

Zechariah peeked at her face. It glowed young and sweet and unlined just as he remembered it from the schoolyard. Cheeks pink from exertion as she spiked the ball over the net for a point or ran the bases after a solid hit into right field.

Fiercely young and fiercely alive.

No less so now, sixty-some years later.

His hand tightened around hers. She responded. Her lips parted. She smiled and ducked her head, no different from a young girl on her first buggy ride after a singing.

She had a lovely singing voice. He began to hum that hymn. "Amazing Grace."

After a second or two, she joined in, but with the words.

Her voice bathed him in a healing pool of anticipation. Something he hadn't felt in years. Sweet anticipation.

He need only lean forward ever so slightly and his lips would touch hers.

What would they feel like? Tender and soft.

Wonderful.

Like love.

Somewhere in the house, Delia's voice cried out. "Mudder, Mudder."

Life whirled between them like a tornado touching down and spiraling away.

Laura withdrew her hand, but the smile remained. "I'll get the tea."

Zechariah turned his hand back and forth, peering at the palm, then the other side. Her touch didn't have miraculous, physical healing power, but something inside him had changed. "Ben meant what he said."

"It's not over until it's over." Her knees popped and her hips cracked as she stood. "It doesn't matter where you live. It's a small community. A short ride. A small effort."

Was she talking about them? It seemed so. *Gott, I hope so.*

Humming, she went to the stove and settled the teapot on a burner. "I don't know much, but I do know every minute on this earth counts. I trust in the Lord and His will for me."

She turned and smiled. The delicate scent of chamomile and honey floated in the air. "And for you."

TWENTY

Laura slipped down the hallway in Solomon's house to the back bedroom. Ben had agreed to give her five minutes with Hannah before the meeting, called specifically to hear her great-granddaughter's confession. It hadn't taken much begging, such was the compassion in Ben's eyes. This was his first official act only one week into his service as bishop. She knocked on the half-open door and peeked inside. Hannah stood at the window, staring out at the frozen landscape in Solomon's backyard.

"Are you ready?"

"Is it time?" Hannah's hands went to her neck as she turned, her face red and blotchy from tears. "Already? I can't decide if I want time to pass quickly so I can get it over with or slowly so I don't have to walk out there yet."

"A few more minutes." Laura hugged her. The girl's thin body trembled. "I just

271

wanted to tell you I'm praying for you. My lieb for you will never change."

"That's what Mudder said." Fresh tears trickled down Hannah's face as she collapsed against Laura's chest. "I'm so sorry I shamed her and you and Daed and everyone." She straightened and wiped her face. "I promised myself I would stop crying."

"You want to get it out of your system before you face everyone?"

"Jah, something like that." She accepted the tissue Laura offered and blew her nose with vigor. "Ben came to me and Mudder and Daed earlier. The elders met with Thaddeus. He didn't want his parents there. Ben didn't tell us much, except that it was agreed that if Thaddeus did not wish to marry me, he would not be forced to do so. He chose not to confess and repent with me. In return, the elders agreed that his decision made it impossible for him to be a part of our Gmay."

"He chose to leave rather than confess and repent?"

"He doesn't want to leave the faith. He told Ben he would go on to Nappanee and meet with the bishop there."

"A hard road for a young man who's never lived anywhere but Jamesport, never been away from his family." Laura sought compassion in her heart. She should pray for him, but right now her heart and soul were with the woman he'd abandoned. "He's seeking a new beginning, I'm sure, but they can be hard to find when old transgressions are left unaddressed."

"I know life isn't fair, but it doesn't seem right —"

"That he should escape this moment?" Laura stood next to her great-granddaughter at the window. A north wind forced tree branches to dip and bow. "He'll have to face it eventually. And it'll be so much worse because he didn't do the right thing to begin with. You're doing the right thing, the brave thing, the righteous thing."

Hannah grabbed Laura's hand and squeezed so hard it hurt. "It helps to know your kind face will be out there."

"I'll be there every minute, I promise."

"It's time." Cyrus's deep voice sounded at the door. He stuck his head through the opening. "Come, Hannah."

Laura went first and found her seat with the other women. She gripped her hands in her lap and kept her chin up as Hannah moved to the front of the room and knelt before the congregation. The girl's gaze remained steadfast on the feet of the men sitting in the first row. Her hands fluttered.

Her fingers touched her throat, but she didn't make a sound. Her thin shoulders shook. The wind whipping in the eaves of Solomon's house and the crackle of the wood in the fireplace broke an otherwise unrelenting silence.

"We are gathered to hear Hannah Kauffman's confession. Hannah has freely confessed her Fehla of fornication to the minister." Ben's voice was gruff and almost unrecognizable as Rosalie's lighthearted, kind husband. Cyrus lifted his hand to cup his ear. Ben's voice rose in volume. "She has confessed that she is with child."

No murmur from the congregation. None of this came as news to a single person in the house. As much as Plain folks didn't talk about this sort of thing, they did. Quietly. Behind closed doors. With hands lifted to their mouths, gazes shifting left and right. Laura closed her eyes for a second, but the image of Hannah's anguished face lit up the breadth and depth of her mind. *Oh, child, child, what have you done to yourself?*

And how could it be right that the father of this baby should not share in this confession and penitence? Not for Laura to question. Her only concern in this moment should be with this soul before the congregation.

Mary Katherine's hand crept onto Laura's and squeezed. Her face spoke of her sorrow and understanding of Laura's pain. Of Seth and Carrie's shame and embarrassment.

Tears threatened. Laura refused to give them heed. This needed to be done. It had to be done. So much was at stake for Hannah and for her unborn child. For that baby to grow up in a community of faith, to know the Ordnung, to know the Holy Word, and to live by it, repentance and punishment were necessary.

A hard truth. Laura took a breath and let it out. *Just breathe. Please, Gott, give her strength and the courage to bear this shame and to learn from it. I know You have a plan for her. Please, Gott, let Your grace envelop her and give her healing.*

She wanted to pray for a husband and a father for the child, but she couldn't. God's plan was God's plan. He knew what was best and it wasn't her place to school Him in how to bring up His child.

"Hannah, are you sorry for what you have done?" Ben's voice held a slight tremor, one that said the emotion of the moment held him prisoner as well.

"Jah. I am." Hannah's whisper quavered.

"I truly am. I'm so sorry."

What must it be like to kneel before her parents, her friends, her family, and admit to doing something Scripture taught was sacred and special, only for a husband and his wife? Plain folks didn't speak of it in private, let alone in public.

Now every person in the community would look at Hannah and remember her sin.

And think of their own temptations. Their own frailties and failures. The image of Eli's handsome face flooded Laura's mind. Those long buggy rides in the evenings. Time spent alone at the pond. Sweet kisses.

One thing could lead to another and Hannah simply had not been strong enough to fight temptation. It could happen to any one of them.

No judgment.

"Has your heart changed, Hannah?"

"It'll never happen again."

While it was true, Hannah would have a permanent physical reminder of the Fehla, once she had completed the bann and had this baby, no one would castigate her. She would be forgiven. The grace of God would be extended through each member of her family, her friends, and her community. Laura hung on to that thought. After repentance, came forgiveness and grace. The beauty of God's plan.

"Leave us then."

With a sob Hannah scrambled to her feet. She wove on unsteady legs down the aisle between the men's and women's benches. Carrie stood. Ben shook his head. She sat.

A young man rose from the back row. Phillip Schwartz. Without looking left or right, he shoved open the door. Hannah trudged through the opening. Phillip gently shut the door.

A small thing. A simple kindness. But still it touched Laura's heart. Phillip's actions reflected an understanding of what went on here today. Repentance. Punishment. Forgiveness. Grace.

"The ministers have met. We recommend six weeks in the bann." Ben wiped at his face with a faded blue bandanna. "All in favor."

Six weeks took them well into the new year. Through the holidays. Even two weeks would've been better, although Hannah would still miss Christmas with her family. They would get glimpses of her at church services, but she would sit near the ministers. After meeting with the ministers for admonition during the *Abrot* at the beginning of worship, she would sit bent over, a hand covering her face during the opening sermon. She wouldn't be allowed to join the meal after the service. But it was called punishment for a reason.

Laura swallowed against the lump in her throat and raised her hand. The vote was unanimous.

Once again, Phillip scurried to open the door. Solomon escorted Hannah back into the house. Her head down, she likely never saw Phillip or the way he looked at her, like a man longing to give a single word of encouragement. He knew better. Her white skin now had a green tinge to it. Hands out as if to catch her, the minister walked behind her to the front of the room. She faced the congregation. Her chest heaved. Her hands went to her mouth.

She looked as if she might vomit on Freeman's and Zechariah's shoes. *Please Gott, no. Spare her that shame.*

The desire to rush to the front and wrap her in a hug overwhelmed Laura. She gritted her teeth and stared at her hands. *Let this be over. Let this be over. Please, Gott, let this be over.*

Not the prayer of a strict Plain member of the Gmay. The prayer of a great-grandmother who couldn't bear to see her girl in such pain and misery.

She hazarded a sidelong glance at Carrie. As hard as this was for a great-grandmother, how much harder it must be for a mother and father. Her face red and tear streaked, Carrie gripped her daughter Jonelle's hand on one side and Evie's on the other. The lessons they were learning today were important for them too.

So important.

"Your penitence has been set at six weeks of bann. Are you willing to take on the discipline of the church?"

Hannah nodded.

"Speak up, Hannah."

"Jah."

"The bann will commence immediately. Cyrus and I will meet with you later to talk about the terms of your punishment. You may go first. Solomon will drive you to the dawdy haus at Martin's. You're to stay there during the bann. You'll be visited by the midwife. And by the deacon. Your needs will be met."

Ben sounded so severe. His job. He's doing his job as a bishop chosen by God.

Cyrus shepherded her from the house this time. No one could miss the fierce glance he cast at Phillip, a glance that would keep a hardier man in his seat. Hannah's gaze stayed on the plank wood floor. That small path from the front of the room to the door surely seemed like a journey of a thousand miles.

The door closed.

"We still have the behavior of Thaddeus Yoder to consider." Ben's voice turned icy. "He chose not to be here today. He has left the Gmay."

A soft murmur ran through the crowd and dissipated. Laura couldn't help herself. She sought out Thaddeus's mother. Susie Yoder's hands covered her face. Her shoulders shook. One of her daughters patted her back.

She surely wondered how much she had contributed to her son's waywardness, just as Seth and Carrie agonized and rehashed their own parenting.

"He was invited to come before us and repent of his Fehla. He declined." Ben stared out at the crowd, his gaze filled with sadness mingled with stern purpose. "Therefore, we are called to determine if he should be allowed to continue as a member. I am calling for a *Rat* of the congregation. All those in favor of terminating Thaddeus Yoder's membership, vote by raising your hand."

The vote was unanimous. How difficult it must have been for Declan and Susie to vote to excommunicate their own son. Shame heaped upon heartbreak for his sin and for his refusal to acknowledge it or his unborn child.

One did not compare sin. One prayed for mercy and grace and the gentling of a headstrong soul.

But for the grace of God, there go I.

Ben pronounced the membership renounced. "If Thaddeus chooses to return and confess his Fehla at any time, his membership can be restored by Rat. Until then, he is subject to Meidung. That concludes this meeting of the Gmay. You are dismissed."

Laura nodded at Mary Katherine and made her way against the flow of bodies toward Carrie. The woman needed support. She needed to know she had not been judged and found wanting as a mother. Children became adults. When they strayed, they had to take responsibility.

As hard as it could be to let them. Laura had been through much with her children's rumspringas. But never this. Never a public confession and bann.

Was that Eli's influence or hers? Both combined. Eli could be brutally swift when it came to punishment. He accepted no excuses for poor behavior. He acted equally swift in loving-kindness.

The knot in her throat grew. On days like today she missed him as if the anguishing, gaping wound had occurred only days earlier. His even keel, his measured words, the soft stroke of his fingers in her hair.

The fingers brushed against her skin as real as the bitter December wind.

And then they were gone.

What kind of father had Zechariah been? The question came hard upon the fleeing memories. She let her gaze wander around the room. There he was. Flanked by Abel on one side, three of his sons on the other. All good men. Every one of his children had been baptized and married in the church. A good father.

The memory of his hand in hers cloaked her like a warm shawl she wore everywhere she went. True, he'd made no move to follow up since that day in the kitchen when their connection had been as real and alive as any she'd ever felt, but neither had she. They needed time to understand what had transpired. If they moved too quickly, the fragility of that shared moment might cause it to be shattered.

If it was real, it would last. No need to rush in where only fools dared to tread.

He turned. His gaze met hers. He didn't

look away. He smiled.

The sweet taste of blueberries in summer lay on her tongue.

He might have kissed her that day if Delia hadn't called out at that moment.

What would a kiss have been like? Like Zechariah. A mixture of rough and softness, gruff and sweet, flannel and worn cotton.

"Stop making goo-goo eyes." A knowing look on her face, Mary Katherine tugged at Laura's arm. "This is no place for mooning over a man. Take it outside, my sweet freind."

"I'm not mooning. Old women don't moon over men."

"Sure they do." Mary Katherine waved at Ezekiel and pointed at the door. They would meet outside. "Just not in public."

How could she moon — as Mary Katherine so delicately put it — over another man so close to the anniversary of Eli's death? She'd always felt his presence this time of year. His tantalizing nearness during the season of his parting always came with a mixture of reluctance and longing. Reluctance to experience it again and longing to feel his touch one more time.

To hear him sing Christmas hymns in that singsong, off-key way as he brought in the wood and started the fire. To hear him hum when he ate gingerbread cookies because they made him so happy. To hear him laugh at the skits performed by the grandchildren on Christmas Eve.

Now, she longed for the touch of another. *I'm sorry, Eli. So sorry.*

But not sorry this Christmas she'd received the surprising gift of sparkly hope that life could still surprise her, still take her breath away, still make her giddy.

What a Christmas present.

Tamara stepped into Laura's path. She leaned in close, her hand on Laura's arm, and whispered in her ear, "That was barbaric."

TWENTY-ONE

What kind of word was *barbaric* for a time-honored, God-fearing Gmay ritual of confession and repentance? Laura scowled at Tamara and placed her index finger to her lips. A discussion of the pros and cons of punishment and repentance did not belong here or now. Tamara had dipped not just her toes in the English ways but her entire body, from the sounds of her impertinent statement.

Laura grabbed her granddaughter's arm. They two-stepped through the barn door, past the corral, toward the long row of buggies. "What are you thinking, talking like that during a Gmay meeting?"

"Hannah made a mistake. She said she was sorry." Tamara scowled back. She jerked her arm from Laura's grip and plowed to a stop. "She'll be alone for the first trimester. She looks like she has severe morning sickness. She could become dehydrated, sick.

She has no boyfriend, no husband. It *is* barbaric."

"Ben will allow the midwife to check on her. He and Cyrus will meet with her before the Sunday sermons. She'll be able to attend. We'll see her. She'll be taken care of. She's not completely abandoned."

They were strict but not inflexible. A punishment imposed with love, not cruel intent.

"She's practically a child herself."

The woman standing in front of Laura took on the aspects of a stranger. "In the Plain world, she's not. She's old enough to commit the sin and old enough to know it's wrong. She took responsibility for her Fehla and she accepted her punishment." A far more grown-up behavior than Tamara exhibited. "She wants to do this so her family can help her raise her kind. Eventually, I hope there will be a man wise enough to see she has learned from her mistake and will make a gut fraa."

"How many people in the congregation failed in the same way and never admitted it? The only reason Hannah did was because she got pregnant. Basically, she got caught."

Laura couldn't answer the question and Tamara's point was surely well-taken. "Why? Have you?"

"Nee. I don't . . . I'm not." For once Tamara looked flustered. "The opportunity has never presented itself."

"But if it did?"

"I would never do anything to jeopardize my chances of becoming a doctor."

Laura had once said the same thing. Then Eli entered the picture.

Tamara needed her own Eli. "What about your chances of being a fraa and a mudder?"

"They don't call to me like medicine does." Her cheeks red from the cold wind that whipped in her face, Tamara tugged on her mittens. "I'm sorry. I know you're disappointed. I know Mudder and Daed are disappointed, but that's the point, isn't it, of rumspringa? If I can't take the vows of baptism with the certainty that I want to live by the Ordnung for the rest of my life, then I need to figure out what I do want. And that is to be a doctor. Stop changing the subject. We're talking about Hannah, not me."

"There's nothing more to be said. Her punishment has been decided."

"And then what? She'll bear the mark of shame on her forehead for the rest of her life? I want to talk to her."

"Nee. You'll only muddy the water more."

"Why? Because I'll offer her other options? Because I'll tell her that her life isn't over? Because I'll tell her to hold her head up?" Tamara's eyes blazed. She put both hands on her hips and stared at Laura as if she were the enemy. "She could come with me. I could take care of her. She could live with me."

The hubris of youth. "How will you support her and a baby and still go to college? Don't create castles in the air. She's mixed up enough without you filling her head with figments of your imagination."

"I know people would be happy to help her —"

"Stop, Tamara. Just stop. Now."

Her anger's ferocity surprised even Laura. She took a breath, then another. "You have gut intentions, but you'll only make the situation harder for her. I promise I will make sure she doesn't suffer. She will be forgiven. Her child will be loved. She will always be loved. Let it be. Please."

"Hey, Tamara!"

The sweet, lilting tones of Molly Hershberger's voice floated between them, taking with it the bitter animosity that had threatened to separate family from family.

Tamara wiped tears from her face with the back of her mitten. "Molly, you look like you're about to pop."

Not something a Plain person said.

It was as if Tamara had fled her life already. Laura bit her lower lip to keep the words prisoner. Only acrimony would result from any more talk. Better to let time heal the wounds of their heated exchange.

Molly would be a good antidote. She didn't have a mean or complicated bone in her chubby body. She had been Tamara's closest friend until she married Anthony Hershberger. "There you are." She waddled their direction, her two little ones following along like babies after a penguin mom. "I was afraid I'd missed you." She waved at Laura, but her gaze returned to Tamara. "I know you're helping out at Rosalie's, but I thought maybe they could spare you for supper tonight."

"If you're making your chicken and dumplings, then I might be able to sneak away." Tamara smiled blithely as if they hadn't been discussing decisions that would affect this life and the next for not only herself but Hannah. "You don't mind, do you, Groossmammi?"

Laura shook her head. Molly clapped. She was like that. A sweet woman with no artifice and a mind only for family and friends. Lovely in her uncomplicatedness.

"Gut. My cousin Emmett Bays has come to stay with us. He'll help Anthony farm in the spring. I want to introduce you."

Ha. From Laura's lips to God's ears. She couldn't help herself. She joined Molly in clapping. Tamara's face darkened. "I don't know. Mary has had a cough since yesterday and Mia is congested."

"Nee, no backing out now." Laura nudged her toward Molly. "I'll make a steam bath for them. Rosalie and I can handle everything for one evening. You go have fun. Meet Emmett."

"Groossmammi."

"Tamara."

Tamara scowled. Laura scowled back. They'd always done a lot of that, simply because of all her granddaughters, Tamara was the most like her. Laura had never seen this as a bad thing — until now.

"Fine." Tamara trudged toward Molly. "But you'll have to give me a ride back to Ben's after dinner."

"No problem. Emmett might want some fresh air."

"Nee. I'm not taking a ride alone with a man I've just met."

"Wait until you see him. You'll change your mind." Molly's smile broadened and her eyes sparkled. "And I've known him all my life so I can vouch for your virtue and his."

Who knew she was such a matchmaker? And this Emmett, was he tall and blond, with blue eyes and big hands and a deep voice?

From Molly's lips to God's ears.

Twenty-Two

The scent of baking gingerbread mingled with the tantalizing aroma of popcorn and something else . . . caramel. The smell of Christmas in the making. Zechariah caught himself humming "Away in a Manger," as he scooped up his binoculars and stuffed them in his knapsack.

The women must be in the kitchen rustling up some Christmas treats. That Laura was making a determined effort to throw off her sadness over her great-granddaughter's six-week bann was apparent, but the confession earlier in the week had been brutal for all those involved. The children's play was in two days and he had spent several evenings listening to Christopher practice.

Ben had said nothing to Zechariah, but he'd overheard his grandson speaking to his wife. Something about after Christmas. After Christmas he would be shunted off to

Michael's. In the meantime he intended to enjoy the season — and his proximity to Laura. He hadn't found the gumption — the bravery — to approach her. How did an old man not allowed to drive a buggy court an old woman?

How indeed? The dilemma gave a deliciousness to his day that had been missing for a long time. That feeling of anticipation. He hadn't known how much he missed it until it reappeared. It felt so much like hope.

A question to be pondered while he enjoyed the annual bird count. Live today and let tomorrow worry about itself. He could ask her along. No. Abel would think Zechariah had gone around the bend. Maybe he had. He glanced out his bedroom window. The thundershowers had cleared. The break in winter weather with temperatures edging up toward a balmy forty degrees would be perfect for the bird count.

Abel better not be late. The old coot sometimes forgot things. Who could forget the annual bird count? Abel Danner for one. He might be younger, but his memory was going before Zechariah's. "Hah."

Zechariah chuckled to himself. Having something over on his friend made a good day even better. Even if it was small compared to his inability to drive a buggy or climb stairs down to the basement. Zechariah tugged on his rubber boots over his work ones and clomped down the hallway toward the kitchen.

Ben stood at the door. He wore his black pea jacket and tall rubber boots. He was supposed to be at Jacob's helping with the addition they were building for his growing brood with his fraa, Iris.

"Did you see Abel out there? He's supposed to pick me up."

"Nee." Ben shifted from one big foot to the other. The man had giant feet, considering he stood under six feet tall. "I told him not to come. He doesn't feel gut, and his fraa was nagging him to stay home. It's best for both of you."

Rosalie, who'd been in the middle of telling Laura and Tamara something about a customer at the Combination Store, quieted. The steady *pop-pop-pop* of the kernels in a huge cast-iron pot on the stove provided a backdrop to several beats of silence. The familiar, enticing aroma mingled with unspoken, startled thoughts.

"Why would you do that? The bird count is today. We've got a lot of ground to cover. I reckon we'll see sixty, seventy species this year. We're meeting Aidan Graber and the others there. I'm looking for a yellow-rumped warbler and a pileated woodpecker. Abel says he saw them both last year, but I didn't get a peek —"

"You can't go, Groossdaadi."

"What do you mean I can't go? I'm dressed. I put on an extra pair of wool socks to keep my feet warm and dry. I've got my binoculars." He patted his knapsack slung over one shoulder. "I packed my guide. I go every year."

"Not this year. I talked to Aidan since he's organizing the group going this year. We agreed you're too unsteady on your feet to be tromping around the lake in the mud. You'll slip and fall and getting you out of there in a buggy would take too long. They'd have to call an ambulance."

"You're creating a problem out of thin air, suh."

Laura moved the pot from the flames and set it down on the counter with a bang that might have been punctuation for his statement. He glanced her way. She frowned, her eyes sharp behind wire-rimmed glasses. Her peeved expression suggested he had support in the room.

"I'll be careful. Abel will be with me. He might act half-witted sometimes, but he's strong as an ox."

"Abel is sick or he has a headache. Some

kind of bug. Jessica is keeping him home too."

Abel's wife didn't tell him what to do. She might argue with him, but Abel had the last word. Until now. "Are you ordering me to stay home?"

If this could be called home.

"I'm saying it's for the best."

"As my grandson or as my bishop?"

Ben's pained expression deepened. He turned and grabbed the doorknob. "This is a family matter, not a church matter." His head bowed, shoulders hunched, he cleared his throat. "We're worried for you, that's all."

"You're consumed with worry about me. Worry is a sin. Have you talked to Gott about that? I haven't gotten this far in life by sitting at home by the fireplace."

"You never had a disease like this before. You've never let a chimney fire get out of control." The pleading tone deepened as did the gruffness of Ben's voice. "Groossmammi's gone. We'd like to hang on to you a bit longer, Gott willing."

"I'm not going anywhere." Zechariah plowed forward. "Except to the bird count. I'll drive myself."

"It's wet and rainy out there. You'll catch Abel's cold." Rosalie spoke up. "You could help the kinner make the popcorn balls and decorate the gingerbread men. They'd like that."

Exasperation blew through Zechariah. The smell of the popcorn turned his stomach. He snorted. "You'd have me sit in the kitchen decorating cookies? I'm not an old woman."

"Excuse me?" Umbrage written all over her frowning face, Laura waved a wooden spoon at him. "Us old women like working in the kitchen."

Ben didn't move. His hand stayed on the doorknob. "It's for the best. We're looking out for you. You'll be fine here. After the holidays, we'll get you moved to Michael's. In the meantime, stay warm and dry. Just don't start any fires."

Zechariah stared at Ben's face. No sign he understood that he was turning his grandfather into a child one decision at a time. No more chopping wood. No more driving a buggy. No more riding horses. No more helping in the fields. No more birding. No more building fires.

No more work. If a man didn't have his work and he didn't have his fraa to love, he didn't have his hobbies. What did he have?

So much for that sense of anticipation. That sparkly hope. "The wood is getting low. I'll bring in some more." He laid his knapsack on the table. Ben didn't move. "Don't worry, I won't mess with the fire."

Ben's gaze burrowed into Zechariah's. Finally, he stepped aside and opened the door. "Just enough for this afternoon. Christopher can bring in more when he gets home from school."

By then Zechariah might be dead of boredom. Or disuse. Or pure self-pity. He squared his shoulders, lifted his head high, and marched past Ben out into the damp air that did nothing to cool his burning face.

Watching a man stripped of his joy left a woman hard-pressed to find her Christmas spirit. Laura pulled another pan of gingerbread men from the oven. Their sad, blank faces matched her frame of mind. Even Delia's high, breathless rendition of "Joy to the World," or "Yoy to the Vorld" as she pronounced it, did little to restore Laura's earlier zeal for making popcorn balls for her fifty-plus grandchildren and great-grandchildren.

"He only wants what's best for Zechariah." Rosalie whipped white powdered sugar frosting with more vigor than necessary. "He wants him to be safe."

"Funny way of showing it, if you ask me."

298

Tamara held up the gingerbread man she was decorating. He had cinnamon dot eyes and a frosting suit with collar and buttons. "Old people have feelings and hopes and dreams too."

"Number one, no one asked you." Laura tried to tamp down the asperity in her voice. The look Rosalie gave her indicated she failed miserably. "Number two, how do you know, Miss Barely Twenty-Two?"

"I watch you."

Nothing fazed this young woman. Lessons in humility were lost on her. Even so, Laura found herself in need of a bit of humility herself. Tamara was smart and she saw the insides of people, not just what they said but what they felt. If Tamara got that from Laura, that was a good thing. *Wasn't it, Gott?*

"I have no dreams that haven't been fulfilled in this life. Gott has given me all I need or want."

"Nice try." Tamara scooped up a dollop of frosting and popped it in her mouth. Her eyes rolled back. "Yum. You make the best frosting."

Delia, who had smeared her cookie with enough frosting for three gingerbread men, climbed into Tamara's lap and opened her mouth wide. Tamara popped in another dollop of frosting.

"Pure sugar. How can you go wrong with pure sugar?"

"It can rot your teeth." Rosalie shooed Delia back to her own chair. "No more frosting, little girl. You'll be bouncing off the walls instead of taking a nap."

"You can't tell me you don't still have hopes and dreams." Tamara smacked her lips and licked her finger. "I see it when you look at Zechariah."

"You're delirious. And delusional." Had her feelings seeped out on her face? A grown woman didn't go around looking moonstruck. "You've been reading so much Englisch stuff, you've turned into one."

"So you never think about getting married again? You never miss having a mann?" Tamara's airy tone said she found both statements impossible to believe. "You never want a special someone around late at night when the wind blows and the tree branches scratch against the windows and you feel all alone?"

"That sounds like something *you've* been thinking about, something a young, single woman such as yourself should be considering for herself." Rosalie finally came to the rescue. She shook her finger at Tamara. "Stop eating the frosting and antagonizing your groossmammi. She raised her kinner.

300

She had a wonderful mann. Gott was gut. She should be content with her lot this late in a long, healthy life."

Rosalie was right, but somehow her summary of Laura's life stuck in Laura's craw. Mary Katherine had a long, happy marriage to Moses. She raised her kinner. Now she had a new, happy marriage to Ezekiel. She had her dream of a bookstore where she spent her days reading stories to kinner and introducing them to the joy of books. Bess had Aidan and her babies. Even Jennie had found the courage to love again with Leo, despite a disastrous first love and marriage to a man meaner than a wild hog. Jennie had a wonderful second marriage and the Combination Store.

That left Laura. She knew exactly how Zechariah felt. Slightly less than useless. That was it. Until she took his hand in hers and he gave her a look that sparked a fire that smoldered someplace under her breastbone.

A look she saw every time she lay down in her bed at night and closed her eyes. The way he rubbed his finger along the edge of her thumb. The hoarse hum in his throat. The wanting in his eyes.

Since that day of the fire, she'd felt a steadily increasing sense of anticipation until she might explode from waiting for him to say something or do something.

To break the silence, to touch her, and to let their unspoken thoughts melt together again.

The sound of wood smacking against wood floated from beyond the doorway. Zechariah must've come in the front door. Likely he didn't want to face the women who'd watched Ben dismantle what little dignity he had left in this life.

With a deep breath Laura wiped her shaking hands on the dish towel and slid two cookies onto a saucer. "The caramel is ready. Start shaping the popcorn balls, will you, before it cools?"

"What are you doing?" Tamara's curiosity matched the three-year-old's across the table from her. "Who are the cookies for?"

"Is that one of the babies crying?" Laura filled a chipped brown mug — Zechariah's favorite — with coffee and added a tablespoon of sugar and a dash of milk. She was nothing if not observant. "You should check on them. Rosalie can start the popcorn balls."

"Laura has a special friend." Tamara sang the words like a jingle as she stood. *"Laura has a special friend."*

Rosalie joined in. *"Laura has a special friend."*

They giggled. Her face puzzled, Delia, never one to be left out, giggled with them. Tamara grabbed the little girl around the waist and hoisted her in the air. They danced about like silly geese, singing their silly song.

"You're ridiculous." With all the dignity she could muster, Laura settled the treat on a tray and strode from the room. "All three of you. The babies are crying. The popcorn is getting cold. The caramel is getting hard."

Breathless and laughing, they kept singing.

Easy for them to sing and laugh. They didn't live Zechariah's life. Living past the point of usefulness. Or maybe it only seemed that way. God had a plan and He was waiting for them to smarten up and figure it out. She marched into the front room. Zechariah dropped an armload of logs onto the stack next to the fireplace. "Don't worry. I didn't touch the fire."

"I'm not worried — not about you." Laura brushed back a lock of hair that had escaped her kapp. She'd never been concerned with her appearance before. She had caramel on her apron and powdered sugar on her dress. Her hands were waterlogged from washing dishes. "I thought you could try the cookies and see what you think. I might have overdone the ginger."

"So now I'm the taste tester." He put his hand on his back and winced. "I suppose that's a job for an old man."

"The cookies tend to sweeten sourpusses, in my experience." She set the plate on the table next to the checkers. "I thought you might be cold so I brought some coffee."

"Sourpuss." He sputtered for a few seconds, then plopped into the rocking chair. "I'm a sourpuss? My grandson is telling me what I can and cannot do."

"Welcome to the club."

"You have an answer for everything."

"I do. What are you making for your grands for Christmas?"

"What does that have to do with anything?"

"They might like popcorn balls and gingerbread men."

"From me?"

Laura settled into one of the rocking chairs. "Why not? If it's from the heart, they'll like it."

"I'm not cooking."

"Nee, decorating. You can make them manly gingerbread men."

"You're a silly woman."

"You're a silly, proud man."

"I'm as humble as the next Plain man."

"Are not." She pulled the checkerboard toward her and realigned the red checkers. "We should finish that game."

"I'm too tired."

"Are not."

"Am too."

"I'll spot you a king if you're afraid of being beaten by an old woman."

He pulled the checkerboard toward his side of the table. "I don't need to be spotted."

She grinned. "I move first."

He picked up one of the cookies. "I can't eat both of those. You might need to help."

He took a bite. She reached for the other cookie. His hand shot out and swatted hers away. "Changed my mind." The words were muffled by a full mouth of cookie. "Gut. Not too much ginger."

She made the first move. Between bites, Zechariah studied the board. He sniffed and pushed his glasses up his nose. He frowned.

"Anytime now. At this rate we'll be here until spring."

"Hmmm. Let me see. Let me see."

The front door opened. Michael entered, followed by his brother Josiah. Zechariah's grandsons carried stacks of empty cardboard boxes.

Zechariah's time had run out.

TWENTY-THREE

If the look on Laura's face was any indication, Zechariah had backup. He would need it. The stack of boxes told the story. Zechariah's grandsons had come to move him to Michael's house. First the bird count, now this. So much for waiting until after Christmas. If that had been Ben's plan, Michael — or more likely Ivan — had others.

Laura stood. "How about some kaffi? We have hot gingerbread cookies fresh from the oven."

Making nice with them or trying to distract them from their mission?

"The rain stopped so we thought this would be a gut time to get you moved." Michael ignored Laura's offer. His gaze danced from Zechariah to the hallway. "Cathy cleaned out Lazarus's old room for you. Still smells like his feet, but we shoved a bookshelf in there that should hold all your birding books."

307

Fat lot of good the books did him when he wasn't allowed to bird. "Ben said I was staying here until after Christmas."

Laura picked up her tray. "We need his help now, with Ben having so much on his shoulders."

Good woman.

Pretty too.

That thought came to him every night when he lay down to sleep since her ministrations after the fire. That moment when their fingers and gazes entwined. It joined him at the table when she sat across from him, eating with such a healthy appetite he envied her.

Zechariah shook his head to dispel the fog. Laura looked nothing like Marian, who had eyes the color of caramel and even darker hair. Her skin had been fair. She was small but shapely. He could pick her up and carry her around with one arm.

Not that she let him. The woman had a mind of her own. In that, she and Laura were identical twins. Could it be that different traits appealed in different seasons of life? He was no longer a man who could pick up a woman and carry her about under one arm in jest. Nor could he love her the way he once had.

His skin went hot. The fire's flames burned

more fiercely. He breathed in and out.

"Are you all right?" Her forehead wrinkled, Laura frowned. "You look flushed."

"I'm fine. But I have no plans to leave."

Her frown deepened. She swiveled and faced Michael. "Where's Ben? I thought he planned to talk to you about this." Her tone was sharp enough to slice a whole watermelon in one swipe. "He also told me yesterday he was inclined to keep Zechariah here until after Christmas."

"We wanted to do it while the weather cooperated." Michael's mulish tone said he didn't like being questioned by a woman — especially one not a member of the family. "It's almost sixty degrees out and the sun is shining. Perfect for making a change before the holiday. We want to get him settled *before* Christmas."

Weather had nothing to do with it. Ivan liked to be in charge. Maybe he felt overshadowed by his son's sudden vault into a place of authority. "Don't talk about me like I'm not here."

"I talked to Ben just now out in the barn before we came up to the house." Michael wiped his boots and strode toward the hallway. "He heard me out. He also told me about the fire. He doesn't want to hurt your feelings, but neither does he want to take a chance with the kinner. He agreed six months with me and then we can see how it's going. By then the twins will be bigger and, Gott willing, sleeping through the night. Rosalie will have recovered."

He glanced at Laura. "By then you'll be back at the dawdy haus."

"I'll go when Rosalie doesn't need me anymore."

"I'll take a cookie." Josiah, the spitting image of his older brother, offered the statement with a hopeful glance at Laura. "I didn't eat enough breakfast."

"How about some hot chocolate with that?" Laura's tone was brisk. "There's no hurry, is there?"

"Another thunderstorm may hit later this afternoon." Michael sounded triumphant, as if he made the weather. "We best get moving."

"What's going on?" A twin — Mia from the looks of her forehead — in one arm, Rosalie trotted into the room. Mia squalled as if she hadn't eaten in a week and wondered why no one changed her diaper. "What are all the boxes for?"

"I'm being evicted."

"Don't be that way, Groossdaadi." Michael dodged Rosalie and kept moving. "We like your company. Come show us what you

310

want to take."

"What's going on?" Tamara, twin number two screeching like she hadn't been fed in a month clutched in her arms, followed Rosalie. "Why the long faces?"

A doll in each arm, Delia brought up the rear. "Michael, Josiah, do you want to play dolls with me? My dolls are hungry. You can feed them."

Josiah, his face suddenly red, lingered near the door. "Maybe later. I have to carry boxes right now."

Michael growled. It definitely sounded like a growl.

"Don't growl at the girl. It's not her fault you came trotting in here like you own the place and are the boss of me. Which you're not, by the way."

Michael's long-suffering sigh said it all. He was the boss and he would have his way. "I'm packing. You can help or not help. I have work to do back at the farm."

How much work could he have to do in the middle of winter? No fields to sow or reap. No hay to bale. No vegetables to pick. "Do what you have to do."

"I will."

Michael turned and clomped back down the hallway.

Josiah continued to linger.

311

"Josiah, get down here and help me."

He shrugged and strode away.

"I think there's still some of that vegetable soup I made yesterday in the refrigerator." Laura brushed past his chair. Her hand squeezed his shoulder. A warm, reassuring touch so swift it might have been a product of his desire to be comforted. "Soup is gut for what ails a man with a cold."

What was she suggesting? A slow smile spread across her face as she trotted to the window. "Seems they left their buggy hitched by the front door. Awfully convenient."

He rose and went to her side. The beauty of her plan — the audacity of it — sent a rush of joy through Zechariah he hadn't felt in years. "You'll be called a bad influence, you know."

"We old codgers have to stick together."

"Hurry. Get the soup before they come out here to mess with my life some more."

"I'm going to say this because I'm an old lady and I can't help myself so please don't be offended —"

Before he lost his courage, he leaned in and kissed her square on the lips. They *were* warm and soft.

She kissed him back. Her hands fluttered. He captured them in his. His heart thumped so hard he could hear it.

They parted and stared at each other. Her cheeks were pink and her eyes wide. "Zechariah Stutzman —"

"I'll be careful."

"You can't just kiss a woman and walk off."

"We're kind of on a schedule, remember?"

"The soup. The soup!" She whirled and skedaddled.

No matter the bird count, no matter Michael's attitude, no matter what, this was officially the best day in Zechariah's life in a long, long time. He'd kissed Laura Kauffman. Not only that, she'd liked it.

He grabbed his coat from the hook and shrugged it on. Still wide-eyed and pink-cheeked, she returned lickety-split with a plastic container of soup gripped in two loop pot holders made by the children. Grinning like she'd just pulled off the best practical joke of the century, she handed it over. "Hurry, hurry. Bring back the pot holders or Rosalie will wonder what happened to them." She made shooing motions. "And don't let Ben see you."

"Isn't he in the barn?"

She peeked out the window. "All clear, run like the wind."

No sarcasm in those words, only the

camaraderie of two people joined together to turn the world upside down for a change.

Lighter on his feet than he'd been in years, Zechariah whipped out the door and heard it click behind him in a definite *you're-really-doing-this* pop.

A few minutes later he manhandled the buggy on the muddy road to Abel's farm some five miles to the east. The heavy, wet air felt more like spring than December. He inhaled. It smelled good. The clouds parted and a thread of light glistened against the puddles of rain and melting snow.

So this was what it felt like to play hooky. Freedom.

Every man should play hooky now and then.

He would never tell his great-grands such a thing.

Every man needed a woman who understood such a thing.

He laughed aloud. The sound startled him. It had been such a long time since he laughed. The sound of a loon, surely.

In half an hour — a peaceful, independent, crisp half hour — he was at Abel's.

Abel and Jessica didn't seem surprised to see him. Nor did Abel look all that sick. Jessica took the soup and warmed it up while Zechariah warmed himself by the fire.

"You plan to tell me what happened?" Abel poked the fire. The wood sizzled and sparks flew. "Ben told me you had been kind of poorly. He said you didn't have the energy for the bird count."

"That's how he sized up the situation, I reckon." Pleased with the spring in his step, Zechariah pulled a rocking chair closer to the fire. His muscles could match a young man's today. So could his bones. Freedom did that to a man. Like a draught of cold, fresh milk. "I'm fine. I'm a grown-up man. If I feel like visiting a friend, I reckon I will."

"Makes sense to me." Abel shrugged and plopped down in the other chair. "As long as I get soup and half-decent company out of it, I'm happy."

The soup took the edge off the chill. Zechariah slurped another spoonful of the savory broth, dropped the spoon in his bowl, and belched. Abel grinned and stuck another big bite of potato, green bean, and corn in his mouth.

Chewing, Zechariah leaned back and hummed. He always hummed when he ate. If he liked the food. Laura made a good vegetable-beef stew. It tasted especially good in light of how and why it arrived at Abel's table in his tiny, sparsely furnished dawdy haus. Even Jessica had giggled behind her

315

fingers at Zechariah's story.

He left out the part about the kiss. His secret. His and Laura's. Having a secret made him feel twenty years younger — fifty years younger.

"You don't look like you have a cold." Zechariah picked up a thick slice of hot bread slathered with butter. Jessica was a passable cook too. "You look like a lazy old man who doesn't give a hoot about the bird count."

"Not my call. I sneezed once and Jessica decided I had pneumonia."

"Not true. Lying is a sin, you yellow-belly sapsucker." Jessica, who hollered from the kitchen sink where she washed dishes, had a quaint way of talking. It made her a perfect fit for a man like Abel, who never knew when to shut up. "You woke me up coughing twice during the night and you snored like a band saw. Plus you told me yourself you've had a headache since yesterday."

"Sinus pressure ain't ever killed a man yet. You could've moved to the other bedroom if I was such a pain," Abel yelled back, but he grinned and stirred his soup. "Or kick me out of bed, if it suits."

"Then who would keep my feet warm?"

Abel's face turned red and he ducked his

head. Seeing a seventy-year-old blush was a beautiful sight. Stifling a chuckle, Zechariah brushed crumbs from his beard. "You're a blessed man. I hope you know that."

"I may be old, but I'm not an idiot."

"I don't know about that."

"Danki for bringing the soup."

"When Michael comes tearing through that front door accusing me of stealing his horse and buggy, you won't be so pleased."

"As long as I get to keep the soup, I'm —"

"We have company." A towel in hands wrinkled from age and dishwater, Jessica stood in the doorway. With her still sandy-blonde hair, clear blue eyes that needed no glasses, and ramrod posture, she didn't look a day over fifty. She was so alive. Maybe they kept each other young. "I just saw them pull up. Michael looks madder than a turkey headed for the Thanksgiving table."

The pounding on the door rattled the windows.

"It's open." Abel settled his bowl on the table and dropped his napkin next to it. "No need to break it down."

The door flew open. His face ruddy from the cold air and his lips turned down in a peevish frown, Michael stomped into the room. Ben, looking slightly less irritated, followed. The two men wiped their boots on the welcome mat. Neither spoke for a full minute.

Zechariah didn't bother to fill the silence. Let them speak their piece. Then he would do the same.

Ignoring Abel and Jessica, Michael folded his arms and stood, legs spread, and drilled Zechariah with a fiery gaze. "You stole my horse and buggy."

"Borrowed —"

"You left without telling anyone —"

"Not true. I told Laura."

"She's as bad as you are, apparently." Michael shook his head. "Ben says he told you no more driving buggies. Yet you took off on wet, muddy roads, on your own, alone."

"I'm not a *kind.*" The bellow surprised even Zechariah. He jerked to his feet. "Now, if you want some of this soup I brought to my sick friend, I reckon he won't mind sharing. Jessica might even be convinced to serve you some kaffi. Otherwise, hush up."

"Hush up," Michael stuttered. "Hush up?"

Even Ben's mouth twitched as if he attempted to hide a smile. He slapped his hand on his cousin's shoulder. "I could use a cup of kaffi myself. Let's sit down and talk this out."

"You're the bishop. You're going to let him

break the rules you set?"

"He's our groossdaadi. Have some respect." Ben nodded toward an open chair. "Mind if we sit, Abel?"

"Not at all." Abel grinned. "I reckon this will be gut."

Ben sat. Michael remained standing, his expression as stiff as his back. Ben rubbed his eyes. "I know this is hard for you, Groossdaadi. We don't mean any disrespect. We only want what is best for everyone."

"I can help you out."

"You can't. Your hands tremble. Your arms jerk. Your feet stumble." His voice held apology for the brutal honesty. "I have no desire to embarrass or shame you. I will miss you. So will the kinner. Your presence in the kinner's lives is important and gut for them. Give me six months. Spend time with the rest of your family. I promise you'll stay with us again."

Like promising a child his birthday would come again next year. Zechariah had been wrong to come here. To make them come after him. To make it harder for Ben. It was foolish. He stood. "Fine." He nodded at Abel. "Danki for the hospitality."

He turned to Ben. "Give me a ride to your house? I have some packing to do."

TWENTY-FOUR

The basket, once heavy with dozens of popcorn balls in caramel, chocolate, strawberry, and butterscotch flavors, swung nearly empty on Laura's arm. The gingerbread men were all gone too. That basket sat on the table next to a Christmas Eve smorgasbord of candy cane cookies, brownies, toffee bars, peanut butter squares, pretzel cookies, thumbprint cookies, spumoni cookies, nut roll-ups, spritz cookies, fudge, peanut brittle, and divinity. Laura had nibbled at more than her share, unable to pick among her favorites. Her stomach rebelled against the thought of one more bite, yet she eyed the divinity with the longing of a six-year-old who didn't know when she'd had enough. The spicy aroma of mulled apple cider mingled with the scent of hot chocolate and coffee.

Every child who participated in the Christmas program had received a sweet from

Laura, whether they were grandchildren or not. The sweets, wrapped in plastic wrap and tied with red and white ribbons, came with a kiss on the cheek whether they liked it or not. The boys mostly ducked their heads and attempted escape, but not without their popcorn balls.

Laura sank onto a bench and rested her aching knees and ankles. Her cheeks ached from smiling. A good ache. Her youngest great-grandchild, Bartholomew, had participated in his first program without even knowing it. Starring as the baby Jesus. Chubby cheeked and pink, he slumbered through most of the evening, awaking with a bewildered squawk during the final song.

Memories enveloped her, even as she tried to fend them off. Eli grinning from ear to ear, clapping after Aaron's and Ruby's turn as Mary and Joseph. The way he piled his plate high with cookies and candies, then insisted it was all her idea. He loved Christmas and she loved him for it. Every year his memory receded further into the past. His laugh, the feel of his whiskers against her cheek, his smell. She could barely recall the color of his balmy blue eyes.

"Did you fall asleep?"

She started at the sound of Zechariah's voice. He stooped, moved the basket to one side, and sat next to her. His eyes were a warm maple-syrup brown and very much alive. She missed his presence in Ben's home. He'd kissed her and then they'd taken him away from her. He'd kissed her and they'd never talked about it. She had told no one. Neither had he, she had no doubt. One kiss did not courting make, but at their age, it was a humongous step forward.

At least she thought it was. She hadn't courted in almost sixty years. Nervous as a blushing bride, she tucked the basket into her lap and wrapped her arms around it. His absence from Ben's house had left a void that couldn't be filled. She admitted that only to herself. No one grunting and growling at her. No one frowning over his morning cup of coffee. No one to beat at checkers. No one to kiss her so unexpectedly she'd barely had time to respond fully. Did he think she wasn't that interested? Did she still know how to kiss?

Soft lips. Slightly parted. Warm breath on her cheek. The scent of peppermint.

She'd been kissed and she still knew how to kiss back. Given the chance.

He felt different than Eli, not better or worse, only different. And nice.

Very nice.

"Are you going to answer me or just sit there looking at me with that goofy stare?"

"Sorry, I'm worn out from making all those popcorn balls and gingerbread men." Embarrassment coursed through her, as warm as the thought of his lips on hers. *Think, think.* Her scattered thoughts hopscotched from one to ten and back. *Think, think.* "How is it at Michael's? The house is quiet without you. I — we — miss you."

"You have chocolate on your lip." He pointed with his trembling index finger so close he almost touched her mouth. His gaze flitted to her eyes and then back to her mouth. He smiled. "Fudge?"

Nodding, she eased back and wiped at her face with her apron. "Or it could be brownie or chocolate chip cookie or toffee bar."

He laughed, but his gaze remained on her lips.

More heat, this time blazing. Her fingers lingered on her mouth, covering it. "There's something about Christmas Eve, isn't there?"

He nodded, the humor in his face fading. "Chockful of memories."

"Eli loved the holidays."

"So did Marian. She started making gifts in August. The house always smelled like peppermint. The candy cane cookies were her favorite."

"Eli liked the gingerbread men."

"So you made those for every one of the kinner."

"I did." She smiled. He smiled back. Such a sweet smile. He should do it more often. "We should be making new traditions, not stumbling around in old ones."

He shrugged. "At our age the trick is to balance the two. What's your favorite cookie?"

"Snickerdoodles."

"I like the thumbprint cookies."

Laura studied her hands. Could two old fogeys make new memories together? Jennie and Leo stood at the refreshment table sharing a cup of mulled cider and laughing over something her youngest, Frances, had done. They looked as if they'd been married all their lives and not a little over two years. They had their second chance at love and it looked good on them.

Old memories and new ones. A balance.

Laura shifted on the hard bench. Zechariah said nothing. He seemed content to watch the children play Simon Says and Here-We-Go-Round-the-Mulberry-Bush in the space where the program had taken place. Two girls played tic-tac-toe on the chalkboard. Botching abounded.

Their youthful exuberance brushed its wings against Laura's skin. Joy and energy mingled. She could walk home if need be, walk to Jamesport and beyond. Christmas joy was like that.

"I figure I won't see you tomorrow." A peculiar hesitancy crept into Zechariah's voice. Laura glanced his way. His cheeks had turned ruddy. His gaze didn't meet hers. His shaking fingers grappled with a canvas daypack that lay at his side. "So I'll give this to you now."

He laid a small, plain package wrapped in brown paper and tied with twine in the space between them. He shoved it toward her with one knobby finger. She glanced around. No one paid them any mind. "I don't have anything for you."

"Don't make a big thing out of it. You already gave me the one thing I wanted." He rubbed his hands together. "Open mine now."

Whatever was he talking about? Either he'd lost his mind or her memory had gotten so bad she didn't remember giving him a gift. "Now?"

"Are you hard of hearing?"

Laura swiveled so she gave her back to Ruby and her other daughters, who gathered with grandbabies in their arms, laughing and talking, giving no notice to her doings. She ripped the paper away to reveal a small pink bag. Inside the bag, small, pink binoculars.

"They're small but powerful." Zechariah's grin held glee. "Just the right size for a woman's hands. Look, they fold in the middle. They have a good field of view up to one thousand yards. They're light too."

"For bird-watching?"

"Nee, for peeking in windows and spying on people. Of course for bird-watching. And seeing other wildlife while you're out there." He crossed his arms and leaned back. "You seemed interested and the bird count at Swan Lake in January would be the perfect place to start. Last year we counted 243 trumpeter swans and 50 bald eagles, not to mention all the owls and snow geese."

They weren't just binoculars. They were an invitation into Zechariah's life. A passion he wanted to share — with Laura. A vaguely familiar tingling feeling zipped up her spine. Her breath caught. That feeling of anticipation. She ran her fingers over the shiny pink. "I feel bad that I didn't get you anything." Her voice sounded funny in her ears. Like the young girl she'd once been. The girl who saw the possibilities and longed to experience them. "But danki. You're sweet."

"I've been called a lot of things lately, but sweet's not one of them." His face went scarlet. "And you did give me something."

"I know my memory isn't what it used to be, but —"

"You didn't treat me like a big baby." His gruff voice grew rougher than steel wool. Laura had to bend closer to hear him. "You gave me cover to run away from home that day. You understood why I needed . . . to go. Besides, I also ate two gingerbread men and a caramel popcorn ball when you weren't looking."

"You did not!"

"Your little ones are quick to share."

A pause filled with the squeals of small children and the big ones' laughter. The socializing could go on for hours. Her gift to Zechariah had been a simple one of faith. He needed someone to have faith in him. "With age comes wisdom. Maybe our kinner will figure that out someday." The sight of Zechariah marching back into the house, head held high, later that afternoon had done her good. He even remembered to return the plastic container, freshly washed by Jessica, and the pot holders. He looked younger and walked straighter. Never mind that he still ended up at Michael's house. The point had been made. "How is it going at Michael's?"

"Fine and dandy." His eyes darkened. Lines around his mouth and eyes deepened. Sadness fought with his attempt at light-heartedness. "Michael's fraa is a gut cook. She has a kind disposition. She's not as cranky as Rosalie. But then she doesn't have twins to feed in the middle of the night. Which means no boplin screeching either."

"You miss Mia and Mary."

"I do." He didn't try to dress the words up. "I miss . . . everyone."

"Me too." She didn't offer to sort out what she meant by that.

Zechariah's eyes narrowed. He laced his fingers in his lap. His legs crossed at the ankles, then uncrossed. "So maybe you'll go see the swans."

"I'll try. Tamara may be gone by then."

"By then Rosalie will be able to care for the boplin on her own."

"It's time to go." Michael tucked his arm in his coat as he walked toward them. His fraa, Cathy, trotted behind him, shooing along their two children. They were about the same age as Delia and Samuel. "It's starting to snow and the roads are icy. The kinner are tired."

Zechariah stood, his back to his grandson. "If you don't be sad, I won't either. Merry

Christmas."

A golden promise from a man who surprised her. Few could at this late date. A lump lodged in Laura's throat. She managed a nod. "Merry Christmas."

He wrestled with his coat. Cathy insisted on helping him. He rolled his eyes and batted her hand away. "I'm not one of your kinner."

"Groossdaadi!"

They bantered their way through the crowd toward the door.

Laura smoothed her fingers over the soft pink bag. Her own binoculars. "Zechariah."

Tossing his gray wool scarf around his neck, Zechariah turned. So did Michael and Cathy. Ignoring their curious gazes, Laura focused on Zechariah. "I might need to borrow that new bird guide you have."

"You're welcome to it." His tone was brusque, his gaze caught somewhere over her shoulder. "I can bring it to you —"

"Groossdaadi." Michael broke in.

"I'll come by for it." Laura shot Zechariah a look he would understand. "It's no problem."

"See you then."

The promise of those three words was the best gift of all.

TWENTY-FIVE

Sometimes it didn't pay to share secrets. Exasperated, Laura retied her bonnet and tried to ignore Mary Katherine's chatter. She found Zechariah's gift of binoculars to be so interesting she'd been talking about it for five miles now. Quiet to contemplate all the meanings of a Christmas gift would have been preferable. But catching a ride with Mary Katherine made Laura's current mission easier. She didn't want to explain a stop at the dawdy haus to Ben and Rosalie. Ezekiel had stayed home with the head cold and cough that was going around. That gave Laura the opportunity she needed. She climbed into Mary Katherine's buggy after the children's Christmas Eve program at the school and settled under the thick fleecy blanket. What did the binoculars mean?

Especially coupled with the kiss. She hadn't told her friend about the kiss. Absolutely not. Mary Katherine would fall over in a faint, the horse would spook, careen out of control, and the buggy would flip, landing them all in a ditch.

All because of one small, feathery kiss.

They'd kissed like teenagers who'd never done it before. Two people, both married for more than forty years, with sixteen children between them, living and dead, kissed like it was the newest thing since wringer wash machines.

"He gave you binoculars. Pink lady binoculars," Mary Katherine said for the fourth time. "I'm so happy for you."

"It's not a proposal."

"I know I've teased you a gut bit about Zechariah, but I really do want you to be happy and he's a gut man." Mary Katherine wiggled in her seat like a little girl at church for the first time. "A little cantankerous, but who isn't at our age?"

"It's only a little gift. It doesn't mean anything."

"Sure it does. I promise you, it does."

"He's old. I'm old. We've had our liebs, our kinner. It's our time to sit by the fireplace and keep our achy bones warm."

"Is it time for us to have that conversation again about The One?"

Mary Katherine was right. Not so long ago, Laura had insisted Mary Katherine consider the possibility that God might give her a second chance at The One, a man she would love more than she thought possible. She loved Moses with all her heart. Now she loved Ezekiel with the same no-holds-barred intensity. Just as he had loved his first wife and now loved her.

Now the kiss was on the other cheek. The One. Could Zechariah be Laura's second chance? At seventy-three? It seemed impossible, but with God, all things were possible. "Can we talk about something else?"

Mary Katherine laughed. Her breath filled the night air with puffy white clouds. "I love Christmas, don't you? It's so full of possibilities."

Mary Katherine could read minds, it seemed. Fortunately, her question required no answer.

For a few minutes Mary Katherine prattled on about how many books they had sold at the store and how good business had been for the holidays. Finally her voice trailed away, leaving the *clip-clop* of the horse's hooves on the icy asphalt and the whistle of the wind in the trees.

"For a woman who generally rivals me in the talk department, you sure are quiet." Mary Katherine's voice softened. "Zechariah giving you a gift must make you think of Eli. I think of my Moses and I know that he's happy I'm happy. Eli would be too."

He would be. But the attention of another man on Christmas Eve, this night of all nights, was strange in retrospect. God's timing? Christmas Eve was a strange, yet glorious, night for Eli to be taken home. He probably grinned about it still. On the other hand Laura remembered each year how it felt to wake up on Christmas morning and find his hands as cold as ice, his lips blue, and his face lifeless. The dawning realization that those lips would never move again. She would never hear him profess his love in that husky whisper in her ear late at night or feel those lips kiss her neck. His fingers would never trace her collarbone or trail across her cheek as his eyes studied her face, trying to decide where to land the next kiss.

He would never laugh or smile or sing or order or scold or love her again.

She had aged since then. The years had not been kind to Zechariah. Caring for him meant facing a future filled with caregiving. A future where she might lose a loved one once again. Could she — dare she — face that again?

The feel of his lips on hers made her close her eyes and sigh.

Teenagers swooned over kisses, not great-grandmothers. It wasn't just the kiss, although it was no small matter in its unexpected delightfulness, but the solidarity, the closeness, the sense of life lessons shared. No starting from scratch, but rather diving in the deep end of the lake of life.

"Nee. I'm fine. I keep busy. You know that." She shivered and tugged the blanket tighter over her lap. If anyone understood how to navigate such a strange new path, Mary Katherine did. She glowed with happiness every time she said Ezekiel's name. He had diabetes. She delighted in finding new sugar-free dessert recipes for him. She adapted to him and he to her. "The program was very sweet this year."

"And you handed out at least fifty popcorn balls and a hundred gingerbread men. I believe I saw Zechariah eat two of the gingerbread men and a popcorn ball. He stole them from Naomi."

"Everyone loves gingerbread men."

Mary Katherine cackled. "Okay, okay, I'll stop. Did you see Tamara sneak out with Emmett there at the end? That's a gut sign, isn't it? She looked like a girl in lieb."

"I did see them." Mary Katherine, ever the optimist, saw what she wanted to see. Laura saw a young woman trying to fit in, trying to make her family happy. "They've only just met, but I'm hopeful."

It was Christmas Eve after all, the night of the greatest miracle in history. Jesus, the Son of God, born of a virgin girl and a simple Nazarene.

"You should be. A grand trying to stick to the path. Speaking of grands, why are you going to the dawdy haus?" She clucked at the horse and the buggy picked up speed. Mary Katherine was a writer and all writers were nosy. The curiosity must've been killing her. "You know you can't talk to Hannah."

"I don't plan to talk to her." Laura shouldn't involve Mary Katherine in her little rebellious plot. Mary Katherine would stay in the buggy, far from the dawdy haus. Laura would only peek to make sure Hannah was doing well. She'd be about three months now. Maybe the morning sickness had passed by now. She was such a skinny girl, she'd probably be showing. Was she warm enough? Did Jacob and the boys leave plenty of firewood for her? "Rachel talked to her yesterday. She said she's passing the time sewing baby clothes and blankets. She is a gut girl. She's fine."

"Then what are we doing here?"

"We may not be able to talk to her, but that doesn't mean I can't leave her a little something." Nowhere in discussing the bann did Ben say anything about Christmas presents. Not a word. "She's still my great-grand and she still deserves a Christmas."

The ministers would disagree. Hannah's sin deserved punishment and that meant no frivolity. She could celebrate the birth of Christ through praise and prayer and thinking about her transgressions.

But one gift wouldn't offset her penance.

Mary Katherine clucked and snapped the reins again. "That's the Christmas spirit."

The dawdy haus was dark except for the flickering light of a lantern in the kitchen window near the back. Mary Katherine pulled up near the front porch so they couldn't be seen from the main house. "Hurry." She sounded pleased as a girl going to her first rumspringa party. "You don't want to get caught, do you?"

A grown woman sneaking around her daughter's house, trying to leave a package for her wayward great-grandchild. Eli would have shaken his head and pulled her into his lap for a good talking-to.

What would Zechariah think of it?

He'd looked exhilarated by his mad dash to freedom the previous week. He would approve. She was sure of it. Not that she needed his approval. Still, the idea that he would be first in line to leave a present on his grand's porch assured Laura she was on the right track.

Her arms wrapped around her package, she tiptoed toward the porch. She peered at the ground in the dark, hoping she didn't fall into a hole or trip over a branch brought down by gales of frigid wind earlier in the day. Women her age didn't bounce.

The wind blew almost as hard now, sending a chill through her. She bent against it and trudged forward. An instant later, she smacked against a solid form.

"Hey!"

"Hey."

"Who is it?" Adrenaline shot through her, leaving a metallic taste in her mouth. Shivering, she back stepped. She fought to keep her legs from buckling. "Phillip? What are you doing here?"

The young man ducked his head. He, too, held a package clutched in his arms, but his was much larger. A huge, heavy-looking cardboard box. In the dark it was impossible to tell what it had held in the past. He eased it onto the welcome mat in front of the door. "What are you doing here?"

"Leaving something for Hannah. You shouldn't be here. If anyone sees you around here, they'll have to tell the ministers.

Hannah's in enough trouble."

"I know that. I'm just . . . I'm not . . . I thought . . ." Rubbing his hands together, he backed away. "I wasn't trying to talk to her. She doesn't know I'm here, I promise. Please don't tell anyone. I meant no harm. I didn't violate the bann. I only wanted to leave something for Hannah."

In the darkness Laura couldn't see his face, but his deep voice, barely a whisper in the wind, trembled with anxiety. He spoke the truth. She had no desire to get anyone in trouble. Besides, how would she explain her own presence on Hannah's doorstep in the dark of evening?

Especially when Phillip apparently had the same idea she did.

"You brought her a Christmas present." The idea delighted Laura. For the first time that day, a burden lifted from her shoulders. The past held less weight. The dark fewer memories. Eli would like this young man. "That's sweet of you."

Considering Hannah's circumstances, his bravery astonished Laura.

"I suppose it is against the Ordnung, isn't it?" He glanced over his shoulder as if expecting Ben or Cyrus or Solomon — or all three — to pop out and drag him away for a confession. "I thought if I didn't actually talk to her it would be okay."

"I thought the same thing." Laura made her voice reassuring. "It is Christmas after all. We're celebrating the birth of Christ and the forgiveness of sins that He represents. Surely, that means we should show grace to poor Hannah."

"What did you get her?" Suddenly, he sounded so much younger, like a little boy comparing notes. "The same as the other kinner?"

He'd been at the program and the recipient of some of her baked goods. He was a tall young man, with a wiry build, but he could put away the cookies. "Sweets, but something special too." Feeling silly, she leaned closer and whispered, even though no one else was around. "A crib quilt for the bopli and a nice shawl for her. I also bought her a book of children's stories at The Book Apothecary."

"She'll like that."

"I didn't know you and Hannah were freinds."

He mimicked her earlier movements by leaning closer and whispering. "We're not. We were in the same class at school. I saw her at the singings, but she always . . ."

Always had eyes for another who had left her high and dry.

Hannah had given her love to someone who didn't deserve it. Someone who might someday, because God was good, regret taking a girl's sweet innocence and giving her nothing in return.

But here Phillip was. He hadn't given up, even in the face of Hannah's obvious, flagrant sin. What a sweet boy. Kind. Perhaps he would like to be Hannah's friend. Like Zechariah could be Laura's friend? Which seemed like a Christmas miracle. Phillip saw through Hannah's weakness and her failing to who she was. "But you're being her freind now and that is very gut of you."

"Everyone makes mistakes. None of us is perfect. We are taught to forgive." He shrugged. "I haven't always done the right thing. Maybe this makes up for that a little bit." His hand waved toward the big cardboard box that now blocked the door.

"Well, aren't you going to tell me what it is?"

"It's a cradle." He shoved his hat down on his head and turned away. "I made it."

"Wunderbarr!"

The dark hid his expression, but his actions trumpeted his caring. He deserved a hug. Before Laura could move, he whirled and headed away in the dark.

A cradle. The baby's father should've made that cradle. What kind of man made a cradle for a baby who wasn't his? A good man. One worthy of consideration. *Gott, let Hannah give him that consideration. Thank You for this blessing You have bestowed on a poor, wayward girl who doesn't deserve it. Any more than I deserved forty-five years with Eli.*

Laura laid her packages on top of the box and turned to leave.

"Groossmammi?"

Laura froze. She swiveled. "I can't stay, my dear."

"Who was that with you? I heard voices. A man's voice."

Laura glanced toward the buggy now retreating in the distance, its reflectors twinkling in the moonlight. "Someone who wants to be your freind."

"No one wants to be my freind these days."

"That's where you're wrong. We're waiting for your bann to be done and then we'll welcome you with open arms. You know that."

"I've had a lot of time to think." Her disembodied voice quivered in the darkness. "I go over and over it and I don't understand how I got myself into this predicament. No one else I know or have ever known has done this. Only me. Me and Thaddeus."

"Many others have done the same, my child." Laura grabbed the porch railing to keep from bursting into the house and wrapping Hannah in a hug. "You're not the first or the last. You only need make sure you don't make this mistake again."

"Never. Never." She hiccupped a sob. "Even if it means I spend the rest of my life alone."

Laura eyed the box on the porch with its homemade gift constructed with kindness and grace. "We don't know what Gott's plan is."

"Tamara came by last night, after dark."

Anger swept through Laura. The girl was a meddling busybody. Much like her grandmother. "Tamara means well, but you must not listen to her. She is going down a path of no return. You don't want to go there too."

"She said I could go with her when I leave. That her doctor freind would help me too."

The road to hell was paved with good intentions and Tamara skipped blithely along it. "You know your family loves you and will love your bopli. Out there you'll only have Tamara, and she'll be busy becoming a doctor. How would you support yourself and the bopli?"

"That's what I told her."

"Gut."

"She told me to think about it. She said she'd be back before she leaves. In case I change my mind."

"You must send her away."

"She doesn't judge me. She says our ways are old-fashioned and the bann is mean-spirited. That it punishes us for being human."

"What do you think?"

"I gave a special gift to Thaddeus that should've been reserved for my mann." Tears choked her words. "I can never get it back. I don't know how I'll explain to my bopli about his daed."

"Cross that bridge when the time comes. For now, concentrate on having a healthy bopli and being a gut mudder."

"I'll try. Danki for coming here to check on me. I feel better just seeing a kind face."

"Actually, I didn't mean to talk to you. I only meant to leave you something."

"A Christmas present?" She sounded nine. Not like a grown-up woman who would be a mother in the coming year. "For me?"

"Nee, for the postman. Of course it's for

you. And the bopli."

"That's so sweet."

"There's also something else. Another gift."

"From the man who was on the porch?"

"Jah. You didn't recognize his voice?"

"Nee. I only heard whispers, one gruff, one soft like yours when you used to tuck me in at night and whisper a prayer over me when you spent the night after Callie was born."

Memories as sweet for Laura as they were for her great-grand. "Then I won't spoil his surprise. I have to go."

"Groossmammi?"

"Jah."

"Merry Christmas."

"Merry Christmas, my sweet girl."

"Next year will be different."

God willing. "We all will be different."

Laura tightened her coat around her and blew on her mittens as she headed for the buggy. The wind picked up and whipped her bonnet strings across her face. Icy snowflakes dusted her nose and cheeks. Poor Mary Katherine would be frozen to the buggy seat.

"You, there in the dark, stop. Who are you? What are you doing sneaking around here?"

Her heart pounding in overdrive, Laura

skidded to a stop. Her chest hurt and the icy air burned her lungs. Like a teenager caught coming in after midnight, cigarette smoke on her breath and gasoline fumes on her clothes. Had she ever been that young? She swallowed the idiotic fear.

Ruby's husband, Martin, approached. His accusatory tone wasn't much different than the one he used when she ate supper with them. He always made her feel as if she'd overstayed her welcome. She couldn't see much in the black, starless night. But the short, rounded form belonged to him.

When Laura had moved into the dawdy haus and Ruby's family took over the main house, she learned the difference between close and too close. She learned to enjoy her tiny space and leave the bigger, familiar, full-of-memories space to her daughter and — truth be told only to her innermost self — least favorite son-in-law. "It's me, Laura."

Martin switched on a hefty flashlight with a beam that scoured the dark far beyond her figure. She thrust her hand over her forehead and ducked her head against the powerful light that danced left, then right, up and down, as if searching her, a pat down as the writers in her mystery books called it.

"What are you doing here at this hour?

Visiting Hannah? You know better."

"Lower the light. You're blinding me." He might be a man, but she was thirty-five years his senior, his mother-in-law, and she was entitled to a minuscule amount of respect for the elderly. "It was my intent to leave her a Christmas gift without speaking. No rule against a groossmammi doing that for her great-grand, even one in the bann."

"You didn't go inside?"

He was debating whether he would have to tell Ben. That would be his call. Nothing weighed on her conscience. "Nee."

"Did you speak?"

"Only because she heard . . . me and called out to see who it was much as you're doing now." A sin of omission. Why not tell him about Phillip? Because the boy's heart was in the right place, even if the timing was wrong. She would pray forgiveness for her sin later. "Don't blame her. Blame a sentimental old lady with bad timing."

Silent, Martin let the flashlight dance across the field behind the dawdy haus. Snow sparkled like tiny jewels in pinpoints of light. Elegant frost hung from stalks of grass. Nature offered its own light display with no need of electricity or wires hung across porch railings, eaves, and the outlines of windows. Laura inhaled the cold night

346

air, trying to assuage the ache brought on by the beauty of Christmas Eve. If only Eli could see it. He would understand.

"Ruby tells me you've been speaking with Tamara. How's that going?"

"It's hard to say." The abrupt change of subject brought relief and a sense that greater problems weighed on this father than the wayward child of another living on his property. He didn't need to know his daughter had visited Hannah right under his nose and tried to convince her to leave too. It would break his already aching heart. "She's still here. She loves Rosalie's kinner and she's born to be a mudder and fraa herself, if she would allow herself to see it."

"If only there were a man who could make her see it." The sound of Martin's boots kicking at the muddy snow at his feet filled the night air. "Courting may be private, but my fraa says she hasn't seen any signs it's happened. Ever. What is it about my dochder?"

He really meant to ask what had he done wrong, where had he gone wrong. Men especially tended to think they played a strong hand in the outcome of their children's lives. They couldn't accept that children grew up and made their own mistakes. They couldn't simply learn from their parents' mistakes. God's design called for something different. Free will.

"She's too smart for her own good." Laura gentled her voice, making it less of a criticism and more of an observation. "She wants to serve. She wants to make a difference. She wants to be who she is."

"You sound as if you agree." Martin turned up the collar of his coat with his free hand. His voice shook with cold, but he didn't seem inclined to end the conversation. "We didn't bring her up to abandon her faith for a wild-goose chase into the Englisch world of medicine. She'll never marry or, worse, marry an Englischer. She'll never be baptized. We won't see her kinner. They won't know us and we won't know them. Is this Gott's will?"

He stopped, but his angry breathing still spoke of anguish.

"I don't know." For the first time Laura caught a glimpse of what her daughter saw in Martin when she married him. A stout believer with a heart for those he loved. A man who loved with ferocity, the kind that could take a woman's breath away. "But, no, I don't agree. However, I do remember what it was like to be that age and to be torn between two worlds. The Gmay gives our young ones this period of rumspringa in order for them to answer the question of whether they want to commit to the faith for the rest of their lives. We don't always get the answer we hope for."

"Then you believe all hope is lost?"

"All hope is never lost. Too many people are praying for Gott's will in this."

"I don't understand it. How could she do this?"

"She wonders the same thing."

"I wouldn't know. She hasn't spoken to me about any of this."

"You're her daed. Does that surprise you?"

Her father and a man. Even Laura, old, wrinkled, and far past any embarrassment on most topics, found this more than awkward, more than embarrassing. She longed to dash past her son-in-law and get lost in the dark shadows.

"Martin, what are you doing? The kinner are ready for bed." Ruby's voice floated from the big house.

"You better go."

"You won't say anything?"

"Nothing to say."

"I'm sorry I put you in this position."

"I'm glad Hannah will have a bit of Christmas. We must always show the grace that was shown to us." Martin pivoted and headed back to the house. His boots crunched in the snow and ice, but his step was sure. The flashlight bobbed in the trees and bushes. "I'm coming, Fraa, no need to shout to the entire world."

Danki, Gott, for the Christmas gift of knowing my son-in-law better. And forgive me for judging him. I could use some of that grace and mercy too.

Even at seventy-three, a woman could learn a lesson. Better late than never.

Twenty-Six

If any day deserved prayer and contemplation, it was New Year's Eve. Laura leaned into the pew in front of her and pushed herself up. The Englisch loved to have parties, champagne, and fireworks. The Plain spent the evening with a service followed by family time and a potluck dinner. Each to their own. Saying good-bye to the old year and praying for God's grace and mercy in the new one.

Laura's knees popped and her legs refused to cooperate. Her behind was numb and her ankles like rubber after all that sitting and kneeling on Solomon's red-oak plank floor. Ruby grabbed one arm and Tamara the other. Together, they hoisted Laura to her feet.

"Danki." It was indeed a sad state of affairs when a woman couldn't kneel in prayer and then get herself back up. "I could've just stayed down there until you're ready to haul me out of here to the house."

"You're so silly, Groossmammi." Tamara giggled. "We love your creaky knees. They make music with all that popping. Like the cereal. Snap, crackle, pop!"

"You're the silly one." Laura loved to see the girl — young woman — smile. She seemed content. She hadn't complained once during her stay. In fact, she seemed content caring for the twins. Diapering, bathing, singing, and playing with them. She and Delia had become best friends with tea parties and story hour every night before bed. It was hard to say who was the bigger child. "You love me so much, why don't you bring me a plate from the smorgasbord?"

"I will." Her grin had nothing to do with food. Her gaze fell on a tall figure standing by the Styrofoam plates and plastic utensils at the first table. Emmett Bays. "What do you want?"

Her tone suggested she likely would not hear Laura's answer. "A little of everything, but especially the five-bean salad and the macaroni-and-cheese casserole. And Mary Katherine's chocolate German cake."

"Got it."

It seemed unlikely, but Laura smiled and shrugged at Ruby. Her daughter's worried gaze followed Tamara. None of the festive holiday spirit imbued her face. She looked scared. "What is it, Ruby?" Laura sat and patted the spot on the bench next to her. "You don't look like you have high hopes for the new year."

Ruby's eyes reddened with tears. Her mouth opened and closed. She mopped her face with a huge white handkerchief.

"Dochder, what is it?" Laura took her hand and squeezed. More tears. More mopping. "What's got you so heartbroken? Is there something I don't know about?"

Ruby was the youngest and most softhearted of Laura's four daughters. Victoria, the oldest girl, didn't have time to be softhearted, what with five brothers and three sisters. Marilyn and Lena, the two middle girls, took turns caring for Ruby, who came at the tail end after three boys. She followed her sisters around everywhere. She was born to be a mother and wife. All Plain women were, but some fell into it more naturally than others.

"I've prayed for forgiveness. I know my worry is a sin." Ruby sniffed. Laura followed her gaze. Tamara picked up two plates. She spoke to Emmett. He took one of the plates and followed her along the tables that groaned with the massive weight of casseroles, sandwiches, ham, turkey, side dishes, breads, and desserts. "I can't bear the thought of losing her. She's too smart for her own gut. Where did that come from, Mudder? I'm not smart. Martin is a gut, decent man who has tried to bring our kinner up right. How could this happen?"

"You know what they say about worry?"

"I do. Worrying about tomorrow takes the joy out of today."

"She's doing better. Look at her. It's obvious she likes Emmett." Laura had tried, with no luck, to find out how much. Two buggy rides didn't a courtship make. But it could be a fine start. It had been with Eli. Tamara managed to duck every inquiry with a self-satisfied smirk. "She's done well at Rosalie's. She's like you, born to be a mudder and fraa. She's seeing that every day."

"You think so?" Ruby's anxious gaze dropped. She kneaded her fingers in her lap. "Martin is beside himself. He says if she runs off to the college, she'll never be welcome in our home again. He says he can't have her influencing the other kinner."

"He *is* right." Laura tried to soften the words. Martin had to keep the two teenagers still left at home free of worldly influence. That was his job as a father. One Ruby shared. "But she could very well change her mind. She understands what an important decision this is. She knows what it will mean to her and to you and your mann. She's not immune to the pain it will cause."

"She's spent three years preparing to leave. Every day she's been preparing to leave." Ruby's lips trembled. She hid them behind her hankie. "And I never even noticed. What kind of mudder does that make me?"

"One secure in Gott's plan for you and for your kinner." The words sounded thin in Laura's ears. She hadn't noticed Tamara's hike off the path either. What kind of grandmother did that make her? "We're not to worry, but to trust and obey."

"She could obey better."

"Agreed, but she is a gut girl. She will make the right decision."

Gott, please.

Her tears replaced by an anxious smile, Ruby nodded. Her hands relaxed. With a deep, audible breath she slipped the hankie into her canvas bag. "Here they come."

They did indeed. Tamara carried two plates piled high with food. Emmett followed behind with two more. Laura forced a bright smile. "Danki, child. That looks so gut. You didn't forget the cake, did you?"

"Nee, of course not. This one with the big hunk of cake is yours. Mary Katherine said to tell you to eat it first. She said that's the license of old age, to eat dessert first."

"I'm not old." Laura took the plate and let her smile extend to Emmett. "How do you like Jamesport?"

"It's gut. I'm settling in." His gaze bounced toward Tamara and back to Laura. "I expected to be homesick, but I'm not at all. Anthony has plenty of work for me to do, and Molly feeds me far too well. And the company has been gut."

No doubt in his meaning. Tamara's cheeks colored a pretty pink. "Give Mudder her plate, will you?"

With great care he handed a plate piled equally high to Ruby. She nodded so hard her head might fall off. "Danki. We're glad you're here. Our district can always use another hardworking, faithful young man. Have you been baptized, then? Or will you do that here? How old are you?"

"Mudder!" Tamara's color deepened to rose red. "I'm going to eat with Molly. She has loads to tell me about something or other." She whirled and strode away, leaving Emmett to fend for himself.

"I'm twenty-four. Baptized at twenty." He didn't seem to mind answering the questions. In fact his blue eyes sparkled. He had dimples that grew when he smiled. His gaze

356

followed Tamara. "I need to find Anthony. He doesn't want to stay too long. He says the weather is getting worse and little Daphne has been fighting a cold."

"Jah, of course. Eat your food before it gets cold." Ruby waved her plastic fork in the air. "Have a Happy New Year."

"I intend to." He made a beeline for the spot where Molly and Tamara sat, next to the two Hershberger children.

"See, I told you."

Ruby sighed. "You're always right. I'm so glad I can rely on that."

"Nee. Rely on Gott. Say your prayers and humbly accept His answer, whatever it may be."

"That's what I meant."

"That's what I thought."

They ate in companionable silence for a few minutes. Mary Katherine was right. No shame could be found in eating dessert first. Especially when it was New Year's Eve and, in a few weeks, she would celebrate the beginning of her seventy-fourth year on earth.

"So Zechariah gave you a Christmas present."

Mary Katherine had a big mouth and no thought for a woman's privacy. "He did. Why?"

357

Ruby chewed and swallowed a big bite of hot German potato salad. "I was wondering if maybe Tamara isn't the only one in the family courting."

"Don't wander too far, you'll get lost." Laura caught several other heated retorts before they slipped out of the corral. "With more than fifty grands and great-grandkinner, there's bound to be more than a few."

She caught most of them. At least Mary Katherine didn't know about the kiss. The single kiss. All alone waiting for another.

"No need to get snippy." Ruby giggled. After her earlier anxiety, it was good to see her smile, even if it was at Laura's expense. She speared a chunk of turkey breast and left it suspended in air for a second. "It would be gut for Zechariah to have someone to take care of him. That's a nasty disease he's got and it'll only get worse. He needs a healthy fraa to give him companionship in his last days."

If Ruby thought Laura was snippy before, she hadn't seen anything yet. "You think that's the only reason someone my age or his age would get married? The only reason someone would marry a man like Zechariah is to be his caregiver? To change his sheets and wipe the drool from his lower lip?"

"Nee. I didn't say that." Ruby's eyes widened. She leaned back as if to escape the fierce flow of words. "I didn't mean anything by it. I just hate to see folks alone in their old age. My mann isn't perfect, but I like having him around. It's hard to imagine what it must be like."

She stuttered over the last words and halted. "You surely miss Daed this time of year." Her gaze fluttered over Laura's shoulder. "No one should be alone during the holidays."

Laura stifled the urge to swivel to see what her daughter saw. "A woman with nine kinner, fifty-two grandkinner, and twenty-eight great-grands is never alone."

"You know what I mean and like I said before, no need to get snippy." Ruby laid her plate on the bench and picked up one of the sorghum-molasses cookies her daughter had stacked on it. "Especially when he's sitting over there all alone in a crowd, likely feeling sorry for himself."

It couldn't be helped. Laura hazarded a quick peek. Indeed, Zechariah sat on the men's side with a full plate of food next to him on the bench. His shoulders were hunched, his eyes hooded under his black hat. He did not look happy.

Laura straightened. "Did you expect me

to do something about it?"

"Nee. I don't want you to scandalize everyone here." Ruby's whole body quivered with indignation at the thought. "I just meant you can see why I feel for him. And he gave you a present so he feels for you. You might somehow let him know how you feel. If you do. Of course."

This conversation had veered so far off course, Laura couldn't find the road for the thickets of trees and weeds. "Are you matchmaking, child, with your own mudder?"

"I might be." Ruby plucked at crumbs that had fallen on her apron. "Would that be so terrible? A dochder who wants her mudder to have a little more happiness in life?"

Laura stood and leaned over Ruby. She kissed her cheek with a big smack. "You've always been my favorite, you know."

"I knew it." Her face pink with pleasure, Ruby chortled. "I know you're teasing, but still, as the last one to come along, it's nice to know you're not getting the leavings."

"Pray for Gott's will in all things." Laura dropped another kiss on Ruby's forehead. The holidays made her this way, full of feelings that seemed to pour from her. Happiness. Joy. Sweet contentment. Love. Happiness that her family was healthy. Joy at the

360

way they had grown through the year. Sweet contentment at her place in their lives. Love for every child and every adult.

That still left that tiny little corner in her heart that said, *what about me?*

What about me?

She glanced at Zechariah.

His head lifted and he stared straight at her. A steely-eyed, cool stare like a barbed-wire fence complete with a NO-TRESPASSING sign.

Too bad. Laura stared right back. Her own steely-eyed, cool stare like a rider on a sleek horse galloping full-out, leaping over that fence right into the heart of the matter.

She marched to the table, picked up a plate, and stacked it with desserts. Candy cane cookies, toffee bars, butterscotch brownies, lemon squares, and thumbprint cookies.

With a deep breath and a silent prayer, she marched to the corner where he'd taken up residence. "I'm the dessert lady." She kept her tone light, her smile lighter. "You look like you can use sweetening."

His gaze faltered. "Danki, but I'm not hungry."

"Eating cookies has nothing to do with hungry." She slapped the plate down next to him and took a step back. "Happy New

Year, Zechariah."

He glanced around. His gaze softened. "Happy New Year, Laura."

"Is something wrong?"

His lips pressed together. He shook his head. "Nee."

"Missing Marian?"

"Always."

"But especially on holidays."

He nodded.

"Danki again for the binoculars."

He nodded again. "No need."

"I'd like to try them out soon." She glanced around. No one paid the least attention. Still, she picked up a cookie and nibbled at it. "Do you still want me to go to Swan Lake with you?"

"It is one of the best birding days of the year." The words held longing. "The swans are beautiful and so are the eagles. You should go."

"With you as my guide."

"I went to the doctor yesterday. There's been progression. The spasticity is worse, which means my ability to walk is affected. Michael says no birding for me."

"With help, you could go. With someone to hold on to."

His head came up. His gaze locked with hers. "You think so?"

"I think where there's a will, there's a way."

The gloom disappeared. He smiled. "You need to use those binoculars."

"I do."

The two syllables hung in the air with the timbre of a small bell.

Heat burned Laura's face.

"Time to go, Groossdaadi."

The ever-present Michael. He tucked his arm under Zechariah's. Zechariah tugged away. "Danki, I'm capable of getting up on my own." With dignity he stood. "Happy New Year, Laura."

"Happy New Year."

He winked.

She glanced at Michael and Cathy. They were busy herding children. She returned the wink. "Until then."

He nodded, scooped up Michael's youngest as if he weighed no more than a doll, and strolled out the door.

The new year had begun early.

TWENTY-SEVEN

The first day of a new year held so much promise. No matter a person's age, the new year stretched forward with 365 days, each one a blank slate, each one an opportunity to work hard and be faithful to family and community.

Laura snuggled under the covers and contemplated staying in bed two more minutes. Only her nose peeked from the warmth of a flannel sheet, a fleecy blanket, and three quilts. The wind whistled outside, smacking branches against her window. A quick gander told her darkness still prevailed. The days were short and the nights long this time of year, especially when dark clouds blanketed the sky from horizon to horizon. Icy pellets of sleet mixed with snow pelted the glass.

She should start breakfast. Ben would get the fire in the fireplace blazing any minute. New Year's Day or not, he had chores to do.

Children had to be fed, holiday or not. Tamara would stoke the fire in the wood-burning stove in the kitchen, as she did every day before bringing out the babies to keep them warm in a cradle nearby while they cooked breakfast. Laura enjoyed her company. She liked to sing to Mia and Mary while she cooked, making meal preparation a festive affair.

Laura stretched and contemplated which muscles ached. Easier to count which ones didn't. She had no right to complain. Her limbs weren't caught in the grips of a disease like Parkinson's.

Which brought her to Zechariah. A few words of encouragement and a chance to do what he loved filled the man with spark, with life. She needed to come through. Somehow they would get to Swan Lake.

She needed a plan.

"Think. Think, old woman." She threw back the covers. "It's not like he's in prison."

The binoculars, safe in their pink bag, lay on the table next to her stack of cards and writing materials for her letter circles. Waiting to be used. She still had a few days to work out the details.

First things first. Breakfast.

Shivering, she rushed to dress. Her icy fingers refused to cooperate, making the braiding and pinning of her hair under her kapp a long, harrowing experience. By the time she marched into the kitchen, her shoulders ached and it seemed likely that her kapp hung askew.

Cold air wafted through the kitchen. No flames crackled merrily in the stove. Instead, cold, dead ashes awaited her. No merry tunes abounded. Only the *tick-tick* of the battery-operated clock on the wall that told her it was six o'clock. Late.

"Someone had a late night." Was talking aloud to herself a sign of impending dementia brought on by old age? Perhaps the sleigh ride with Emmett had born fruit. Maybe Tamara also saw bright possibilities in the new year — opportunities that would come to her only if she stayed with family and community. "Best let her sleep in a bit."

Despite frozen fingers, Laura managed to get the fire going in short order. Wonderful, blissfully hot, aromatic coffee next. Pancakes and bacon sounded good. Between the coffee and the bacon, the smells would bring everyone scurrying to the breakfast table. Maybe even Tamara. Laura applied herself to whipping the batter. She sang her own song. Not as festive as Tamara's, but "How Great Thou Art" was her favorite English hymn.

"My, you are bright eyed and bushy tailed this morning." Rosalie shuffled into the room in terry-cloth slippers. She held a baby in each arm. Dark circles spoke of what kind of night she'd had. New mothers always paid a price for staying up late on special occasions. "Is the kaffi hot?"

"It is and there's milk if you'd like a dab."

"And sugar. Lots of sugar." Rosalie laughed as she laid her precious cargo in the cradle they shared. Both girls were wide eyed. Mia had a milk stain on her nightgown. Mary yawned and fussed.

"No fussing, either of you." A look of pain on her face, Rosalie put one hand on her hip and stretched. "You've been changed, fed, and burped. Mudder's turn." She grabbed a fat, green ceramic mug from the counter and filled it to the brim with coffee. "Where's Tamara?"

"What do you mean, where's Tamara?" Laura dropped a dab of lard on the griddle. It sizzled. She added six half-dollar-size puddles of batter. "Isn't she in her room, sleeping in?"

"Nee. She never came in to check on the boplin, but I figured she was out late with her special friend. I figured that was a gut thing." Rosalie cupped the mug with both hands and blew on the steaming liquid.

"But when I called to her this morning to bring me some clean diapers, she didn't answer. So I peeked in her room. Her bed hasn't been slept in. That's a whole other ball of wax. Ruby and Martin will be so disappointed in her. And this Emmett, what do we know about him, really?"

The coffee in Laura's stomach heaved in an acidic wave. Her throat burned. "Watch the pancakes and bacon for me?"

"Surely, but she's not there. I looked."

Not there. What would be better? Staying out all night with a Plain man like Emmett Bays? Or slipping away to an Englisch life?

The first. It could be forgiven and forgotten if it didn't happen again. She might be in her rumspringa still after all these years, but Tamara knew the rules. So did Emmett, no doubt, even if he'd grown up in another settlement and another church district. Teenagers returned home and slipped into bed before light dawned. They didn't rub their families' noses in their antics.

It wasn't done.

But then Hannah knew that too and she now spent her holidays alone under the bann.

Her hands tight around a ragged dish towel, Laura trudged down the hallway to the last bedroom. That little room more like a closet than a bedroom. She forced herself to peek inside. Clean and neat. And empty. No clothes on the hooks. No brush or pins on the table. No books. Nothing except a white envelope on the pillow that lay on a Hearts and Nine Patch quilt. Laura's name had been written in sloppy letters that suggested great hurry and stress.

Her heart already heavy with words still unread, Laura tugged the single sheet of notebook paper from the yellowed envelope.

Dear Groossmammi.

I'm sorry. I feel I should start with those words even though I'm not sorry for what I'm doing. Not really. I'm sorry for your hurt and for the pain this will cause Mudder and Daed. I'm sorry for the holidays we won't spend together and the hundreds of everyday family things I will miss. But I'm not sorry that I'm doing this now. A clean break is best. The time spent with Emmett has helped me see clearly what I want to do. He's been a gut listener. He's a gut man and I know there is a fraa for him in the future. But it's not me. He doesn't know me well enough to be hurt by that so that's one less burden I carry into my life. I didn't lead a man on or break his heart.

Emmett came here for a new start so he understands the need for one. He understands my need to follow my heart and my dreams. I hope you can too. Tell Mudder not to worry. I know where I'm going. Today and in the future. I have a place to stay. I have a job. Next week, I'll start classes. Dr. Reeves says she'll help me any way she can. I'm not alone. I'll never feel alone because I know you'll always be with me. I carry a million memories in my heart. Nothing can change that.

I can't in good conscience not offer the same hope to Hannah. I hope you understand that. She desires a second chance not sullied by the sly glances of men who know "what she did" and the frowns of women who don't want her example to lead their daughters astray. I know all about forgiveness and how we say we forgive, but we so often do not forget. Hannah's too young to suffer this fate. I have to do what I think is right.

Happy New Year.

Love, Tamara

Underneath, she'd signed a bunch of x's

and o's. Hugs and kisses. Laura plopped on the bed and stared out the room's only window. The sun had crested over the horizon, backlighting woolly black clouds that hinted of more sleet and snow.

Her heart plummeted. Hannah. Had Tamara taken her?

Tossing the letter on the bed, she shot to her feet. *Gott, please keep these girls safe. Guard them and keep them. Please don't let Hannah be led astray too.*

"Laura?" Rosalie met her at the door. "What is it? What's happened?"

"Can you get breakfast?"

"Of course I can."

"I have to get to Hannah. And talk to Ruby and Martin." Offices were closed today, but tomorrow she would pay a certain doctor a visit as well. This was not over. Not yet. "Among other people."

Understanding dawned in Rosalie's face. "I'm sorry."

"Me too." It would take courage to show the letter to Ruby and Martin. And humility. "I was sure the time with the babies would make her see. Make her feel."

"What I feel?" Rosalie hugged Laura. "What it's like to be a fraa and a mudder?"

"Jah."

"You did your best, Gott will do the rest."

371

He should get on with it then. Stifling that thought, Laura hugged her friend back. "We better get out there and make breakfast. Life goes on, one way or another."

She looked back. Not a hint that Tamara had graced this room. Would the rest of their lives be like that with her gone? Out of sight, out of mind?

Her place here was marked and now it stood empty. The paths of many lives would be changed by her absence.

Including Laura's.

Twenty minutes later she pulled up to the dawdy haus. Smoke spiraled from the chimney. Ice glistened on the windowpanes. The house looked so peaceful. *Please Gott, not Hannah too.*

She climbed down and rushed up the steps.

The door opened. Hannah, a shawl wrapped around her shoulders, squinted against the glare of the sun bouncing from the snow. "What are you doing here? And so early. Is everything all right?"

"You're still here."

"I'm still under the bann. Where would I go?"

Danki, Gott, for her gut sense, her faith. "Is Tamara here?"

"She's already gone."

Puffing from exertion mixed with relief, Laura drew a deep breath and paused on the porch. "You didn't go with her."

Hannah shook her head. "Did you really think I would?"

"It might seem like a way to escape your fate."

"The baby goes where I go. There's no escaping that. Besides, I've had a lot of time to think." Hannah's hands went to her belly in a protective gesture. "My faith hasn't changed. I would never leave my family."

Relief swept through Laura. She wouldn't have to tell Seth and Carrie their daughter had left Jamesport for another way of life, taking with her their grandchild.

"What's going on here?" Martin marched across the expanse of snow that separated the corral from the houses. His nose was bright red with cold. "Why are you here, Laura? Again. Once I could ignore but —"

"Tamara is gone."

He halted. His body swayed. His gaze drifted out to the barren pastures where he would plant corn and alfalfa in the spring. He sniffed, turned, and walked toward the house. "Ruby needs to know." He tossed the words over his shoulder. They sounded as icy as a winter storm.

"I'm going after her."

His shoulders hunched against the wind that whistled through the bare tree branches, he kept walking. His boots crunched in the snow. "She's made her choice."

"We must still try."

"Nee." He stomped up the stairs to the porch and disappeared into the house.

"She's not coming back." Hannah rubbed her hands together and blew on them. "She told me she can't wait to see the world. She can't wait to fill her head up with all that medical stuff about muscles and bones and organs and diseases and how to treat them. She was so happy."

"I have to try."

"I know."

"I have to go now."

"I know."

Laura shivered. Life could go along perfectly fine and then suddenly hit bump after bump. It changed in a fraction of a second. She knew that, yet it always surprised her. "I'm glad you didn't go."

"Me too." Hannah's wave was a tiny flutter. "See you soon."

"Talk to you soon."

"Wait."

Laura looked back. Hannah still stood in the doorway. A tentative, almost scared, look on her face. "I have to go, child. You know that."

"Just tell me one thing. Who left the cradle?"

Maybe this piece of information would shore up her hope for her future. Maybe it would help her see that her life was not over. "Phillip."

A smile replaced the hesitation. "It's nice. He did a gut job with the finish."

"It was sweet of him."

"Why would he do that for me?"

"A question you'll have to ask him one day."

"I couldn't."

"We never know what we can do until we have to do it."

Thanks to her indiscretion, Hannah would learn this lesson over and over again.

Laura followed Martin into the house. The fire had been allowed to sink low and the living room was cold. Ruby sat on the couch. Martin had joined her. They sat side by side, not touching, both staring at the glowing remains of logs that now generated little heat.

Ruby bit her lower lip. Her eyes were red rimmed and her skin pale. Her gaze met Laura's. "She's really gone?"

"I'm afraid so." Laura eased into a rocking chair. Her throat ached with the effort to hold her own tears back. Crying might be considered a sign of weakness but often brought a catharsis unparalleled by any other activity. "But rest assured, I plan to talk to Dr. Reeves and find out where she is. This isn't over."

"It is over. She's chosen." Martin cleared his throat and stood. "It's time to get breakfast on the table."

Ruby didn't move. Her gaze faltered and landed on her hands in her lap. She clasped them so tightly her knuckles were white. "That's it, then. We'll never see her again."

"Unless she recognizes her error and decides to return. We always take our lambs back into the fold." His voice sounded gritty, like a man with a chest cold. He turned so his back was to Laura and placed one callused hand on his wife's shoulder. "Now we all must live with it, Fraa."

Ruby stared up at her husband. A sob escaped. She put her hand to her mouth as if to corral the others that would surely follow and nodded. "I have a breakfast casserole in the oven." Her voice trembled. "I better check on it."

Martin's shoulders hunched. His hand lifted. "Go on then."

Ruby rose, but tears trickled down her

cheek. "Will I be allowed to write to her?"

"I reckon there's no rule against it." He brushed away her tears in a tender gesture that brought tears to Laura's eyes. "But I don't know that it'll serve much purpose."

"She's still our dochder."

Laura wanted to flee herself. This was a private grieving between a father and a mother whose child had gone astray. She edged toward the door. "She's still my granddaughter. It can't hurt to talk to her one more time. And to Dr. Reeves, who arranged all this."

"It can hurt. It creates hope where there is none." His eyes were cold and empty. "It does hurt."

"There's always hope."

"Leave it be." He worked his jaw. "Stay for breakfast. If I know Ruby, she made enough casserole for ten."

"I have to go. Rosalie will need me, with Tamara . . ."

"Then I reckon we'll see you on Sunday." He strode from the room so quickly it seemed as though his thoughts chased him.

"Mudder."

Ruby's soft entreaty tugged Laura from her spot by the door to her daughter's side. She encircled her in a hug and they huddled on the sofa together. "There's always hope,

Dochder, always."

There was hope and then there was acceptance.

"He's my mann. He's a gut mann."

"Jah, he is."

"He's right. We should let it go." Ruby rested her head on Laura's shoulder. "If it were anyone else's dochder, I would say she's made her choice."

"I know."

She rubbed her eyes with a crumpled handkerchief. "Try one more time, Mudder."

Sometimes it was hard to know when to let go of hope and embrace acceptance. Especially when it came to mothers and daughters. "I will. I promise."

TWENTY-EIGHT

Germs far and wide. Laura never used to worry about germs. Now it seemed any little cough from one of the children and she had the cold or the flu. Old age. She waded through Dr. Reeves's waiting room, filled as usual to the rafters with croupy babies and feverish toddlers and children with green faces that suggested it might be good to have a vomit bag on hand. All those who'd been sick over the New Year's Eve holiday were now in the doctor's office. A wizened elderly man with a pained expression rubbed his head with both hands. A man in a package delivery uniform dozed in a seat two chairs down. Surprised that she didn't recognize more of her English neighbors, Laura managed to make it to the receptionist's window without stopping.

"Do you have an appointment?" The woman on the other side of the window, dressed in pink uniform pants and a shirt covered with Winnie the Pooh bears, looked puzzled. "I don't see your name."

"Tell her it's about Tamara Eicher. I'm sure she'll want to squeeze me in." Shoving her way through the door into the exam rooms wouldn't be too drastic a measure, considering the situation. A weeping Ruby and grim-faced Martin were beside themselves with grief over Tamara's sudden, early departure. Martin's scowl left no doubt he blamed Laura. After she read Tamara's letter, Ruby's gaze faltered as well. The words "How could you?" were written all over her wan face.

Emmett's contribution had been a somber recitation of Tamara's monologue on why she had to go. And why he couldn't make her stay.

"I didn't have time to make her love me."

The man looked stricken at the thought.

While it was sad, the fact that Tamara didn't love her family and her God enough to stay was more bothersome.

A woman shouldn't be baptized if she didn't have the faith of her convictions. Simple as that.

Not simple. Laura had to give it one more try. She'd done everything in her power to keep Tamara from straying. And now she would try to get her back. Once she found her.

A few minutes later the nurse ushered her into the recesses behind the door and down a long hallway past exam rooms, some occupied by crying babies and mothers who looked at their wits' end. Laura didn't miss those days of waiting with a sick and crying child while toddlers attempted to explore the exam rooms from magazines to trash cans to biohazardous material containers.

The nurse showed her into Dr. Reeves's office. "She'll be right with you."

Which in doctor time meant within the next hour or two.

Laura spent fifteen minutes examining Dr. Reeves's diplomas and certifications and planning the big speech. The doctor was an educated woman with many pieces of paper to prove her worthiness of being trusted with family medicine. Laura had trusted her with Tamara, a precious gift from God.

"I've been expecting you." Dr. Reeves hustled into the room on rubber-soled Crocs that squeaked on the tile. They were covered with purple flowers as was her uniform shirt. The pants were a solid purple. She looked like a lovely flower with her short, curly black hair and lilac eyes. "Have a seat, please."

With a deep breath Laura sank into the soft leather chair on the other side of a massive oak desk covered with files and framed photos. Something tinkled and the doctor glanced at her computer. "One second, please." She typed for a minute with an amazing rapid-fire ferocity. The doctor's phone dinged. She spent another minute typing with only her thumbs. "Okay, you have my undivided attention. I promise." She glanced at her watch. "For about five minutes. Patients are waiting and you know how frustrating that is for them. They had appointments."

Guilty, but nevertheless Laura pushed forward. "It's a simple question with a simple answer. Where's Tamara?"

"She's safe and sound. I can also promise that." The doctor leaned back in her swivel desk chair, hands clasped over her midsection. "She doesn't want you to know where."

"What, is she afraid we'll come and drag her home by her hair?" Despite her best intention to remain cordial, Laura snorted. The doctor played a role in Tamara's flight, but she didn't instigate it. "We don't do that. I only want to give her one more chance to rethink this choice and to say good-bye. Did she tell you how she did it? How she left?"

"No, but when she showed up at my house on New Year's Day, I suspected."

"Did you tell her it was cowardly?"

"What Tamara did was unbelievably hard. It took great courage." Dr. Reeves frowned. Lines formed around her eyes and mouth, making her look older. "I suspect you know that and you respect it yourself."

"That doesn't make it what's best for her."

"Your granddaughter is one of the brightest, most intelligent women I've met in a long time." Dr. Reeves sat forward. She gripped the edge of her desk with both hands. "If you think I enabled her on a whim, you're mistaken. I look at her and see a woman with a great future ahead of her, given the opportunities and the education she needs to succeed. I can help her get that. I understand the cost to her and to her family. So does Tamara."

"I'd like to have this conversation with her, not you."

"I understand that. I have two daughters myself." Dr. Reeves touched a pink butterfly-shaped frame that held a photo of two dark-headed, elfin-sized girls with their arms around each other. They grinned at the camera. Both were missing front teeth. "I look at them and I feel so blessed that they'll never have to make those kinds of decisions. I hope they're as brilliant as Tamara. And as brave."

"If she was truly brave, she'd say good-bye to me face-to-face."

Dr. Reeves sighed and shook her head. "I can't."

"I'm an old woman. I may never see her again."

"She said you'd play the old woman card."

"She knew I'd come looking for her."

"She said if you couldn't be discouraged — which she knew you couldn't — I was to tell you to give it your best shot."

"I thought I had."

"She also said her stubbornness comes from you." Dr. Reeves scribbled something on a yellow stickie note and held it out. Laura took it. An address. "She's staying at a boardinghouse in Trenton that rents to students. She'll work there in exchange for a reduction in room and board. The place converts to a B and B in the summer, which means they'll still need her services for tending to the tourists. She's also starting this week as a filing clerk at a medical practice owned by a friend of mine. She has a lot on her plate."

"When will she go to class? When will she study?"

"She'll learn to juggle like every poor

medical student does. I think you'll find she's blessed to do this kind of work instead of waitressing or tending bar like so many students do. She has years of this ahead of her. These experiences knock the wheat from the chaff. Many students don't make it. I think she'll be one of those who will."

Or maybe she would come home. Only God knew. "If she had to do this, I'm thankful it's with the help of someone who can make the path a little bit easier." Laura managed to sound appreciative despite the desire to breathe fire on the other woman. "She's not out there in the Englisch world simply waiting for someone to take advantage of her."

"It's a hard world, no doubt, and it's not only Plain girls who tempt the ugly evildoers out there." Dr. Reeves stood. "English girls — and boys — are often victims as well. They may have more exposure to the world's ways, but they're still young and naive and away from home for the first time. I will do my best to stay in touch with Tamara and guide her. I've made a commitment to mentor her. You never know, she may come back to Jamesport one day and take over my practice."

As nice as that sounded in theory, it might also be agonizing to have her so close and yet no longer a part of the community. By that time Laura surely would have left this world. God's will be done. She stood. "Thank you for the information."

"Tell Tamara I said hi. Tell her not to be late for her classes next week. It sets a bad precedent. They may not take roll, but professors notice." She glanced at her watch and headed for the door. "Can you see yourself out? I have two strep throats and a possible case of pneumonia waiting for me."

"Go." For a fleeting second Tamara's image superimposed itself over Dr. Reeves. Younger, more vibrant, more energetic. This would be her future. Unless Laura could convince her otherwise.

Should she or was she meddling in God's plan? How could this be God's plan?

Gott, my pea-sized brain doesn't understand. I'm not smart enough to divine Your plans for this girl or for myself. Forgive me if I'm muddying the waters. I pray Thy will be done. And for the peace to accept whatever comes.

After I speak my piece.

Fifteen minutes later she was on the road out of Jamesport in Dineen Talbert's rust-encrusted blue minivan.

Dineen agreed to make one stop at Michael's before they headed to Trenton.

Laura had another errand to run on this second day of the year. "I'll wait here." Dineen settled back in her seat with the paperback romance novel she favored. They always had men's bare, chiseled chests on them and women in extravagant, low-cut gowns. Laura averted her eyes whenever she could. "I'm at a good part."

How she defined good part, Laura could imagine but tried not to. She marched up to the door and knocked. To her surprise and relief, Zechariah opened it. He looked bleary eyed, as if he'd just rolled from bed. His shirt was wrinkled. He squinted against the midday sun and smiled. "You're here. It's not bird count day, is it?"

"Nee, but I need you for something."

He stepped through the door and closed it behind him. He stretched and stood taller. "How can I help?"

"Two things. I need the book we discussed. And I need you to come to Trenton with me to convince Tamara to come home."

"Why? What's she doing in Trenton?"

"Becoming a doctor. Keep up."

"I can't just leave."

"Why not? You're a grown man."

That lopsided smile appeared. "That I am." The smile faded. "Abel's here."

"Bring him too. Make it snappy. Dineen's

waiting."

"You're bossy for an old woman."

"Because I'm an old woman. I don't have time to waste. Who knows how many days we have before we keel over. Get a move on."

"No need to get snippy. Moving."

The door closed. Laura scurried down the sidewalk and squeezed into the front seat with Dineen, who didn't look up. Chuckling, her head nodding, she licked her index finger and swiped from one page to the next. "Lord have mercy. These hot flashes will be the death of me." She fanned herself with her bookmark — a coupon for cottage cheese at the Hy-Vee grocery store in Chillicothe. "Are you ready to go?"

"Two more passengers. Zechariah Stutzman and Abel Danner."

Dineen slapped her dog-eared paperback shut, tossed it on the dash, and whistled. "Now you're talking. Are you sure you don't want to sit in the back seat? One of them could sit up front. Which one you got your eye on?"

"I don't know what you're talking about." Laura wiggled in her seat and fixed her gaze on the windshield, but the heat on her neck and cheeks told her they had gone red. Dineen might not be the best chaperone.

"I'm perfectly fine sitting in the front seat. I need their help to convince Tamara she should come home."

"Why not get Mary Katherine and Jennie or Bess? Women?"

Because they didn't need reminding that they were still useful. Zechariah did. Abel always had something good to say. He could help.

Two minutes later, Abel hustled down the walk. Birch cane in hand, Zechariah tottered behind him. Talking — or bickering — they stuffed themselves in the back seat.

"Hurry up. Shut the door." Zechariah slammed his harder than necessary. "We're in. Let's go."

"Easy, easy." Dineen put the van in drive and turned the wheel. "Be good to poor Kittie. She's all I got and she ain't getting any younger."

"He's in a tizzy because his lady friend came calling." Abel snapped on his seat belt and chortled. "I haven't seen him move that fast in ten years."

"She said she needed help. Time's wasting."

"Keep your pants on." Dineen accelerated. The landscape zoomed by. "You two settle down back there and let Miss Laura explain the mission. You're here for support, so try to keep the bickering to a minimum."

Something brushed against Laura's shoulder. She glanced back. The bird guide. "Danki."

"Keep it safe. Now what about Tamara? When did she take off?"

Laura told the story. "Dr. Reeves is convinced Tamara is doing the right thing and she's helping her stay gone. She has no right to meddle in our affairs."

"I reckon you told her that." Zechariah's chuckle was dry, humorless. "She's lived around here long enough to know better."

"I managed to keep my mouth buttoned up."

This time both Abel and Zechariah laughed aloud. Dineen joined in.

"I doubt that." Abel hooted. "You and my fraa are just alike when it comes to speaking your mind."

"It doesn't seem to bother you." Laura twisted and gave him a snoot full of sass. "And she puts up with you, so I figure you're even."

"It does bother me." Frowning, Abel rubbed his forehead. "It gives me a headache. Try to keep the noise down in here."

"You're always complaining of a headache. Maybe you need glasses."

"I don't need glasses —"

"Enough, kids, enough." Dineen eased around a buggy. She leaned past Laura and waved at the owner — Aidan Graber.

Laura caught herself ducking her head and managed to wave without so much as a hiccup of guilt. Aidan waved back, but his startled expression followed her down the road thirteen miles to Trenton. Now everyone to whom Aidan talked would know about the road trip with Abel and Zechariah. And word would spread like head colds in winter. Twenty minutes later they pulled up to the boardinghouse at the address on the yellow stickie.

White picket fence and white snowy grounds decorated bright-yellow faux-wood siding on an old three-story frame house converted to rooms for rent. The empty flower boxes that lined the front porch likely gave the place bright splashes of cheery color in the spring. The English tourists unable to get rooms in Jamesport would like it. No matter, Tamara wouldn't be here in the spring. Leaving Dineen to her novel, Laura tromped through the muddied slush to the front door and rang the doorbell.

"Why are you ringing the bell? They rent rooms. People come and go. Go on." Abel reached past her and grabbed the screen door. "Go in."

Zechariah touched his friend's arm. "Nee. We don't walk in. We're not students."

"So what — ?"

"Okay, you two —"

"What's going on out here?" Tamara shoved the screen door open and stared down at them. "I can hear you three jabbering in German all the way in the kitchen. What are you doing here? No, don't answer that. I know what you're doing here. Go on home, all three of you."

"Not until we see that you're all right." Laura's breath hitched in her throat. She swallowed a lump the size of her pillow at the sight of her granddaughter. She wore pants. Black pants and a blue polo shirt with the name of the boardinghouse embroidered on the pocket. A kapp still covered her hair. *Danki, Gott.* She hadn't gone so far as to display her hair in public. Hope sallied forth and did a masterful handspring. Laura eased past Tamara. "We came all this way. The least you could do is invite us in."

"I'm working. I can't have visitors right now." Tamara's lower lip protruded, but her eyes were luminous. Wet. Could she be glad to see her old granny? "Why would you bring Abel and Zechariah? Seriously, Groossmammi, you are too much."

"They're here to talk some sense into you."

"I don't need more talking. I got plenty of that from Emmett. I need space."

"Space? Jamesport is smaller than Trenton. It's in rural Missouri. It's all wide-open spaces."

"That's not what I mean and you know it."

Tamara's shrill tone, only slightly dampened by her attempt to whisper, set Laura's teeth on edge. "What I know is you left without saying good-bye. You didn't have the decency or kindness to let your parents know you were leaving. That is a cowardly act in my book."

"Mine too," added Abel.

"It's understandable, but your family expected more from you." Zechariah squeezed past Tamara and limped toward the closest of several overstuffed chairs arranged around a big-screen TV and fireplace in the living room. Puffing, he plopped into the chair. Despite the cool air that had followed them through the open door, he wiped his forehead with his sleeve. "They deserve more. If you don't plan to be a member of the family anymore, the least you could do is say so to their faces."

"Understandable." Laura sputtered. She

glared at Zechariah. He pursed his lips, frowned, and nodded. What was he trying to do? "Understandable? Nothing about this is —"

"They knew of my intent," Tamara intervened. "Not exactly when, but my decision to leave couldn't have surprised them. Unless they stuffed their heads in the sand like a bunch of stubborn ostriches."

Stubborn ostriches? Stubborn ostriches! "You don't get to be disrespectful to people who raised you and loved you —"

"What do you do here?" With a quick scowl directed at Laura, Zechariah put both hands on his cane and leaned forward. "It looks like you're settled in."

"I clean the common areas. We provide sheets and towels, too, stuff like that. Students can purchase the service."

"You like cleaning for strangers?"

"They're not strangers anymore. I've met everyone." Tamara grabbed Laura's arm and propelled her down the hallway and into an airy kitchen painted yellow and filled with an enormous pine table with a dozen chairs. It smelled of coffee and cinnamon rolls. "I know what you're trying to do and it's not going to work. I'm not coming home."

Two young men seated at a table cluttered with coffee cups, books, and laptops looked up. Laura frowned at them. They went back to their computers.

"Wearing pants is more important to you." Laura managed to keep her voice low. "Dressing like a man and living with men."

"I don't live with men." Tamara's voice rose. The man in black sweats and a green Jason Aldean T-shirt looked up again. He grinned. Tamara smote him with a scowl. He went back to his laptop. She sighed. "I have my own room and now, I have my own life."

"This is your last chance. You know when we walk out the door, we can't come back."

"I know that. I have made my peace with it."

"Well, I haven't."

"I know." Tamara's voice dropped to a whisper. She wrapped her arms around Laura. She smelled of cleanser and minty toothpaste. "I'm so sorry. I'll miss you. I'll miss everyone. But I have to do this. I can't be baptized. You know I can't. Not with these feelings in me."

Laura drew back. Swallowing the lump in her throat, she snatched a paper napkin from the table and wiped at her face. The showdown was over. If Freeman — or Ben — were here he would pronounce the situation at an impasse. No more begging. The choice had been made.

"We'll go home then."

A home that would be bereft of this child's presence.

Not a child, a woman who'd made her choice.

"I am sorry."

"I know."

"Tell Mudder and Daed I'm sorry."

"You can always change your mind. Any time. If God softens your heart and you decide you want to be baptized, you can come home. You'll be forgiven."

"I know that."

"Never forget it."

Tears trickled down her face. "I won't."

"We should go." Zechariah stood in the doorway. He put one hand on Laura's shoulder. "We can do nothing more here."

Laura allowed him to lead her to the front door and out to the van. He didn't let go. Abel said nothing. At the van door Laura allowed herself one glance back. No one peered through the screen door. It was closed, like the door to Tamara's life with her family and friends in Jamesport.

"Gott's will be done," Zechariah muttered. "Gott's will be done."

"I don't understand it."

He held the van door open for her. "I

don't understand much, but this I know. We're not smart enough to figure these things out."

"I let Ruby and Martin down."

"You are not bigger than Gott."

"I know that. I only wanted to save them from feeling this pain."

"Gott surely has His reasons."

"Do you believe that, or are you just saying it because that's what we say at times like this?"

Zechariah swished his cane back and forth in the slush around the van tires. He looked tired and cold and ancient. "Sometimes faith is all we have. I never want to find out what it's like to try to survive without it. Do you?"

"Nee." She slid in and he closed the door with a gentle nudge.

Dineen turned the key. The van's engine stuttered and then caught. "No luck, eh?"

Luck had nothing to do with it.

TWENTY-NINE

Laura stared up at the golden arches and managed a smile. Fast food wasn't quite comfort food, but it would do. Her shoes crunched in the icy slush as she followed Dineen and the men into the Trenton McDonald's. Abel and Zechariah's bickering over whether a Big Mac or a Quarter Pounder was better made her chuckle. She didn't expect to do that only an hour after her encounter with Tamara at the bed-and-breakfast.

"You see, life isn't so bad." Abel tossed that comment over his shoulder as he pushed through the door and held it for Dineen. "They even have a senior discount here. I might get a milkshake."

"In the winter?" Laura wanted a cup of coffee, chicken tenders, and fries. Fries dipped in extra catsup qualified as comfort food in her book. "You'll freeze your lips together."

"Maybe he'll stop talking so much." Zechariah seemed tickled at the idea. "Don't try to discourage him. Order him two of them."

"Ha, ha, ha."

They made their orders and picked up their condiments, straws, and napkins. Apparently, Dineen thought she was herding children — what with the large stack of paper napkins she grabbed. She slapped them on the table. "I'm headed to use the facilities. Get my order for me if it comes up."

Considering the crowd in the restaurant, it didn't seem likely, but Laura nodded as she stirred sugar into her steaming cup of coffee.

"Me too." Abel swaggered after her. "Don't let Zechariah touch my Quarter Pounder."

"I'll guard it with my life."

In the silence that followed, Zechariah dumped another packet of nondairy creamer in his coffee and gazed out at the packed playscape, filled with greasy-handed children with catsup and mustard stains on their faces. Their shouts were carefree and full of that live-in-the-moment joy children always seemed to have.

"Have some more sugar." She pushed another packet across the table. "It'll sweeten you up."

"You're a fixer." He pushed the packet back. "You can't fix this and you can't fix me."

"When it comes to Tamara, I'll keep trying as long as there is breath in me." She tore open the packet and dumped it in his coffee. "I'm not trying to fix you."

"Lying is a sin."

"Fine. The truth is, I don't like to see people I . . . care about unhappy."

"I'm not unhappy."

"Lying is a sin. You're wrinkled and disheveled and smell like you slept in your clothes."

"Dressing and undressing, along with other things, has gotten harder. Sometimes I don't have the strength to mess with it — any of it."

"Ask for help."

"Why do you care so much about an old man you didn't give the time of day back in school?"

"I don't remember that far back." Not true. Early memories were shiny, like baubles hanging in the trees with sunlight bouncing off them. The newer memories, those were the ones fading into old clothes washed and worn too many times. "Things change. People change. They grow. You can't figure out why I care, Zechariah Stutzman, then you're a bigger idiot than I thought."

Out of breath and surprised at her own outburst, Laura huffed. Had he forgotten their kiss already? Would he blame old age for that too?

Zechariah stared at his knotted fingers, covered with fine black hair, splayed across the plastic table. His cheeks turned scarlet. His eyes were hooded.

Laura tore her gaze from his face and turned to watch the children play through a greasy-fingerprinted wall of thick-plated glass. A cluster of children obviously related dashed to and from their tables by the door, eating french fries dipped in catsup as they ran to climb through the tubes and slide into a sea of red and blue balls. They looked so happy. To be that carefree again.

"Look at me."

His gritty voice tugged her back to the table and reality. Tears pricked her eyes. She was too old for this rigmarole. She had great-grandchildren and a great-great-grandchild on the way. "I'm not hungry anymore. I want to get back. I'll wait in the van."

"Look at me."

With reluctance that felt like a load of cinder blocks on her shoulders, Laura forced herself to face him.

"If I made you uncomfortable in some way, I'm sorry."

"Uncomfortable? You thickheaded old man."

"If you're going to keep calling me names, *I'm* going to wait in the van."

"You do that. Was my kiss that odious to you?"

"Nee. I enjoyed it. Thoroughly. More than a thickheaded old man should."

"Gut. Because I don't want to paint you a picture. I'm not very gut at painting."

His grin appeared. "Laura Kauffman, I do believe you have a crush on me."

Dineen strolled from the hallway that led to the bathrooms and made her way across the sticky floor. "We should've waited until we got to Jamesport. We could've eaten at the Purple Martin." Her raspy voice carried over the children's laughter and the parents' chitchat.

"I'm not a teenager who gets crushes. I'm a full-grown woman who has experienced true love between a man and a woman." Laura rushed to get the words out before Dineen arrived at her destination. The last place she expected to have this conversation was in a fast-food restaurant filled with English folks enjoying burgers and play. "I recognize it when I see it."

"You surely kiss like a full-grown woman."

Dineen stopped to pick up their orders.

Her cheeks hot all the way to her neck and beyond, Laura leaned closer. "That's not a proper thing to say to a woman."

"Did you say love?" A perplexed look teetered on Zechariah's face, then fell away, replaced by what could only be abject fear.

Fear of what, Laura couldn't say.

Dineen slapped a crowded tray of burgers, fries, and shakes on the table. "Don't mind me, I'll get the rest of it."

Zechariah stared at the large orders of salty, hot fries. "My doctor wouldn't be happy with this meal."

"Which means you'll love it." Dineen returned and squeezed her generous backside into a swivel chair too small for her. She began dousing her fries in catsup. "You look hot and bothered. Still arguing about Tamara?"

"Nee," they responded in unison.

"She called me an idiot," Zechariah offered.

"Weee, doggie, this is getting good. What did you call her back?"

"I didn't. Because she said she loved me."

"Did not."

"Did too."

"Calm down, kids, before I make you sit in the hallway and eat all your french fries myself."

Dineen had been a third-grade teacher before she retired. When she used her teacher voice, people listened. "Speaking of which, where is Abel?"

"I guess he had a lot of business to tend to." Zechariah unwrapped his Big Mac and took a healthy bite. A look of pure joy spread across his face. "Once a year, once a year, I get one of these. Marian never would let me."

"Because she loved you."

Zechariah laid the burger on the wrapper and wiped his fingers. Laura pointed at his face. He wiped his lips and beard. "I'll go tell Abel his food is getting cold."

"Hurry back."

He grinned. "So you can yell at me some more. I wouldn't miss it for the world."

Unscrambling his brain would take more time than a trip to the bathroom and back. Zechariah shuffled through the door. Abel needed to return to the table before his fries turned into ice cubes and his shake melted. The room was empty except for his friend, who stood at a streaked mirror, his back to Zechariah.

"What are you doing? You know those fries are best when hot."

One hand on the white ceramic sink, Abel swiveled halfway toward Zechariah. "Somethingggs wwwrrrong my-my-my faccccce."

His words were so slurred, Zechariah had to sort them out. "Your face?" He looked closer at the image in the mirror. The right side of Abel's face seemed to droop. Zechariah stepped closer and took Abel's arm. "Turn around and look at me. Smile."

The left side of his mouth turned up, but not the right.

"That's strange. Let's go tell Laura. She'll know what it is."

She was a midwife, but Laura knew a lot about other sicknesses. She doctored with a lot of folks. Which was why Tamara's decision bothered her so much. It wasn't the eternal damnation thing — well, it was — but the fact that she was living out Laura's dream. His body might be falling apart, but Zechariah still had half a mind.

He guided Abel toward the door. He had to let go to open it and still hold on to his cane. Abel swayed and started to sink to the floor. "Hey, hey, don't do that, freind."

Abel's arms flailed. Better said, his left arm flailed, but his right arm drifted and returned to his side.

The weak leading the weak. Zechariah got a better hold on Abel and churned toward the eating area. "Laura. Laura, we need help."

Laura shot from her chair. Dineen followed at quite a clip for a big woman.

"His face won't smile and his words are all messed up. He's staggering like he can't get his balance."

Laura tipped Abel's chin up. "What's going on, Abel? Can you talk to me?"

"Headdddd hu-r-rrrr-ttts."

"Let me see you smile."

Same results as the first time.

Dineen had her cell phone to her ear. "Our friend may be having a stroke. We're here at the McDonald's on Ninth Street. Send an ambulance. Now!"

"A stroke. Are you sure?"

Laura helped Abel into a chair. His gaze unfocused, he rubbed his head. Dineen squatted next to him and peered up at his face. "Have you ever heard of F.A.S.T.?"

Zechariah shook his head. He had enough trouble keeping track of his own symptoms.

"Take my word for it. He's having a stroke and the most important thing is to get help fast."

His friend, the picture of health, was having a life-threatening emergency. The sirens sounded within minutes. Zechariah backed away to give the EMTs room while they administered aid to a befuddled man who kept mumbling his wife's name. He needed Jessica.

"Can you call Ben's phone shack?" Zechariah turned to Dineen, who leaned against one wall, along with Laura and many of the customers who'd given up any semblance of eating or talking to watch the EMTs work on Abel. "He can go to Abel's and get his fraa and hire a driver to bring them to the hospital. The kinner will want to come."

"Where will you take him?" Laura called out to a youngish-looking bearded EMT who didn't glance up as they loaded Abel onto the gurney. "We need to get his wife to him."

"Wright Memorial. The folks there will take good care of him. We gotta go."

There was no time to say good-bye.

Instead, they prayed. Zechariah took Laura's and Dineen's hands. They bowed their heads and prayed silently as the noise playing, sirens blaring, and people talking resumed.

Gott, I'm so sorry for being such a selfish man. Not only selfish, but envious. I wanted the health Abel had. Please, if it is Thy will, restore his health. You are the Great Physi-

cian. The great I Am. Guide and direct the doctors. Give Abel strength and peace. Give us what we don't deserve. He's my freind.

God knew Zechariah didn't have many of those.

Laura squeezed his hand. She didn't let go.

Danki, Gott.

THIRTY

The smells emanating through the corridors of Wright Memorial were the same as every hospital. Cleansers mixed with sickness. Memories of Marian's stay here assailed Zechariah. He shoved them away. This was about Abel and his stroke. Not Zechariah. The wait was long. The specter of bad news loomed. After two hours, Ben, in his role as bishop, and Jessica arrived, with half of the Gmay behind them. Abel's three sons and three daughters with their husbands and wives. Grandchildren. Brothers, sisters, those that still lived. Like most people his age, Abel had lost a few loved ones along the way. He was the second youngest of six. His younger brother Carl showed up at the door just as the doctor arrived in the waiting room.

"What is it, Doctor? How is he? Did he have a heart attack? The man is an ox, healthy as a horse —"

"Let the doctor get a word in edgewise, Carl." Ben intervened. "We all want to hear what he has to say."

The doctor, a young Hispanic man whose name tag identified him as D. Lopez, explained that a CT scan showed a bleed on the left side of Abel's brain. "We were able to determine the type of stroke, the location, and the extent of the damage. He's had what we call an ischemic stroke. What that means is that fatty stuff we call plaque has collected in his arteries, causing them to narrow. A blood clot formed and went to his brain."

"That sounds bad." Jessica's hands fluttered and went to her neck. Laura moved closer and wrapped an arm around the woman. "Will he be all okay?"

"His friends did the right thing calling 911 immediately. We've already started a treatment to dissolve the clots. There will be some damage to address with rehab, but with time, he should make a complete recovery."

Jessica wobbled. Her legs collapsed. Ben grabbed one side and Laura the other. They guided her to a chair. She bent over, head between her knees, her breaths coming in gasps.

Laura rubbed her back in widening circles,

murmuring comforting words that only Jessica could hear. Clearing his throat twice, Zechariah edged closer to the doctor. "Why was only one side affected? The right side of his mouth, the right arm. He seemed to list to one side."

"That's because each side of your brain controls the opposite side of your body. The blood clot was on his left side, so the right side of his body is affected."

"You said he'll need rehab. What kinds of things are affected? What kind of rehab?"

"It's a little early to say exactly what ill effects we're dealing with." Dr. Lopez stroked a thin mustache that curled around his lips. His gold wire-rimmed glasses glinted in the fluorescent lights, making it hard to see his eyes, but his tone was kind. "Generally, we're talking about a physical therapist to work on movement and balance, an occupational therapist to deal with relearning to eat, bathe, and dress one's self, a speech language pathologist, who helps with relearning to speak clearly. Sometimes language skills are lost and have to be relearned. It can be very frustrating for the patient. And for the family members who serve as caregivers."

It sounded so familiar. *Gott forgive me.* He had coveted his friend's life. His health.

411

His happy family life with a wife as healthy as he was. A wave of nausea washed over Zechariah. His lunch of hamburger and french fries threatened to fill his throat. He swallowed until it hurt. He was a selfish, selfish, utterly despicable excuse for a friend.

"It's not just rehab, although that comes first. After that he needs to change his eating habits and his lifestyle." The doctor's gaze swept past Zechariah to Jessica. "I suspect he knew he had high blood pressure. Did he ever say anything about heart disease or high cholesterol?"

"Never. Not a word." Zechariah spoke for Jessica, who had covered her face with her apron. "He was the picture of health and whenever he went to the doctor — which was once in a blue moon — he came back saying he was healthy as a horse and would live to be a hundred."

Jessica let her apron drop. "Big liar. Wait 'til I get my hands on him." Her voice quivered, but her chin went up.

Dr. Lopez's expression became stern. "You can help by changing the way you cook."

"So it's my fault — my cooking — that made him have a stroke." The apron went back up. Jessica's shoulders shook with the force of her sobs.

"No one is saying that." Laura shot the doctor a scowl. "Mary Katherine has some gut cookbooks at The Book Apothecary. We'll get you one. Or two or three. It'll be fun to try new things."

New dry, no-fat, no-taste foods. Better Abel than Zechariah. He might have Parkinson's, but his heart was strong. "Can we see him?"

The doctor frowned and hesitated. "Two groups of two. No more. For a minute or two. He's groggy and disoriented. It might be good for him to see a familiar face. But then you should all go home. You can come back tomorrow when he's had a good night's rest."

No one ever got a good night's rest in a hospital. They saw to it with hourly visits to check vitals, dole out medicine, and generally harass a patient. Zechariah turned to Ben. "Who's going in?"

"You go in first. He'll want to see you." Jessica spoke before Ben could. She wiped at her face with her sleeve. "I need to get myself together. If he sees me like this he'll think he's dying for sure."

"May I go with him?" Laura stood and looked at Ben. He shrugged and looked beyond her to Carl.

"I'll go with Jessica." Ben waved off the

disappointed chorus from Abel's children. "You'll get your turn tomorrow. You heard the doctor. Go home. Come back tomorrow. We don't want to overwhelm the man."

No one overwhelmed Abel. He wouldn't allow it. He'd smile, sit back in the rocker, and start telling some whopper of a story.

A different person lay in the bed, his face gray against the white pillow. The wires and machines seemed to dwarf a shriveled man. Zechariah studied the machines, better to do that than stare at his friend. Blood pressure 122 over 80. Not bad for a man with heart disease. They had it under control. Respiration 68. Low by all accounts.

In other words, heavily medicated.

"Abel?" Laura touched his hand.

One eyelid popped open, then closed. He coughed, then groaned. His lips moved, but no sound came out.

"What's that? Jessica's outside. She'll be here in a minute or two. She wanted to gussy up first. Like it was your first date or something."

Both eyelids fluttered open.

"Deadddd — ddee—ddd?"

Zechariah exchanged glances with Laura. "Dead?"

Abel muttered something that sounded like *dead.*

"Nee, you're not dead."

"Toooooooo baaa—ddddd."

Too bad. "Jessica wouldn't agree."

Abel's hand twitched. Laura picked up a pad and pencil. She handed it to him. His hands shook, but Abel grasped them, his face the picture of grim determination. He formed the letters like a child just learning them would. Squiggly, frail letters on the chalkboard of his fractured schoolhouse memories.

Me first. Selfish. Nothing to fear.

It was selfish, but Zechariah would've preferred to go first too. Like his friend, he didn't fear what lay beyond this world. Only the pain death left behind.

Abel's fingers moved again. The letters were so distorted Zechariah could barely decipher their meaning.

French fries?

Laura laughed. Zechariah shook his head. "No more french fries or cheeseburgers for you, buddy."

Abel flung the pencil across the room and let his head drop back on the pillow. His eyes closed.

"Better check your breath and straighten your gown. We're sending Jessica in." Laura started for the door.

"I'm right behind you." Zechariah kept

415

one hand on the bedrail.

"He knows." Laura smiled. "Just like I know."

She couldn't have looked sweeter.

He might have to kiss her again.

But not now. "Tell Jessica to come on in. I'll keep him company until she gets here."

After the door closed, he turned back to Abel. "I'm sorry."

Abel's eyes remained closed, his face slack in repose.

"Forgive me for being so envious of your life. I coveted your health and your life. Your wife. Not Jessica, but you know what I mean."

Abel fidgeted, but his eyes didn't open.

"I know you can hear me, you stubborn old coot. I don't expect you to say anything. You've got your own mountains to climb right now. I just want you to know I'll climb them with you. Right by you." He swallowed the stupid bundle of tears that stuck in his throat like year-old crackers. "Doc says you have to do some rehab. I've been putting it off myself. So I figure we could do some of it together. Misery loves company."

Abel's lips moved. He murmured something unintelligible.

Zechariah leaned over the railing and strained to hear.

"I'm not really dying, am I?"

Or words to that effect. "No, you're not dying."

"Gut."

"Get some sleep."

"See you soon."

Or at least that's what Zechariah presumed the words *seeee yuuuu soooooon* meant.

"Tomorrow." That was a promise.

He let Dineen take him to Michael's. She thankfully required no conversation. He was worn to the bone. Peace, quiet, and a good night's sleep were the prescriptions he needed.

Zechariah almost made it into Michael's house without being waylaid. A shaky old man with a cane could not expect to make a stealthy entry. He leaned against the wall outside his bedroom and waited. Sure enough. The sound of brisk steps followed the clang of his cane dropped from his grip onto the wood floor.

"There you are. Where did you and Abel disappear to?" Michael barreled down the hallway. "I was about to run out to the shack to call Ben to get a search party going."

And Ben wouldn't have been there. "Would you mind picking up my cane?"

Still scowling, Michael snatched up the

cane but didn't offer it to Zechariah. "You didn't answer my question."

"I'm not one of your children. I don't have to account for my whereabouts to my own grandson."

Michael tapped the cane on the floor in a *rat-ta-tat-tat* rhythm. "You'd rather worry us."

"I'm safe and sound, as you can see."

"LeeAnn saw you getting into Dineen's van with Laura."

"So you know I was in gut hands." He held out his hand for the cane. Michael stared at him. Finally, he returned it. "Danki. I don't really need it, but it's a habit and it makes your daed happy."

"What were you doing with Laura?" Michael's curiosity gleamed in his eyes. He thought he needed to know, but really, he simply wanted to know. "Why isn't she taking care of Rosalie and the twins?"

"She's staying with them because she's needed." Only obstinacy kept Zechariah from answering the question forthrightly. *Don't be a grouchy old man. It's not becoming.* That's what Laura would say. Now the woman was in his head. "We went to Trenton to see about Tamara." No need to go into the whys and wherefores of that situation. "Abel had a stroke. He's in the hospital. I'm surprised you haven't heard."

Gossip usually spread like the flu through the Gmay. Michael's curiosity turned to concern. "Daed was here. We were talking and painting the kitchen. How is Abel? Will he be okay?"

"With time. And rehab. His fraa and his kinner are with him." His legs weak with fatigue, Zechariah leaned on his cane and tottered to his bedroom. "I'll help him with his rehab. I know how it feels. I'm tired. I'm going to bed."

"You haven't had supper." Michael motioned toward the hallway. "Cathy kept a plate warm for you."

They were kind people. Loving grandchildren. He didn't deserve such largess. "That was nice of her." The thought of the hamburger and french fries Abel hadn't touched and would never be allowed to eat now caused nausea to rear its nasty carcass in Zechariah's stomach. "I guess the day's events have caught up with me. I need to rest."

Michael followed him into the bedroom. He settled into the room's only chair. "Ivan came by for more than painting. He wanted to talk to us — all of us."

That couldn't be good. "Now where am I moving?"

"It's not you who's moving." Michael stared at his hands, fisted in his lap. "It's Ivan. He's moving to Nappanee with Micah and Dillon."

THIRTY-ONE

The Swan Lake National Refuge was closed in the winter, but the doors opened to volunteers for the annual bird count. Laura had it all planned out. Abel remained in the hospital on January fifth, but she and Zechariah could still enjoy the bird count and make it a celebration of his seventy-sixth birthday in a few days. Nothing would stand in her way.

The sound of Dineen's minivan engine humming in her ears, Laura strode up the steps to the porch and knocked on Michael's door. She had her arguments lined up. Zechariah needed this and Mary Katherine had agreed to stand in for Laura for the day at Ben's house. She'd even brought a big pot of chili and her famous cinnamon-applesauce cake. Laura would keep an eagle eye on Zechariah at the refuge. He would be perfectly safe with her and the refuge staff. One long, deep breath and she rapped on the door.

After a few minutes, the door opened and Cathy appeared. Her eyebrows raised, she shoved the screen door ajar. "Hey, Laura, it's good to see you. I wasn't expecting company, but I've got strudels in the oven and kaffi on the stove. Come on in."

"Actually, I'm here for Zechariah. The bird count is today." The words sounded tinny and awkward. More than she expected. Here for Zechariah. What woman said that about a man? "I told him I'd get us a ride out to the refuge in celebration of his birthday."

"What a wunderbarr idea." Cathy pushed the screen door wider. "Come in while I roust him from his room. He'll need to dress warm. Men. You'd think they'd use the brains Gott gave them."

Her double chin quivering with laughter, Cathy trotted into the living room ahead of Laura. "Have a seat, have a seat. Help yourself to kaffi in the kitchen, if you want."

Too stunned at first to reply, Laura sank onto the crocheted-blanket-covered sofa. "Wait, Cathy, so you think birding is a gut idea for Zechariah?"

"Jah, I told my mann as much. Not that he listens to me." Cathy puffed as her short, round body plowed toward the hallway. "I told him there's no sense in coddling a man that age. Someone who's lived that long doesn't need coddling. It'll drive him nuts."

She might be only twenty-four, but the mother of three had garnered more than her share of wisdom.

"Whew, I'm glad we agree on that." Laura settled back and waited for Zechariah. A mere ten minutes later they were on their way with Cathy's promise to head off Michael's objections as much as possible.

"Are you dressed warm enough?" For the first time since Laura rushed him to the van, Zechariah spoke. "Did you put on an extra pair of socks and bring two pairs of mittens?"

"I'm gut. And you?"

"Gut."

His gaze returned to the snow-blanketed, windswept landscape that whizzed by in a blur. He looked and sounded morose.

Maybe he didn't like surprises.

Maybe he'd given those stolen moments, those stolen kisses, a second or third thought.

"I thought we'd agreed to do this, but if you'd rather stay home —"

"We hadn't talked about it with everything that happened with Abel. I wasn't sure we were still going."

"When I make a plan, I stick to the plan. Why are you so quiet? Thinking about Abel? He's much better. They're sending him to the rehab center tomorrow."

Dineen's curious gaze connected with Laura's in the rearview mirror. The other woman had insisted Laura sit in the second row with Zechariah. Dineen being the chauffeur and all. Laura frowned and shook her head. Dineen's gaze returned to the road.

"It's for the best, but I wish he were coming home. But I'm not quiet. I'm conserving energy."

"When did you ever conserve energy?"

"I don't want to prove Michael right. I want this trip to be uneventful."

Miffed for a reason she couldn't identify, Laura focused on the view from her window. She wanted the trip to be uneventful too. In the sense that she didn't want an accident or a fall or getting lost in a sudden blizzard.

"Ivan has decided to uproot his fraa and go to Nappanee with his boys."

No wonder Zechariah looked morose. "Is he out of his mind?"

"He says they asked him to go and he decided they need him more than the kinner here. They're younger. The boys here are settled. They have their farms."

"You couldn't talk him out of it?"

"He's retired. He can go wherever he wants."

"That doesn't make it a gut idea."

"Agreed."

They lapsed into silence.

Cold fingers curled around hers. She jumped. Zechariah's woodsy scent enveloped her. She looked up at his dark, sharp eyes.

"What are you so nervous about?" He'd unbuckled his seat belt and slid halfway across the chocolate-brown leather seat.

"That we'll have an accident and you won't be buckled in."

The grin that made a spot beneath her rib cage warm and buttery appeared. "Are you saying Dineen is a bad driver?"

"Hey." Dineen scowled into the rearview mirror. "Put that seat belt on, mister."

"Yes, ma'am."

But instead he leaned closer and whispered in her ear. "Danki for coming for me. Getting out of the house is gut medicine." He slid back across the seat and did as he was told, but the grin stayed.

Heat rushed headlong up Laura's spine, spread over her neck, and toasted her cheeks. The overzealous heater surely caused it, but it might also be the memory of his fingers around hers.

"Here we go." Dineen pulled off the gravel road and into the parking lot at the refuge's visitor center, a tan metal building with a mishmash of square and rectangular pieces and a high roof that sat near the entrance to the ten thousand-plus acre refuge. Volunteers dressed in bulky thermal jackets in bright blues, greens, and reds spilled from cars and streamed into the building with little delay, no doubt due to the subfreezing temperatures. "I'm headed into Sumner. I'll get myself some coffee and read my book. I'll be back before dark. If you finish before that, ask one of those park rangers to call me on my cell."

Twenty minutes later Laura and Zechariah padded through brown stubble and naked bushes to their appointed sector on the west side of the lake near viewing scopes that squatted along the nature trail. In the short walk they'd seen a white-tailed doe, a raccoon, and three cottontail rabbits. It might be winter, but the refuge was alive with wildlife. Laura had been to the lake many times in the summer, but never in winter. It had its own quality. Despite the frigid wind out of the north and the cold of the snow under her rubber boots, she liked it.

The hardwood trees on the other side of the lake looked like sentinels standing guard, dressed in dark browns, grays, and rust. Some might find it desolate, but winter had its own majesty and much life hid under that blanket of snow. Sun peeked through the silver-matted clouds and sent a spray of light across stretches of ice on the lake, sparkling like spun sugar. This was a perfect location for two elderly folks, one of whom used a cane.

Visitor Center staffer Neil Davenport hadn't blinked an eye when they reached the front of the line at the sign-in table. He simply pushed back his dark-brown cap, grinned, and ribbed Zechariah about having a girlfriend. He gave them their assignment with no argument.

As it should be.

"I like this spot." Pulling a pair of black-rimmed sunglasses from his pack, Zechariah squinted against an on-again, off-again sun. "It's perfect."

"Me too. It's close to the center. Not too far to walk back."

Zechariah hid his dark eyes behind the sunglasses. "I like it because we get to count the trumpeter swans. *Cygnus buccinator.* Look, there's a few strolling around on the ice." He pointed and then tugged the bird guide from his backpack. "Did you know they are the largest living flying birds in the world?"

They were gorgeous birds, regal in their bearing, with long, graceful necks. Their black beaks stood out against the snow and ice. "I did not." Zechariah no doubt could recite the facts of the trumpeter swan from memory, but the book gave him even more credibility. Laura feigned interest while she memorized his face and the way his breath, white and puffy, came quicker over his beloved bird facts. "They look too big to fly, but I know they're migratory, so they must."

"Some of the males weigh as much as thirty pounds and have the biggest wingspan of any extant species of waterfowl. Some exceed ten feet."

Extant? She would not tell him the word was unfamiliar. "How do they fly?"

"Very well. They just have to get a running start. Give them at least one hundred feet of runway and they're off."

What would it feel like to fly? A bird of great proportion, the swan could soar through space, wings outstretched, and escape whatever earthly turmoil pursued it. Laura had never flown. It was against the Ordnung, which never made much sense to her. If God let birds fly, why not humans? She had learned long ago to keep such thoughts to herself.

At that moment one of the snowy-white birds flapped its wings and squawked at the bird in front of it — a sound reminiscent of a brass instrument. A bugle. They were arguing or mating. Laura certainly wouldn't ask Zechariah which one.

The black bills would make them easier to count. The one part of their body that didn't blend with their surroundings.

"They eat aquatic plants. If that's not available they will eat the planted crops. That's why the US Fish and Wildlife Department lets farmers plant some of the land on the refuge." Somehow Zechariah's spouting of information made him seem nervous. As if he had a need to fill the space between them with facts and not feelings. "They get a percentage of the crops, but the rest is left for the birds."

"If it helps restore the bird numbers, that is gut, I reckon." Laura found his mouth much more interesting. She couldn't take her gaze from it. *Stop it.*

Until recently, it had been eight years since she'd kissed a man. She hadn't thought about it for years. Now, she couldn't stop thinking about it. "Do you want some kaffi? I brought a thermos."

"Something else I find interesting." Zechariah cleared his throat and pointed his finger at the birds. "They mate for life. And both parents raise their young."

"Smart birds."

" 'Course, mating for life means less than twenty-five years. It's not like us humans where marriage can mean fifty or sixty years stuck with the same person."

"You just like to get me all riled up, don't you?"

"I like to see you smile."

Despite temperatures in the low thirties, hovering near freezing, Laura felt inordinately warm yet comfortable. They were alone. The only place in the world they could be alone, it seemed, was here at Swan Lake with the trumpeter swans that mated for life and raised their babies together.

Worse places existed.

"Look, here come four more." Zechariah pointed toward the south. They flew with grace, their wingspan enormous, flight seemingly effortless. "Aren't they beautiful?"

Beyond the swans were flocks of geese and ducks and other birds Laura couldn't identify. She'd leave that to Zechariah. This was his specialty and she wanted to share it with him. She slipped her arm through his and grasped his hand. Somehow it just happened. No thinking, simply doing. Taking one step at a time along a road she hadn't known existed a few weeks ago. Together, they watched as the birds swooped down and settled on the lake as if coming home. "Gott's creatures. Like us, only pretty. What else do we count? How do we count them?"

"Counters will be at different vantage points throughout the park watching the many varieties of birds as they take off to go feed. Northern harriers, American tree sparrows, we could even see bald eagles. Last year they counted 126 of them. There's mallards and snow geese and hawks. It's a bird lover's paradise."

"But it's not an exact science."

"Nee. But it gives the US Fish and Wildlife Service a gut idea of how many birds are making their homes here in the winter, and they can track the trends from year to year — see how the bird populations are faring. It's important work."

"And you like it."

Zechariah leaned into her space. His cheeks and nose were red, his eyes as bright as Laura had ever seen them. "I do. Danki for the birthday present."

"Happy birthday."

"There's something else I want."

"Cake and ice cream? I thought we would stop at the Purple Martin for supper. The desserts are the best even if Ezekiel doesn't have a hand in making them anymore."

"That sounds good. But it's not what I meant." He leaned still closer. His cold lips met hers. She put both hands on his chest and let herself go.

No hurry. No rush. No embarrassment. An exploration under the winter sky with only the birds to see. His gloved hands moved to her cheeks, brushed against her skin, squeezed her shoulders, then trailed down her arms. Winter turned to spring. He kissed the tip of her nose and moved to her eyelids, then her forehead. His forehead leaned against her shoulder for a second.

Spring turned to summer heat. August heat.

Laura didn't open her eyes. She didn't want his tender touch to end. He moved her in a way no one ever had. Not even Eli. She could admit that. Eli's love had been different. Wild like an unbroken colt. And all over the place. Excited, breathless, fearless.

Zechariah's touch, his kisses, were so much more tender, almost tentative, as if testing the waters. A little, a little more, even

432

more, until she could hardly breathe, let alone stand. She wanted his touch like she'd never wanted anything before. She felt like a young woman all over again. Such an unexpected gift in her old age.

Danki, Gott, danki.

"You'd never know it's January." His whisper tickled her ear. She shivered. "It feels like August."

"I was just thinking the same thing. Or Fourth of July, complete with fireworks."

His gaze caressed her face. "Do you think this is what it feels like to fly?"

She slipped closer so she could lean her head on his chest and gaze at the sky. "I think so. It's like floating on your back on the lake in the summer. But instead of the clouds being above you, they're below you. They're soft and warm."

His gaze moved from her face to the sky. "I think it must feel like hope."

The longing in his voice filled her with the desire to fulfill all his needs. "You have every reason to be hopeful." She imbued the words with her own hopes and dreams. "We both do."

"Flights of fancy, indeed." His lips twisted in a sardonic grin. "A person would think we're teenagers."

"We don't have to be young to be hopeful, only faithful. Gott is gut."

"Until your first kiss, I would've said I was too old for this."

"We're never too old, just too scared or too stupid."

"Speak for yourself." He raised his head and kissed her ear.

She considered fainting, knowing the snow would soften the fall, but decided it would scare Zechariah too much.

He stepped back. His boots slipped on the icy path. His arms flew out, cane in one hand. He wavered, floundered two steps forward. Laura threw her hands out to catch him. Her fingers snatched air. The cane flew and landed a few feet away. He fell to his knees, then on all fours.

"Ach, Zechariah, are you all right?"

"Fine." He kept his head down as he attempted to scramble to his feet to no avail.

"Let me help you."

"Nee. I don't need your help." He crawled to a nearby pine tree and clambered to his feet. For a few seconds he stood with his back to her. Then he turned. His face was scarlet. Snow caked his knees and gloves.

He sighed deep, almost guttural. Regretful.

"The trail is icy. It could happen to anyone."

"But mostly to a foolish old man."

"Then I'm a foolish old woman."

"Nee. A strong, healthy woman who has done her time taking care of a mann and her kinner." His gaze settled on her mouth. He sighed again.

"Enough with the sighs. What are you trying to say?" Without moving he retreated further and further away, beyond her reach. "I know what kissing you means to me. I need to know what kissing me means to you. We need to talk about it."

"Women and their talking. Talk, talk, talk."

"Zechariah Stutzman, if you don't tell me how you feel, I'm walking back to the visitor center and have them call Dineen. I'm leaving, and you'll be stuck getting home on your own."

"No need to get huffy. How do I feel? I feel like maybe there might be something I'm still gut at." He brushed at the snow on his clothes. "But we can't do it anymore."

A completely different kind of heat blew through Laura. The heat of anger and the fear of rejection. "Why? Am I not gut at it too?"

"I have a disease that makes it so I can't take care of myself."

"In my old age I want someone I can share in the caring with." She wanted to stomp her feet like a belligerent child. How could he do this? Two steps forward, ten steps backward. "What makes you think I won't have a need too? Isn't that what people who . . . care for each other do?"

"I won't do that to you."

"Wouldn't you rather spend your last years with someone, rather than alone, with joy rather than loneliness? With company at night by the fire, with checkers and hot cocoa and kisses and hugs and warm feet under the quilts?"

"You paint a nice picture, but it's only words." He pulled his binoculars from his knapsack. "A whole bunch of other things have to be done. Washing and shaving and picking me up when I fall down and helping me eat and trips to the doctor and medicine, lots of medicine. Day-to-day living with a man who has Parkinson's looks very different than the picture you're painting. Did you know I could hallucinate and have dementia?"

He was afraid of her seeing him in his humanity. "As if you won't have to take care of me. My arthritis makes my whole body hurt. I can't sew anymore. I can't stand on my feet for hours anymore. I can't do half the things I used to do. I have to make lists or I forget what I'm supposed to be doing. I don't mind you seeing my frailties. You're a coward."

"Nee, I'm a realist." A man with enough strength of character not to rise to her bait. Instead, he sounded resigned.

She pulled her pink binoculars from her canvas bag. "Our path remains to be seen. We don't know how things will turn out, but we can trust that Gott does."

Gott, don't make a liar out of me. Please.

She raised the binoculars and did her best to count the milling mass of birds, a task as confusing as trying to understand her own feelings — and those of the man at her side.

THIRTY-TWO

Not even the scent of chamomile and lemon could relax the iron grip of the headache that throbbed at Laura's temples. A day spent outdoors in the cold and wind combined with the whirly-bird up-and-down exchange with Zechariah had left her exhausted but unable to sleep.

She settled into a chair at the kitchen table and glanced at the clock on the far wall. Ten o'clock. She should be sleeping, not wandering the house in the dark, her thoughts a mixed-up bundle of hurt and hope that confronted her every time she closed her eyes. How could this man kiss her one minute and disown the feelings between them the next? Only a man could do that.

No, that was uncharitable. Not all men were like that. Only most of them.

As if she had so much experience. Eli had been The One for her and he'd never faltered in his pursuit of a life with her. She sipped the scalding hot tea and breathed in its warmth, trying to recall his features. They were fading with time. The flame that flared in his eyes when he beckoned her to come to bed at the end of a day in the fields. The feel of his thick, curly hair in her fingers. Bits and pieces that still haunted her in the middle of the night. He was so alive. So full of vigor. So full of laughter. In all fairness, Eli had been young and healthy with no traumatic experiences of loss to deter him in his quest for love. Their life had been an uneventful, ordinary, exceedingly happy life.

They had been blessed beyond belief and beyond anything they deserved.

Zechariah, on the other hand, had climbed some mountains and crossed some dark valleys in his life. His resistance to more of the same was understandable. Yet frustrating.

She sighed and stirred more honey into her tea. She needed sweetness to deter the bitterness that threatened to worm its way into her heart. She'd been content with her evenings on the porch, watching the purple martins making their homes high in the birdhouses Eli had built.

Now her contentment lay in ruins and her heart raced every time she thought of this cantankerous man with his crooked smile, fierce independent streak, and love of the earth.

Gott, I'm too old for this.

A person's never too old for love. Never.

The words were as clear as the blue sky on a breathlessly hot summer afternoon. As clear as if they'd been spoken aloud.

Old or not, she needed love and so did Zechariah.

The question was whether they were meant for each other. Zechariah didn't seem to think so.

An insistent wail broke the silence. Cup of tea halfway to her lips, Laura paused. A spate of coughing followed. One of the babies had a nasty cough. Poor Rosalie. If that cough were any indication, the woman wasn't getting much sleep. She'd recovered nicely from the C-section, but like most mothers of twins, she was constantly sleep deprived. With Tamara gone, Laura would step in more to help at night. She should make herself useful instead of spinning woolly thoughts.

Starting now. She rose and took her cup to the sink. When she turned, Rosalie stood in the doorway, a fussy baby in her arms.

"Ach, Laura, you scared me." She had dark circles under her red-rimmed eyes. "I didn't expect anyone to be out here."

"Which one is it?" Laura trotted over to her and took a peek. "Mia, poor baby."

A fist stuck in her mouth, Mia stared up at Laura. Her cheeks, which had grown pudgy over the past six weeks, were rosy. Her eyes looked glassy in the lantern light. She needed her nose wiped.

"It's both. They're taking turns. Poor Ben hasn't got a wink of sleep and he doesn't feel all that great either."

Leave it to Rosalie to worry about her husband. She looked half dead on her feet. "Let me take the bopli. If she's congested, she's probably having trouble sleeping because she can't breathe."

"It's the cough that worries me and the fever. They're both getting worse." Rosalie sank into a chair. "This has been going on since Christmas. Let me see if feeding her first will help."

"It's probably hard for her to eat if she can't breathe."

"Which means she might be hungry."

"I'll stoke the fire."

Having done that, Laura made two fresh cups of peppermint tea with a liberal dose of honey and a splash of lemon juice. The cold night air seeped through the cracks and crevices of the old house. Ben needed to do some caulking. "Drink this. You need to keep plenty of fluids in you too. You look peaked."

"It's the lack of sleep." Rosalie leaned her head against the back of the chair as the baby suckled between aggravated snuffles. "I knew I shouldn't have taken them to the Christmas program. They haven't been right since. Everyone wanted to hold them. There are so many colds and ear infections going around this time of year."

"Kinner cooped up together all day long keep the sickness going."

"She feels warm. Does she feel warm to you?"

Laura laid her palm on Mia's tiny forehead. "A little. A slight fever, I'd say."

"Me too."

Eyes squinted against the light, Ben shuffled into the room, Mary in his arms. "The other one is squawking too."

Laura held out her arms and he deposited the baby in them. "I'll bring the other rocking chair."

After pushing the chair close to the fireplace, he shuffled out.

"Not a night person?"

Rosalie managed a smile. "He's a gut mann. He's never cross, even when they keep waking him up." She shook her head.

"That one seems to know when I pick up Mia from the crib. She wants to be held too."

"Two halves of the same apple." Laura settled into the rocking chair. Her diminutive arms flailing, Mary fussed until her face turned red. "Ach, the poor apple of my eye. You'll get your turn with Mudder. Be patient."

"You should go to bed. You need your sleep. Don't feel like you have to keep me company."

"I couldn't sleep anyway. I'm here to help, remember?"

"Then tell me how your birthday celebration went. Did Zechariah like it?"

Rosalie had been the one person in whom Laura had confided her plans. The other woman couldn't hide her surprise that Laura would go to the trouble for Zechariah, but she didn't try to deter her.

"It was fine."

"Your words say one thing, but your face says another." A smile tickled the edges of Rosalie's lips despite the exhaustion etched on her face. "Tell me something to keep me awake, or I might doze off and drop the bopli."

"We counted birds."

"And what else? There's something else, I

443

know it."

Nothing she could share. Those kisses were private. So was the conversation that followed.

"Zechariah is taken with you, that's for sure."

"You're delusional from lack of sleep."

"I may be, but I know what I saw — and everyone else — on his face at the Christmas program."

"He probably had a stomachache."

"Or was lovesick."

"Men his age don't get lovesick."

"Men his age get lonely and sometimes it amounts to the same thing."

"That's not a reason to get close to a man — because he's lonely."

"It is when you're lonely too."

"Who can get lonely with a hundred kinner running around?"

"You are as crotchety as he is. You're like a matched pair of salt and pepper shakers. A little different looking, but meant to be together all the same."

"You need sleep."

Mary coughed with such force it wracked her entire tiny body. Her face turned red, then blue. Finally, she inhaled, a high whoop sound that made Laura's own breath stall in her throat. "Ach, the poor apple of my eye. That doesn't sound gut."

Her forehead wrinkled with concern, Rosalie moved Mia to her shoulder and began to pat her back. "Whooping cough? What do we do?"

"For now, we need to boil water." She laid Mary in the crib by the woodstove. The baby fussed and then coughed some more. With each cough she struggled to breathe. The more she struggled, the more she cried, the more congested she became. Simply watching the battle made Laura tired — and worried. "We'll fill the tub in the washroom and close the door. The steam will help them breathe. In the morning we go to the doctor."

A long day turned into a long night. Laura and Rosalie took turns carrying fresh, hot water to the washroom and holding the babies, who were as tired as their caretakers. No one slept. The coughs grew worse.

Laura sank onto a straight-back chair on the other side of the wringer wash machine. Her back ached, her neck hurt, and her shoulders screamed for rest. Sweat and water soaked her dress and hair. "It'll be light soon."

"I'm praying for it." Rosalie had dragged the cradles into the washroom. She laid a sobbing Mia in the first one and hunched over, hands on her knees. Hair that had escaped her kapp straggled down her back. A few wisps hung in her bloodshot eyes. "My throat hurts and my nose keeps running. Can grown-ups get whooping cough?"

"It's highly contagious." Laura dug through the files of medical information stored in the back of her exhausted brain. "Antibiotics are needed to stop it. That's why we have to go to the doctor. The kinner have had their vaccinations, but they can still get it. We need to do booster shots."

"It's so cold out there. I hate to take them out."

"We'll bundle them up gut. And take some hot water bottles to help keep them warm."

Laura didn't share the rest of the information that pricked her tired brain. Babies under six months who contracted whooping cough were susceptible to bronchitis and pneumonia. Some died from the disease.

Rosalie didn't need to know that.

"Mudder."

They turned to find Delia at the door still dressed in her nightgown, her feet covered with wool socks. "My throat hurts." She coughed. A high *whoop, whoop.* Then she started to cry.

Rosalie looked as if she might join her.

"You better get Ben up." Laura cleared

446

her throat. "He needs to go to the phone shack to call Dineen to take you into the clinic as soon as they open."

THIRTY-THREE

Physical therapy wasn't so bad. Zechariah stifled a small grin. Especially when it was Abel's turn. Zechariah had done his share of PT in recent years. He often thought of it as a form of senior citizen torture, but he hadn't told his best friend that. He and Jessica timed their visit to coincide with this foray into the rehab center's PT room as a form of support. Stationary bicycles, treadmills, a set of parallel bars, rubber balls in various sizes, rubber mats, a rack of hand weights, and half a dozen other contraptions Zechariah couldn't identify filled the room.

Patients grunted, groaned, and scowled as they received their cup of torture. True, some smiled, but they probably had a heaping helping of painkillers. Windows from ceiling to floor filled three of the four walls and gave patients a second-floor view of undeveloped property behind the medical building. Bare trees and snow to the horizon provided a calming view of Missouri winter in the second week of January. Abel's thoughts on his new home away from home had taken some time because of his speech, but Jessica had filled in many of the blanks — something Dr. Hassan chided her for. Abel needed to do his own talking.

Speech therapy, like physical therapy and occupational therapy, had begun his first day in the hospital and continued here at the rehab center. With hard work and a good attitude, according to Dr. Hassan, Abel could go home in as little as two weeks.

The carrot dangling in front of the horse. Abel wanted more than anything to go home.

Jessica only wanted to help. Zechariah smiled at her. She sat in the chair next to him in the small waiting area that allowed them to see most of the room, but most importantly, to see Abel. She chewed her lip. Her foot tapped. Her fingers rolled and unrolled the edge of her apron.

"He's fine."

"I know." She unrolled the apron. "They have him walking with those bars. Without the walker. He'll fall."

"The PT assistant is right there with him. Thalia is her name."

"I know her name."

Jessica seemed to think she could've staved off the stroke, if only she'd been with them at the McDonald's that day. Her expression said she had no intention of ever leaving her husband in Zechariah's hands again.

"Maybe we should've come later in the day."

"He needs me."

"If Abel is anything like me — and you know he is — he doesn't want help." Zechariah chose his words with care. Jessica didn't need a lecture. She had suffered a traumatic event only slightly less daunting than her husband's. Abel had been her rock for more than fifty years. "He wants to get strong again. He wants to be able to take care of himself."

And in doing so, he would be able to take care of his wife, as he'd always done.

"I know." Jessica wiggled in her chair. "He will. He's a strong man. They caught the stroke early. The effects aren't as bad as some folks get them."

"He'll work hard."

"He will."

Abel shuffled from the bars to a table and the aide helped him lie down. She tucked a huge blue ball under his legs and he began to push the ball forward and backward, using both legs. An easy task for a person with full use of his legs. Not so for Abel. Still, his chuckle was audible across the room. Followed by a mishmash of words something to the effect that he was playing ball on his first day of PT.

"He has a gut attitude." Suddenly warm, Zechariah shrugged off his jacket and folded it on his lap. These places with their central air and heat were always too cold in summer and too hot in winter. Abel's can-do attitude convicted Zechariah. He acted like a big baby. No wonder his children passed him around so much. He could do better. He would do better.

Starting with Laura. He let his gaze sideswipe Jessica. He'd known her for more than sixty years. Even before she deigned to marry his closest friend. Plain men and women who weren't related didn't have many conversations beyond "supper was good" and "it looks like rain." She surely qualified as family by now, didn't she? "You're a woman."

She giggled. "Last time I checked."

"Can I ask you something?"

"Surely. But I won't promise to answer."

He studied the tree branches bending and swaying in a north wind outside the windows. "Do you think I'm too old to get married again?"

Her smile widened. "It's Laura, isn't it? That's wunderbarr. I'm so happy for you both."

"Don't be getting ahead of yourself. Can an old *hund* learn new tricks?"

The aide removed the ball and began to guide and stretch Abel's legs in a variety of positions. More chuckles from Abel. He would be more flexible after his stroke than he had been before.

"An old hund probably has a better chance of learning new tricks than a stubborn man." Jessica rolled her eyes. For a second Zechariah saw the grinning teenager who hopped into Abel's two-seater after a singing and waved. No tiptoeing around, trying to keep their love a secret. She would've used a megaphone to announce their courting, if it had been available. "If anyone can whip you into shape, it's Laura."

"I don't need to be whipped —"

"This is Abel's fraa you're talking to. Who do you think kept him moving all these years?"

"Understood." Zechariah contemplated the ceiling. "Don't you think it's unfair to dump a disease on a fraa who is as old as I am? She'll end up being a caregiver in her

452

final years."

"In sickness and in health." Jessica shook her finger at him. Her expression reminded him of the many times he'd seen her scold one of their children. "How do you know you won't be caring for her too? You will. You'll care for each other. That's the nature of the vows. The beauty of the vows. She'll do it because she cares for you."

"What if I can't take care of her?"

"That's what's really bothering you." Jessica's eyes were getting almost as good a workout as Abel's arms and legs. "Whatever happened to Gelassenheit? Your shoulders aren't so broad that you can't accept help. She has dozens of grandchildren and great-grandchildren. She has family, as do you. You have the Gmay. It's never up to you alone."

She punctuated the diatribe with a snort, then sighed. "Not to speak out of turn. I'm only a fraa and a mudder."

"Don't give me that humble fraa speech." He laughed. A man on a stationary bike in front of a TV screen with the low sounds of a news program floating from overhead smiled as if sharing in Zechariah's good humor. "You know what you think and you're not afraid to speak."

"When it's my place to speak. In this case,

you did ask."

"I did indeed."

Jessica had confirmed his suspicions. The only one standing in his way when it came to a second chance at happiness was him.

THIRTY-FOUR

Laura fed Samuel and Christopher supper. It was a quiet meal punctuated only by the creaking of the house in a northerly January wind. Both boys asked repeatedly about their sisters all day, but Laura could tell them little. The girls were at the doctor. They were getting medicine to make them feel better. That was good.

The kitchen door opened. Ben strode in. Delia, wrapped in a blanket over her coat, clung to his hip. He settled her on a chair next to her brothers.

"Where's Mudder?" Samuel hopped from the chair and ran to his father. "And the twins? Are they out there?"

He started to dodge Ben and head for the door. Ben scooped him up in a hug. "Suh, they're not out there." He caught Laura's gaze. His was full of carefully contained worry. "They're spending the night in the hospital. The doctor wants to make sure their cough doesn't get worse, so it's for the best. Mudder is staying with them. They'll be home soon."

Delia coughed and began to sniffle. Ben patted her head. "It's okay, Dochder. We have medicine for you too."

He held up a white paper bag. "We have medicine for everyone." He nodded at Laura. "Even you. The doctor says our immunizations lose their potency, and since we've never had boosters, we're susceptible to pertussis — that's another name for whooping cough — too. She says there's quite the epidemic of it across the country for reasons that aren't important right now."

"I'll get the boys started on it right away." Thank goodness thinking had changed over the years regarding immunizations. Some Old Order communities didn't vaccinate their children, but most Plain communities did in this day and age. Each to their own, but it seemed that God intended for them to be good stewards of their bodies and of their children's health.

Laura took the bag and turned to the children. "Boys, go get ready for bed. I'll be in with your medicine and a story in a few minutes."

She picked up Delia and hugged her. "My bopli, how are you doing?"

The little girl snuggled into Laura's arms. "My throat hurts and my nose keeps running."

"The medicine will make you better."

"It tastes yucky."

"How about a muffin to get rid of that taste?"

Delia shook her head. "I'm not hungry."

"She hasn't eaten all day." His face creased with worry, Ben shook off his coat and hung it by the door. "Her fever is down, though, and the doctor says she'll be fine. Rest, lots of water or juice, and the medicine."

"And the twins?"

"It's harder. They weren't due for their first immunizations until two months." He glanced at Delia, who closed her eyes as she laid her head on Laura's shoulder. "They're so tiny. Their lungs aren't strong to start with. They're doing breathing treatments and giving them fluids through IVs. They'll be there a while. The big fear is they'll get pneumonia."

"They're in gut hands." Laura breathed in Delia's scent of little girl. "And we'll pray for Gott's healing."

He nodded, but he didn't look convinced. "Rosalie is staying with them as much as possible. We got a hotel room right by the hospital. I'll come back and forth to check on things here."

More bills. Laura made a mental note to ask Mary Katherine for another mention in *The Budget.* Ben would meet with Solomon and Cyrus later to discuss support from the Gmay. The emergency medical fund was intended for situations like this one. "We'll be fine. You just take care of Rosalie and the twins."

He took Delia from Laura. His gaze held hers over the little girl's head. "I know it's wrong to worry, but they're so tiny. They're struggling to breathe and that cough — it sounds so bad."

"It's human to worry, but we have our faith and we know Gott is gut. Pray."

He cleared his throat. "You're right. No matter what happens, we'll be fine."

The days were long, but family stepped in to help. Nadia organized meals to be brought to the house. Cathy, June, and Cassandra took turns stopping by to clean and do laundry. More than anything, their company helped stave off worry and gave Laura a chance to take much needed naps after sleep interrupted by sick children. Ben came home at night but spent his days at the hospital.

Taking care of the children kept Laura from thinking about Zechariah — most of the time. She read Delia stories. She played checkers with Christopher, and Life on the Farm with all three. The week passed. Some days the news was good. Other days, Ben seemed more burdened than ever. Friday night he didn't come home at all.

Did that mean they'd taken a turn for the worse? *Gott, please perform a miracle of healing in these two tiny babies. Heal their lungs. Take away their cough. Give us strength to bend to Your will.*

By Saturday, Laura's joints ached, her muscles hurt, and her head pounded. "No point in feeling sorry for myself," she said to no one in particular. "I'll make bread pudding. That will feel gut on sore throats."

Despite knowing that Nadia would stop by with some delectable dish later in the day, Laura got busy in the kitchen.

"They're here, they're here!" Samuel rushed into the kitchen. "They're here!"

"Who's here?"

"Mudder is home. The twins are home."

She looked out the back window. Sure enough, they were home. "Gott, danki." She sank onto a chair and closed her eyes. "Danki."

Samuel grabbed the door and swung it open. "Coat."

He wavered just long enough for her to

tug his coat on. She followed suit and rushed out to greet them. "Why didn't you let us know?"

"We wanted to surprise you." Rosalie looked better. Still exhausted, but lighter, less worried. "Besides, we didn't find out until yesterday that they were considering releasing them today. And it wasn't for sure until this morning."

"Get inside, get inside."

Everyone tromped inside. Samuel, jumping and hopping and whooping, led the way.

"They're still coughing." Rosalie eased into a rocking chair with Mia. "The doctor says it can linger for months. But their lungs are clear and they're better off at home now. Fewer germs than the hospital."

Ben, who looked as exhausted as Rosalie, rocked a crying Mary in his arms and paced the length of the living room. The homecoming reminded Laura of the first time she'd seen them. Zechariah sat in the rocking chair, holding Mia. Grinning. Happy. She shunted the memory away.

"Everything here is under control."

"Before I left the hospital I called my sister." Rosalie leaned her head against the chair and managed a watery smile. "She'll be here later this afternoon from Seymour. It's time we let you go home. You can stay with Ruby and Martin until Hannah's bann is up."

Laura opened her mouth, then shut it. Time became a gaping hole in front of her. She hadn't thought about leaving, not since she arrived. This had been her place, her task, her work. Her usefulness dried up like an old box of raisins. "There's no rush."

"We've been so blessed by you." Rosalie's eyes were wet with tears. "You've helped us so much. I don't know what we would have done without you. We don't want to take advantage. We might need you again sometime."

Pain sculpted the woman's face, making her seem older than she was. She ducked her head. "I mean . . . you know what I mean."

"I do. Anytime." There would be no new babies at the Stutzman house. "It's been my pleasure. I've enjoyed it." Laura swallowed the lump in her throat. They thought she wanted to go home. They weren't throwing her out. Still, it felt like the end of something important. Like when she stopped being a midwife. The end of her usefulness.

Just as Zechariah felt. The stubborn old coot.

Perhaps she was just as stubborn.

Be that as it may.

461

"Pack up your things and I'll run you over to your place." Ben laid Mary in Rosalie's free arm. "Rosalie will put the boplin down for a nap in the meantime and get ready for her sister."

"I can help —"

"I'm fine." Rosalie cuddled the babies to her chest. "The kinner will help. It's time you get some rest."

Who said she needed rest? Laura nodded. No sense in arguing. She hugged Delia, who cried, and Samuel, who demanded she tell a quick story, and patted Christopher on the back. He was not one for hugging. An hour later, Ben pulled the buggy up to the hitching post in front of Martin and Ruby's home.

"You know you need to stay away from the dawdy haus for two more weeks."

"I know."

"She's used her time well. Her repentance is genuine." Ben shoved his hat back and leaned into the sun. "Even so, when the time comes, she'll need the wise counsel of a person such as yourself."

A nod to her long years of experience, even though she was a woman. "I'll do my best to guide her through it."

"Do you think it was best for Thaddeus to leave?"

Laura studied his face. For a man, a bishop, to ask her, a woman, this question spoke of his concern for truly doing what was right by Hannah. "To be unevenly yoked for life to a man who made his wish to flee known is not a fate I would want for anyone, man or woman."

"I agree. Solomon argued otherwise." Ben winced, as if the memory of those discussions still pained him. "Cyrus was somewhere in the middle."

"So you ultimately made the decision."

"A difficult one for a new bishop."

"Marriage is a precious bond and not one Thaddeus showed himself to be ready for."

"I know Gott has a plan for Hannah and I tell myself not to be so prideful as to think my decision will affect how she spends the rest of her life." He ducked his head and cleared his throat. "Just between you and me, I worry — as sinful as it is — that my decision will deprive her of a life with a mann."

"Hannah's story isn't over. Her journey is just beginning." Laura closed her eyes and let the sun warm her face. The cold would return, no doubt, but for now the sun warmed bones icy from the long winter. "We have no idea what Gott has in store for her. Only that He is gut. Trust and obey."

"Trust and obey." Ben hopped down and came around to her side of the buggy. He offered her a helping hand. "With age comes wisdom. The problem is I need it now."

Laura eased to the ground. Her ankles and knees ached. "You have shown your wisdom by seeking counsel. You hear all sides. You pray. You seek Gott's will in all things. I'd say you're doing fine."

His expression rueful, he shook his head. "I know you don't think we did right in sending Zechariah to Michael's."

"It's not for me to say. You're his family. I'm not."

"You've never lacked for an opinion before."

Zechariah had made it clear he didn't want her in his business. Despite kissing her. Or her kissing him, as the case might have been. "It's the idea that he should be sent here and there that bothers me."

"I only want what is best for everyone."

"And it's your decision." She turned toward the house. "Just remember, his body may be failing, but his mind is as sharp as ever. If you want to seek wise counsel, his would be a good place to start."

"More wise words."

Ruby opened the screen door and peered

out. "Howdy! Come on in. I've got kaffi on and a cinnamon strudel cake just out of the oven."

Ben waved. "Danki, but I'm meeting my daed to talk about a few things and I'm already late."

The move to Nappanee no doubt.

"If Rosalie ever needs more help —"

"You've done so much already." He smiled. "We know we can count on you. We appreciate it."

Plain folks didn't set much store by expressing thanks. It was a given. But Ben's expression said it all. Laura returned the smile. He swung back into the buggy and drove away. Laura heaved herself up the steps. "Kaffi would hit the spot about now."

"Don't get too comfy. There's half a dozen little ones in the backyard, making mud pies. They'll need baths later on."

No time to stew or whine. Just the way Laura liked it.

THIRTY-FIVE

The next two weeks passed more quickly than expected. Laura found herself engulfed in wave upon wave of great-grandchildren. Ruby had a revolving door, it seemed. Or there was a concerted effort to keep her occupied. From helping with meals and laundry to bandaging real and imaginary boo-boos to overseeing sewing projects to playing checkers and Life on the Farm to story time, she had little opportunity to ruminate over her time spent at Ben and Rosalie's. She missed the babies, but she had more than a few great-grandbabies of her own.

That didn't stop her from wondering how Zechariah was doing. Not that she would ask. He was a stubborn old man. If he thought she would trot after him, he was sadly mistaken. He'd made his feelings clear. She would finish out her days doting on all her grands from newborn to grown-up and married.

That included Hannah. The girl had emerged from the bann to do a kneeling confession at their members' meeting. She'd answered the necessary questions regarding whether her punishment was deserved. She promised to live more carefully and to live up to the promises she made when she was baptized. Her sins were pardoned. She was reinstated. Her bann was over.

Sweet relief. Hannah had emerged from the experience looking more like a woman and less like a girl. She still had a hard road to walk, having this child without a husband, but she would have the full support of her family and her community.

Which meant Laura could move back into the dawdy haus as soon as Hannah's parents came to pick up her meager belongings. Laura's packed bags were on the porch as soon as breakfast was over.

"Shall I have Martin carry them down?" Ruby dried her hands on a kitchen towel. "He's headed into town this morning. He could give Hannah a ride to Seth's."

"I reckon Seth and Carrie will come for her," Laura called over her shoulder as she trudged down the steps. Raindrops splattered across her face. She tugged her bonnet tighter against a north wind. "Ask Martin to give me a few minutes before he brings the suitcases. I'd like a chat with Hannah."

"He'll be chomping at the bit, but I'll try to hold him back."

The image of Ruby holding her husband back made Laura chuckle. Feeling lighter than she had in weeks, she trotted through the wet weeds and mud to the dawdy haus, anxious to talk to Hannah. The girl had made it. Now she could take the next step toward returning to life in her community.

Laura rounded the corner. Hannah sat on the bench, the overhang on the porch protecting her from the rain and north wind. She was a dark figure, all dressed in black, against the white backdrop of the dawdy haus.

"Whoa! I wasn't expecting you to be sitting out here." Surprise took Laura's breath away. "You scared me."

"I reckon Daed and Mudder will be here to get me after a while."

"I reckon you're right." Laura settled onto the bench next to Hannah. She shivered. "I know it's warm for winter, but this dampness still gives me a chill. Is there a reason you're sitting outside?"

Hannah rubbed her pale face with her

black knitted mittens. "You'll think I'm crazy."

"I doubt that."

"I don't think I can do it." She paused, her voice full of tears. "I don't think I can go back and act like everything is the same. Wash dishes. Do laundry. Cook with my schweschders. Garden and can like nothing has changed."

"Life will go on, whether you're here or out there."

"I feel like I'll be . . . naked out there." Her voice dropped to a whisper. "Before, no one can tell. Now everyone can see that I'm, I'm, you know."

"In a family way." Laura doubted that. Hannah was slim, but even so, at three months, she barely showed. More likely, her shame and guilt made her feel as if everyone would stare at her belly. "Everyone knows, but everyone loves you, just the same."

"I know Mudder and Daed. They're so hurt. They'll try not to look it, but they will be ashamed."

"And here you can hide from those looks."

"I've been here for six weeks, by myself, morning, noon, and night. At first it was so quiet, I thought I'd go crazy. But then I had a routine and I cooked for myself, and cleaned for myself, and did my laundry, and read, and sang to the baby — I know that's silly —"

"It's not silly. You were alone, just you and your baby. You felt safe."

"Safe. Exactly." She brushed away tears with a damp mitten. "Only now, I have to face the world."

"Not the world. Just people who've been your friends for your entire life. And family. Those are the people who matter."

"I wonder if I'm being selfish."

"What do you mean?"

"Maybe I shouldn't keep him." She cast a painful, shy glance at Laura. The changes in her wrought by this situation wrenched Laura's heart. "I think of the bopli as a him. I wonder if maybe I should give him to a family who can give him a mudder and a daed, a regular family. He deserves that."

"That is a choice you'll have to make." Laura grappled for words of understanding, support, and most of all, grace. Rosalie's face as she acknowledged she would have no more children flitted across Laura's mind. "There are families who would jump at the chance to love another bopli. Some who can't have one or can't have more. But you would have to relinquish your feelings for this *kind*. You can't have it both ways. It wouldn't be fair to the bopli. Or the family who adopted him. Or her."

"I know," she whispered. Her gaze went to the gray, gloomy sky. "That's the thing. I don't know if I can do it."

"The decision doesn't have to be made today."

"Can I stay here with you?"

"You know you're always welcome here, my sweet girl." Laura put an arm around her shoulder and hugged. "But you can't hide from your life either."

"I know." Hannah sighed, such a soft, plaintive sound.

"There's still time for a cup of tea, I'm sure. I'm chilled to the bone."

A smile of relief revealed the Hannah she'd once been, the Hannah who could never be again, simply because she now had a responsibility she hadn't had before. "I made peanut butter cookies yesterday. That would be nice with the tea," she said as they entered the dawdy haus.

"Indeed, it would."

"I still can't believe Thaddeus left without saying good-bye."

"Or that he's sorry?"

"That too." Hannah's tone was tart. "It's not fair. The choice was to make him marry me against his will or let him leave. Leaving allows him to escape all the knowing stares. I don't want him to marry me if he doesn't want to, but it's not right that he can walk away."

"Women do have it harder, I'd agree with that. But we also have the joy of giving birth. Would an apology have made you feel better?"

"Honestly, nee." She tugged the box of teabags from the shelf and handed them to Laura. "I've struggled long and hard with forgiving him. I can forgive him for abandoning me. But our bopli? How can I forgive that?"

A good question. One Laura grappled with herself. "A person has to work at it. It's called taking the high road." She moved the teakettle to the front burner and lit the flame. "You can't control what another person does, only how you react to it. Gott forgives us for our sins. How can we not forgive others?"

"Gott sets a high standard."

"Indeed, He does. One we can never meet."

"Not just me?"

"Nee. Everyone struggles."

The struggle apparent on her young face, unmarred by time or circumstance, Hannah took two mugs from the shelf, added teabags, and set a honey bear next to them. The entire time, she shook her head without speaking. She probably didn't even know she did it.

"What is it, Hannah?"

"Nothing." She glanced up and scowled. "It's just strange. I thought what I felt for Thaddeus was lieb. Now he's gone and I feel like gut riddance. He is the daed of my bopli. A few times since Christmas, I've thought of Phillip and wondered . . . Is it wrong of me to think of him?"

The young wanted to do everything fast, everything now. They had no concept of the mistakes that littered a road traveled too fast. "Not wrong. But too soon. Phillip gave you a lovely gift, but he acted too soon. He surely understands that. With time, maybe. But not yet."

"It's silly, I know, but I feel so alone. I'm surrounded by people who still care for me despite what I've done." Her face crumpled. "If I don't return Phillip's interest, will there be anyone else? Will I always be alone?"

Laura brought the girl into her arms and hugged her. "If Phillip really cares for you, he'll wait until the time is right. He's been walking around with all these bottled-up feelings. Now he sees a chance to grasp for his happiness. He'll understand if he's the

473

man I think he is. You need time to figure out if your loneliness is driving you toward him, or whether you really have feelings for him. Don't settle for less than true lieb."

Hannah drew away from Laura's arms and straightened. "I've learned a lot from what I've done. I don't want to make the same mistake twice. I'll be fine, but I think of the bopli and maybe he will be better off with parents who are mann and fraa. The way it's supposed to be."

Laura poured water over the teabags and handed her a cup. "No one in this Gmay will fault the bopli for your mistake. He or she will find only acceptance here."

"No one will say anything to his face, but they'll talk. I know how it is. Whispers behind my back and his back. Looks. And what will I tell him when he asks about his daed? With a family he'd have the chance at a better life."

"You still have months to make that decision." Laura settled into a chair and motioned for Hannah to do the same. "In the meantime, you can spend a few weeks with your parents and then ask them if you can stay here with me. We'll find plenty to do and you'll help Ruby at the big house. Life will go on."

For them both. If Zechariah never opened

his eyes to what was right in front of him, Laura would continue with a life full of family and friends. She'd help her great-granddaughter through this difficult time, and this task would help Laura through her own difficulties.

God knew what He was doing.

THIRTY-SIX

The vans and U-Haul trucks lined the dirt road, pointed toward the north, ready for the journey. On the other hand, Zechariah was not ready. No way, no how. He tucked his hands under his jacket's armpits and stared at the slush on the ground. Mother Nature couldn't decide. Did the first week of February usher in early spring or was it still winter? The northern wind said winter hadn't given up yet.

He gritted his teeth to keep from growling. Ivan was making the rounds, saying good-bye to his children and grandchildren. He would get to Zechariah soon. What could he say that wouldn't spoil a good-bye that made no sense?

"Let it go, Groossdaadi." Ben chucked Zechariah's shoulder with a gloved fist. "They're going."

"You're the bishop. Stop them."

"You know better."

Zechariah stared at the horizon where the first hint of sun touched the sky, radiating soft pastels of pink and yellow. "Families should stay together."

"We hold tight to our principles, to our way of life, but we also examine every possible change in the light of how it can help our families survive in a world that will change with or without us." Ben scooped up Delia and nuzzled her head with his chin. She snuggled against his chest. "Our ancestors rubbed up against the world from the time they arrived in this country. We continue to do that today. Yet our way of life has not only survived, we have thrived."

"I'm not blind to those facts." Zechariah held out his arms. After a moment's hesitation, Delia returned the favor and Ben handed her over. Her warm hands patted his face and she grinned. Her sweet breath smelled like cocoa. "I have trotted this move around in my brain over and over. I don't see how working in factories preserves our way of life. Not in the least."

"I consider it an experiment." Ben's voice dropped to a near whisper. "I also expect them home within the year. But don't be spreading that around. Daed is a straight thinker. His being there with them will help keep our families on the right track."

Something was afoot here. Zechariah kissed Delia's head. "You asked him to go, didn't you?"

"I suggested it might serve us all well to have an older, wiser man in the caravan, that's all."

Ben was a good, if young, bishop. He would only get better with time. That boded well for the Gmay. And Zechariah's grand-children and great-grandchildren. God knew what He was doing.

"When will you realize you can't fix every-thing?"

"I'm already there."

"Gut." Ben clapped his gloved hands twice. "Now you can make yourself useful showing the little ones what it means to be a gut and faithful servant to Gott. It's an important job."

"That it is." A job that — in his grief and his anger at his lot in life — he hadn't taken seriously enough. "I won't let them down again."

"I reckon Laura can help you with that."

"Don't meddle."

Ben laughed. "A bishop's prerogative."

"You're still my grandson and I can still take you to the woodshed."

He put up both hands and shook his head. "Bishop, remember."

"The women have pancakes on the griddle." Zechariah set Delia on her feet. "Tell your mudder to save some for me. And don't use all the maple syrup."

"I share mine." Delia trotted away.

"I need to say my good-byes." Zechariah craned his neck. Ivan stood with his three daughters who would not be making the move. Waterworks looked imminent. Ivan didn't deserve to be saved, but Zechariah would throw him a lifeline for old time's sake. "You go talk to those van drivers, make sure they understand what the words *speed limit* mean."

Still grinning, Ben headed that direction while Zechariah hobbled over to save Ivan.

Ivan held up both hands. "No need for a last-minute lecture."

"No lectures." Zechariah settled for a quick man-hug complete with back pats. He glanced at the women. "Give us a minute."

"We'll say good-bye to Nadia again."

Zechariah waited until they were out of earshot. "You could've told me Ben asked you to go."

"In the end I made the decision."

"A tough one. I respect it."

"You would've done it if he asked you."

"They'll listen to you better than me."

Zechariah cleared his throat and memorized the mud caked on his boots. "You'll be missed."

"We'll be back to visit." Ivan waved at Dineen, one of the van drivers, who tapped her wristwatch and jerked her head toward her minivan. "Weddings, funerals, baptisms. We won't miss any of the important stuff."

"Important stuff is sitting down to supper together, volleyball games after church, and sitting on the porch talking about the weather."

Ivan drew a line in the mud with the toe of his boot. "It'll be a different world in Nappanee, but we'll still do all those things."

"See that you do. Don't get so caught up in those RV parts that you forget where you belong."

"I'm an old man, stuck in my ways." Ivan lifted his hat and settled it again. "I'm a lot more like you than you think. I know what's important."

"I know you do."

"We need to get on the road. It's a long drive." Ivan slapped Zechariah on the back and winked. "I reckon we'll be back sooner rather than later."

Zechariah would hope and pray for their return. "Why is that?"

"For the wedding, what else?"

"Whose wedding?"

Ivan laughed and ambled away.

"Whose wedding?" Zechariah crossed his arms over his chest and harrumphed. These young folks thought they knew everything. "Nobody likes a smarty pants."

Ivan was a smart man.

Zechariah, on the other hand, was an idiot.

THIRTY-SEVEN

Hell hath no fury like a woman scorned. Zechariah set his coffee cup on the table with a deliberate *clink*. It made sense that Laura hadn't spoken to him in a long while, what with the babies being sick, then helping with the grands, and then taking Hannah under her wing. But she'd been at church today and had made every effort to avoid him. When he tried to get close, she went the other direction, every time.

Here he sat at Aidan's with the after-church crowd, and the one person he wanted to see had gone home as soon as the service ended. He growled to himself. He was an idiot. The fall at Swan Lake had taken him by surprise. Like it always did. Which made him an even bigger idiot. It happened. She didn't care. She made it abundantly clear that she didn't care. Why couldn't he accept that? Accept her grace and her offer of the kind of friendship that could only be had between two people who were real friends, on their way to being more?

"You looookkkk dddeeepp in thththt-hooouught."

Zechariah scooted over on the bench so Abel could maneuver his walker and plop his hunched body next to him. All things considered, his friend was doing well. His leg dragged and he held on to the walker so hard his hands turned white when he navigated, but he was on his feet. He embraced physical therapy with the enthusiasm and determination of a man intent on winning back his good health. As a result he'd been allowed to return home.

"Just thinking what a big idiot I am."

Abel snickered. His mouth worked. His eyes closed. He so wanted to make every word clear. His speech therapist had been greatly impressed by his improvement in a month's time. "So whatttt's new?"

"Danki. Laura left without saying hello." He'd already told Abel about his fall at Swan Lake. Abel didn't laugh at that. He now understood how easily balance could be lost and how hard it was to get it back. Getting a woman back whose affection had been rejected only minutes after one of the best kisses known to an old man was proving to be equally difficult. "She's still mad and she has a right to be, but I figured she'd want to forgive me. That's what she's supposed to do."

Abel shrugged. His lips curled. His jaw worked. "Will, but won't forget."

Or something like that.

"Where's your fraa?"

"Fluuuuu. Dochder brought me."

The flu had thinned their ranks frequently during this long winter season. Spring, with wide-open windows and breezes to clear out the germs, would be welcome.

"Zechariah, Abel!" Anna sped toward them, her youngest, Jason, on her hip. Her coat slung over her other arm. "Have you seen Donny? He was here a second ago. Now I can't find him anywhere."

She sounded more perturbed than worried. Donny had a penchant for wandering off. They had to keep a constant eye on him or he'd be in the barn loft sleeping on a bale of hay or "feeding" the hogs Cheerios or stealing eggs from the chicken coop so he could "cook" breakfast for his dad.

Zechariah glanced around. Folks still visited in thick clusters. The after-church crowd didn't thin quickly on a winter day, even though a tiny hint of spring floated in the air on this first Sunday in February. The temperatures had climbed to the fifties in the last two days, melting the snow, leaving puddles of water on the roads that splashed under the buggy wheels. Water filled the ditches. He'd even heard bluebirds warbling when he hoisted himself into Michael's buggy that morning. "He probably followed the other kinner outside to play hide-and-seek."

"Or play in the mud." Anna scowled and hoisted Jason higher on her hip. The boy was getting too big to carry around like that. "If he gets his church clothes all dirty, I'll tan his hide."

What child could resist a puddle or mud? "He's around here somewhere."

"He better be."

She strode away, the spitting image of her grandmother when she was headed toward the oak in the front yard to cut a switch.

"I better go find him before she does." Zechariah used Abel's broad shoulder to pull himself to his feet. "I'll be back. Don't let them take my kaffi cup."

Abel nodded and helped himself to the cup with his good hand.

"Hey, that's my kaffi."

Abel's grin was slightly less crooked than it had been only a week ago. Coffee dribbled from the corner of his mouth. He grinned wider and swiped at it.

Nothing bothered the man. Zechariah could take a tool from his toolbox.

He hobbled outside. The children ran like crazy people through the front yard, to the corral, and then the barn in a wide game of tag. He grabbed Christopher's arm as the boy tried to dodge him. "Have you seen Donny?"

"Nee. I have to go." The boy's chest heaved. His face was scarlet and sweat trickled down his forehead from under the brim of his Sunday hat. "Caleb is it and he's fast."

"Are you sure you haven't seen him?" Zechariah cupped his hand and hollered after his retreating back.

"He walked down the road."

"Which direction?"

Caleb dashed past Zechariah.

"Have you seen Donny?"

"He went that way." Caleb's thumb pointed at the dirt road that led to muddy, fallow fields to the east. "I think."

Ten minutes later, Zechariah turned around and headed back to Aidan's house. Anna stood on the porch with her husband, Henry. The looks on their faces made it obvious they hadn't found their special child. Now, the children were engaged in searching for Donny in all the nooks and crannies a boy could find on a farm.

If he went for a walk, how far could his little legs carry him? Farther than Zechariah's old, tired legs. He avoided the front porch and slipped in the back door. Abel still sat on the bench in the living room. Ben and the other men donned coats and filed out the front door in a flurry of activity. They bandied about the words "outbuildings" and "911" and "thirty more minutes." They were mounting a search before calling the sheriff. If they waited much longer it would be dark, and the search would become more difficult. The sheriff's deputies would have four-wheelers and spotlights.

"Do you want to go for a ride with me?" Zechariah laid a hand on Abel's shoulder and whispered in his ear. "I could use company."

Abel cocked his head toward the walker. "Me? They told me to sit tight and let them take care of it."

His exquisite effort to pronounce each word resulted in an almost understandable sentence.

"They'd tell me the same thing if I asked." Zechariah plucked Abel's coat from a hook by the front door and helped him put it on.

"So I'm not asking."

Together they tromped out to the row of buggies next to the barn. Abel climbed in Michael's buggy while Zechariah hitched the horse. They were headed east at a canter when Josiah waved at them from the path trail that led to a small pond. "Where are you going?" he called. "He's not down at the pond, praise Gott."

"We'll look down the road at Abel's and by Michael's and then swing back." Zechariah kept the buggy moving at a steady clip.

"But Michael won't want —"

"Tell Michael we'll be back as soon as we find Donny." Zechariah didn't look back.

"Mad?"

"I imagine. Keep your eyes peeled on that side. I'll look over here."

Nothing in the mile that brought them to the turnoff to the highway. What if someone picked him up? An Englischer wouldn't understand a word Donny said. He hadn't been to school. He spoke no English. "Left or right?"

Abel hooked a thumb right.

Toward town. Would Donny know that? Who knew how much knowledge Donny retained? He counted to ten, but he couldn't make change. He sang hymns in church but couldn't read from the Ausband. Nor did he know his left hand from his right.

An innocent wandering around in a world fraught with peril.

"Most people around here know Donny. If they see him, they'll bring him home." The reassurance was more for Zechariah than Abel. "They probably found him already, walking with Michael's hund, pretending to hunt deer."

"Probably."

No point in more inane remarks. They rode in silence on a mostly empty highway. An occasional car out on a Sunday afternoon zipped around them. The fields were empty too. The sun dipped toward the horizon.

They eased around a bend and an eighteen-wheeler came into view ahead of them. Its engine revved and hummed. The gap between them increased as the truck pulled ahead.

"Maybe we should go back." Squinting, Zechariah peered into the sun. Despite a cold breeze, it warmed his face. "Maybe they have found him."

Abel grunted. "Maybe."

"There's a buggy up ahead coming this way."

The truck and buggy passed from opposite directions.

The horse neighed and strained against the harness. The buggy swayed and lurched. The horse screamed and swerved off onto the shoulder. The buggy teetered and rolled. It disappeared down a drainage ditch.

The sound of the horse screaming mingled with the long screech of the semi's brakes.

Nee. Gott, have mercy.

Zechariah snapped the reins and leaned forward as if he could make the buggy move faster. Its brakes still squealing, the semi pulled to the side of the road. Hazard lights blinked like orange beacons in the gathering dusk.

"Giddyup, giddyup, come on, girl." Zechariah snapped the reins again. "The buggy rolled. They'll be hurt."

Abel held his hat with one hand and grabbed the seat with the other. "Go, go."

Zechariah pulled in facing the long, shiny silver eighteen-wheeler. Signs painted on the sides told of a cargo of dairy product.

The driver, a chunky man with black skin and a shiny bald head, leaped from his cab. "I don't know what happened. I'm on the other side of the road. I didn't even get close." He raced across the highway, still yelling in that way folks did when they're in shock. "I called 911. They're coming."

Zechariah followed as quickly as his legs

490

would carry him. Abel struggled to get down from the buggy, but Zechariah didn't have time to wait for him.

The buggy landed on its top, upside down in four or five feet of muddy water. The harness entangled the horse so he couldn't move. Which was good. He couldn't hurt himself or the occupants of the buggy any more than they already were.

"Are you hurt? Can you hear me?" Zechariah spoke in Deutsch. The driver stopped yelling and let him do the talking. "Let us get you out of there."

"I'm okay. Get to the kinner." A familiar voice, although now shaky and filled with panic. "Donny? Hannah! Are you all right?"

Laura.

A high voice mingled with her words. "I'm fine, Laura. My nose hurts, though." A boy's voice. Donny. "The water's cold and Mudder will be mad I got my church clothes dirty."

Together, Zechariah and the truck driver waded into the muddy water and pulled at the shambled boards that had once been a buggy. Donny emerged first. He had an egg-sized lump on his forehead and two black eyes. Still, he grinned. "The buggy flew. We flew."

The driver caught him up in his arms and

set him on higher ground away from the highway. "You sit still, little man. Don't move until help comes."

Donny rubbed grubby hands across his face. "My nose hurts."

"Help is coming." Zechariah turned back. He slung pieces of the roof and seat aside to find Laura. She tried to scramble to her feet. Water soaked her dress and apron. The dead weight held her back. He grabbed both hands and tugged her forward. She staggered into his arms. "Hannah, help Hannah."

Zechariah handed her off to the driver and slogged through the water. Hannah lay on her side on a back wheel. She held both arms across her middle as if to protect her belly. She raised her head. "Zechariah. My arm hurts. And the bopli. The bopli has to be all right."

He didn't know much about these things, but Marian had fallen from a stepstool once before Esther's or Michelle's birth — one of them, he couldn't remember which. She broke her collarbone, but the doctor said babies had a lot of padding and a watery world that protected them during small falls. "Let's get you out of here."

He put his hands under her arms and tugged her upright. Despite being in a family way, the teenager weighed no more than a hummingbird. Groaning, she tried to stand. Her shoes slid and slipped in the mud. "Hang on to me." He tightened his grip and led her from the miry pit and into Laura's waiting arms.

"Danki." Laura nodded at him over Hannah's shoulder. "I've got her."

He wanted to say, "I've got you," but he couldn't. The words couldn't bulldoze through the lump the size of a cantaloupe in his throat. Her kapp had fallen down her back, revealing a straggly bun of silver hair. Mud caked her cheeks and chin. Blood trickled from a deep gash across her forehead. She looked awful, but never better.

He cleared his throat. "Anyone else?"

"Nee. I was taking Donny back to Henry and Anna. I found him skipping along the road." She eased Hannah onto the brown stubbled grass on the edge of a field of mud and puddled water. "He said he was going into town for candy."

She tottered over to the horse and smoothed his tangled mane. The horse neighed and shook his head. His eyes were still wild. His breath came in ragged snorts. "He's desperate to get out, poor thing. He's town safe. I've never had a problem with him spooking for a car or truck."

"Who knows why now. We'll get Martin down here to untangle him and take him home. The horse knows him."

"I don't know anything about horses." The truck driver stuck out his hand. "I'm Joe Haag. Maybe the sheriff will help or the firefighters."

Zechariah wasn't crazy enough to think he could do it by himself. If the horse reared, he'd be hamburger in short order. "We'll get some of our men here. If you let me borrow your phone, I can call the phone shack at my great-grandson's." It could be hours before any thought to check the messages. Unless they called 911 about Donny. He let his gaze skip to Laura's. "Anna and Henry are beside themselves over Donny."

"I figured they would be. I scolded him good and put him into the buggy." She slogged back to Hannah and began wiping dirt from the girl's face. "Where does it hurt, child?"

"My arm." Her voice quivering, Hannah hunched over. "I'm afraid for my bopli."

"We'll get you checked out." Sirens howled in the distance. "See, they're on their way."

"You need checking out too." Zechariah scrambled out of the ditch, using both hands to pull himself along. His legs shook, but they didn't fail him. "All three of you."

"I'm fine." Laura rolled up her filthy apron and wrung it out. Dirty water streamed from it. "I need to get to Aidan's to let Anna and her mann know Donny is found."

"You're not going anywhere until they look at that cut on your head." Anna and Henry were suffering, not knowing where their child was. They needed to be told. But Laura was hurt. Abel couldn't drive the buggy by himself. Zechariah wrestled with his thoughts. "I'll take Abel back to the farm. We'll tell Anna and Henry. But I'll be back."

"Everyone okay?" Daviess County Sheriff's Deputy Dan Rogers slogged down the side of the ditch and through the water. His dark-brown pants turned an even darker brown. He shoved his wide-brimmed hat back and gave them the once-over. "It's been a while, Zechariah, Miss Laura. I'm sorry it's under these circumstances. You look a little worse for wear."

"Laura, Hannah, and Donny need medical help." Zechariah beat Laura to the punch. "We need to get the horse untangled."

Two volunteer firefighters from Daviess County Fire and Rescue followed Rogers down the incline. One was Doug Barnes, a longtime farmer Zechariah often saw eating at the Purple Martin. The other was Shep Laird, Zechariah's optometrist. Deputy Rogers took Joe Haag aside and began to question him, giving the firefighters time to check for injuries before he talked to Laura.

"Doug and I will split up the wounded," Shep offered. "After we get a look at everyone, Doug can figure out what to do with the horse."

"Sounds like a plan." Laura was in good hands. As much as Zechariah wanted to stay, now was the time to ease Anna's and Henry's minds. "I'll take Abel back to Aidan's. We'll tell Anna and Henry." He squeezed closer to Doug, who was busy running his hands over Hannah's arms and frowning. "Where will you take them?"

"The ambulance is on its way. They'll go to Chillicothe to the medical center."

"I'm not going anywhere in an ambulance." Laura struggled to her feet and charged down the incline that led to the highway. "I got Donny into this mess. I'll be the one to tell Anna and Henry."

"Settle down, Miss Laura. You need stitches." Shep frowned as he held up two fingers and asked Donny how many he saw. Fortunately, Donny could count to ten.

"And they'll want to do a CT scan. You most likely hit your head when you got that gash."

"Don't Miss me," Laura grumbled. "A little B&W ointment and it'll be fine."

"You'll have a dandy of a headache before it's over, and don't be putting ointment on anything until a doctor looks at it." A concerned frown on his chubby-cheeked face, Donny wiggled from the firefighter's grasp and ran to Laura. Shep leaned back on his heels. "You're scaring this little guy, and he seems like he's had enough excitement for one day."

Laura put her arm around Donny. He had a sweet nature and never met a stranger he didn't like, but doctors were another matter. He didn't like them much. A few tears left tracks on his dirty face. "I want Mudder. Laura, you said you were taking me to Mudder."

"As soon as we get you fixed up." She hugged him tight to her chest. "I'll be right there with you all the way."

"With me too, Groossmammi." Hannah's voice sounded stronger, now that help had arrived. "I'd rather go back and have Rachel look at me."

"She can't do anything about your arm," Zechariah pointed out. "You'll need an

X-ray and they can check on the baby. Do whatever it is they do. I'll tell your folks so they can get a ride to the hospital and carry you home when the doctors get done with you."

His muscles and sinews united to keep his boots planted on that empty field next to the highway. His brain scolded him, but his heart clamored to stay. He breathed. *Get going. The sooner you go, the sooner you'll see her again.*

He ducked his head and began the arduous trek — for him — back to the highway.

"Zechariah."

He swiveled to look back. "The ambulance is here. Sit down and wait for the paramedics."

Laura tottered after him. "Danki for saving us."

"You would've saved yourself, if I hadn't happened along the way."

"But you did. You found Donny and you took care of us. A very useful day you've had."

She was right about feeling useful. It was a good feeling. "I have to take Abel back. And talk to Anna and Henry."

"Tell them I'm sorry."

"You have nothing to be sorry for. You found Donny and would've brought him back to them if it wasn't for a contrary horse and a semi."

She nodded. "See you soon?"

It was a question. "See you soon."

His was a statement.

THIRTY-EIGHT

Laura huddled closer to the blazing fire. The wood popped and embers sparked. She took a sip of the peppermint tea Ruby had brought her before she went to bed. It burned her tongue. Still, she couldn't get warm. Her hands shook. Everything shook. She set the mug on the table and tugged the shawl tighter around her shoulders. The silence comforted her, somehow.

Hannah had insisted she stay wherever Laura stayed. Ruby and Martin insisted they both sleep in the big house. Hannah had gone to bed, worn out from the accident and the trip to the hospital. She couldn't get over the sight of her tiny baby on the ultrasound machine. The pulsing sound of his or her heartbeat. *Whoosh, whoosh, whoosh, whoosh.* The most comforting sound in the world when a mother was worried about her baby slipping away. An X-ray revealed no break in her arm. The doctor had pronounced it a sprain and recommended ice and ibuprofen.

Laura's date had been with a CT machine that engulfed the top part of her body. Lying perfectly still with her head on a small prop had been hard. Her body didn't want to stop shaking. Poor Donny needed a sedative for his CT. He found the big donut too intimidating and refused to lie on the table. Fortunately, in both cases, the results had been negative. Martin said her head was too hard to be cracked by a simple dunk in a ditch full of water.

Eight stitches later she'd been out the door. She couldn't leave fast enough. Now every muscle ached. Her head ached, despite the two ibuprofens. Her stomach rocked with nausea every time her mind replayed the scene. Which was every time she closed her eyes.

The *clip-clop* of the horse's hooves on the highway. The scent of wet earth on the springlike breeze. Scolding Donny about his unannounced trip to town. Donny's giggle. Discussing the pros and cons of adoption with Hannah. Encouraging her to see the possibilities of a future with someone . . . someone who would not abandon her. Laura didn't give the semi a second thought. She saw them on Highway U all the time.

Billy was traffic safe. That's why Martin allowed her to use him.

Then it happened. Billy reared and bucked. Laura fought to hold the buggy on the highway. Neighing, Billy jolted back and forth, back and forth. The reins jerked from Laura's hands. Billy swerved away from the truck. They careened toward the shoulder, then the ditch.

They rolled to the right.

The buggy slammed into the ditch.

Water rose to meet her. The taste of muck and wet, brown stubble dirtied her mouth. She gasped and swallowed more of it.

Her stomach lurched as the buggy slung her head over heels. Pieces of buggy slammed her from all sides. Her knees and elbows collided with Hannah. The girl screamed.

Laura grabbed at her, but her hands groped air.

The buggy rolled. Then it bucked to a stop on its side. Laura landed on top of Donny. His cries broke her heart. Hannah shrieked and shrieked. Laura gasped for words of comfort, but her lungs were flat. No words came out.

The world spun in a dizzying whirl, even though the buggy had stopped. Every bone, every muscle, down to the sinews that held them together, hurt.

Hannah. The baby. Donny. She needed to help them.

Then help came. The sight of Zechariah's worried face would be a blessing she never forgot until the day she died. His hands on her arms, the way he clutched her to his chest and led her up the incline to safety.

His care for her shone in his face. A light that would lead her wherever he wanted her to go. She couldn't wait to tell him that.

When everything didn't hurt. When she wasn't bruised and bedraggled and bereft in her confidence in her ability to handle a horse and a buggy and its precious cargo.

Billy never acted up.

Not in all the times Martin let her borrow him for trips to town or frolics. Now Martin would feel guilty. Like his horse's sudden aversion to trucks was his fault. She breathed, in and out, in and out. It was over. They had survived. No serious injuries. They were lucky, the doctor said.

Not lucky. Blessed. By the grace of God, Hannah's baby was protected. Donny's small frame had not a single broken bone. Only a slight concussion, bruises, and cuts.

Even so, Laura felt guilty because Donny and Hannah were hurt at all. The truck driver felt guilty his semi scared the horse.

Zechariah felt guilty their paths hadn't crossed sooner. Hannah felt guilty about everything under the moon and stars.

Only Donny didn't feel guilty, even though his running away set everything in motion. He didn't have the capacity to understand cause and effect or consequences beyond being sent to bed early without a cookie. God had blessed Donny with perpetual innocence.

He would sleep well tonight.

Zechariah. Laura took another sip of tea and let the hot liquid seep into her bones. His arms were so strong, his legs planted and firm, when he tugged her from that horrible pit, that ditch of dirty water.

Did he know it was his horrible pit of miry clay? He'd saved her and in the process, Gott had saved him from feeling useless. He carried Donny out and guided Hannah to safety. He'd never looked more vital and alive.

He'd saved himself.

She leaned back in her chair. She couldn't wait to tell him. If he hadn't figured it out himself. Men were so thickheaded, he probably hadn't.

She leaned back in the rocker and rested her head against the solid wood. The floor creaked. She straightened.

"It's only me."

Laura pressed her hand against her chest and breathed. "Hannah. What are you doing up? You were sound asleep the last time Ruby checked on you."

"She's so sweet. I drank too much of that tea she kept offering me."

With the baby, trips to the bathroom would become more and more necessary, even without the tea. Laura gestured to the other rocker. "Keep me company for a minute."

Hannah grabbed a crocheted blanket from the back of the chair and wrapped it around herself. She snuggled into the chair, looking more like a grade school girl than a woman who would have a baby in a few months. "I had bad dreams."

"It'll take a while to get back to normal." Laura rubbed her forehead. Maybe she should take some more ibuprofen. She felt like a big blob of hurt. "We all had quite a scare. Do you want some more tea?"

"Nee." Hannah shook her head vigorously, then giggled. "But danki. Do you think Tamara will ever come back?"

"That's what you're thinking about tonight?" Laura rose and added one more piece of wood to the fire. A little longer, then they both needed to get some sleep. "I prayed. Then I left it at Gott's feet. What happens is up to Him. It always has been. As a semi-wise man once told me, I can't fix everything. When I think I can, I've made myself into a god. I think I control what happens. That's wrong. Sinful. I'm not doing that anymore."

"Why do you think Phillip made the cradle for me?"

"I think you're smart enough to figure that out."

"He never said anything to me at the singings. He never asked me to take a ride."

"Maybe he noticed that you only had eyes for Thaddeus."

"Thaddeus didn't hesitate to ask for more than a ride."

"If Phillip had asked, would you have said jah?"

"I don't know. Probably not. Thaddeus was so sweet and so handsome. I know that's not supposed to mean anything, but every time I got close to him I felt so . . . caught up in him."

"So you couldn't see anyone else. No one likes to be a third wheel."

"Which brings us back to why Phillip made the cradle."

"Thaddeus let you down. Maybe Phillip wants a chance to show you he never will."

"How can he even look at me like this? With another man's bopli. Won't he see what Thaddeus and I did every time he looks at me?"

"He sees a bopli, a special gift from Gott. Something Thaddeus apparently did not."

"I'll never leave."

"I'm glad to hear that. Your parents will be too."

Hannah wrapped a loose strand of hair around her finger and bit her lower lip. She looked eleven. "I'm keeping the bopli, no matter what happens. Mann or no mann. Without Thaddeus. Phillip or not."

"Gut for you. I'm glad."

"Me too. I've never been so scared as when that buggy started doing flips. All I could think was my bopli, my bopli. I wasn't afraid for myself. Only the bopli."

"That's what happens when you become a parent."

"I saw that little blob on the screen and heard his heartbeat and I knew." Staring at the fire as if the memories resided there, Hannah smiled and sighed. "This is my bopli. Gott gave me this gift. He had His reasons for doing it now. It's not to teach me a lesson or punish me. A person doesn't give away a gift like this. At least I don't, when I know I can take care of him and love him."

Waiting for the knot in her throat to dissolve, Laura inhaled and blew out the air. *Danki, Gott. We had an accident. We went to the hospital. We were fine, but lessons were learned. Wisdom gained.*

Zechariah learned he shouldn't listen to others who inadvertently, through their love and caring, made him feel useless. He could drive a buggy. He could help them from the pit. He could deliver messages. He could take care of Abel. Donny's parents would remind him every time he left the house not to go far. They would remind his brothers and sisters to watch over him. They would check on him more often. A blessing nearly lost was held closer to the chest in tighter arms.

Even if he did wiggle to be free.

What had she learned? That sometimes she needed to be saved. Whether she liked it or not. Sometimes she needed help. She might not be helpless, but she could let others help her. And in doing so, she helped them.

She might let someone else drive the buggy. Like Zechariah.

She smiled. "I think . . ."

Hannah's eyes were closed. Her head reclined against the rocker. Her hands were tucked inside the crocheted blanket.

Time for bed for a tuckered-out mother-to-be. And the old woman who, despite her aching body, didn't feel quite so old.

THIRTY-NINE

"Laura. Laura! Wake up."

A hand shook Laura's shoulder. She forced her eyelids open. Pain registered first. Her back. Her legs. Her arms. Her hands. Her head. Her fingers went to her forehead. Stitches. She rolled over. Ruby stood over her. "There you are. Zechariah is here. He's determined to talk to you." Her delighted expression matched the slight giggle in her voice.

Laura rubbed her eyes and tried to absorb the meaning of her daughter's words and the enthusiasm with which they were conveyed. "What time is it?"

"Early. I just put biscuits in the oven. I'm starting the eggs."

"Breakfast time and Zechariah is at the door?"

"Nee. I gave him a cup of kaffi in the living room. He said he went to the dawdy haus first, then came up here pounding on

510

the door, all in a tizzy. He thought you were still in the hospital and no one told him." Ruby scurried to the wall hooks and grabbed the dress on the top. A new dark-blue one she'd sewn for Laura. She pushed her glasses up her nose and examined it. "I didn't know he needed to be told your whereabouts, but I told him you were still asleep because you had a hard day yester-day."

Laura dragged herself up on her elbows and squinted at the window. "Why is it so dark?"

"Cloudy. And the temperature is dropping instead of going up this morning. Welcome to February. That little bit of spring we had is over." Ruby whipped back to the bed and used her free hand to drag back the blankets and quilts. Icy air wafted over Laura. "Get up, get up. This dress is clean and looks fresh. Get dressed. He's waiting."

"You'd think he was the bishop or some-thing." Despite her protestation, Laura swung her legs over the side of the bed and hobbled across the room on the cold wood planks to examine her other dresses. Blue brought out the green in her eyes. What was she thinking? She put her hand on her hip and winced. "You'd think I tumbled out of a buggy yesterday."

"I'll get the ibuprofen and the B&W ointment." Ruby thrust the blue dress at Laura.
"Wear this one."

She bustled from the room and returned
so fast with the first aid that she surely
must've run up and down the stairs. "Hurry
up."

After her daughter departed again, Laura
took her time getting dressed, pinning up
her hair, and brushing her teeth. A woman
didn't rush down to see a male visitor. She
took the ibuprofen but left the B&W on the
bathroom counter. She didn't want to smell
like aloe and comfrey.

Taking a deep breath, she said a quick
prayer and descended the stairs. Zechariah
sat on the couch. He looked spiffy in his
black pants, blue shirt, and suspenders.

Instead of going to him, Laura strolled to
the windows and stared out. "Did you steal
Michael's horse and buggy again?"

"Aren't you the funny one?" The clack of
his cane on the wooden floor signaled his
approach. His scent of soap and peppermint
toothpaste told her he stopped close by.
"Michael didn't object. He didn't say much.
Mused a bit over how gut Gott was to bring
me to your accident yesterday. He almost
told me to be careful of the puddles that
have turned to ice, but he caught himself

512

about halfway through."

"Did he want to know where you were going?"

"I told him. To see a freind."

"He probably thought it was Abel."

"Nee. I told him it was you."

It was good to have friends. Close friends. She gave him a sideways glance. "Why would you come to see a freind so early in the morning?"

"It's not that early. Some folks just lie around until all hours of the day."

"Hardy-har-har." She concentrated on his scent and the sound of his soft, gruff voice. "It's not that late. Ruby just put the biscuits in the oven."

"Gut. Then I'm not too late."

"You invited yourself to breakfast?"

"Nee. I'm inviting you to breakfast." He held out her coat. "I'm taking you to the Purple Martin Café."

In Ezekiel's day the restaurant hadn't been open until ten. Burke opened it for breakfast because it was his favorite meal to cook. Laura accepted her jacket, but she fixed her gaze on Zechariah's face. "You're taking me into town? Just you and me? To the Purple Martin?"

"Jah, unless you have an objection."

They would be the talk of the Gmay.

"Nee." She stuck her head through the doorway to the kitchen and informed Ruby she would be going into town for breakfast.

"Bundle up," was her daughter's only response.

A few minutes later, Zechariah helped her into the buggy and slid in on the other side. He tugged a fleece-lined, blue-plaid blanket from the back seat and unfolded it. "It's cold." He grinned as he laid it over her knees and then tugged it over his. "And it's a long drive."

Indeed.

At first they chatted about the weather. Then Zechariah told her all about the sightings of the purple martins along the Gulf Coast and how some had been sighted in Austin, Texas. That meant they should arrive in northeast Missouri in early March.

Was this what he wanted to talk about — bird-watching and the weather?

"How are you feeling this morning?"

Or her health. "I'm fine. Thanks to you."

"The truck driver was there. He would've gotten you out."

"Hannah has decided to keep the bopli — not give him up for adoption."

"It'll be a hard road."

"But worth it."

He was silent for several minutes. The

Jamesport city limits came into view.

"Did you have something you wanted to talk to me about, or is this really about Burke's Spanish omelet?"

"I like his ham-and-cheese omelet better." Zechariah's voice, hoarse with cold, dropped. "But you're right. It's not about breakfast. Although I am partial to breakfast. I'm also partial to the thought of eating it with you . . . every day."

He wanted to take her out to breakfast every day. The implication broke over her in an enormous breathtaking wave. She swallowed a squeak of excitement or trepidation or both. "That could get expensive if you plan to take me to a restaurant every day."

"Don't be dense, woman."

"Zechariah, you're driving me into town in freezing temperatures and an icy wind. A hard snow is about to dump all over us. You're talking about weather, birds, and omelets. Spit it out."

Scowling, he pulled the buggy into the parking lot behind the restaurant and halted. At this early hour only a few cars dotted the lot. It would fill up as the morning wore on. "You're such a sweet talker, you know that?"

"I gave up sweet talking in my twenties. I'm old and acutely aware of the passage of time. We have little to spare."

"Tell me, are you going to keep trying to fix me?"

"Nee. I gave that up. I learned my lesson with Tamara. It's not my job to fix people." The hardest lesson of her long life, just behind learning to accept death of loved ones as an integral part of the circle of life and God's plan. "It's my job to step out in faith and try to help people. But fixing them is Gott's job. I pray and leave the rest to Him."

"I learned some things too." He slid his gloved hands under the blanket. His fingers found Laura's. She inhaled. The cold air hurt her lungs. He slid closer. The warmth of his legs seeped around hers. "Lessons I thought I'd already learned."

"Like life is short."

"Jah. I knew that, but when I heard your voice coming from inside that banged-up, upside-down buggy, everything inside me went topsy-turvy too." His hand tightened. She put her free hand over it. "I keep thinking of how much worse it could've been."

"By the grace of Gott, we're fine."

"That cut will leave a scar." His gaze fixed on her stitches. "It will always remind me of how close I came to missing my chance."

He took his hand from hers, removed his

glove, and with his bare finger traced a line just below the jagged stitches. "I'm burying my pride and my fear side by side. I will not miss this last chance."

Here she sat in the middle of a parking lot, under a dark sky that looked ready to drop a load of snow, and the cold left Laura. From her feet to her head, a toasty heat surged through her. A snowflake landed on her cheek. Then another on her lips. "What chance?"

His expression bemused, he raised his face to the sky. Snowflakes dusted his eyebrows and his beard. "It's snowing."

"Zechariah Stutzman."

"The chance to ask you to marry me."

"So do it."

"I thought I just did it."

"You'll have to do better than that."

Grinning, he turned on the seat so he faced her. His hands gripped hers. "I've wanted to do this since that day at Swan Lake. I knew I was being a stubborn old codger, but I was afraid. I'm not afraid anymore. Laura, will you marry me?"

"Jah, jah, jah."

"Three times jah. In my book, that means three kisses."

"I like your book."

He tugged her closer. Their lips met. His

warmth, his stubborn aliveness, flowed through Laura. His hands released hers and his arms slid around her waist. "Come here, woman," he muttered. "Closer still."

His lips warmed her from head to toe. No more aches and pains. Nothing but sweet release. "I can't breathe." She leaned back and smiled at him. "You know how to warm up a woman."

"Just you."

"Better be."

She snuggled against him. The scratchy wool of his jacket tickled her nose. He kissed her kapp and then her forehead just above the stitches. "When?"

"When do I want to get married?"

"Jah."

"As soon as possible. As we both know, life is truly short." She dared to touch his cheek. "And we're old."

"Hey, you two are going to freeze to death out here."

They shot two feet apart on the buggy seat. Zechariah waved briskly at Burke, who slung two bulging garbage bags into a Dumpster. "Hey, Burke, don't you have enough help? You're bringing out the trash yourself?"

"All work is honorable." Chuckling, Burke cocked his head toward the back door.

"Bring your lady friend in for kaffi and a hot cinnamon roll. I just took them out of the oven. I'll have them frosted in a few minutes. I add a nice chunk of real butter when I serve them."

He broke into a Christmas carol as he headed for the door. It didn't seem out of place at all. Christmas came year-round in Jamesport, Missouri. Hand on the door, he turned. "Or stay out here necking like teenagers. Looks like a lot more fun."

"Necking?" Laura had heard the term, but she'd never been accused of such behavior. "We're not necking —"

The door slammed behind Burke.

Zechariah laughed first. The giddy sound of a man in love. Laura liked the sound so much she joined in. They laughed so hard her stomach hurt and tears rolled down her face.

"First time in a long time I've been accused of doing anything like a teenager." Zechariah wiped at his face with his sleeve. "I like it."

"Me too." Laura slid back across the seat. "I think we need to neck some more."

"You're my kind of girl. You choose kissing over a hot cinnamon roll."

"I think I can warm up more out here."

Zechariah hooted. "At your service."

Eventually, they did go inside. But not before the breakfast menu had been replaced with the lunch menu and all the cinnamon rolls had been eaten.

Laura didn't mind. From this day forward, she would have plenty of chances to make cinnamon rolls for Zechariah. And eat them with him.

Life would be sweet, spicy, and warm, no matter the season.

EPILOGUE

Clang, clang. Laura sat bolt upright in bed. She opened her eyes. Darkness enveloped the dawdy haus bedroom. It couldn't be time for breakfast yet. She'd just laid her head on the pillow. She patted the tangled mass of sheets. Still warm. Zechariah. She smiled at the thought, just as she did every time it hit her again like a bolt of lightning since their wedding almost five months earlier. "Zechariah?" She liked saying his name. It had weight and substance. "What are you doing?"

No answer. She slipped from bed and padded barefoot to the kitchen. The windows were open to let the faint whisper of night-cooled July air waft through the house. Little good it did. The nights weren't much cooler than the days. The light of a kerosene lamp flickered on the walls in the kitchen. Zechariah stood at the counter, a cookie in one hand and a glass of tea in the other.

"Midnight snack?"

"I couldn't sleep."

"So I see. Caffeine won't help. Didn't you get enough supper?"

"I ate two helpings of your chicken-fried steak, mashed potatoes, and gravy."

His renewed appetite never ceased to delight Laura. Or the way he smiled at her across the table. Or his bashful request for more dessert. He'd put on a few pounds in the last few months. The doctor said this was good. The Parkinson's hadn't progressed a great deal in six months. A small miracle.

Being happy and in love helped, the doctor said.

As if they didn't know that.

"I'll take a cookie."

Laura waited while Zechariah placed half a dozen peanut butter cookies on a saucer and brought it to the table. On the second trip he brought a glass of tea. "We can share. Otherwise, both of us will be up half the night going to the bathroom." He settled into a chair. She did the same. "Not that we aren't already up."

"It's nice to be able to share the middle of the night in our very own place, just the two of us."

"I wanted my own place." He nudged the

cookie plate toward her. "Sharing it with you makes it perfect. Moments like this are the best."

"I agree." She selected the biggest cookie and nibbled at an edge. "Why are you really awake?"

"Jerky legs."

"The doctor can adjust your medicine."

"I don't want to talk about that right now." He offered her the glass. She shook her head. He sipped and returned it to the table. "I like the way you look in the middle of the night with your hair down, no glasses, and wearing a nightgown."

Words of denial rose in her. She resisted them. If he liked what he saw, she was glad. She was grateful. Grateful for every second of every day. "You don't look so bad your-self. No glasses. Bed shirt. Messy hair."

He rubbed his bald pate. "Ha. Not much hair."

Pounding buried the night noises. "Laura, Zechariah!"

Ruby. Laura rose and swept through the tiny house to the door. She jerked it open. "What's wrong?"

"Nothing's wrong. Seth came to the door. Hannah's in labor." Ruby whirled and sped down the steps. "I told him not to wake you, but he says she's asking for you."

"I'll get dressed."

Sweet Hannah with her freckles and her love of volleyball, a mother. Laura flew to the bedroom and dressed. Zechariah insisted on coming with her. Seth paced the floor in the small living area when they came out.

"Let's go, let's go."

A half hour later they rolled into Seth's front yard. She hopped down and trudged into the house while the men put away the horse and the buggy.

The smile her great-granddaughter offered was weak but still a smile. "He's coming."

"You keep saying 'he.' " Laura grabbed a washrag and wiped Hannah's face. "Do you want a boy?"

"Nee, not necessarily." She gasped and panted. "The pains are strong. Rachel says soon I'll know one way or another."

A sob punctuated her words. "Did I make the right decision? Should I give him up? What if I can't be a gut mudder? What if I'm terrible at it?"

"You won't be terrible. You're a natural. And you'll have all of us to help you."

"Phillip came by yesterday. He brought me watermelon. Cold watermelon. I was so hot and it tasted so gut. How did he know I needed watermelon?"

"He's a smart man."

The gasping turned to a shriek that bounced off the walls and flew into the night through open windows where the sun had just peeked over the horizon. "I don't want to do this anymore."

"It's time to push." Rachel smiled at Hannah. "You're almost done. Take a breath, let it out, and then give a gut hard push."

Four good pushes and a little girl slipped into Rachel's hands. She crowed with delight. "You have a daughter, Hannah, a sturdy little girl with all her fingers and toes."

"Let me see, let me see." Hannah struggled to prop herself up on her elbows. "Are you sure she's fine?"

The baby uttered her first cry. Loud and not the least bit shy.

"Lungs are gut." Rachel snipped the cord and clamped it. "Color is gut. Everything looks perfect."

She handed the baby to Laura, who took a quick peek. "She has your hair. Just a few wisps, but definitely red. Another carrot-top."

"Gut. She doesn't look like her daed."

Hannah still had forgiving to do. "You're bound to see Thaddeus in her."

"I know." Hannah kissed the baby's forehead and cooed. "And it's okay. Looks don't have anything to do with the way a person acts. I'll teach her to take responsibility for her actions."

"You have set the example." Laura squeezed onto the edge of the bed and rested her weary legs. "What will you name her?"

Tears trickled down Hannah's cheeks and one dropped from the tip of her nose. She sniffed and smiled. "Evelyn Rose. Daed says that was your mudder's name, his groossmammi."

"Evelyn Rose." Laura swallowed her own tears and breathed. "Such a pretty name. You would've liked her. She never had a cross word for anyone and she always listened before she decided who to punish. With eight kinner she needed that patience."

"She was like you then."

"I'm like her, I hope."

"I hope Evelyn is like you."

"Can I show her to Zechariah?"

"Jah, but bring her back soon. I just met her and yet, I know I'll miss her."

Laura carried her precious bundle out to the front room where Zechariah sat rocking by himself. He waggled his eyebrows. "You look so gut with a baby in your arms. Seth went to do chores and Carrie is starting breakfast."

"This is Evelyn Rose. Evelyn, meet Zechariah Stutzman. He's your great-great-groossdaadi."

"I am, aren't I?" He stood and peered down at the baby. "Another carrottop. Carrottops are gut workers. Are you a gut worker?"

"If she's anything like her namesake, she will be."

"Your mudder. I vaguely remember snickerdoodles and gingersnaps when the singings were at your house. And a smile a lot like yours. What do you think she'd say if she could see us now? You and me?"

She'd be smiling, for sure. She was smiling now. With Laura's father. "She'd say you did well for yourself."

Zechariah laughed, a sound so hearty Evelyn began to cry.

Laura touched her soft cheek. "Don't cry, bopli, this is the start of something you'll like a lot. We'll be here to rock you when your mudder is tired and change your diaper —"

"Speak for yourself." Zechariah pinched his nose with both fingers. "I'm not a fan of stinky diapers."

"I'll change your diaper and groossdaadi will sing you songs and teach you 'This

Little Piggy Went to Market.' Life will be hard sometimes, but for as long as we're here, we'll take care of you."

Zechariah tucked his arm around Laura. He kissed Evelyn's head and then Laura's cheek. "Just like we do each other. That's a promise."

Laura leaned into him and inhaled the fragrance of her husband and this newborn, equally sweet. "You can count on us." She couldn't resist. She didn't want to resist. Kissing Zechariah topped the list of things she loved about married life. Top five for sure. She kissed his lips, then his cheeks, and his nose. "That's a promise."

A promise for every season.

A NOTE FROM THE AUTHOR

It's hard for me to believe this is the last book in the Every Amish Season series. I've enjoyed writing all four books, and I hope readers will continue to enjoy reading them. My thanks to the HarperCollins Christian Publishing team for all its hard work in producing them. *With Winter's First Frost* represents the great work they do in every aspect from editing, to titling, to formatting, to cover illustrations, to printing, to marketing and publicity, to sales.

Much of the material for this story comes from my life. My husband and I are in that season when we're coping with our own aging and that of our parents. No need to do much outside research when the hurdles regarding health and independence are at our own front doors. My love goes out to Mary and Stan Irvin and Larry and Janice Lyne. Our lives are enriched by the multigenerational nature of our lives. We're blessed to have these experiences.

I truly appreciate the readers who make it possible for me to continue to write these books. Thank you for reading in an age when there are hundreds of other ways to fill your days.

Thank you to our Lord Jesus Christ. Every blessing flows through Him.

DISCUSSION QUESTIONS

1. The Amish educate their children through the eighth grade. They believe their children learn enough "book" education in this manner followed by "vocational training" for farm- and home-related tasks for the remainder of their youth. How do you feel about not offering higher education to children? Do you see value in steering children away from formal education in order to better control their exposure to outside culture?
2. Tamara wants to be a doctor. In order to continue her education, she must leave her family and her faith. Could you make that choice? Why or why not?
3. The Amish believe premarital sex is grounds for excommunication. How is this different from what the world tells us about confining sex to marriage? Has the church shifted in its acceptance of worldly views on this topic? How do you feel

about this shift or lack thereof?

4. Hannah is required to do a kneeling confession in front of the congregation and spend six weeks under the bann. Do you feel that this is too harsh or not harsh enough punishment for her sin?

5. Scripture tells us we are to forgive the sin and accept the repentant sinner in our midst. If you were Hannah's parents, could you forgive her sin? Could you forgive Thaddeus for his role in her situation?

6. Thaddeus decides not to marry Hannah despite being the father of her child. Do you think he had an obligation to marry her despite his feelings? Why or why not?

7. Not only did Thaddeus not marry Hannah, he chose not to beg forgiveness. Instead he left Jamesport. How do you feel about his choices? Do you think he'll be able to leave behind the situation, or will it follow him to Indiana?

8. The Amish care for their elderly family members at home. It is rare for them to go to assisted-living facilities. They live in a dawdy haus and continue to contribute to the family. In Zechariah's case, his disease limits his ability to function on his own, but he doesn't want to give up his independence. Have you had to help an

elderly family member who refuses to give up his or her independence? How have you handled it? Do you think Zechariah's family handled it well? What would you have done differently?

9. The Amish choose their church leaders by lot. They have no additional training for preaching sermons or leading services. That also means the men cannot choose to become ministers. How do you feel about this method of choosing leaders? What are the pros and cons of this practice? How do you feel about women being unable to assume church leadership roles?

10. A member of an Amish church district is able to approach leadership and confess any sin with the understanding that he or she will be forgiven if repentant. This includes sins that may also be criminal such as spousal abuse. Do you believe the leadership is obligated to report these church members to legal authorities? Why or why not? Could you forgive someone who confessed to these types of crimes and repents? What is the role of the church in these situations?

ABOUT THE AUTHOR

Kelly Irvin is the bestselling author of the Every Amish Season and Amish of Bee County series. *The Beekeeper's Son* received a starred review from *Publishers Weekly,* who called it a "beautifully woven masterpiece." The two-time Carol Award finalist is a former newspaper reporter and retired public relations professional. Kelly lives in Texas with her husband, photographer Tim Irvin. They have two children, two grandchildren, and two cats. In her spare time, she likes to read books by her favorite authors.

Visit her online at KellyIrvin.com
Facebook: Kelly.Irvin.Author
Twitter: @Kelly_S_Irvin